TAHOE BLOWUP

Other Titles by Todd Borg:

TAHOE DEATHFALL

TAHOE BLOWUP

by

TODD BORG

THRILLER PRESS

First Thriller Press Edition, September 2001

TAHOE BLOWUP

Library of Congress Card Number: 00-111553

ISBN: 1-931296-12-X

Cover design and map by Keith Carlson.

Manufactured in the United States of America

For Kit

AUTHOR'S NOTE

Unfortunately, this novel requires that Owen drive off-road in some of the mountains surrounding Tahoe. This commits offense against all of the indigenous plants and animals.

Although this story gives serious treatment to the role of fire in maintaining a healthy forest, I want to also stress that forest health can never be achieved unless we all tread lightly in the woods. A good rule of thumb is this: If the road isn't paved, don't drive on it. Further, one cannot really enjoy the sights and sounds and smells of the forest unless one is unencumbered by engines and motors and their attendant noise and exhaust.

ACKNOWLEDGEMENTS

Although many people were helpful in writing this novel, special thanks go to South Lake Tahoe Fire Department Division Chief Merle Bowman. He taught me a great deal about fire departments and fire fighting. While any mistakes I've made are my responsibility alone, Merle deserves the credit for whatever I got right.

Thanks also go to Sandy Bryson, dog trainer extra-ordinaire. What I know of search and rescue dogs I learned from her and her books Search Dog Training and Police Dog Tactics.

I'd also like to thank the U.S. Forest Service and all of Tahoe's fire-fighting agencies. They do an admirable job at what sometimes seems like the thankless assignment of looking after Tahoe's forests. In addition to charting an intelligent course through the maze of government regulations and current forest science suggestions, they also have to navigate the preferences of many groups who have strong opinions about the stewardship of the forest.

Many thanks as well to Kate and Tim Nolan. They provided great help with the countless details of making the characters of this story come alive. I smile with gratitude every time I think of Kate's Post-it notes. Each one was a golden trail marker on my path to a better story.

Thanks again to my agent Barbara Braun. Her suggestions on this novel were especially good and helped focus the story. She has helped in more ways than she knows.

And as with Tahoe Deathfall, Tahoe Blowup is blessed by a great cover and map designed by Keith Carlson.

Finally, my wife Kit is a writer's greatest companion, support group and editorial staff all rolled into one person. I could never thank her enough.

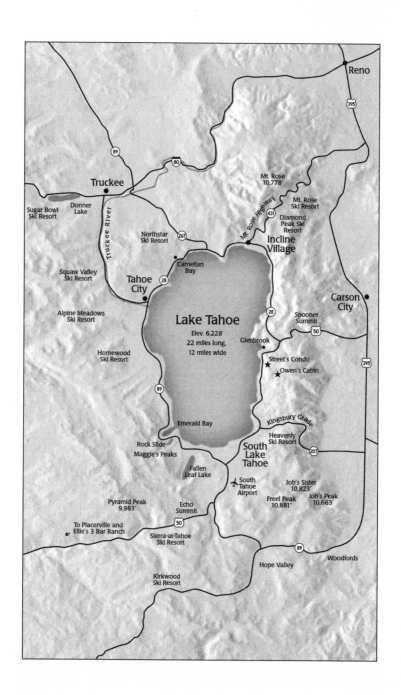

PROLOGUE

When the match touched the sleeve of Jake's gasoline-soaked shirt, flames flashed up his arm and across his back.

Jake threw himself to the ground and rolled over to try and put out the fire. But the tall dead grass was sun-dried and it ignited as he writhed on the ground. A hard wind spread the fire and in a moment the entire end of the meadow was engulfed in angry orange flames. Jake scrambled to his feet and ran into the forest toward Highland Creek. The small stream was only fifty yards away, down at the bottom of the ravine. If it still flowed with water at the end of summer, and if he sprinted...

A guttural scream ripped at the back of his throat as Jake fumbled with the buttons on his shirt. The fabric was synthetic, and before he could peel the shirt away it melted to his skin.

He plunged through the trees, a literal fireman carrying fire into the twilight. His fingers clawed at the melting synthetic that ran in rivulets of fire down his body. Skin came off under his fingernails.

The acrid smoke from his burning flesh caught inside his lungs, but it was nothing against the searing on his skin, a thousand red irons pressed on bare nerves.

Jake jumped and slid down the steepest part of the ravine. He tripped on a root, fell forward into the dry stream bed and hit his head on a rock. He lay motionless, his blackened body still burning like a torch.

A clump of dogwood, baked to tinder by a summer with no rain, caught fire. The flames spread to a maze of manzanita and from there touched a dead white fir that still had a full dressing of dried needles. The tree exploded like a firebomb and the growing inferno lit up the night sky.

ONE

My first glimpse of the forest fire came as I was barbecuing a Salmon steak out on my deck.

It was about nine in the evening on September 18th when Spot, my Harlequin Great Dane, gave a little growl. Little, of course, is a relative thing when it comes from a one hundred and seventy pound polka-dotted foot rest. I ignored the comment, hunched as I was over the short barbecue, trying to stay warm. If I were in Kansas City or New York or even Minneapolis, a mid-September evening would be a pleasantly cool precursor to fall weather. But the deck on my little cabin sits at 7,200 feet of elevation, a thousand feet above the east shore of Lake Tahoe. When the sun goes down the temperature plummets like a skier in a tuck.

The weather forecast predicted that our first winter storm would hit tonight. After the standard summer of one hundred straight days of hot sun in clear blue skies, precipitation is an elixir from heaven.

Like other Tahoe locals, I was more than eager to put up with chill and wet in order to dampen the fire danger in the forests. Besides, the snow level in the coming storm was supposed to be at 7,000 feet which meant that Spot and I would be enjoying that famous Sierra white stuff while the poor people down below in their lakeside mansions would suffer a cold, cold rain.

I shifted my chair closer to the coals and moved the fish to make it sizzle. The wind threw ominous clouds across the moon. Spot was sprawled on the other side of the barbecue, the arc of his body wrapping halfway around the black metal cooking pot. His throat rumbled again. This time he actually lifted his head off the deck boards, an indication of seriousness.

"What, your largeness, are you making a fuss about?"

Spot jerked himself to his feet. His claws scraped the cedar decking like sixteen-penny nails. He upped the amplitude of his deep growl one notch, just enough to make his jowls quiver. His square body pointed over the water like a German tank above Omaha Beach.

"Okay," I said. "Let's take a look." I pushed my chair back, stood, walked to the edge of the deck and looked down. Lake Tahoe lay below me like a twenty-two mile long puddle of black ink. The moon stabbed through the clouds and made a silver glow on the water. I leaned on the railing, listening for the sound of an intruder, wondering if yet another bear had decided to scratch its backside against the posts that support my deck.

I heard nothing. Which ruled out bears because they are noisy. That still left the possibility of a mountain lion or coyote or even a person, all of which have been known to be silent. Spot increased the rumble.

"I know," I said. "You're pretty tough."

Spot turned and looked at me, wagged his tail a quick one-two, then went back to his growling.

I gazed across the water, the second highest big lake in the world. Nothing appeared. I was turning back to the barbecue when my peripheral vision sensed a light just beyond the cliff ridge below my cabin.

I looked down toward where the land dropped off into the big ravine where Highland Creek ran all the way down to the lake. Nothing moved. Aware that a faint light like a faint star is less visible when you look straight at it, I looked away.

Staring into the black clouds that presaged the coming storm I sensed a vague glow in the air. Spot growled louder. I smelled something that prickled the hair on the back of my neck. I grabbed the deck phone off its cradle and dialed the number I know best.

"Yeah?" a sleepy voice answered after five rings.

"Street, my sweet, wake up. You're in bed early."

"I'm sleeping," she said groggily.

"Still got jet lag from the Honolulu bug conference?"

"Yeah. All the bugs are asleep. Me too."

"I can tell," I said.

Street was one of those rare people who slept as if they were under the influence of anesthesia. When I first met her I thought it was her norm, a happy, blissful somnolence. Later, I witnessed the first of what are regular wrestling matches, her slender muscles roping and twisting the sheets to the point of tearing, her jaw clenching while frightening whimpers escape from her throat. If you wake her at that point she'll spend the next two hours shaking and refusing to say a word. But if you don't wake her, her sleep will calm and she'll later awaken happy and refreshed. The fact that she'd answered the phone at all told me I'd gotten her at a good time.

"Just do me a quick favor," I said, "and look out your window, up the mountain toward my cabin. Tell me what you see."

"Owen."

"I know. You're sleeping. Look. Tell. Then back to bed." I heard the phone bang on her night stand. I heard the rustle of covers and a loud, frustrated sigh, then blinds being raised. Her gasp was frightening.

The phone was picked up, dropped, grabbed again. "Owen, Owen! My God, Owen!"

"What do you see?"

"Owen! You have to get out!"

"Sweetheart, perhaps you could elaborate."

"Owen," she said, now low-voiced and calm. "The mountain is on fire. As I'm standing here watching, the flames are racing up the ravine toward your cabin. I'd give you three or four minutes at the outside."

Just after I hung up the phone, the first crest of fire rushed over the ridge a hundred yards below my deck.

TWO

I picked the Salmon off the grill, slapped it onto a plate and went inside my old, four-room log cabin. Spot followed, sniffing the air behind me. The fish went into the fridge along with the Pinot Noir that I'd opened.

The prospect of my cabin burning was more than I could fully contemplate in a few seconds, so I concentrated on what I could quickly carry out. My first thought of what to save was my art books, but I decided human lives took priority.

I called 911 and explained that there was a forest fire just below my house. The operator told me they'd already received several reports.

In the drawer near my phone is a list of my wealthy neighbors, all of whom live in glass and cedar contenders for Architectural Digest. I didn't particularly care about their houses, but I wanted no bodies on my conscience. I took the time to call each one and let them know the mountain was burning. I got two answering machines, one voice mail and a pager. The only actual person who answered was Mrs. Duchamp, the woman with the toy poodle named Treasure who periodically tries to teach Spot how to do handstands and pirouettes. I once had asked Mrs. Duchamp if she was any relation to the artist Marcel Duchamp and she thought I meant a hair and nails boy down at the Mountain High Salon in Carson City.

"Mrs. Duchamp?" I said when she answered. "Owen McKenna. I'm calling to let you know our mountain is burning and the fire is coming our way. I don't know how serious it is, but we should leave fast."

"What?!" her voice shrieked in a falsetto worthy of a Parisian drag queen.

"Do you want to drive yourself, Mrs. Duchamp, or would you like a ride?"

The woman started blubbering about poor little Treasure and how the dog had once knocked over a flea-killer candle while watching a Pet Care video on Nail Polish for Poodles. The flame had singed her fir and made the most God-awful smell. Now Treasure hasn't allowed Mrs. Duchamp to light candles, or even a fire in the fireplace, ever since.

"I'll pick you up!" I yelled into the phone. "Two minutes! Be ready!"

I hung up and shook my head at Spot. "You ever start watching dog videos, I'm selling you to Elmer's Glue." Spot stuck his nose into my hand and pushed it around, lightly grabbing my fingers with his teeth.

My stereo is normally tuned to public radio, so it took me a few seconds to dial in the local AM station. I turned the radio up loud, in case they reported fire news, while I collected my art books. There was no way I could gather them all in a short time, so I shoveled the ones from the main shelf into plastic Safeway bags.

Over on the end table next to my recliner was the book I was reading, an Abrams publication that contained a nice color plate of my current favorite painting, Bierstadt's The Sierra Nevada In California. I stuffed it into one of the bags.

The air outside was filled with smoke as I dragged my Safeway bags out to the Jeep. Spot got excited when we pulled into Treasure's driveway.

I ran up and rang the bell and heard another shriek from Mrs. Duchamp. I tried the door. It was unlocked.

"Mrs. Duchamp?" I called out as I turned the huge brass handle and pushed open a heavy oak door that stood eight feet tall and four feet wide. "Are you ready?"

Treasure came running. I bent down and she jumped into my arms and proceeded to lick my chin with a tongue so tiny it could barely moisten a postage stamp. But then, my perceptions may be lopsided what with owning a dog who could irrigate Southern Somalia in a single drool.

"Mrs. Duchamp, we have to go," I yelled.

"But, but..." she cried hysterically.   She ran into the hallway, high heels clicking on the hard maple floor. She turned and faced me, all two hundred pounds of her quivering with fear. She was wearing a peach-colored silk evening gown. Her large feet overflowed the edges of her red enamel, strapless heels. Through the toe opening I saw bright red nails. "I'm not even dressed!" she cried.

"Mrs. Duchamp. Treasure is right here. You need nothing else but your coat."

"But..."

I picked up Treasure, turned and walked out the front door. Mrs. Duchamp came out a moment later. She was wrapped in a huge mink and she took fast tiny steps in her heels as she waddled toward my Jeep. I opened the door and she climbed in.

"Treasure! Oh, Treasure!" she exclaimed. "Are you here?"

Treasure was in the back seat leaping all over Spot, oblivious to Mrs. Duchamp's cries.

"She's in back, Mrs. Duchamp." I backed out of her driveway and headed through thick smoke and falling ash down the long private drive I share with my neighbors. Halfway down the mountain we passed a wall of flames racing up through the Jeffrey pines and manzanita. The fire was fanned by the wind of the approaching storm and was oblivious to the few big rain drops that began to strike our windshield. Mrs. Duchamp shrieked as I drove past the flames.

We rounded a corner and saw another crescent of flame trying to out-flank the first. Mrs. Duchamp shrieked again. The road turned around another switchback and we entered a dark forest with no sign of additional fire. My neighbor settled down to a steady whimpering.

When we came to the highway two miles below, the first fire truck turned in, lights and siren on. It struggled in low gear up the steep road. Another fire truck was coming down the highway at high speed. A third followed in the distance. I was glad for their effort, but I knew that when it comes to forest fires, firemen are often impotent. If the wind is strong enough and the fuel sufficient, the fire will go where it wants.

The rain increased to a steady patter. It probably wouldn't dampen the enthusiasm of the fire, but it couldn't hurt. And if the storm came in as forecast, the weather would help in containing the fire.

I pulled onto Highway 50 and headed toward Street Casey's condo. Mrs. Duchamp and I did not speak, both of us unwilling to voice our worst fears.

Street was standing in her open doorway when we pulled into her drive. She was wearing her black coat. Under the hem hung the longer fabric of a sheer nightgown. As always, just seeing the silhouette of her calves probably added a year to my life. Men have painted large triptychs with less inspiration. Street's thin, angular form did not fit the typical American standard of beauty, but to me she was gorgeous.

Although Street figured I'd come straight to her after leaving my cabin, I could see by the look on her face that she hadn't bargained on Mrs. Duchamp. Nevertheless, Street was gracious to a fault and she ran out into the cold rain in her bare feet and opened the passenger door.

"Mrs. Duchamp," she said. "It's good to see you again, but I'm so sorry about the fire."

Mrs. Duchamp got out, threw her meaty arms around Street's slender body, bowed her head on Street's shoulder and started crying in great heaving spasms. "Are we safe, here?" she cried out, panic in her voice. "Will the fire come this way?"

"The fire is on the mountain above us," I said. "It will travel up the slope, not down. So we are completely safe, Mrs. Duchamp."

"Come, now," Street said, turning the woman, patting her on the back and walking her into the condominium.

Once inside, Mrs. Duchamp sat rigidly on Street's couch holding Treasure so hard to her lap I thought the dog was having trouble breathing. Mrs. Duchamp sobbed that her entire life was in her house and that it was all in ashes. Street fussed over the woman, making assurances that the fire might miss the houses. Street's administrations were so smooth that soon she had Mrs. Duchamp in Street's own bed and, with the aid of a healthy glass of cognac, sound asleep.

Street and I sat by her fire in the living room. It was ironic that we could be comforted by the warmth and crackle coming from the fireplace when a forest fire raged just a couple of miles above us. Spot lay on the floor. Treasure sat next to his head and leaned her tiny jawbone on his neck. Treasure turned her ears when Mrs. Duchamp's snoring rose above the volume of the Pretenders CD that Street put on.

"Do you think the fire will get the houses of your neighborhood?" Street asked.

"Don't know," I said.

"It must be snowing pretty hard up there now."

"From what I saw the fire was hot enough that it won't matter. Too much fuel, too dry for too long. What will matter is the wind. Either way we'll know in the morning."

"Don't you want to call Terry Drier and find out?"

"Something tells me that a Fire Department Battalion Chief has more to do right now than talk to me about my cabin." I got up and fetched a Sierra Nevada Pale Ale from Street's fridge. "I'll call him in the morning. If it's good news, great. If it's bad news I'll sleep better if I don't know." I put my hand on Street's leg, feeling the curves of her thigh through the nightgown fabric. "Then again, there are other sleep aids."

Street looked at me. "How many fires do you think I can handle in one night?"

"But this fire is easy to put out."

"So I recall," she said, giggling, pushing me back on the couch.

THREE

Before I had a chance to call Terry Drier the next morning, he called me, waking me up.

"You knew I was at Street's?" I said after I had dragged the phone off the table next to the foldout couch. The clock on the living room wall said 6:15 a.m. Street was sprawled at a diagonal next to me. Mrs. Duchamp's snore was still seeping through the cracks around Street's bedroom door.

"Logical guess," Terry said. "I'm calling with fire news."

"I lost my home?"

"No. Your cabin is fine. Singed, but fine. The fire went up the mountain just south of your house and took out most of the mature pines nearby. The fire went between yours and Duchamp's. In fact, no structures were burned. But your area looks like hell.

"As Incident Commander on this fire I didn't want to take any chances. I called in an Overhead Team right off and we had a chopper carrying water up there all night. It's not contained yet, but with this snow, we'll circle it by tonight."

I rolled toward the window and looked out at the dull gray of early dawn. A dark blanket of cloud covered all but the bottom of the mountain. Most of the fire path, including the area near my cabin, was obscured. There was only a dusting of white on the trees visible below the clouds. Which meant that my cabin probably had no more than a few inches. The storm had turned out to be all promise and little delivery. Enough to help slow a fire, but not enough to put it out.

"Where is it burning now?" I asked Terry.

"Up above your place, toward Genoa Peak. The fire is approaching the tree line and the snow has covered the brush above that. We're concentrating on cutting fire breaks to the sides of the fire. If we can keep it from spreading sideways across the mountain, we'll have it contained. It's too steep to get our Douglas County vehicles in, so all we've got is Forest Service trucks and the chopper. Most of the work is on foot. Slow going."

"How do the Forest Service trucks get in where yours can't? Are they smaller?"

"Theirs are Type Three. Four-wheel-drive. Those jerks call our trucks Pavement Dollies. But I guess it's true that our trucks aren't much good in the woods.

"What about the snow?" I asked. "Doesn't it slow the fire down?"

"Slows it maybe, but not much. Lot of wind last night. The snow didn't accumulate in the pines. For awhile this was a crown fire, not a brush burner. It jumped from tree to tree. You could hear some of them exploding now and then. Sounds like the shells the highway boys shoot for avalanche control on the slopes above the passes. Anytime you get a crown fire, you worry about it exploding out of control like what happened in the Oakland Hills. Luckily, between our efforts and the snow, we got it settled down."

"How much has burned?" I asked.

"About a thousand acres."

"Any houses in danger?"

"Luckily, the fire stayed in the ravine until it got to your cabin. It was still burning in a narrow swath as it went between your cabin and Duchamp's house. It spread out some when it got higher up, but as long as the wind doesn't change and we can keep it from jumping the firebreaks, no houses will burn because they're all off to the side and at lower elevations than yours."

"Any idea yet on how it started?"

"That's why I called you," Terry said. "I wonder if you can come down to the station. Got something to show you."

"Sure. When do you want me?"

"Now," he said.

"I'll be right over."

I keep a razor in Street's bathroom and while I shaved I scanned the enormous selection of bottles and jars that Street had lined up on the edge of the tub, in the medicine cabinet, and across a towel shelf. It always amazed me to see how many lotions and potions were required to maintain a female body.

I put a note to Street and Mrs. Duchamp on Street's fridge while water boiled for a mug of Street's instant coffee. I gave Spot and Treasure a pet and was in my Jeep a minute later.

Across the lake on the California side, the clouds were breaking up. The sky was turning bright cobalt blue and the snow-covered mountaintops were luminous with alpenglow from the first rays of sun. Mount Tallac was a sharp triangle of rock and snow and reminded me of the mountains in the Bierstadt painting.

Terry Drier came out of the fire station as I pulled up. He was a hard, narrow, sinewy man who stood a half foot shorter than my six-six. But his slight frame belied an out-sized strength of both muscle and will. Terry Drier was afraid of nothing, bear or beach bully, avalanche or forest fire. He'd made Battalion Chief at the young age of thirty through intelligence and his ability to focus the efforts of other firefighters. That he would one day be Fire Chief seemed accepted knowledge in the department.

We shook hands and went inside. "Chief Phillips wanted to be here," Terry said. "But he's got an early meeting. Said he didn't want me to wait to call you." We walked into Terry's office. "Have a seat," Terry said. "Coffee?"

"Already tanked up, but thanks." I sat in one of the white plastic deck chairs that Terry keeps in front of his desk. Terry thought nothing of submitting budgets for hundreds of thousands of taxpayer dollars on fire-fighting equipment. But he didn't waste a cent on office decor. He sat down behind a dented, gray metal desk and opened a file drawer.

He pulled out a clear mylar sleeve containing a piece of paper. "We found this in our mail slot. It has no address or postage, so it was hand-delivered. Yesterday, this was a threat. Now it is evidence in a felony. Officials from seventeen agencies want to look at it. But Phillips wanted you to see it before we turned it over." He handed it to me across the desk.

The note was on standard white copy paper. The font looked like Helvetica.

Tahoe is going to burn.
This is punishment for years of
crimes against the environment.
The first fire will take only trees.

There was nothing else on the note. I set it on Terry's desk. "This was a warning for the fire that started last night."

"Yes," Terry said.

"What do you think?" I asked, gesturing at the note.

"Can't know for sure. But my guess is the arsonist just wants to make his crime sound fancy. I think this guy is like other firestarters. He likes to light fires. Turns him on."

"Why me?"

Terry picked a mug up off his cluttered desk and slurped from it. "Because Chief Phillips and I consider all possibilities. Which means maybe I'm wrong and the firestarter really does have some terrorist agenda. If so, a standard search for the arsonist may not be productive. Maybe we'll catch this guy ourselves, but what if we don't?"

Terry sipped more coffee. "Captain Mallory told me about a firestarter you caught in San Francisco back when you were on the force. The apartment building where the little girl burned up? Mallory said you nailed the guy two years later by tracking the source of the propane bottle he used to start the fire."

"Yeah, but I really don't know much about arsonists."

"Look," Terry said. "You are outside the system and that gives you a perspective that the local police and fire officials don't have. You've solved every case you've had as far as I remember. And you caught a firestarter. In our book that makes you more qualified than Smoky Bear. So maybe you're not a fire expert. You're tenacious as hell and we need help."

Terry drained the rest of his coffee and put the mug down on his desk. "Will you? We've got some room in the budget. Put you on at least a couple weeks."

"Okay," I said. I pointed at the note. "Guy says this is the first fire. Implies there's going to be more. He also says the first one would only take trees. Which suggests the next one will take something else."

Terry shrugged. "Maybe."

"You've called Diamond Martinez?"

Terry nodded. "I guess you heard that the Douglas County Sheriff's Department recently named Diamond the Fire Investigator for this area. We've told our people to give him anything he wants." Terry leaned forward, elbows on his desk. "Diamond might know more about fire than anyone else in the Sheriff's Department. But the truth is, none of us, Diamond included, have that much experience with arson."

"The few fires I was involved with in San Francisco were all buildings," I said. "In each case the insurance company sent in a specialist which was a big help. But there's no insurance with trees."

"Right," Terry said.

"We've got the warning note, but are we certain the fire actually was arson?"

"There's a meadow in the woods east of the highway down below your cabin. This guy was real bold. Struck a wooden kitchen match and tossed it into the dry grass. We found the charred match. The breeze was strong enough that the fire fanned out from the match and the match blew out. Made it easy to find. The arsonist didn't want us to have to go to any effort to identify the source of ignition."

"Taunting you?" I asked.

"Maybe. Or he just didn't care that we figure out his method. Lights the match, drives away in his car and watches from a distance."

"And his prediction was accurate."

"About burning only trees? Pure luck," Terry scoffed. "That fire started a half mile down the mountain from your house and ended up burning forty feet from your deck and a hundred feet from Mrs. Duchamp's. Any shift of wind and both your houses would be ashes."

I fingered the letter in its mylar sleeve. "What do you think he means about crimes against the environment?"

"Who knows? Could be one of those wacko environmentalists who thinks we shouldn't be putting out fires in the woods. Those guys think burning Bambi to death is natural for chrissakes." Terry's disgust was heavy on his face. The circles under his eyes were as dark as his eyebrows.

I looked at the warning note again. There were no markings on it. "If you get another note will you call me before the suits take it away?"

"That's the idea."

I thought about it a minute. "You got someone who can tell me the other side, the wacko environmentalist perspective?"

Terry smiled. He returned the mylar sleeve to his file drawer. "One name in particular comes to mind. Arthur Jones Middleton the Sixth is a member of The League To Save Lake Tahoe. Mostly lives in San Francisco. Rich, old money, time on his hands. You know the type. An actual pocket watch in his vest pocket. His family's money goes back to the gold rush. I guess they did that type of mining where they used a high pressure water cannon to wash away whole hillsides and flush out the gold."

"Real rape-the-wilderness stuff," I said.

"Right. Now Mr. Middleton is dealing with his environmental guilt by coming up to Tahoe and filing lawsuits to stop development. He and his make our lives miserable. You call Middleton if you want the latest environmental correctness."

"What about someone less narrow minded?"

Terry paused in thought. "I'd talk to Linda Saronna. She's with the Forest Service. Runs the Lake Tahoe Basin Management Unit. She hears it from all sides and can give you a balanced view. I've got her number here somewhere." Terry flipped through his address book and wrote it on a yellow Post-it note.

"I'll check around," I said, "but it's hard to see where I could add anything to what Diamond will give you. "

Terry leaned forward, putting his elbows on his desk. He spoke in a hushed voice. "You were once a cop. You know the constraints of playing by the rules. If Diamond wants to look around somewhere, he needs a search warrant. If he kicks someone's butt, they suspend him while the citizen's committee investigates."

"You think the laws don't apply to me?" I said.

"Maybe not so much, huh?" Terry said.

FOUR

I went back to Street's condo. She'd left a note saying she was at her lab. I gathered up Mrs. Duchamp and the dogs and drove back up the mountain to inspect the damage.

Mrs. Duchamp started emoting when her house came into view, although I could not discern whether hers were tears of happiness that her house was unscathed or tears of sadness that the nearby trees were all burned to charred trunks. Nevertheless, she calmed when I got her inside and put her into her love seat with Treasure on her lap and a cup of hot tea by her side. I told her to call if she needed anything, then left.

The snow was melting fast and making a mess as the slush combined with the ash from the burn. In addition, the firemen had showered our houses with their fire hoses. The torrent of water, while possibly saving everything we had, splashed ash and mud across our homes. It would be months before our homes looked normal, decades before the forest returned.

When I let Spot out of the Jeep he immediately ran around, investigating the new snow and the strong smells coming from the burn. I carried my bags of art books back inside.

The phone rang as I was poaching eggs for breakfast.

"How bad is it up there?" Street asked.

"My view has been expanded. All the trees that previously blocked my vista of Heavenly are gone. If I get a telescope this winter I'll be able to watch the skiers trysting inside the gondolas."

"At least you're putting a positive spin on things," Street said.

"Now that you say that, I realize the irony of the fire. Everything near my cabin burned up. That leaves me safer from fire than I've ever been."

"Tough way to achieve fire safety," Street said. "But I'm glad my favorite little cabin is okay."

We said goodbye and I went back to my breakfast.

Later, I went out and surveyed the burn. The landscape was as surreal as a Dali painting. I shoveled the ash-laden snow from my deck, then stopped and looked down the ravine where the fire had come up. The words on the note came back to me. The first fire will take only trees. I took my walking stick and eased my way down through the snow to the escarpment below my house. At the top of the cliff I moved laterally until I came to a more gradual incline. Spot came along and skidded his way down the slippery slope. Hazy plumes issued from smoldering tree trunks.

A hundred yards below my cabin I stopped and looked down. The ravine had strong ridgelines at the sides and it arced down the mountain like a giant bobsled course. Before the fire, the trees had been thick in the center of the ravine and thinner at the edges. I wasn't certain, but from where I stood it looked like any fire in the ravine would stay confined as if in a chimney. Unless, of course, there were strong cross winds. I remembered Terry's conviction that it was pure luck that our houses didn't burn. But I was beginning to think that maybe the firestarter knew what he was doing.

I climbed back up to my cabin and went inside to call the woman whose name I'd gotten from Terry Drier.

"U.S. Forest Service," a woman answered. Her voice was harried.

"Linda Saronna, please," I said.

"I'm sorry, she's busy. Would you like to leave a message on her voice mail?" Another phone was ringing in the background. "Hold on," the woman said.

When the secretary came back on I said, "This is Owen McKenna calling on behalf of the Douglas County Fire Department. I've been asked to look into the fire on the east shore. I'd like to stop by and talk to Ms. Saronna. Will she be around this morning?"

"Let me see. How about ten-thirty? Only I can't promise. Linda is wearing three hats today. But I think it'll be okay."

I told her I'd take my chances.

I drove through South Lake Tahoe and pulled up at the Forest Service building on Emerald Bay Road at the appointed time.

Linda Saronna saw me in her office. She was a tall redhead in her late forties wearing beige Forest Service slacks and shirt. Her impatience filled the room as she finished one phone call and answered another. She tapped a pen on a yellow pad as she talked. During a third call she got up and paced like a caged animal. "Look," she said after she hung up and we exchanged names, "I'm really busy. Can't this wait?"

"Until the arsonist lights another fire?"

Her eyes flashed with exasperation. She shut them for a moment, sat down, took a deep breath and leaned back in her desk chair. "Sorry," she said at last. "We've had a lot of confusion around here. The phone hasn't been quiet for thirty seconds all morning. I've talked to every agency in the Tahoe Basin at least twice. The fire is still burning up by Genoa Peak."

Linda Saronna rolled her head around while she massaged her neck with both hands. Her red hair swung back and forth. "I don't think it's been this hectic since the Freel Peak Fire."

"When was that?"

"You must not have been living here or you'd remember. Let's see. I moved here a year after the fire and I heard all about it. So that would make it fifteen years ago."

"I was a cop in San Francisco."

"Oh?" She paused, re-appraising me.

I was used to it. People always rethink what they've said when they find out you're an ex-cop. You go from being a regular guy, even if you're a private detective, to someone they can't understand. "Tell me about it," I said.

"What? Oh, the Freel Peak Fire. From what I learned, it was a crown fire that started below High Meadows. Burned past the tree line all the way up through the brush at the saddle between Job's Sister and Freel. Every Fire Department from the Tahoe Basin was involved. And the California Department of Forestry pretty much demonstrated their claim that they have the largest fire-fighting air force in the world."

"The Freel Peak Fire was obviously very large."

"Right." Linda Saronna nodded in the nonchalant way of someone who regularly dealt with situations that the rest of us would find extreme. "In addition to the Carson Valley and Sacramento teams, they also had crews come in from Boise, Idaho and Flagstaff, Arizona. From what I understand, the main concern was that they could lose much of the south shore."

"You mean the town of South Lake Tahoe."

"Right," she said. "Except for the hotels, the entire town is made of wood. Houses, shops and a million dry trees." The phone on her desk rang and she picked it up fast. "Linda Saronna. What? No. I'm in conference. I'll call you back." She hung up and looked at me. "Where was I?"

A vague memory of the Freel Peak Fire story was coming back to me. "Didn't someone die in the Freel Peak Fire?"

"Yes. They lost a woman who was in a cabin in the fire path. The woman soaked herself down with water and breathed through wet clothes." Linda Saronna went silent, her mind no doubt replaying images from what she'd learned of the fire. "She may have known the Hotshots were coming, could have heard the airplane. But they got there too late."

"The Smoke Jumpers?"

"Right. They came up from one of the Gold Country units. Hotshots are to firefighting what Top Gun is to Air Force pilots. They parachuted down to the cabin, but the woman was already gone." Linda turned and looked out her window toward the pines. She didn't seem pensive so much as it seemed she was trying to keep me from seeing her face.

FIVE

Linda Saronna glanced at her watch, rubbed her eyes and turned back to face me. "Look, I'm sorry, but I've got an eleven o'clock readiness meeting with four fire departments." She pushed a button on her phone.

"Frederick?" she said. "Could you come in here please? Thanks."

"May I call you back when I have more questions?" I asked.

"Of course."

"When is a good time?"

Linda Saronna puffed out her cheeks like Dizzy Gillespie and then let the air out in a rush. Her breath smelled like coffee mocha. "I don't..." She paged through her calendar. "Okay, tomorrow morning I'm out, but the rest of the week I'll be in if you call before seven-thirty in the morning or after six at night."

"Your energy is impressive."

"When Tahoe's on fire, I'm focused. I'll take some time off when we have six feet of snow on the ground."

The door opened and a clean-cut young man came in. He was of indeterminate age, a youthful 35 or a mature 25. "Yes, Linda?" he said, glancing at me. He wore a green short-sleeved golf shirt that was snug enough to show off hard biceps and triceps and abdominals like cobblestones. His hair was short and combed into a schoolboy flip above his forehead. He smiled when he spoke Linda's name, revealing teeth bright enough for toothpaste commercials.

"Owen McKenna meet Frederick Mallicoff. We hired Frederick because he is an expert in fire science. Frederick, Tahoe Douglas F.P.D. has Mr. McKenna looking for the east shore firestarter. Can you be his liaison? I'm slammed for the next few days."

I was about to thank Linda Saronna for her time when her phone rang. She picked it up and started talking nonstop as Frederick ushered me out of her office.

"I should apologize for Linda," Frederick said when we were in the hallway. "She thinks the world is on her shoulders right now and, to be fair, it kind of is."

"Your job here," I said. "What do you do?"

"I'm a fire risk analyst. I study fuel levels in the forest, monitor moisture levels, wind patterns and topography as it relates to fire danger. Superimposing these factors over population density allows us to rate any area of the Tahoe Basin in terms of fire danger to the residents." We turned from the hallway into a lunch room.

"There are a host of other components we look at as well," Frederick continued. "Insect damage to the trees, its direction and rate of spread, snowpack, runoff, long term meteorological forecasts – you get the idea. Fire science is an emerging field. We know dramatically more now than we did thirty or forty years ago. And this knowledge should increase exponentially in the future."

His speech, which sounded like something he prepared for his job interview, was interrupted when a small young man walked into the lunchroom. Frederick reached out and slapped him on the shoulder. "Francisco, here, is the number one grunt. He refers to me as Mallicoff the Magnificent when I'm not around. Right, buddy?"

"More like Mallicoff the Malevolent," Francisco said, grinning.

"Insubordination!" Frederick said with a chuckle. He and Francisco locked hands for a moment.

"Anyway," Frederick said, "I work with whatever Linda gives me. Some of my overload paperwork goes to Francisco. Francisco, meet Owen McKenna." We shook. Francisco got a Coke out of the machine and left.

"Your job sounds fascinating," I said.

"I love this job. It was my dream, growing up in Bakersfield, to get in with the Forest Service and be assigned to a place like Tahoe. I'm learning all the ropes. Linda's a good teacher. I'm actually putting to use most of the forest management I learned at Sac State. On top of that there's about a million pages of Forest Service protocol to memorize. If I do a good job, who knows? Someday maybe I'll have Linda's job. Of course, it's more likely I'll get transferred. I'd love to stay in Tahoe, though."

"Tell me," I said. "Does the Forest Service have a position on why an arsonist would want to light forest fires?"

"You mean an official position? Not that I know of. Some crazies like to light fires, I guess. I don't imagine there is any doctrine specifically about forest arson as opposed to burning down buildings. The main focus of the Forest Service as regards arson fires is that they try to prevent them at all costs, and if - I suppose I should say *when* - an arson fire occurs they try to put them out at all costs. Some would say at too much cost."

"What do you mean?"

"Just that same old environmentalist crap about too much fire suppression leads to too much fuel stock in the forest. The liberals think that we should let the forests burn the way they did thousands of years ago. They ignore the tiny little differences between then and now, like the existence of people, for instance. We put out fires because we're trying very hard to keep people from burning up. And we are constantly doing controlled burns to eliminate fuel buildup."

"When a fire starts, what decides who fights it?"

"Depends," Frederick said. "If it is small, then the local fire department will usually be first on the scene and sometimes they get it put out before the Forest Service can get their rigs and men in there to help. In a big fire, we throw everything the Forest Service has at it. The neighboring fire departments also join in along with the California Department of Forestry and the Nevada Division of Forestry. There is a group called the Sierra Front that oversees the coordination. They're comprised of eight local F.D.s and F.P.D.s in the basin plus all the other groups."

"F.D.s are Fire Departments. F.P.D.s are..."

"Fire Protection Districts," Frederick said. "The nomenclature is confusing, but they are all agencies that fight fires."

"It sounds complicated."

"I suppose it is. But the bottom line is this: We have a Mutual Aid Plan that basically says everybody agrees to help wherever and whenever they're needed."

"What about the East Shore fire? Are there lots of these groups fighting it?"

Frederick nodded as he sipped his coffee. "This has been a medium response. Not so much because of houses being threatened because there aren't that many. But this fire is big enough that by the middle of the night we had the Forest Service, a couple of local F.D.s and a chopper on the scene." Frederick drank the last of his coffee. "If we get an even bigger fire, or if many structures are threatened like the Autumn Hills fire on Kingsbury Grade a few years ago, then everything comes out. Every man and rig in the Tahoe Basin as well as Hotshot teams from around the Western States. And many distant fire departments send a truck if they can spare one. Plus, if need be, the search and rescue groups bring in dog teams to find any missing persons."

"It sounds like a high level of co-operation between the different groups," I said.

"A miracle woman with the title of Mutual Aid Coordinator does the legwork." Frederick smiled. "That's what I love about this business. Everyone chips in. Of course, the payback is that if a department, say, in the Sacramento Valley sends up a truck and crew to help us, then they'll expect us to do the same for them if they ever get a big fire."

"It sounds like coordinating every resource would be like fighting a war."

"It is," Frederick said, nodding. "The Mutual Aid Coordinator works with every fire-fighting organization. At each fire an Incident Command Post is set up near the fire. The Command staff is often comprised of a fireman, a cop and a Forest Service official."

"It sounds like there is a lot of opportunity for confusion. Do people ever pull rank or fight for jurisdiction?"

"Yeah, it can get ugly." Frederick actually looked a bit embarrassed. "Sometimes one of the local departments and the Forest Service will both be trying to set up Incident Commands. We've even had it where the Forest Service and a local department are both fighting a fire without even talking to each other about it."

"Boys and their fire trucks."

"Yeah. But really, when you look at it, it is no different than the different factions on the school board or city council fighting over procedures or plans." Frederick looked at his watch. "I better get back to work. If you need anything, call me at this number. It is my cell phone so you won't have to deal with the switchboard and the secretary." He handed me his card.

"Thanks," I said.

We stood, shook hands again and I left. I drove back across town and headed up the mountain to my cabin.

Spot showed his excitement at seeing me by bringing me his big metal food bowl and holding it in his teeth. He stood there thumping his tail against the dishwasher. The bass drum in the high school marching band wasn't as loud. I told him to wait while I dialed Diamond Martinez on his pager and punched in my number.

My phone rang in a minute and Diamond said he was in the area and would stop by. His new white Explorer with the Douglas County Sheriff's emblem on the door pulled up to my cabin fifteen minutes later. He got out with a serious frown on his dark brown face. Diamond scanned the devastated landscape and scowled. Spot ran up to him and stuck his nose in Diamond's hand.

"Congratulations on being appointed Fire Investigator," I said.

"Just in time to help you gringos with a bad-ass firestarter." Diamond grabbed Spot's ears and rubbed them like he was kneading tortilla dough. "We don't have these situations back home."

"What, no forest fires in Mexico?"

"Not like this one. Smoky Bear doesn't go south of the border. Up here old Smoky's been suppressing fires for so many years, fuel builds up to dangerous levels. When a fire finally does happen, it is difficult to control. In Mexico, regular fires clear out the back country. More natural. The people come out and watch them burn. It's just as well because we couldn't afford the fire fighting equipment anyway." Diamond walked to the edge of my deck and looked down at the ash-covered landscape. "This fire that went through your back yard, Owen, it's probably the first fire here in a hundred years or more. Whereas, before white man's glorious arrival, lightning-caused fires swept Tahoe every five to seven years on average."

"How do they know that?"

"Tree cross-sections. And species distribution. Regular fires used to keep the forest open, and the ratio of pines to firs was much higher."

"Pines being more fire-resistant," I said.

Diamond nodded. "In fact, one of the early white guys wrote that Tahoe's forests were so open you could ride through them on a horse at full gallop. Now the forest is so dense, it's hard to walk through in places, especially on the west shore where they get more precipitation."

"You seem to know a lot about this stuff."

"Been studying," Diamond said. "The darker your skin, the more you gotta know."

"You're not including me in with the pale faces, I hope."

Diamond looked at me. "You are pretty pale. But no, I'll be magnanimous. Don't want to automatically assume guilt by association."

"Magnanimous," I said. "You got some big words for your second language."

"I'm learning," Diamond said. He sat down on one of my deck chairs. Spot sat next to him and lowered his head onto Diamond's lap, hoping for more pets. "Is he going to drool on me?" Diamond asked.

"Probably. He hasn't eaten lunch yet."

Diamond looked disgusted, but didn't move his hand which was rubbing Spot's ears. "You should be glad you're on the Nevada side of the lake where it's drier. Less growth. Less fuel. Probably why your chateau didn't burn."

I looked at my little cabin. "Chateau?"

"Palatial estate where I come from."

I nodded. "About this perp," I said. "I thought a dog search might turn up something."

"Can't hurt," Diamond said. "I thought about it myself now that I've been appointed Fire Investigator. But we've got one deputy out on disability because of his back, another on vacation, and a third sick with the flu, or so he says. Anyway, for the near future I'm Fire Investigator in name only." Diamond looked at Spot. "Tell me. If you were to find a person poking around the crime scene, is there some way a dog can tell if it's the firestarter or not?"

"If we can find an article specific to the firestarter, then we could have the dog scent it. If the dog then alerts to a person, that could be the perp. But you and Terry Drier's guys found no articles, so it is unlikely. Besides, what arsonist is going to hang around to be sniffed by a dog? I didn't have a specific idea of what a dog would find, just that it might be worth the trouble."

"Sure. Bring Spot out there and let him run."

"Actually, Spot is only trained for finding live humans and he isn't that great at it anyway. But I thought I'd bring in a dog that is trained on fires. Accelerants specifically."

"We don't have a dog in our department," Diamond said. "But the South Lake Tahoe P.D. has one."

"Right, but I don't know if it is accelerant trained. I thought I'd call Ellie Ibsen, the woman who trains them. I met her last spring."

Diamond gave a slow nod as the memory came back. "It was her dog found the body of Jennifer Salazar's sister."

"Right."

"Let me know if you find anything," Diamond said.

After Diamond left I looked up Ellie Ibsen in my little book and dialed her number.

"Hi, Ellie, Owen McKenna calling," I said when she answered.

It took her a moment. "Owen! How are you and how is that wonderful animal of yours?"

"I think he misses you. Misses Natasha, too. Ellie, I'm wondering if you have a dog that is trained on accelerants."

"Both Natasha and Annie are. Although Natasha's better. Besides, Annie's laid up with a torn toe ligament. What have you got?"

"The arson fire on the east shore. I'm wondering if any accelerants were involved."

"Natasha's your dog," Ellie said. She paused. "I told my assistant she could have the afternoon off. And you know I'm getting a little old to drive these mountain roads. But if you want to come and get us we've got nothing on our schedule."

"Ellie, remind me to give you a kiss when I get down there."

After I hung up, Spot saw me look at him. He picked up his bowl again, teeth grating on the metal, and resumed thumping the dishwasher with his tail.

"You can drop the bowl now."

It clattered to the floor and rolled like a lost hubcap until it hit the closet where I keep his Science Diet.

"How did you do that?" I said.

Spot wagged some more.

I gave him a small serving what with the car ride in front of us. He waited, two strings of Pavlovian saliva quivering from his jowls, until I gave the okay. Then he inhaled his food faster than I could have with a shop-vac. No manners.

Spot napped in back as I drove up the Sierra crest, out of the Tahoe Basin and down into gold country. For most of an hour I followed the American River canyon as it cut deeper into the mountains.

I turned off in Placerville, drove past where they discovered gold in 1849, and found the turnoff to Ellie's Three Bar Ranch. Spot was awake and excited as I came to a stop. I reached over the seat and opened his door.

Ellie came out of her house and waved. Natasha, her black German Shepherd, appeared beside her and raced into the huge yard.

Spot had met the shepherd before and he ran toward her with enthusiasm. For a moment I worried that they were going to have a head-on collision which could cause serious injury to Natasha considering that Spot out-weighs her by 110 pounds. But they slowed in time and Spot veered off. Natasha, quick as a cat, reversed direction and caught up with him in seconds.

Ellie approached me as the dogs disappeared behind her immaculate house. "Owen, I'm so glad you called again."

Ellie was a tiny woman in her eighties, but energetic as a 50-year-old marathon runner. She reached up and shook my hand with both of hers, squeezing my fingers as if the obvious arthritis in her knuckles was nonexistent. "You said you'd give me a kiss." She grinned and turned her cheek up toward me.

I bent down to her four and a half feet and pecked skin as thin and soft as flower petals. Her wispy white hair felt like goose down brushing my cheek, and she smelled of lilacs.

"I was thinking of you," Ellie said, "because I got a call from your young friend Jennifer Salazar." Ellie was referring to the girl from a murder case I handled the previous spring. Jennifer Salazar had hired me to find the murderer of her twin sister. It was one of Ellie's dogs that had located the body on the rock slide above Emerald Bay.

"I thought Jennifer was off at Harvard," I said.

"She is. She's doing an independent study project on animal intelligence for her psyche requirement. She called me for an expert testimonial. Her words, not mine. I told her I'm just a dog trainer, but she insisted. She is going to fly out here to interview me! Can you believe the extravagance! I worry I won't give her her money's worth."

"Don't worry. You're obviously important to her project. Anyway, she has lots of money." I pictured the French Renaissance mansion on the east shore of Tahoe, all hers now by court decree.

"So I gathered, but I still hope I won't disappoint the girl."

"You won't, Ellie. It's not possible."

Ellie picked a small bag up off the front steps and then called the dogs. Spot and Natasha came at full speed. Again I worried that Spot might cause an injury, this time to Ellie. But the old woman was a master and had my giant dog heeling at her side in a moment. They marched off to the Jeep, Ellie's arm held up high to rest on Spot's back.

We all piled in and headed back up into the mountains while I told Ellie about the forest fire that had nearly burned up my little cabin.

"The motor fuel that runs our cars," Ellie said. "I don't say the G-word in front of my dog as she would recognize it. We call it petrol when we don't want them to know what we're talking about." She glanced in back toward the dogs who were each hanging their heads out opposite windows. "You think petrol is what started the forest fire?"

"I have no idea. The firemen found a burned kitchen match, nothing more. The meadow was so dry, possibly a single match was all it took. But I want to find out if petrol or something similar was used. It seems worthwhile to see if a dog would turn up something. No matter how hot the fire, petrol leaves traces, doesn't it, traces a dog can smell?"

"Yes. In buildings, it seeps into floors and under the walls. Outside, it seeps into the ground. Rarely does it burn up completely. Even in hot fires." She reached into her little bag and handed me a small vial with an eye-dropper cap. Her movements were casual in a way that was meant to escape notice by the dogs. "I need to ask you to arrange to put some petrol in this vial. Of course it needs to be done out of sight of the dogs. Then you must wash the outside of the vial and your hands thoroughly. A strong detergent is a good way to erase the smell on the vial."

"What if the firestarter used an accelerant other than petrol?" I asked. "Turpentine or lighter fluid or alcohol are all available in most peoples' homes. We're scenting your dog on petrol. Will she find any of those other fluids?"

"Yes," Ellie said. "They are all volatile organic compounds. Sensitizing the dog to any of them will work. Think of perfume. There are hundreds of them. But let's say I asked you to smell a typical perfume. Then I sent you to the opera to sniff the ladies and find out if any of them were wearing perfume. You would alert, so to speak, on all standard perfumes, ignoring only those strange scents like musk and such."

I thought about where I could get gas as I drove up into the Sierra. Getting gas in a vial was not so easy as it would appear. A gas can was rarely full enough that one could touch the surface of the liquid with an eye-dropper. I decided to stop at the fire station when we got back to Tahoe and see if they could help.

Terry Drier was out so I explained my problem to one of the firemen and showed him the vial.

He looked at it with skepticism and then glanced toward the Jeep where Ellie and the two dogs waited in the parking lot.

"The dog handler needs gas to pre-scent the dog," I said. "I thought maybe you would have a can. Or maybe we could get some from out of your snowblower."

"That old woman is a dog handler?"

"The best Search and Rescue trainer in California."

He shook his head in disbelief. "Give me a break."

"Remember the avalanche in the back country near Kirkwood last year?" I said. "When the Kirkwood Search and Rescue dog ran up the mountain and immediately started digging where that ten-year-old skier was buried?"

"Of course," he said. "It was little Jimmy Jackson that dog saved."

I looked over toward Ellie in my Jeep. "She trained that dog."

The fireman looked at Ellie, then at me. "Follow me," he said. "We've got gas in the garage."

We poured some gas into a coffee cup and then used the eye-dropper to transfer it to the vial. "Any chance you've got some detergent to wash this with?" I asked.

"There's liquid hand soap in the bathroom. Will that work?"

"Sure," I said. "Thanks much. I'll tell Terry how helpful you were."

Back in the Jeep I showed Ellie the vial which smelled like perfumed soap.

"Perfect," she said. "Now we'll go catch an arsonist!"

SIX

"Do you need a rest stop?" I asked Ellie. "Food or coffee? We've been driving a long time." I didn't know how much stamina I could expect from a woman in her eighties.

"No, I'm ready to go. I'll rest later. Where is the fire?"

"Just ahead." I drove another two miles and pulled off where the burn started its long swath up the mountain.

We let the dogs out, and they ran around in the burned-out meadow while Ellie explained the procedure.

"I'll stay here by your car and talk to the dogs while you walk out of sight over beyond that rise." She pointed toward the forest. "Put one drop of petrol on the ground in a spot that you'll remember. Then come back to us in a different way so the dogs have not seen where you've been. Be careful not to get petrol on you or on the outside of the vial."

"Will Spot be in the way? He's never done a search for accelerants."

Ellie's eyes brightened with enthusiasm. "No, not at all. He'll learn from following Natasha." Ellie looked up at the dogs across the meadow, then put four fingers in her mouth and whistled loud enough to hurt my ears. Natasha came running fast, followed by Spot. The impression was of a streaking fighter jet with a big transport plane lumbering behind. "Okay," Ellie said to me. "I'll wait for you to come back."

I hiked off across the blackened meadow while Ellie held both dogs with nothing more than her kind voice for a leash. When I was well out of sight I came upon a burned fallen tree trunk that would be easy to find again. Twisting trails of smoke issued from one end. Near the other end I put a single drop of gasoline on the ground and then carefully re-inserted the eye-dropper into the bottle so as not to get any gas on the outside of the vial or on myself.

"Everything go okay?" Ellie said when I returned.

I nodded.

"Let me take your arm," she said. "The ground looks uneven. Let's walk this way. The dogs will follow. My dog will find the petrol drop. It is a reinforcement technique."

We set off across the meadow in a new direction, the dogs bounded this way and that. Eventually, we circled around toward where I'd put the drop of gasoline. Natasha was trotting some distance away, a stick in her mouth, when she stopped. She dropped the stick, sniffed the air and then started a search pattern, her nose to the ground. In seconds, her nose was where I'd put the drop of gas.

"Gasoline!" Ellie said to Natasha. "Natasha, find the gasoline!"

Natasha immediately changed from a dog at play to a working dog with an intense focus on the task at hand. The transformation was so impressive and complete, it was as if she were a different animal. She kept her nose to the ground and started off at a trot.

At first, I didn't perceive a pattern to what looked like a random search. But after a minute, it was clear that she had a method. She went in a zigzag fashion away from where I'd put the drop. Then she made a gradual circle, larger and larger so that she described a rough spiral of sorts.

Spot sensed that she had a purpose but the befuddled look on his face showed that he had no clue what it was.

"Spot!" Ellie called out. He came running while Natasha kept up her widening search. "Smell here." She pointed to the ground where I'd put the drop of gas.

I was amazed again as Spot did what she said, demonstrating that this woman had magic with these animals. He stuck his nose in the dirt, inhaled, pushed dirt around with his nose and inhaled again.

"Gasoline, Spot! Gasoline! Find the gasoline!" Ellie gave him a little smack on his butt and Spot ran off, joining Natasha in her search. Although I'd never worked him on any search training except humans, it seemed clear that he understood that this was the same process. But his constant looks toward Natasha suggested that he realized that the fastest way to find gasoline smells was to follow her rather than strike out on his own. The sight of the Great Dane trying to mimic the dedicated movements of the small German Shepherd was a little like watching a Disney movie.

It was only a minute before Natasha alerted. Ellie pulled on my arm and pointed.

"Look. She's found something."

I watched as Natasha ran to where Terry Drier had said the fire started. She stuck her nose in the ground, pushing ashes and dirt. The dog became nearly frantic as she moved away, nosed more dirt, then moved away again.

"A trail!" Ellie said, her voice quivering with excitement. "She's found an accelerant trail!"

Natasha trotted along with her nose to the burned ground. She jerked to stop, reversed, turned, ran off again. Not far from where the fire started was a large blackened tree trunk. Natasha rushed around it and stopped. Spot joined her. We could see their tails held high and wagging with excitement.

Ellie and I hurried toward them. When we came around the tree we saw the reason for their excitement. A small gas can, its finish burned to a blackened crisp, lay on its side in the ashes. I walked over to an unburned area and found a stick. I poked it through the handle of the can so I could lift it up without marring it.

The small can was circular in shape with rounded edges and looked like it would hold no more than one gallon. Being so small it was the type one would use for filling a weed eater or a similarly small engine with a tiny gas tank. I couldn't think of any other practical use for it. Unless one wanted to start a forest fire?

I set the can back down. "We can retrieve this later," I said. "Can you ask your dog to look for more petrol?"

Ellie turned to the dog, held out her arm and pointed her finger toward the burned forest. "Natasha! Find more gasoline!"

Natasha immediately understood. She put her nose to the ash-covered ground and resumed her search pattern.

We picked up our pace as Natasha, followed by Spot, headed out of the meadow and into the burned landscape that used to be forest.

The dogs went over a rise, through a maze of charred, smoldering tree trunks, then down a slope. Natasha repeatedly jammed her nose in the dirt and wiggled it around. Then she ran forward and pounced on the next spot of scent as if seizing a mouse. Spot was less focused but he followed directly behind.

"Are you okay with this hiking?" I asked Ellie as we tried to keep up. "I can run after them and then come back and get you."

"No way," Ellie said in a voice more like a teenager's than an octogenarian's. "I want to see what she's tracking!" Ellie tugged on my arm and clamored even faster over the uneven, rocky landscape.

We followed the dogs down an increasingly steep slope that was littered with fallen smoldering logs. The air was thick with the stink of wet smoke. At one point, Ellie's foot slipped and rolled off a stick. She gasped and I thought she had sprained her ankle or worse. But after a moment she insisted on continuing.

Natasha and Spot got ahead of us and disappeared among the blackened trees. But a minute later we saw them at a distance. Their noses were to the ground, tails held up, their excitement undiminished.

Ellie and I did our best getting down the long slope. I realized we were heading into the ravine where Highland Creek flowed, the same ravine that went up the mountain and ended just below my cabin. Why anyone would bring gasoline into the ravine was beyond my imagination, but I did not question the fact, so focused was Ellie's dog.

At the bottom of the ravine, Highland Creek flowed lightly from the melting snow on the mountain above. But I had no doubt that it was dry prior to the storm as evidenced by the complete burn of all the dogwood near and in the creek bed. Ellie and I paused to catch our breath. The dogs were out of our sight around a turn in the ravine.

"Listen," Ellie said. "Natasha's whining. She's found something. Something bad."

We hustled upstream and around the bend. Both dogs came into sight. Spot was standing still, looking back toward us. Natasha was moving back and forth near a large black object on the ground.

Neither Ellie nor I knew what we were looking at until we got much closer. Then Ellie stopped with a sharp intake of breath. I finally realized what it was.

Contorted in a grotesque position, seemingly wrapped in black peeling layers of what must have once been skin, was a body. The only parts that weren't burned black were its teeth. They were darkened brown by the smoke, and exposed in a hideous final grimace.

SEVEN

We didn't spend more than a few moments at the macabre scene. It was unsettling for Ellie and me as well as the dogs. Ellie called Natasha and Spot over and pet both of them extravagantly, telling them how smart they were. The dogs showed little enthusiasm, and, although I'd never witnessed a dead find before, I understood that it was a very depressing experience for dogs. While Spot seemed to mope, Natasha, in particular, hung her head and whined as if she'd been physically hurt.

"We need to do a live find as soon as possible," Ellie said. "This poor creature will be a wreck until then."

"Let's go back to the Jeep, first, so I can report this body on my phone. Then I can go hide. Will that work?"

Ellie looked up at me and nodded. It was only then that I saw the tears in her eyes. As a search and rescue handler, she'd no doubt seen sights as bad many times. But that didn't lessen her sensitivity.

We made our way back up the steep incline of the ravine, Ellie holding my arm tight and letting me lift her up the steepest sections. The dogs followed behind us without veering or running around. There was no more play in them and no more searching. They understood that their job was over.

We made it back through the woods and across the meadow to the Jeep. I helped Ellie up into the passenger seat so that she could rest. Despite her incredible energy level, she wasn't used to the low oxygen of high altitude. The dogs stood unmoving outside her open door, literally hanging their heads. A periodic whine issued from Natasha's throat.

I got through to Diamond on my phone.

"The search dog found a gasoline trail," I told him. "There is a gas can not far from where the fire started and down in the bottom of the Highland Creek ravine there is a body."

"Do you recognize the victim?" Diamond asked.

"It is in an area thoroughly burned. Identification will no doubt require dental records."

"That bad, huh?" Diamond said. "Can you stick around until we get a unit over there?"

"Certainly."

I hung up and turned to Ellie who was leaning back in her seat and suddenly looking nearly as old as she was. "How should we work the live find?" I asked.

Ellie rallied somewhat as we shifted our attentions to a new task. "Do you have an article of your clothing we can use? Gloves in the back of the Jeep or something?"

I dug under my seat and pulled out a baseball cap.

"Put it on a moment to freshen up your scent," Ellie said.

I did as told, rotated it on my head and then handed it to her.

"I'll keep the dogs with me," she said. "You hike out of sight and hide. Tell me how high to count before I send the dogs looking."

I thought about it a moment. "Let's see. How about one hundred. That should give me enough time to go back over the rise, then double back and hide in a different direction."

"Okay. At one hundred I'll scent them on your hat and send them off." She got out of the Jeep and turned to the dogs. "Natasha, Spot. Come here. Sit-stay."

The dogs moved slow, but did as told, depression heavy on their faces. I went back into the burned forest and, once out of sight, found a large depression under a rock where I curled up, invisible to anyone who didn't have a damn good nose. Sooner than I imagined possible, Natasha ran around the corner at full speed as if she'd known all along where I was going to hide. She lightly bit my arm, tugging at my sleeve, trying to pull me into the open. Her tail wagged furiously. Spot was less graceful as he followed on her heels. He leaped onto me. His mass knocked me out of Natasha's grasp and onto my back. I grabbed him and we rolled around in the dirt and ash. Natasha wanted to get in on the act and tentatively pawed at us while her tail wagged like windshield wiper on high, but her good sense no doubt told her to be careful before jumping into a four hundred pound wrestling match.

I separated myself from Spot's grasp, vigorously pet them both again and walked with them back toward the Jeep.

Ellie saw the changed mood of the dogs from a distance and she grinned. "A live find always makes them so happy," she said as we got close.

At that moment Diamond pulled up, followed by two young cops in a cruiser. Diamond got out and looked me up and down. Then his eyes went to Spot. Covered with ash and dirt, Spot and I must have resembled Hollywood extras for a disaster movie. "You have a big nose, even for an Anglo, but does it work so well that you've been down in the dirt, sniffing with the dogs?"

"Dead finds are depressing for dogs," I said. "We did a live find to cheer them up. I was the find."

"Inscrutable gringos," Diamond muttered and turned to the young cops who were walking up. "This man has a body to show us. I want one of you to stay with the vehicles and..." He looked from me to Ellie.

"Diamond," I said. "I'd like you to meet Ellie Ibsen. She is a search and rescue trainer. It was her dog Natasha who found the body. Ellie, Diamond Martinez."

Diamond and Ellie nodded and smiled at each other.

"Natasha," Ellie called out from the passenger seat. She pointed at Diamond. "Please meet Officer Diamond Martinez." Natasha trotted over, sat in front of Diamond and lifted her paw.

Diamond, who prides himself on showing little emotion, broke into a large grin and shook his head. He bent over and shook the dog's paw. "We got deputies ain't this smart," he said, looking at the two younger cops.

The dogs stayed with Ellie and one of the cops. The other cop walked with Diamond and me out to the ravine. I pointed out the location of the body without walking back down the slope.

"You think this corpse was killed in the fire?" Diamond asked.

"I don't know, but it makes sense it was the fire."

"Well, we know when the fire started," Diamond said. "So maybe we should call in Street."

"Sure. She can do a time-of-death estimate. Although it's hard to see how there could be any bugs on the body after a forest fire."

"But if there are any bugs, Street's report and the coroner's autopsy should tell us if the perp is just an arsonist or a murderer as well."

"Right. Okay if I take Ellie home? She could probably use some rest. It's been a long day."

"Sure," Diamond said. "I'll call you with any questions."

EIGHT

I brought Ellie up the mountain to my home for refreshments before the long drive back down to the foothills.

When I pulled into the drive my eyes immediately went to an unusual dark object in front of my door. All my internal warning sensors went off. I angled the Jeep so Ellie wouldn't see. "I'll get your door," I said. I jumped out, went around the back and trotted over to my front door. The object appeared to have been a stuffed animal before it had been burned black. Reaching down, I felt for heat. Sensing none, I picked the creature up by an ear and quickly carried it, clumps of stuffing falling out, over to the garbage can, put it inside and snugged the lid down tight.

Hoping the burn smell would blend with all the other smells from the forest fire, I wiped my hand on my pants and hustled over to open Ellie's door. I helped her out, then opened the rear door. The dogs bounded out with Spot immediately running and sniffing around the garbage can. I ushered Ellie and Natasha past the garbage can and into my cabin.

"What a cute little place!" Ellie exclaimed. She walked through the living room and out onto the deck. "And the view of the lake! Kings and queens don't get to see this!"

"It's true." The dogs must have been warm for they both sprawled on the deck, a good thing being that they were covered with ash. I grabbed a towel and quickly wiped them down. "What can I get you to drink, Ellie?" I was mentally cataloging my lack of selection.

"I'd take a little scotch if you had any."

I tried not to show surprise as I ushered Ellie in from the early evening chill. "I don't think there's any scotch in the cabinet, but I might have some Jack Daniel's," I said.

"J.D. will work as well," Ellie said. She sank into one of the chairs by the wood stove, leaned back and put her feet up on the hassock.

"How do you like your libation?"

"Straight up with water on the side, if you please," she said.

"Coming right up." I washed the soot off my hands and was getting out a shot glass for Ellie and a beer glass for me when the phone rang. It was Street.

"I just got a call from Diamond," she said. "He said you found a body?"

"Yeah," I said, moving into the bedroom so that Ellie would not hear me talk about it. "A burn victim."

"He wants me to take samples."

"He mentioned it to me," I said. "Can you do that? Are there bugs on a burned body? I'd think the fire would have torched all the bugs in the area."

"I'm sure it did. But flies will come from miles away if they smell a body."

"But they have to lay eggs on the body. How are eggs going to hatch on charred skin? I would think it would take much longer for maggots to develop and it would throw off your time of death estimate."

"Actually, a burn will speed things up a bit because there are usually multiple cracks in a burn victim's skin and the flies lay their eggs in those cracks. The maggots get a jump-start at getting into the body."

"A lovely image," I said.

"Anyway, I thought I'd come by after I'm done. Want some company?"

"We'd love it."

"We? Having a party?"

"You'll remember Ellie Ibsen, the search and rescue trainer I told you about. She's here with the amazing dog Natasha. Only thing we need to make the evening complete is you."

"I'll be there as soon as I'm done," she said, then hung up.

I brought Ellie her Jack Daniel's with water on the side.

She picked up the shot glass. "Here's to keeping the old ticker motivated," she said and downed a third of the whiskey.

I toasted with her, then put some paper and kindling in the woodstove and lit it. As the flames grew behind the glass I wondered who would put a burned, stuffed animal on my doorstep.

Ellie looked at my shelves. "You have a lot of art books," she said. "Are you an artist?"

"No. More of a dilettante."

Ellie scanned the number of volumes on my shelves then turned back to me. "You're being self-deprecating. You certainly have large appetite if not large scholarship."

"I guess I'm just continually amazed that artists toil away to make something which has no earthly purpose other than for the rest of us to look at. What good fortune that is, don't you think?"

Ellie nodded. "How do you do it, studying art? Do you just read the books straight through? Or do you make sketches of your favorite paintings?"

"I kind of poke around in the books, reading, looking at the reproductions. I'm not at all focused in my approach. An academic would be horrified."

"I'll bet," Ellie said, the first touch of sarcasm that I'd witnessed in her. We spoke about art for a long time while Ellie sipped her whiskey and I drank a couple beers.

"Would you show me some art?" Ellie said just as I was thinking she must be bored with the subject. Something you like?"

"Sure," I said after thinking a moment. I was reaching for a book when I heard a car pull up outside. "Excuse me, Ellie, while I check and see if that is Street."

Ellie nodded as I went out.

Street got out of her VW bug to the enthusiastic greetings of the dogs. She was wearing a white blouse, black skirt and tights and low black pumps.

"You took samples in your skirt?" I said.

"No. I wore jeans in the woods and put this on in the car. A change of clothes helps me change the mood. She spun in a circle and her skirt billowed enticingly. Her exceptional posture gave her the grace of a dancer. I kissed her.

Street lowered her voice. "So how did you find the body? It was practically hidden down in that ravine."

"Natasha, here, traced gas, I mean petrol, down into the ravine and found it." I turned to the dog. "Natasha, I want you to meet Street." The German Shepherd immediately sat and raised a paw.

"Oh my God!" Street exclaimed as she shook hands with the dog. She turned to my dog. "Spot, are you watching this?" He stuck his nose in her stomach, then raised his head and licked her neck.

Street turned her head toward me as she hugged him. The bright red gloss on her full lips and the dark eyeliner made her high cheekbones and distinct jaw line look a bit severe. Although Street was a woman of impeccable grooming, she used no other makeup. In the same way that she didn't try to hide her excessive thinness with bulky clothing, she preferred to let her acne scars remain uncovered. It was clear that her efforts were not designed to make herself look prettier, but instead to make her look dramatic. Even so, she was still beautiful.

"Can you tell anything yet from your samples?"

"Probably. I found a lot of first instar maggots and a few in the second instar stage."

"Meaning?"

"The first flies' eggs were probably laid while the body was still smoldering. They would hatch in about ten hours and those first instar maggots would begin molting into second instars in another ten or eleven hours. Which would mean death came about twenty one hours ago, or just about the time the fire started. But this is still speculation," she said.

"You have to raise the maggots to adult flies to verify the species and their specific growth patterns, right?"

"Exactly. I also left a hygrothermograph at the scene so I can get temperature data over the next few days. That could alter my findings. Even so, it looks like the victim perished just about when the fire started, whether from the fire or not."

I gestured toward my cabin door. "Before you meet Ellie, I should say that finding the body was somewhat upsetting to Ellie and, for that matter, the dogs as well. So we're kind of trying not to talk about it."

Street looked up at me and fixed me with a penetrating gaze from narrowed eyes. "But a big macho guy like you isn't even fazed by such discoveries."

I smiled. "Of course not," I said as I directed her inside. "Unless lying awake the next three nights qualifies."

When we were inside I said, "Ellie, I'd like you to meet Street Casey, woman of my dreams."

"I'm delighted," Ellie said with scintillating eyes and smile.

"And I'm pleased to finally meet you, Ellie," Street said.

Ellie brightened at Street's vivacious presence. As always, Street was like fresh air in a room, and she seemed to fill my entire cabin with life.

"Ellie," Street said, "You should know that when Owen met you last year he spoke about you at some length. How did you describe her, Owen? Oh, I remember. He said you were as light and luminous as a Japanese paper lantern."

"Stop, you're embarrassing me," Ellie said.

"Me, too." I said.

Ellie sipped more whiskey and turned to Street.   "Owen was going to show me some art."

"Indeed," I said as I got out a beer and glass for Street.

Street poured a couple of inches or so into the glass while I pulled a book off the shelf, squatted down next to Ellie's chair and paged through the book. "Here is a painting I've come to really admire."

"Oh, my, look at that jagged, snow-capped peak." Ellie took the book into her delicate hands, slipped on the glasses that had been hanging on a gold chain around her neck and looked at the painting up close. "And that beautiful lake with the waterfalls plunging into it! Is that by Thomas Moran? He was always my favorite landscape painter."

I raised my eyebrows in surprise. "Close. Albert Bierstadt. This one is called 'The Sierra Nevada In California.'"

"It's a mythical place, isn't it? I suppose this peak is like Mt. Whitney, only more majestic. And the waterfalls are as perfect as those in Yosemite. Deer and ducks, and a forest that looks like Merlin lives there... it's a perfect fantasy!"

I left the book in Ellie's lap, sat down in my rocker and drank some beer.

Street walked behind Ellie's chair and leaned over Ellie's shoulder to see the reproduction. One foot was cocked back. I could see her ankle. It was perfect. Her lovely ankle bones looked delicate and vulnerable, although I knew better of it having struggled on many occasions to keep up with her as she rocketed down ski slopes or scrambled up cliffs on a mountain hike.

"Owen," Ellie said. "Was Bierstadt one of the first people to see the Sierra Nevada? Was this painting a way to show what the West looked like to all the people back east? If so, it would kind of fool them, wouldn't it? It's not as if the whole West looks like this."

"Right," I said. "Imagine that you're an Easterner in the Nineteenth Century. You've never been past the Mississippi. You see this painting and you think that's what the West looks like. It would take hold of your imagination and not let go until your wagon broke a wheel in the middle of the Oklahoma prairie."

"So what makes it art, Owen?" Ellie asked. "Is this more than just a pretty picture?"

Her question surprised me, revealing an acuity of thinking that few lay people brought to art. I supposed it was what made her a great trainer of search dogs. She knew that to look at a scene for its obvious attributes was to be partially blind. It was only when one looked beneath the surface, literally and metaphorically, did one begin to really see.

"Yes," I said. "I think it is more than just a pretty picture."

Ellie looked at me. After a moment of silence she grinned and said, "Well?"

"My guess is that Bierstadt was exploring the difference between the natural landscape and a man-made landscape. Even though he came long before shopping malls, I think he understood that man had violated the essential grandeur of nature. The perfect places in the world, places that man had not trampled, were beginning to disappear. So he wanted to paint those places and make them as perfect as he could imagine." I leaned forward in my chair and pointed to the reproduction. "Look at the way these misty shafts of light come though the clouds. Amazing."

"It's almost too much," Ellie said.

"You're echoing what an art critic said at a talk in Reno a few months back. He was explaining that Nineteenth Century landscape painters like Cole and Church depicted the untrammeled American wilderness as sacred. But when Bierstadt went west of the Mississippi, he went wild with ostentatious detail and overboard metaphors."

"Meaning," Ellie said, "that the light shafts coming through the clouds are supposed to represent God's presence."

"Exactly," I said. "Even so, I like it. I think Bierstadt was saying that these mountains were God's vision of a perfect place, and that they should remain pristine."

"If this painting shows God's idea of perfection," Street said, "then where are the insects?"

Ellie raised her eyebrows.

"Street's an entomologist," I said. "Sees the whole world in terms of bugs."

"And so should God," Street said. "If it weren't for bugs..."

"I know," I interrupted. "Without the insects pollinating the plants, which are the basis of all food chains, we wouldn't be here."

"Among other things," Street said. She sipped her beer so slowly it was if she were savoring each molecule. The level in her glass had already dropped a quarter of an inch.

"How does an entomologist find work in Tahoe?" Ellie asked.

"It's not plentiful," Street said. "But I've been doing an increasing amount of forensic consulting recently."

"Forensic?" Ellie said. "You mean insects can tell you..." She trailed off.

"Right," Street said. "Time of death. Sometimes even cause of death."

"Oh, my," Ellie said. "That doesn't sound pleasant."

"Street also does consulting for the Forest Service."

"Well, at least that sounds less macabre," Ellie said, grinning.

Street was deadpan when she responded. "I did a study comparing the gallery patterns chewed under tree bark by Ips beetle larvae in pine and Scolytus beetle larvae in firs. Pretty exciting, huh?"

Ellie grinned like a child. "Yes! It is! Tell me more."

Street looked embarrassed. "Well, the more robust the galleries, the quicker the trees die. Yet a few of the trees that are infested show inexplicable resistance to the beetles. It's like those rare prostitutes in Africa that seem to be immune to AIDS. The more we learn about the trees, the more..." Street suddenly stopped talking. "Sorry, I go on. But it is fun, actually."

"I can see," Ellie said, sincerely amused. "So what kind of bugs should Bierstadt have put in this painting?"

"Let's see," Street said, still looking over Ellie's shoulder. Street pointed to the picture. "We've got all the boreal zones up to arctic alpine. Within that range are a greater diversity of insect species than all other plant and animal species combined."

"I'm envisioning a single grand mythic bug for this painting," I said.

"Oh yes!" Ellie exclaimed. She held her arms up and her eyes sparkled. "A Kafka bug thirty feet tall! Scratching its way up the glacier on this mountain!" She made clawing motions in the air with her hands.

"Actually, bugs do live on glaciers," Street said, grinning at Ellie. "For example, there is a type of Springtail, Achorutes nivicola, that swarms in enormous numbers on snow. They're commonly referred to as snow fleas, although they aren't fleas at all."

"Okay!" Ellie said, barely containing her excitement. "Owen told us about art. Now you tell us about an insect! Pick a bug. Any bug. Something strange that would live in this landscape."

Street sat on the arm of Ellie's chair and gazed at the reproduction of Bierstadt's painting.

Ellie drank the last of her Jack Daniels and looked up at me, more life in her eyes than I rarely saw in a person, never mind someone working through their ninth decade. "Owen? While Street thinks, maybe I should have another J.D.! Don't you agree?"

"Absolutely."

"Oh!" Ellie said. "I haven't had this much fun in years!" She was nearly bouncing in her chair.

I brought Ellie another whiskey and myself another beer. I didn't refill Street's glass because, after all, she still had an inch left which would last her another hour.

"Okay," Street said. "There's an obvious insect wherever you find dead wood." She pointed to the picture. "Like the rotting stump of this tree. Underneath there is likely a termite colony."

Ellie scrunched up her nose. "I hate termites. The pale, crawly things give me the creeps."

"They'd give you worse than that if you were an invader in their nest. You know how social insects like ants and bees have evolved specialized behaviors among their members? Queens lay eggs. Workers find the food and tend the eggs. Well, the only job of soldier termites is to protect the nest. And they've evolved an extreme way of doing so."

I looked at Ellie. "Knowing termites, I have a feeling we're about to hear something gross."

Ellie turned toward Street. The old woman's eyes were wide and alert.

"Worse," Street said. "When the threat to the nest is severe, the soldier termite turns around and attacks with a blast from its rear end. Except, in this case the effort is so severe that it blows its entire rear end off."

"Does the termite die defending the nest?" Ellie asked.

Street nodded somberly. "Altruism in the extreme."

"This, uh, artillery shot," I said. "What do entomologists call it?"

"Explosive defecation."

Ellie and I looked at each other, our eyes locking.

"Definitely a Kafka bug," Ellie said.

We ended up discussing insects and art for another hour during which time I got out some salsa and cheese and leftover roasted chicken, rolled up some enchiladas and popped them in the oven. While they baked, I opened a Sonoma Valley Zinfandel, got out spinach and lettuce and washed a bowl of cherry tomatoes. When the enchiladas were hot I sprinkled shredded sharp cheddar over them. I put a couple more logs on the fire and, because I don't have a dining room never mind a table, I served us an enchilada dinner in our living room chairs.

After a time, Ellie said that she didn't remember the last time she had such an enjoyable evening, and could she extend it by sleeping over? I understood that she was too tired to ride back down to the foothills. My first thought was that I didn't have a fold-out couch and maybe Ellie should sleep at Street's. But then I remembered that Street had just put up Mrs. Duchamp. And the previous spring my client Jennifer Salazar had taken refuge there. Despite Street's generosity, it wasn't right to put all of my temporary housing needs on her doorstep.

"Of course you can stay over," I said. "You'll take the bedroom."

"Are you sure?" Ellie said.

"Certainly. I'll sleep in the living room with the dogs. Natasha will be more comfortable in a strange place if she has company.

Street stayed a few minutes longer and kept Ellie company while I put fresh sheets on the bed. Then Street headed home.

"She seems like a very special girl," Ellie said as I returned to the living room. "So... full of life." Ellie looked up at me, her eyes searching. "Do you think you'll get married some day? Mind you, I know that's prying, but when you get as old as me you can get away with it!"

"I'd love to," I said.

"Get married to Street?"

I nodded.

"She doesn't want to?"

"It's not real clear. I've asked her a few times, but she declines."

"But she seems to like you so much. You two get along in a special way." Ellie's face showed confusion. "Is there another man?"

"No, nothing like that," I said. "It is more about having complete control over her life. I think she feels she would be losing some independence." I was surprised at myself. It wasn't like me to reveal such thoughts to another person. But Ellie had a way of opening me up.

"If she has a measure of fear about losing control," Ellie said, "there must be a reason."

"There is. The last time she wasn't in control was when she was a child and her childhood was rough to say the least. Some ugly things happened to her. She ran away from home when she was fifteen and hasn't spoken to either of her parents since."

"Where do they live?"

"At the time Street left, they lived in St. Louis. Her mother was an alcoholic and her father had been in and out of prison, mostly in. We don't know where they are now. I offered to find out, but Street doesn't want to know. She shut the door on her childhood and won't open it back up."

"Does she have siblings?"

"She had a brother, two years her junior. But he died a few days after a beating by the father. The coroner said the cause of death was pneumonia, but everyone else thought it was the beating. Street left the next day."

"Oh, Lord, I'm so sorry," Ellie said. "Maybe I shouldn't have asked."

"No, it's okay."

"Where did Street live when she ran away? Fifteen is so young."

"She took a Greyhound to Memphis where she had cousins by her mother's sister. She called from the station and they came to pick her up. But the first thing her aunt did was call Street's parents. Street could hear her father yelling in the background. She was so frightened of him coming and taking her home that she slipped out in the middle of the night and started hitchhiking."

"I can't imagine anything so terrifying," Ellie said.

"Me neither. But she got a series of good rides and headed west to San Francisco."

"Did she know anyone there?"

"No. And she didn't quite make it that far. Her last ride let her off in Berkeley early one morning. She wandered around for a couple of hours and spotted Cody's Bookstore. She was still standing there when they opened.

"Let me guess. She got a job."

"Yes. She lied about her age and said she would be good in the science section. The manager asked what she knew of science and she gave him a lesson on the insect Order called Lepidoptera."

"How did a fifteen year-old girl know about that?"

"She'd always wanted a pet as a child, but her mother wouldn't allow it. So Street collected insects. Her favorites were Monarch butterflies. She learned everything about them. I forget their scientific name, but I remember the Lepidoptera Order they belong in because we've joked about her time at Cody's books as a type of adoption. She refers to it as the Lepidoption. She says Cody's saved her life."

We were silent awhile. Ellie had a few drops of wine left and she held her glass upended to let them drip out into her mouth.

"I suppose it is a good balance," Ellie said. "You two live apart, Street has her independence, but you get together often. That is why I never married. In my day a man's needs were everything. Now people are finally realizing that women are just as important. You respect Street's needs."

"Yes, I do."

"That is a good thing. More important than marriage."

We sat for a time in comfortable silence, then said goodnight and Ellie turned in.

Now that I was alone, I quietly stepped outside and opened the garbage can where I'd put the stuffed animal. I pulled it out and turned it over in the weak light of the front entry.

Most of the outside had been burned black. The fabric had melted in places and then cooled into a hard brittle covering that was cracked and broken. The inner yellow stuffing was singed and it too had cooled hard and rough.

I pulled two of the bent legs back into what may have been their original position and looked at the animal from different angles. I now understood that it had been a toy dog. But as I rotated it I saw that it had unusual proportions, thick through the chest and neck, but with long thin legs. On its flat belly was a patch of unburned fabric. Although soiled, it appeared to be mostly white with a bit of black on the edge.

Goosebumps raised up across my back. The toy stuffed dog, burned to a crisp, was supposed to be a Great Dane. A Harlequin like Spot.

NINE

I spent the night in my sleeping bag in front of the wood stove, the dogs on either side. Although little of my fitful dozing could be called sleep, toward dawn I finally achieved a couple hours of slumber, then awoke to the smell of coffee. Ellie must have already been up and busy in the kitchen. I unzipped the sleeping bag and shuffled outside onto the deck where Ellie reclined on the chaise lounge. The dogs lay on the far side of the deck, their noses on the edge of the boards, appearing to project over the lake. The fall sun was bright and hot and Lake Tahoe looked like a giant blue crystal a thousand feet below.

"Good morning," I said.

"I made coffee," Ellie said. She reached over to the tray she'd put on the table and poured me a steaming cup from the thermos. "I found no cream or sugar, so I'm assuming you like it black."

"Blacker the better."

"I dreamed of your Bierstadt painting," Ellie said. "It was so peaceful."

"With or without Street's insects?" I asked.

"Without." She looked at me, eyes flashing. "No Kafka bugs at all!"

We had a leisurely breakfast of strawberries and cantaloupe and did not speak of the fire or the dead man. Afterward, we loaded the dogs into the Jeep and drove back down to the foothills. We had an animated conversation about Ellie's favorite pastime, gardening, as we wound through the American River canyon. Ellie's take on the business of planting and weeding and harvesting was that gardening wasn't much about vegetables at all, but instead was very much about rejuvenating one's soul. To see things grow, blossom, mature, get old and die, and then watch nature start all over with a new beginning as fresh and eager as if the process weren't a cycle but a singular miraculous event, was to Ellie a cleansing of her deepest places.

By the time I dropped Ellie and Natasha off at her Three Bar Ranch she'd gone from being a pleasant acquaintance to one of my good friends and someone I would consult in the future on matters much more varied than search and rescue.

When I got back to Tahoe, I stopped at my office on Kingsbury Grade. The only mail in my box was junk and bills. The day's paper was on the floor in front of my door. The headline was huge and the story was under my friend Glenda Gorman's byline.

BODY FOUND IN FOREST FIRE

A body found in the east shore fire was burned beyond recognition according to Douglas County authorities. The unidentified corpse, believed to be that of a large male, was discovered by a search and rescue dog brought in by local detective Owen McKenna. McKenna, who could not be reached for comment, is believed to be working for the Tahoe Douglas Fire Protection District. Battalion Chief Terry Drier would neither confirm nor deny McKenna's involvement. Nor would he explain what motivated McKenna's search and whether or not he expected to find a body.

Diamond Martinez, Fire Investigator for the Douglas County Sheriff's Department, confirmed that the fire was set with gasoline in a meadow near the bottom of the Highland Creek ravine.

According to a source in a local fire department, the fire may have been started by an environmentalist

upset with the fire suppression policies of the U.S.
Forest Service. Linda Saronna, head of the Forest
Service's Lake Tahoe Basin Management Unit, said that
the Forest Service is continually reviewing its fire
suppression policies. Saronna further stated that while
controlled burns are increasingly used to reduce fire
danger as well as to restore a natural balance to parts of
the forest, it is Forest Service policy to use all
available resources to put out fires near populated areas.

I tossed the paper on my desk and played the messages on
the answering machine.

There were two from Glenda Gorman at the paper and
one message from Diamond Martinez.

I dialed Diamond back first and he answered immediately.

"Got an ID on the body," he said. "A Mr. Jake Pooler of
Jake Pooler Construction in Truckee was reported missing yesterday. We sent a courier to Truckee to get old man Pooler's records
from his dentist. Dr. Aaron Ashley did the forensics."

"*Old man* Pooler?"

"Sixty-eight."

"Doesn't sound so old to me," I said.

"Old where I come from. You work the fields on your
hands and knees, you're old by forty. Anyway, Mr. Pooler had a
bridge, some crowns and a lot of fillings. They all matched up."

"Who made the missing persons report?"

"His wife."

"Has she been notified?"

"Not yet.

"I'd like to talk to her," I said.

"Feel free. The Truckee officer who took the missing persons report said she didn't seem too upset by his disappearance."
Diamond paused. "Makes you wonder if she lit the match. Maybe I
could ask you to do me a big favor, being that half of Truckee's finest are down in Sacramento at a tactics seminar and they wondered
if I could..."

"You want me to do the tough stuff," I said.

"Sensitive guy like you would be perfect for the job. Besides, you're on the Douglas County payroll. You're practically a public official. Makes sense you'd inform the widow."

I paused. "Okay."

"Let me know what you find out."

"Any word on her? Does she collect life insurance? Is his business worth much?"

"I asked a friend who works for one of the building supply companies in the area. Sounds like old man Pooler had more liabilities than assets. His name was near the top of their receivables list."

"Not much motive for the widow," I said.

"No."

"One more thing that may connect with this." I told him about the burned stuffed animal I found on my door step.

"Do you think it could be our arsonist trying to warn you off?" Diamond asked.

"I would, except that at the time the stuffed animal was put on my doorstep almost no one knew I was on the job."

Diamond sighed. "I guess you didn't see yesterday's paper. The article on the fire had a mention of you just like today's paper. Said you'd been hired by the Tahoe Douglas F.P.D."

"What? I thought I was supposed to be kept under wraps."

"You were. So either we've got a leak or someone was very careless. Anyway, there's a lot of psychos out there, Owen. Anyone could have read about you and decided make a sick joke. Then again, maybe someone found the burned, stuffed animal in the woods and put it on your doorstep thinking you'll want to see all possible evidence. Either way, I'd watch your back side. It ain't a reach for an arsonist to leave a threatening sign before they do something more serious. Could be a copycat, too. Some jerk who wants to get in on all the fun the firestarter is having. I'll send a deputy up the mountain to pick up the evidence. Never know what leads us to a firestarter. You going to be there?"

"No. I put the stuffed dog in the garbage can."

"We'll pick it up." Diamond said goodbye and hung up.

I dialed the Herald and punched in Glenda Gorman's extension.

"Glennie," I said when she answered. "This is your favorite detective returning your call."

"Owen, honey! Where have you been? You're solving the world's hottest fire mystery and I'm in big need of a scoop. Do we know who did it, yet?"

"Nope."

"How 'bout an ID on the victim?"

"Nope."

"Any clue on the motive?"

"Nope."

"There you go again, loquacious as Larry King. How am I going to fit it all into ten column inches?"

"Don't know," I said.

She paused. "How is Street?"

"Wonderful as ever," I said.

"God, what I'd do to have a guy like you say that about me."

"Glennie, you *are* wonderful and I've said so before."

"But wonderful doesn't make for love, does it?"

"For the right guy, it does."

There was an uncomfortable silence. "Owen, you know that time a long way back when we almost had something? You and I fit together pretty good." Her voice wavered. "How did you put it? 'Like Zinfandel and garlic bread. A lot of spice and flavor, but still not the main course.'"

"Did I say that?"

"Yeah," Glennie said. "The most heart-breaking words I ever heard."

"Sorry," I said.

"If Street ever..."

"I know. If it happens, I'll call you first."

I put on a windbreaker and got in my car with Spot. I drove around the south end of the lake and headed up the west shore toward Truckee. Late September is the beginning of what locals call the shoulder season in the Tahoe tourist trade, yet cars filled the parking lots at Emerald Bay and camera-toting tourists crowded each other at the overlooks. All the snow from the storm had melted at the lower elevations and the wind was calm, leaving the lake smooth as glass near the shore. Out in the middle were odd calligraphic patterns traced by wind on the surface. In the distance across the lake I could see the dark scar from the fire and the smoke plume on the mountain above my cabin.

I drove past Homewood ski area with its lonely ski lifts waiting for the heavy snows of winter. In Tahoe City I turned left on 89 where the Truckee River spills out of Lake Tahoe and winds down the valley to Truckee, then Reno and on to Pyramid Lake, its final destination before the water ultimately evaporates in the hot Nevada sun. I went past the entrance for Alpine Meadows ski area and, a minute later, the Olympic rings that announce Squaw Valley. When I came to the historic mining town of Truckee, now brimming with coffee houses, boutique shops and art galleries, I got out my map to find the street listed in the phone book under Jake Pooler Construction.

The company's offices were in a small building, up steep, narrow stairs. The thin wooden front door was warped and had peeling paint. Several letters had come off of the company sign so that it read, "Jake Poo   Con ruction" A woman in her sixties sat behind a desk typing on a manual typewriter. She looked up at me with eyes that were weary behind a face stretched tight by an aggressive face lift. Her skin looked as if it would rip if she laughed.

"Good afternoon, my name is Owen McKenna. I'm working with the Douglas County authorities. I understand Jake Pooler is missing. May I talk to you a minute?"

"Sure. I'm Betty Williamson. Is he okay?"

"Your boss," I said, ignoring her question. "How long has he been missing?"

"He didn't show up for work the last two mornings. He went home early the day before yesterday, about two-thirty. He isn't dead, is he?"

"We're just trying to track his movements," I said truthfully, wondering about her conclusions. "You're sure it was two-thirty when he left?"

"Two-thirty, quarter to three. I remember because we had a window rep show up for a three o'clock appointment and Jake was already gone. Anyway, he left, apparently didn't show up at home, and hasn't been seen since."

"Have you spoken to his wife?"

"Sure. But Lenora doesn't know where he is, either. She was calling from the get go and demanding to know exactly when he left here. As if I had anything to do with where he's run off to."

"Any idea where that might be?"

Betty Williamson exhaled forcibly enough that I smelled a mint-flavored breeze. "With one of those young sluts, I suppose."

"Do you mean prostitutes?"

"They may as well be. You know the kind. Rings in their noses. Circles under their eyes so dark it's anybody's guess what kind of drugs they're on."

"Where does he meet them?"

"Who knows," Betty said. She briefly looked at the ceiling. "Probably waits outside the high school and catches the dropouts." She scowled at the sheet of paper in the typewriter. "If you want to know more you can ask Winton. Oh, speak of the devil."

A door had opened up and a thin young man came into the office. He had long brown hair greased straight back, a pencil moustache and a pointed goatee. The little beard glistened as if it were dipped in polyurethane. His sleeves were rolled up exposing fuzzy tattoos on both forearms. In one hand was a clipboard, in the other a mug of coffee. His slouching posture was so bad that his back, viewed from the side, made a pronounced S-shape.

"Winton, have either of the crews heard from Jake yet? This man is looking for him." Betty pointed toward me. "I'm sorry, I'm really bad with names."

"Owen McKenna," I said.

The skinny kid made an exaggerated lean backward to take in my height, and gestured at me with his coffee. He stunk of patchouli layered over three-day-old body odor. "Hi. I'm Winton Berger."

"Winton?" Betty said again.

The kid shook his head. "No. The Jake brake ain't been seen or heard." He had a thin, reedy voice and a slight speech impediment such that he gave the S in the word 'seen' a touch of an SH sound. He was a cliché of trailer trash, and yet I had a clear sense of a sly intelligence lurking beneath his dirtball façade.

"Winton, I've told you not to call him a Jake brake. He isn't part of a truck. He's your boss. I won't ask you again."

"Your boss, too. You should hear what part of a truck he calls you."

"Winton!" Betty Williamson colored a deep red.

Winton set down the clipboard on a cluttered desk, rummaged around until he found a pencil, stuck it behind his ear and walked back out.

"Maybe I'll come back another time," I said. "I'm off to see Jake's wife. Can you tell me where they live?"

Betty calmed and worked at smoothing her skirt under the desk. Then she told me where Mrs. Lenora Pooler lived.

"What does Jake drive?" I asked.

"A white Chevy Dooley. With a white topper."

"Dooley?"

"You know, one of those monster pickups with dual rear wheels."

"Thanks, Betty. You've been very helpful."

She gave me a sad smile as I walked out.

TEN

To get to the Pooler residence I drove out to Donner Lake, a long finger of water just below the granite crest of Donner Pass. The scene was majestic enough that I wondered if Bierstadt had ever painted it. I reminded myself to check in my books someday.

The house was a ramshackle affair with a filtered view of the water. Sided with weathered cedar shakes, it looked as if three old lake cabins had been dragged together and mated at odd angles. It seemed a strange house for someone in the construction business. As I approached and parked in front of an enormous Ponderosa pine, I struggled with a moral dilemma. Should I tell Lenora Pooler right off about her husband's death and risk not learning anything in the resulting emotional upheaval? Or should I ask questions first, hoping to learn anything that might help find the arsonist?

I decided that a person had a basic right to the truth about all things central to their lives even if that compromised an arson and murder investigation. I left Spot in the Jeep, his huge head hanging out an open window, walked up to the door and knocked.

The door was opened by a trim woman who, like Betty Williamson, was also in her sixties, but with a normal face. Her short, carefully-brushed gray hair looked soft as cashmere, and when she craned her neck to look up at me I saw pretty blue eyes that looked permanently mournful. A blue cardigan that matched her eyes was draped over her shoulders. Her demeanor showed the same fatigue that imbued Betty Williamson, and I wondered if all the women around Jake Pooler had the same affliction.

"Mrs. Pooler?"

"Yes?" she said in a tiny voice.

"My name is Owen McKenna, calling on behalf of Douglas County, Nevada. I'm very sorry ma'am, I have bad news."

"What?"

"Mrs. Pooler, your husband Jake was found dead yesterday afternoon. He wasn't identified until this morning."

I didn't know what reaction I expected, but it wasn't what I got.

Lenora Pooler looked at me without a change in her sorrowful expression. "You'd better come inside," she said.

I followed her into the house. She sat on a peach-colored loveseat, perching on the edge like a bird, her ankles and knees primly together. She motioned me toward a big, leather easy chair where Jake no doubt took up residence when he was home.

"Where did they find him?" she asked. Her voice, although weak, was calm.

"In Douglas County. In a ravine just up from the east shore of Tahoe."

"How did he die?"

"They won't know for certain until after an autopsy is completed. But the body was burned in the east shore forest fire, so the fire may have been the cause of death. I'm very sorry, Mrs. Pooler."

"Please call me Lenora." She paused, looking inward. It seemed that whatever emotional parts of her that might have collapsed at the news had already imploded long ago. "What do I need to do now?" she asked.

I watched her, wondering if she could have murdered him and then lit the fire to cover it up. While it seemed that the news of her husband's death was not devastating, I realized she nevertheless felt completely lost. That didn't mean she wasn't a killer. But it was hard to imagine.

Of course, most people have the capacity to kill. It is a wide spectrum. Some people kill because someone looks at them wrong. Others would need to have their entire family slaughtered in front of their eyes before they could work up the nerve to pull the trigger. But they have the capacity.

Now, looking at Lenora Pooler, I wondered if she had the capacity to kill. Her diminutive voice, age and physical stature didn't mean anything. There are tiny, meek women who can run a piano wire through their husbands' brains and then sit down for their favorite TV show. But whatever the language is that communicates the potential to kill, it wasn't talking to me now.

Her question came back to me. "I'm not well versed in these things, Lenora. But I think the thing to do next is to call a good friend, someone who knows your situation. You'll need help with the phone calls from the authorities and making funeral arrangements. Later, you may need some help figuring out what to do with your husband's business and such. Do you know someone you can call?"

Lenora Pooler shook her head. "I don't have any friends anymore." Then she bent her head down and mumbled something I couldn't make out.

"Excuse me," I said. "I didn't hear you."

She mumbled again.

"I'm sorry, Lenora, I still didn't hear you."

She lifted her head and looked at me, her sad blue eyes larger and tinged with pink. "I said that he went to bed with all my friends."

Such words from this woman were shocking. She didn't speak in anger, but with resignation. "I'm sorry," I said.

"It didn't matter who they were, what they looked like or how old they were," she said. "If they were female, he went after them. And with Jake it was like saying no to a charging horse. Nothing stopped him." Lenora hung her head. "To make it worse, once he made his conquest it was the women who would come back for more. He'd be chasing the next one while the last one would beg him. I listened in on some of the phone calls. Even my best friend Lucy." Lenora's eyes suddenly streamed tears. "So one of them finally torched the bastard," she said, the first hint of anger in her voice.

I thought of what Betty Williamson said about Jake Pooler chasing young women, or even girls. "Perhaps you have a male friend or relative who could help you out," I said.

Once again Lenora Pooler seemed to turn inward. I had the feeling that she spent a lot of time in this private place inside her mind.

I decided to probe in a new direction. "Lenora, did your husband have a gas can?"

Her gaze shifted from her inner world to me. "Certainly. Several. You know, on the truck, for the machines and such. And here in the shed. For the snowblower."

"Do you know where the truck is?"

"No. That truck was the only thing he really cared about. Besides chasing other women. He even had a name for it. Molly. Can you imagine anything more stupid than naming your truck?" She turned and gazed vacantly out the window. The granite of Donner Summit reflected in the blue water of Donner Lake. "He told me that Molly had more curves than I did."

It took me a moment to think of something to say.

"May I see the gas can in the shed?"

Lenora looked surprised. "I don't see why not." She stood up and walked to the door. From a closet nook she pulled out a long coat. I helped her pull it on before we went outside into a day that was bright and warm.

Lenora took a long look at Spot hanging his head out of the Jeep window. His tongue dangled from his mouth and, with each panting breath, flicked drops of saliva onto the side of my car. "Pretty dog," she said, not mentioning his size which may have been a first. But then, for a diminutive woman who lived with a big man who had even bigger appetites, maybe nothing else seemed out-sized.

The shed was around the side of the house. It was built as a lean-to and had a fiberglass roof that joined the house just under the eave of the main roof.

Lenora unlatched the door and pulled it open. "He keeps the snowblower and some tools in here. And the gas can is right there." She pointed behind the door.

There was no gas can.

Lenora looked elsewhere in the small shed and then turned and looked up at me. "I was wrong. The gas can is not here."

"Do you remember the last time you saw it?" I said.

Lenora thought a moment. "No. But it's been here for years. So perhaps it went missing with my husband." Words came easier to her now as if problem-solving took her mind off his death. "Makes you wonder if he lit the fire, doesn't it? Knowing Jake, I wouldn't put it past him to accidentally burn himself up."

Her suggestion was a surprise. Did she know the fire wasn't from natural causes? I hadn't seen a paper anywhere in their house, nor was the radio or TV on when I arrived. "Do you have reason to believe the forest fire was caused by arson?" I asked.

"No, but it seems logical when you asked about a gas can."

"Has your husband ever lit fires before?"

"No, Jake isn't an arsonist, at least not in the way of someone who gets their kicks out of burning things down. But he is a hot head. Was." She looked away toward the trees in their backyard. "If someone made him very mad, I suppose I could think of a scenario where he might put a match to something and it got out of hand."

"Do you remember what the gas can looked like?"

"Oh, you know, normal, I guess. A small, red can. It was circular and had a flexible spout." She had described the can that Ellie's dog found.

We backed out of the shed and Lenora shut the door. She led the way back to the front door.

"Did Jake ever have any disagreements with the forest service?"

Lenora turned on the front step and looked up at me. "Mr. McKenna, if you want to understand Jake you need to know that he had disagreements with everyone. I mean everyone he ever met and everyone he never met." Lenora's eyes narrowed. "Jake was the orneriest son of a bitch you could have ever known. If you never knew him, count yourself lucky."

I nodded understanding. "Did Jake have a computer?"

Lenora opened the door and led me inside.

"Actually, he just bought one. He used to think that computers were part of a United Nations conspiracy to take over America. He'd heard of computer viruses and he was convinced that they would come out of the machines at a certain pre-arranged time and kill us all off. Then brown-skinned men in turbans would rise up and take over the world."

"But he bought a computer anyway?" Jake was beginning to sound like a true nutcase.

"Yes. He had started to imagine that there might be something he could use one for."

"Which was?"

"Nothing of any substance that I could see. I said he should give it to Betty at work. My God, she still types on a manual typewriter. But he wouldn't hear of it. He kept it in his office where he could watch porn movies or whatever it is that comes from the internet."

"I stopped by the construction business, but I didn't see any computer."

"Oh, no. He is much too private to have his office at work. He uses the back room here at home."

"May I see it?"

"Sure. But I'll warn you that it is an awful mess." She led the way through a door in the corner of their living room. Inside was a desk piled high with papers and vendor notebooks. On one corner was the computer, still running. The screen saver was a naked woman cavorting through a forest.

"May I?" I asked, my hand poised above the mouse.

Lenora Pooler nodded from the doorway, watching me, not from suspicion but from curiosity. I guessed that she'd never worked one.

I clicked and the Windows format came up. I looked through his files for any obvious file names that would indicate a note saying that "the first fire would take only trees." Nothing came to my attention. I loaded Word, typed a few words and clicked on the print icon to see what the default font would be. The laser printer hummed and out came the paper. The font looked like the same size and style as on the note delivered to Terry Drier's fire station. None of it meant that Jake Pooler typed the note and lit the fire that burned him and half the mountain. But it appeared to be a possibility.

"Lenora," I said as I left Jake's home office and stepped back into the living room, "do you have any children?"

Her eyes were painful to look at as she answered. "I don't," she said, pausing. "He may."

I thanked her, told her I'd be in touch and then left with the paper from Jake's laser printer in my pocket.

ELEVEN

After leaving Lenora Pooler, I went and made a report to the Truckee police. It turned out that Diamond had already called them and the Placer County Sheriff's department. He explained that I was on the case and that I was informing Jake Pooler's widow of Jake's demise.

I told the sergeant on duty about Pooler's missing gas can and showed him the paper I'd gotten from Pooler's computer printer with the type font that looked like the arsonist's note. All of this was just professional courtesy because the crime of arson had taken place on the Nevada side of the lake and was out of their jurisdiction. Nevertheless, I knew that all people in law enforcement appreciate shared information and they despise those agencies, like the FBI, who dispense information only on a need-to-know basis.

When I rejoined Spot in the Jeep I wasn't sure of what my next move should be. I thought about a matinee and popcorn. Yet I was being paid by the Tahoe Douglas County Fire Protection District and they deserved fair value. Maybe I could consult with Street Casey. I drove back around the lake, stopping at the store for a baguette, cheese, wine and a rose.

Although I have a key to Street's condo, I knocked and held the single red rose behind my back. Spot sat like a gentleman dog next to me. Maybe he'd learned some manners after hanging around Natasha.

Street must have just gotten out of the shower. She was wearing her red satin robe when she opened the door. She looked ravishing.

"Do you always dress like that when you answer the door for strange men?" I said.

"Most aren't as strange as you." She held the doorjamb as she leaned forward, raised up on tiptoes and kissed me. Her hair was still wet and was delightfully mussed up. She smelled like apples. Probably the shampoo. "Besides, I have the peephole," she said.

"What if the man at your door is short and looks like he goes to church with his mother?"

"Then I put on my Kevlar vest, get my gun and sneak out the back so I can come around and surprise him from behind that bush." She motioned her head off to the side. Her full lips looked as seductive as ever. I bent down and kissed her again, sucking on her lower lip.

"Easy, cowboy. I haven't even had a sip of wine yet."

"Why I brought you this." I held the groceries out, then pulled my arm out from behind my back.

Street immediately put the rose to her nose and inhaled deeply, her eyes closed in bliss. I liked that a woman who found so much beauty in creepy crawlers would still be affected by the beauty of a rose. Without being particularly careful of the thorns, she put the rose in her teeth, then took the groceries in one hand and the wine in the other. "Ah," she said, holding up the wine. She rotated on her perfect bare foot and walked inside.

She set the bread and cheese and wine down on her kitchen counter and got out the corkscrew as I snugged my arms around her from behind, feeling her curves through the slippery satin.

"Is sex all you think about?" Street said, trying to work the corkscrew.

I sang like an off-key crooner,
"I've got a one-track mind 'cause
 you've got a one-track body."

"Please," she said. "Now you're writing country songs? Anyway, I'm too thin and you know it."

"And I'm too tall and you know it. Too thin doesn't change what you do to me. And it isn't just chemicals or whatever it is that you say bugs are teaching us about." She turned to face me.

Spot stuck his nose between us and wedged himself into our embrace. He was about as subtle as a bulldozer in a boudoir.

"You mean pheromones," Street said. "Insects use them to attract each other.

Street slipped out of my hands and poured us each some wine, three inches in a large glass for me, maybe six or eight drops for herself. I wasn't certain if the bottom of her glass got thoroughly moist. Nevertheless, we clicked glasses and both drank. "Mmmm," she said and licked her lips.

"Remember, there is a rabid temperance movement in this country," I said, pointing at her nearly empty wine glass. "You don't want the wine police hauling you off to detox camp."

She shook her head, her eyes flashing. "Your detecting," Street said as she munched a chunk of bread. "Has it revealed dark secrets yet?"

"None at all. All I've learned is that the victim was an ornery bastard who had more sex drive than a Brahman bull."

"More than you?" Street acted shocked.

"Maybe," I said.

"Sounds like you've spoken to some of his conquests."

As soon as Street referred to them in plural, I realized that Jake's secretary, Betty Williamson, also belonged to the group. Which would explain her animosity toward the girls she called young sluts. I went back over my conversation with her, trying her out for the role as killer.

"Well?" Street said.

"Sort of," I said. "I've spoken to his secretary and his wife. From what they said, he pursued every woman he came in contact with and was successful with most of them."

"He was that good, huh? Makes me curious."

I raised my eyebrows at her.

"Just scientific interest. You hear about men who seem to have magic power over women. I'd like to get a whiff of their special potion as it were. Maybe it's those pheromones. I'm curious about how it would affect me. Not that I'd act on any impulse, of course."

"No, of course not," I said. "But then I seem to recall that you acted on an impulse with me the first day we met. Remember?"

Street sipped her wine drops and looked at me with a poker face. "But you tricked me with all that romantic talk about Diebenkorn's Ocean Park series. There should be a law preventing single women from going to art museums. The atmosphere is much too dangerous. Makes women vulnerable to the guile of men."

"You're equating art talk with sexual trickery?"

"That and all that one-track body stuff. You men forget that we women want to believe. That's why we're so fragile."

I set my wine glass down. "But in this case it's all true," I said as I ran my hands over her red satin robe.

"And what are you doing now, if not using sexual guile?" Street said as she reached up and kissed me.

"Investigating."

"What?" she asked through our kiss.

"Primal needs," I said.

"Whose?" Her lips were soft and wet.

"Yours," I mumbled.

"Bullshit," Street said as she pulled me into her bedroom.

TWELVE

Street had to retire early in order to be at her lab first thing in the morning to check on her maggots. So Spot and I drove up the mountain to my cabin. I was wary of what I would find, but my entryway was free of stuffed animals.

I let Spot out to run. Normally he explores in the woods and comes back and paws the door after ten minutes or so. Twenty minutes later he still hadn't come back and I began to worry.

I went out on the deck and called his name. All I got in response was the high squeak of a late season bat flying through the dark. A light breeze washed over me, thick with the sickening scents of smoke and water-logged coals. I walked around the cabin to the drive and called Spot's name again. Nothing. Turning back to the cabin I heard sounds from down below the deck.

"Spot? Spot, is that you?" I said, expecting him to bound out from the shadows, wagging proudly and showing off some log or something he'd dragged out of the woods. I looked down the mountain from the deck. The sounds seemed to be coming closer, but were still a bit distant. I went inside, got the big flashlight from the kitchen drawer and returned to the deck.

I turned it on and shined the beam down the mountain. The sound was louder now. Walking sounds, but muffled as though through ashes. And high cries.

There was a flash of reflected light as I swept the flashlight beam. I slowly shined it back and forth until the beam found the movement.

Spot was coming up the slope. His head was down and his whimpering mixed with heavy breathing. There was something with him, under his feet. Then I understood.

I ran down the deck stairs, then down the slope toward Spot.

"What have you got, boy?" I called out, concern washing over me as the shape beneath him took on color and size. From a distance I thought he had a tawny colored duffel bag and I worried about more bodies. As Spot dragged it closer the duffel bag became furry and it grew ears and eyes.

A mountain lion.

"Spot!" I yelled.

Spot let go and the lion slumped to the ground. I was horrified to see blood all over Spot's jowls. The mountain lion's neck was covered as well, the fur red. "Jesus, Spot, what the hell have you done?"

He looked up at me, the strangest look in his eyes. As if he'd only wanted to play with the lion and didn't mean to hurt it.

"Spot, come here! Now!"

Spot left the apparently lifeless lion where it lay and came up to me. Where he wasn't bloody, he was nearly black with ash and his neck was wet with his own saliva.

I shined the light back on the lion and saw movement.

"Spot, come!" I yelled and ran back up to the cabin. I keep a chain on the deck. "You stay here," I said as I clipped him in.

Next to the list of my neighbors' phone numbers are a few emergency numbers. One is Dr. Richard Siker, the vet who periodically gives Spot his checkups. I dialed him at home.

"Dick," I said when he answered. "Owen McKenna. Are you busy?"

"Not unless sitting down with this Silver Oak Cabernet qualifies as busy."

"I've got a serious problem."

"Let me guess. Large and covered with spots."

"Related. My dog just dragged a mountain lion out of the woods."

"Good Christ! Spot killed a mountain lion?"

"It's not dead yet. I saw it move its head. But it is lying in the dark down below my deck."

"Owen, this isn't my area. I deal with house cats."

"C'mon, Dick. Who else am I going to call?"

"All right. Give me fifteen minutes."

I was outside when Dick drove up. He got out of his Explorer carrying his bag. "You got a gun?"

"No."

Dick gave me a puzzled look. He knew I was an ex-cop, but the subject of guns had never come up between us.

"Then take my pistol." He dug it out of his glove compartment and handed it to me. It was a Beretta nine millimeter.

"You'll have to be close to hit a charging lion with this. Let's hope we won't need it. Down here?" he pointed to the stairs that went down from the side of the deck."

"Yes."

Dick Siker walked down, pausing to look at Spot who was sitting in the corner of the deck. "You're in deep shit, Spot, if you start killing mountain lions."

Spot hung his head. His eyes drooped in shame.

I trotted after Dick. I'd found another flashlight in the garage. I shined both of them on the lion as Dick and I hiked down toward it.

We stopped about twenty feet away.

"I don't have a tranquilizer gun," Dick said. "Don't usually need them with poodles and tabby cats." Dick shook his head as he gestured toward the lion. "This kind of situation could get a guy killed."

Dick bent down and picked up a stick. He tossed it toward the lion and missed. The lion didn't move. He tossed another, then a third which bounced off the lion's flank. The lion groaned but remained motionless.

"Okay," Dick said. "Better have that piece ready. Expect this guy to move fast and maybe even snarl at me. But don't shoot unless he tries to put my head or neck in his mouth." Dick looked at me. "Understand? He might want to swat at me or even grab me with his paws. But I can still get my syringe into him."

"Got it," I said.

Dick nodded, then set his bag on the ground, got out a big syringe, stuck the needle in a vial and drew out the liquid. He left the bag, took one of the flashlights and moved slowly toward the mountain lion.

I stood off to the side, gun in one hand, flashlight in the other.

Dick started talking, soft and low, as he got close. "Okay, you big pussy cat. Let's you and me get friendly. Atta boy, I'm just gonna sidle up next to you, gonna stay away from your paws in case you wanna leave some love marks on me. There you go, real easy."

Dick continued his talk and inched closer while I tried to keep the gun and light steady and on the target. My hand vibrated with tension and I thought I was crazy to have put my friend in this position. I knew Dick would walk up to any animal short of an angry grizzly, but that was perhaps a lack of judgement, the result of twenty-five years of practice where the most dangerous creature he ever dealt with was a mother Doberman with young puppies. Furthermore, Dick was the kind of guy who could not walk away from an injured animal, dangerous or not. It could be a prescription for disaster. One thing I knew was this:

I wasn't going to wait for the lion to put his teeth around Dick's skull.

I aimed for the heart and my finger tightened on the trigger.

Dick reached a long, thin stick out and brushed it along the back of the lion's neck. The animal twitched but nothing more.

Dick brushed the animal again. This time it did not move at all. Dick kept talking as he moved closer.

I knew he had more guts than I did when he reached out and laid a hand on the lion's bloody neck. He slid his hand down in a gentle pet. His hand went up to the lion's head, where his fingers looked small between the ears. I reminded myself that Spot's head was bigger and probably his teeth were too and Dick wasn't afraid working on Spot. But that rationale didn't do anything to calm my pounding heart. Just when I was expecting Dick to stick in the needle he stood up and walked back to his bag.

"Any wild animal that doesn't move in a situation like this has about a one percent chance of making it through the night. I better listen to his insides before I shoot him full of anything." He pulled out his stethoscope and went back to the mountain lion.

Once again, he approached slowly, calling the lion a pussy cat and talking about love making and full moons.

I concentrated on being a good sentry while Dick put that stethoscope all over the lion's chest.

Finally, Dick stood up again. "I won't know for sure until we get this pussy cat down to the hospital and up on the table, but I don't think there's any chance of survival. There's a lot of fluid in the lungs. And it looks like the blood loss is substantial. This cat's in shock and we've only got a few minutes if we've got any hope at all. I'm going to give him a shot while you run up and get a heavy blanket we can carry him in."

"But what if he reacts when you give him the shot? I should be ready with the gun."

"Trust me, Owen. This guy isn't going to react. You better hurry. We are down to just a few minutes."

I sprinted up to the cabin and took the deck stairs three at a time.

The strongest blanket in the house was the Hudson Bay red plaid on my bed. I yanked it free and ran back to Dick who was bent over the mountain lion.

"Spread it out here," he said. "Okay, I'll reach around the chest, you reach under its abdomen. Gentle now. Up onto the blanket. Corners together. Ready to lift?"

I nodded. We both stood. The stink of blood and smoke rose from the lion's fur.

The lion was relatively light. Dick, carrying the chest and head, was lifting the most weight, but I didn't think the lion could weigh much more than a hundred pounds.

We hustled up the slope and slid the animal into the back of my Jeep. I left Spot tied where he was. Dick jumped in his Explorer and led the way down the mountain and south to his animal hospital not far from my office on Kingsbury Grade.

Dick parked at the back entrance. I stopped next to him and we had the lion in the back door of the animal hospital and up on his table in seconds.

"Remember where my office is?" Dick said to me as he pulled some instruments out of drawers and opened the cabinets above.

"Last door down the hall?"

"Right. Look in the address book on my desk. Solomon Reed lives down in the Carson Valley. Get him up here fast. If there is any possibility of saving this guy, we'll need Solomon." He shifted the lion on the table. "Oh. I mean this girl."

I got Dr. Reed on the phone and explained the situation.

It took a moment for him to respond and his voice sounded groggy as if he'd been in a deep sleep. "It'll take me thirty minutes to get up the mountain at the fastest. I better tell Dick a couple things that can't wait 'til then."

"Okay, hold on."

I ran back to the examining room. "Reed says he better talk to you before he jumps in his car."

Dick picked up a wall phone, stuck it in the crook of his shoulder and continued to work while they talked.

I didn't understand any of it. They spoke of various drugs and pulmonary this and histamine that. I walked over to the lion's head and looked at her eyes which were half shut. Her breathing was labored and I could hear the wheezing in her lungs. The big cat's fur was wet and dirty from being dragged. And the smoke smell was so strong that it was clear that the lion had been dragged through a lot of ash. Had the lion been injured in the fire before Spot got hold of her? Or was that thinking my bias at work?

Dick had already done some work on the neck wounds. He'd gotten in several sets of stitches to staunch the blood flow. But blood was still oozing. I stared at the injuries, astounded that Spot would do such a thing as attack a mountain lion. I tried to convince myself that there was a reason, that maybe the lion had attacked first and Spot was merely defending himself.

You feel an instant connection to an animal in such a situation, hoping desperately that its life be saved, yet feeling helpless. A single incident like this back in high school would have sent me into the veterinary profession. Looking back now, it seemed a much more rewarding career than the police work I'd pursued for so long before moving up to Tahoe to engage in the slightly more genteel work of private investigation.

As I stared at the bloody lion, my eyes blurring, I saw again the robber who'd come running out of the Wells Fargo Bank down by the Wharf. I was in a cruiser bringing in a repeat sex offender. The call came on the radio while I was moving east on Bay Street. I was near the bank branch. I jerked the front wheels onto the sidewalk, slammed it in park and did a sideways roll out the door.

I crawled up to the left front wheel and had my .45 up and over the hood when he came out. The bank door opened so hard and fast it broke the hydraulic dampening arm, bounced up against the wall and exploded the tempered glass into a million diamonds.

He ran out fast, his long, lean legs bare below the gangsta pants. Little pebbles shot out from under his Air Jordans as he turned down the sidewalk.

I played it by the book and shouted the warning. After his gun came up and he took a rough and bouncing aim at my face over the hood of the cruiser, I shot to kill.

Weeks later, after three committees and a half dozen officials investigated and ruled it justifiable homicide and even gave me commendations for valor and bravery, I turned in my badge and gun for good.

When you kill a twelve-year-old, all the justification in the world can't make it better.

I reached out and gave the lion a gentle stroke on her neck and thought that being a vet would have been a far better way to spend my working years.

Dick hung up the phone and turned back to the animal on his table. "How's she doing?"

"Doesn't look to be any change," I said even though I knew that he had only asked to put the noise of some words into the heavy silence that surrounded the wheezing of the lion.

Dick pulled out an oxygen tank, set it on a rolling cart and rigged a mask over the lion's snout. Next, he hung an IV bag on a pole. He shaved some fur on the lion's leg and inserted a needle into a vein. Fluid dripped into the clear plastic tube that ran into the animal.

Dick lifted her jowls. "She's young, maybe two years old if I'm any good at reading her teeth. Solomon will give us a more accurate idea when he gets here. Hope that is soon."

"Sounds like her lungs are worse," I said.

"Yeah, that's what I've got to fight. She's likely to drown in her own fluids. Next hour or two will tell." He picked up the note he'd written on while talking to Solomon.

"Anything I can do to help?"

"We need to weigh her before I stuff anymore drugs into her system. I'll hold her body, but her head will droop. You can hold it up."

I held the lion's head and the IV pole while Dick scooped her slack body up and walked over to the scale. I helped slide the weights. Then we laid her back down while Dick weighed himself.

"One hundred twenty-four pounds," he said after he did the subtraction. "Next thing would be for you to watch out front for Solomon." He slid a rectal thermometer into the lion while he spoke. "Drives a green pickup. Direct him around to the back door so he doesn't waste time pounding on the front door."

I took that as my cue to make an exit and get out of his way, so I went out the back door, checking to make sure it wouldn't lock behind me, and went around the front to wait for the other doctor.

Solomon showed up twenty minutes later, whipping his old pickup into the lot like a cop. He jerked to a stop and was out the door in a second, a big, black bag in his hand. The man was a generation older than Siker and I. His hair was white and stood up as if he were under permanent electric shock. "Solomon Reed here to see Doctor Siker!"

"Around back, doctor." I led the way at a trot.

"You found the lion?" he said.

"My dog did. I don't know how bad he hurt her. She may have been dragged pretty far."

"I don't get it," Solomon Reed said. "Your dog dragged the lion? What the hell kind of dog is that?"

"Great Dane."

"Oh," he said.

I opened the back door and showed Dr. Solomon Reed to the room with the lion.

Dick looked up as we came into the room.

Solomon rushed over to the lion, opened her eyes, looked in her mouth, then put his ear down to the lion's mouth and nose and listened. He grabbed Dick's stethoscope and listened several places. "Let's see the blood work."

Dick handed him some notes.

Solomon studied them for a minute. Then he once again used the stethoscope to listen to the lion's insides, more thoroughly than before. When he was through he sighed and spoke. "Only fair thing is to put her down."

It hit me hard, this pronouncement of death for an animal my dog had wounded. "Isn't there anything you can do?" I asked.

Solomon looked up at me as if I were a troublesome, over-grown child. "Yes, there's something we could do. If we had the facilities of a big university's veterinary school, we could put this cat on life support, open her up and do some serious arterial repair where your dog's teeth tore her up. Problem is, we'd have to do it in the next couple of hours. Furthermore, it would cost many thou-sands of dollars, and even then she'd probably still die." The old vet's watery blue eyes looked enormously sad. It was obvious that he wanted the lion to live as much as I did.

Dick spoke up. "The Sierra Wild Animal Network," he said. "Wouldn't SWAN pay for her treatment?"

"We could take her to the university in Reno," I said.

Solomon turned away from me, put his hand on the lion's neck and gently caressed her. "Davis has the best vet school in the country," he said. "If she's going to have any chance, we'd have to take her there. But there isn't time to drive. We'd have to fly."

"There's a charter company at the local airport," I said. "They might have a plane ready. Or, for that matter, I can fly. If I can rent a plane on short notice, I could have the lion at UC Davis in an hour."

"What if the Sierra Wild Animal Network won't pay for it?" Solomon said. "Flying an animal to Davis is only a small portion of the expense. Her treatment will be a lot more."

I thought of what my dog had done to the lion. I thought of how quickly we dispense with animals when their welfare becomes too expensive or inconvenient. "I'll pay for it."

Solomon turned away from the lion and looked at me for a long moment. Then he spoke to Dick. "Siker, you got the number for Davis?"

I left the room and went down to Dick's office while they spoke. I went through the Yellow Pages, called every possible source for an airplane and got nothing but answering services.

When I went back to report my lack of success, I heard Solomon on the phone. He spoke in a loud and rising voice.

"I don't care if everyone at the hospital is asleep! Last I heard you don't need anymore sleep in Davis than you do in Tahoe! Wake them up! Tell them we're bringing in a beautiful mountain lion in the next two hours! If she doesn't get proper treatment, she'll die before morning. Do you want that on your conscience? No, I didn't think so. I don't care what it costs. We've got the expense covered." He hung up the phone. Solomon and Dick exchanged a few words and I sensed that there wasn't much else they could do.

"I'm having trouble locating a plane," I said.

Solomon looked at me. "Hang around. UC Davis is going to call. They might be able to send a plane up. We may need you to meet it at the airport."

I went out to the waiting room and tried to read magazines, but kept thinking about the unconscious lion desperately trying to suck oxygen into fluid-filled lungs. I thought of Spot. What was I going to do with him?

I'd wandered into Dick's office when the phone rang. I answered it. A woman said she was from the University of California at Davis. She asked for Doctor Solomon Reed. I ran and told the doctor.

"You won't have to run to the airport," Solomon said after he hung up. "The UC Davis Veterinary Hospital is sending an air ambulance chopper up to take the lion down to their hospital. They're coming directly to this parking lot. It's large enough, isn't it?"

"I can make that easy," I said. "I'll call Diamond Martinez. He'll help."

"Thanks," Dick said.

I dialed Diamond's pager. He called back in less than a minute.

"Diamond," I said when I picked up the phone. "I'm in Dr. Richard Siker's animal hospital on Kingsbury Grade. We've got a mountain lion here, severely wounded."

"It's at the animal hospital on Kingsbury?" Diamond's voice was filled with alarm. "I can be there in a minute. I'll radio for help on the way. Don't worry. We'll take it down before anyone gets hurt."

"Whoa, Diamond. It's inside the hospital on the table. Unconscious. UC Davis is sending a helicopter to pick it up. They want to land in the parking lot. I'm not sure there's enough room here. I thought maybe you could help."

"Got it. I'll call you back later."

This was obviously Diamond's kind of mission as evidenced by what happened within minutes of my call.

Kingsbury Grade was closed off. Four South Lake Tahoe police cruisers came across the state line and joined three Douglas County Sheriff vehicles to make a large circle in the middle of the street. They all trained their spotlights on the asphalt in the middle of the circle and lit up the landing zone.

Diamond got patched through directly to the pilot and talked him out of a cloudy sky on a fast track to this corner of town.

The local press picked it up on their scanners and there were several reporters and photographers on the scene by the time the chopper roared above and settled down into the circle of flashing red lights.

Dick, Solomon and I had the mountain lion wrapped back up in my Hudson Bay blanket. Dick and I carried the lion while Solomon carried the IV pole and an oxygen tank. We had the big cat out to the chopper by the time the doors opened. Solomon supervised the paramedics as they strapped the cat down.

A photographer and a familiar face from the Herald emerged from the crowd. "Owen, my God, it's you!"

"Hi, Glennie."

"We hear they found an injured mountain lion." She had to practically yell in my ear as the helicopter had revved up. It roared as it slowly levitated off the ground. "What did you have to do with it?" Glennie shouted.

"Spot found it."

"Spot!? What happened to the lion?"

"Not sure."

"Where did Spot find it?"

"Down below my cabin."

Glennie's eyes got wide. "Oh, my God, what a story!" She turned to her photographer and pointed to the helicopter which was just clearing the Jeffrey pines. "Are you getting pictures? Go on!"

The photographer snapped away as the big machine tilted forward and then roared off into the sky.

Glennie turned back to me. "How many stories can I do about you in one day?"

"What do you mean?"

"I already wrote one about the burn victim. You'll see it in tomorrow's paper. If I hurry, I can get this one filed before the paper goes to print. You're a one-man news machine, Owen."

"But this story is about a lion, not me."

Glennie nodded and wrote in her notebook. "So you brought it here to the animal hospital," Glennie said. "Then UC Davis came to pick it up."

"Right," I said.

"We need to humanize this for the paper. Give me an angle, Owen. Tell me some details."

"I don't know, Glennie." I didn't want to commercialize the story. I just wanted to go home.

"Come on. Something. What kind of mountain lion was it?"

"I didn't know there were kinds. Female. Smallish. One hundred twenty-four pounds."

"Name?" she asked and then started laughing. "God, you'd think I was after a criminal. It's just automatic."

"Pussy Cat."

"What do you mean?"

"That's what Doc Siker kept calling her. Pussy Cat. Look, Glennie, I have to go. Nice seeing you." I carried the Hudson Bay blanket back toward my Jeep.

"Thanks, Owen," Glennie called out to me. "Say hi to Street."

I drove home, feeling worse the closer I got.

Dogs can get under your skin, and when they do something very wrong it is as upsetting as if they were children instead of pets. In some ways it is worse, because they can't talk and tell you whatever it was that motivated them.

I parked and walked over to Spot who was still chained to the deck railing. He crouched down, tail between his legs, eyes infinitely sad. He knew he'd done something terrible to the mountain lion and that it displeased me very much.

I squatted down next to him and unhooked the chain. He was covered with ash and dried blood and shivering from the cold.

He lifted his nose off the deck and looked at me, his eyes breaking my heart.

"C'mon," I said. "Let's get you cleaned up." I brought him around to the hose and, despite knowing he would temporarily freeze, I washed off the dirt. Back inside, I got a fire going in the wood stove, put out a big towel for him to lie on, then put another towel over him.

I drank a beer while I worried over my dog. The Bierstadt book was on the end table. I flipped through it. I didn't know what I was looking for. Solace, maybe. I didn't find it, so I went to bed.

THIRTEEN

I was awakened before dawn the next morning by a phone call from Terry Drier.

"Are you awake?"

"Yes. No. Give me a minute," I said as I fumbled with the light above my bed. "Okay. Kind of."

"What?"

"Kind of awake."

"We got another note. You'll want to see it."

"Of course," I said, suddenly alert as adrenaline surged through me. "You at the station?"

"Yes."

"I'll be there in a few minutes." I opened the door to let Spot out, but he just hung his head and looked out the open doorway. I eventually dragged him to the Jeep and drove down the mountain through the dark as I considered the implications of a second note. Another note meant the writer wasn't Jake unless he had intended it to be posthumous. In which case, who delivered it? Another potential fire meant Jake probably didn't set the first, unless this note was the work of a copycat. Maybe Jake didn't burn himself to death, accidentally or not. And the identity of the person who put the burned, stuffed animal on my doorstep was not made any clearer by another note. It was still appropriate to consider the stuffed dog a real threat.

I got to the station just as the mountains were taking on shape against the lightening sky. I left Spot in the Jeep and walked up to the heavy firehouse door.

The morning paper was on the door mat. The headline was as large as the day before, and the story was again under Glennie's byline.

It said that the gas can we'd found at the fire matched one missing from Jake Pooler's shed and that authorities were considering the possibility that Jake had accidentally burned himself while starting the forest fire.

Glennie's story recapped everything else that was known about the fire and posed several of the questions I was trying to answer.

I nodded at one of the firemen and carried the paper into Terry's office.

Terry picked up a mylar sleeve with the second note in it. His face was pale and his voice grave. "This was slipped through our mail slot sometime between two and four in the morning. Mike and Jose were on duty. Mike took his coffee break at two and walked by the basket. He is sure it was empty. Jose found the envelope in the basket at four and called me at home immediately." Terry handed it to me.

It was the same kind of paper and type as the first note, and looked just like what came out of Jake Pooler's printer.

> The crimes of the government
> continue. So do the fires. The
> second fire will take out two houses.

"Not much to go on," I said.

"No, the sick S.O.B. is toying with us. Wants to make us sweat. Well, I'm here to tell you, he's going to fry when we catch him." Terry was taking it personally. "You got any ideas?" he said.

"I'm wondering why he brings the note to this fire station. There are fire stations all over."

"I thought about that, too," Terry said. "Could be he lives on the opposite side of the lake and picks the farthest station. Or maybe he lives on this side and picks the most convenient one. You can read it almost any way you want. Or it might be that he likes the way our station is in a dark and uncrowded area and he can sneak up without being seen."

I stared at the note, then set it on Terry's desk. "We should probably start going over maps and see if there is any obvious place in the basin where a fire would burn just two houses."

"You believe that?" Terry was incredulous. "It was pure luck that bastard didn't burn houses last time. What makes you think he can set a forest fire and control where it burns this time?"

"We have nothing else to go on, that's all. If, for example, there are any pairs of houses with no others around, they would be possible sites to watch."

Terry seemed disgusted with the suggestion. "Have you found out anything yet on the last note?"

I decided not to mention the similar font in Jake's computer. "No. I've only had time to pursue the fire victim."

"Heard it was Jake Pooler."

"You know him?" I asked.

"Sure. Everyone did. Talk of the town up in Truckee where I used to live."

"How so?"

"Just that he broke up more marriages than a Las Vegas divorce court, for one. And he was a brawler, for two. Had it coming to him, let me tell you. If we looked for people with motive to burn him, then we've got a couple hundred candidates just in the Tahoe/Truckee area." Terry put the arsonist's note in the Xerox machine. When the copy came out he handed it to me. Then he paced around the small office, frustration making his nostrils flare.

"You call anyone else on this note, yet?" I asked.

"No," Terry said. "I'll give the chief a ring first, then Diamond.

I told Terry I'd let him know the moment I learned anything, then said goodbye.

I thought about the note as I went out. There were many possibilities. The first was that Jake was not the firestarter. Unless, I realized, the writer of the note did not light the east shore fire but knew that Jake was going to and decided to complicate our investigation by sending us a note in advance. Now, a second note was making us think there was going to be another fire. Maybe it would happen. Maybe not.

Then again, the note writer might be actually intending to set a second fire, copying Jake's first fire. Either way, the new fire-starter would be hard to catch because we would not be certain about which clues from the first fire pointed to Jake and which, like the note, pointed to the second party. The possible confusion was without limits.

Back in the Jeep, I drove south through town to Emerald Bay Road and the U.S. Forest Service.

Linda Saronna was busy, but when I explained what I wanted they made a space for me in her schedule. Eventually, I was shown to her office which was empty. Linda rushed in a minute later.

"Sorry," she said. "Chicken Little was right, and I've got no place to hide." She took off a light coat and tossed it on a rack in the corner of her office. "I've heard all about your exploits already," she said. She removed a scarf from around her neck and shook out thick, red hair. "I'm curious. What made you look for a victim?"

"Nothing. It was the last thing I expected to find."

"But you went to the trouble to bring in Ellie and her dog. Just a hunch?"

I nodded. "I thought there might be something to learn. You know Ellie?"

"Oh, yeah. She's the best. We've used her several times. Lost hikers. Back-country skiers who go down the wrong side of the Sierra crest and can't figure out a way back."

"Did you hear about the latest note?"

Linda Saronna nodded, her face suddenly serious. "I almost can't believe this is happening. When you found the body I thought, 'thank God this is over.' Now it is worse than I could have imagined."

"What will be the Forest Service's response?"

"There isn't really much we can do other than have all our units ready to go. I was in my truck just now when Terry Drier called me about the second note. So I've been on my phone trying to crank up our preparedness. We're officially on Red Flag Alert. We've already got a chopper on the way. With that and all the local departments ready, we should be on any fire within seconds." Linda leaned back in her chair and rubbed her eyes. It was obvious that she needed rest.

"What about scouting for locations where a fire would burn just two houses?"

"I thought of that and called Frederick. He agreed with me that it didn't seem promising, but that he would get on it immediately. Let's see where he's at with it." She punched some buttons on the phone. "Frederick? I've got Owen McKenna here and we're wondering about your two-house survey. Find anything yet?"

Frederick Mallicoff walked in a moment later. He had several rolled maps. "Hey, Owen," he said as he spread them on the table. "Heard you found the body. God, that must have been... I don't know, horrible." He seemed embarrassed by what he'd said and focused on his maps. He lined up four topographical maps into a large square, the intersection being in the middle of the lake. Together, they covered the Tahoe Basin. "The problem," Frederick said, "is just as we thought. There are several dozen sites where a fire might only take out two houses. We could never watch all of them." He pointed to the little black squares that dotted the maps and represented houses.

"The last fire was set just off the main highway," I said. "The firestarter might want to use a vehicle for a quick getaway as before. What if we narrowed the sites down to those where the fire could easily be set from the main road?"

"That would still leave too many possibilities. Besides, this guy lit the last blaze below several houses and burned none of them, just like he said. If he's as good the next time around, he might set a fire where there are many houses but plan it so only two burn."

What Frederick said seemed possible and as such was frustrating. I looked at Linda who sighed and chewed her lip.

"I'm not saying," Frederick continued, "that we shouldn't post lookouts at the most obvious places. Only that we shouldn't expect too much. Let me show you how I think the arsonist would plan."

Linda got up from her chair and we all leaned over the maps while Frederick explained.

"There are several ways for a firestarter to guide where a fire will go. One is to use mountain slopes because fires burn up. The steeper the slope, the more direct the burn. This assumes, of course, that there will be little or no wind to direct the fire sideways. But in any event, fires don't move well down-slope even when the wind is going that direction.

"The second way to direct a fire is to know which way the wind is going to blow. But that is almost impossible to predict. Even when we know the prevailing wind, the local topography creates so much turmoil that it can blow one way at one elevation and the opposite direction just a thousand feet up or down. So my guess is that the firestarter will want calm conditions.

"The third way to control a fire is to use natural firebreaks. Scree chutes like the two big vertical stripes of rock up on Trimmer Peak are hard for a fire to cross." He pointed to an area on the map just south of the town of South Lake Tahoe.

"You mean the ones that look like ski runs in the winter?" I said.

"Right. It is so steep that the constantly sliding rocks make it impossible for trees to grow. They look like narrow ski runs from town. But in reality they are a couple hundred feet across. Makes a great firebreak. Other firebreaks are ridgelines. Fires like to race up to the top of the ridge and then follow it up sideways. But fires don't readily go over the ridge and head back down. Cliffs and other rock outcroppings are difficult for fires to cross." Frederick pointed to the maps. "Here, near Emerald Bay, and over on Mount Tallac, for example.

"Then, there are the not so natural firebreaks that are in many parts of the basin, some wide, some not so wide, but all capable of directing a fire to some degree. These, of course, are the roads."

"You've really studied this," Linda said. She almost seemed alarmed.

Frederick Mallicoff nodded. "I took every course they had in fire science and have been to two or three seminars a year ever since school." He leaned over the maps again and pointed to a highly populated area. "In several places all these factors come together. For example, over here we have a steep slope with a ridge on one side, a scree slide on the other, and down below where it is not so steep there are roads that would direct the fire. Strike a match near the highway and almost for certain you would take out these two houses on the escarpment above but not any of the several dozen nearby."

"Frederick Mallicoff, you're scaring me," Linda said. She was pale. "How many places like that are there in the basin?"

"I have no idea," he said. "But certainly a dozen or more."

"So, combined with all the lonely pairs of houses out there, we could never watch them all." Linda's voice was soft.

Frederick said, "I think the best policy is maximum preparedness."

"Owen?" Linda Saronna said. "Any thoughts?"

"I agree with Frederick. You're already doing everything you can."

"Okay," Linda said briskly. She was in command mode. "Frederick, see if you can bring in anymore rigs from Carson and Sac. We'll put spotters with radios on high lookouts twenty-four hours a day. Owen, do you have a cell phone?"

I pulled out a card. "The number is on here. Please call at any time."

I left and drove to my office. I practically had to drag Spot up the stairs and down the hall.

My copy of the day's paper was in front of my door. I picked it up and unlocked my door. The phone started ringing as I walked in.

"McKenna Investigations," I said

"I thought I'd explain how Glennie got the picture," Street said.

"What picture?"

"You have a paper?"

"Sure."

"Turn to the back of the first section."

I did as she said. One of the headings said,

LOCAL DOG FINDS INJURED
MOUNTAIN LION

Underneath was a good-sized picture of Spot hanging his head out of my Jeep. Below that was a short article on Pussy Cat with all of the information Glennie had gotten from me including weight and sex.

"Glennie came to my condo late last night. She told me about the lion. She begged so hard for a picture, I gave her the one she put in the paper. Anyway, I just thought you'd like to know your dog is upstaging you again."

"Always has, always will," I said.

"So what happened to the lion? Glennie only had the vaguest idea. She said Spot found it below your deck?"

I told her the whole story about Spot dragging the lion up the mountain.

"Oh, my God, Owen, I'm so sorry. I can't believe he'd do such a thing. Are you sure?"

"What other conclusion is there? Either the lion attacked him which is highly unlikely considering his size, or he attacked it. I want to think that they surprised each other in the woods. If the lion thought she was cornered, she might strike and then Spot would defend himself."

"What are you going to do?"

"I don't know. I may have to keep him chained up at all times. I may even be open to prosecution. I think it is illegal to hunt or harm wildlife in the Tahoe Basin. And pet owners are responsible for the actions of their pets. I feel so bad about that cat. Let's just hope she lives."

We talked some more and I could tell that Street was getting upset over the problem. She was as attached to my dog as I was. I decided it was best to end the conversation, so I asked if she wanted to come for dinner and she said she had too much work to do. So I told her I loved her we hung up.

I went home and spent the evening ruminating on arson and murder and the cat. I sipped Sierra Nevada Pale Ale in front of the woodstove while Spot, morose as ever, lay in the corner of the living room. Although the evening was cool, I kept thinking about the warm turn in the weather. All vestiges of the Pacific system that had brought some moisture to the mountains were now gone. The air and forest were crispy dry. Worse, the forecast was for warmer weather still, with hot, southwest winds picking up in the afternoons for the foreseeable future. It was the worst that could happen with the arsonist threatening another fire.

I got another beer, picked up an art magazine and read an essay written by an art educator named Sister Wendy. She'd become well-known through PBS specials on art, shows that, lacking a TV, I hadn't seen. Sister Wendy had an intriguing definition about art. She said that great art is what draws you back again and again. Much of the time great art possesses a captivating beauty. But Sister Wendy thought that homely art and, sometimes, even sacrilegious art can possess the power to repeatedly bring the viewer back to observe.

As I read on, I was surprised to discover that her essay seemed to apply to my current investigation of the arsonist. Sister Wendy was illuminating an idea that, to my point of view, drew parallels between some art and the forest fire and threatening notes.

She was talking about conceptual art. She thought that while conceptual art was valuable, it served society like newspapers. You quickly get the point and then move on. An example she gave was the scandalous Piss Christ. The piece, which depicts a crucifix in a bottle of urine, is by most people's judgement revolting and crude. Sister Wendy didn't think it was great art, but she was open-minded enough that she found some value in the questions it provokes about how we view religion.

I had always looked for nothing other than beauty in art. This approach, in which beauty was not necessarily paramount, suddenly got me thinking about arson as a heretical concept.

The book with the Bierstadt reproduction was on the floor to the side of my chair. I picked it up and flipped through to the picture. The image of The Sierra Nevada In California was clearly about beauty, the exquisite grandeur of nature, the untouched realm of God. It was similar in many ways to the scene of Tahoe out my window. A pristine, natural beauty. Yet someone was trying to burn it down.

I sipped my beer as I tried to reconcile the conflict between the sacred and the sacrilegious.

What if Jake had died by accident? What if the firestarter only intended to burn trees? If so, was burning the forest like putting a crucifix in urine? Could we, like Sister Wendy, learn from an apparently violent act? All conventional thought said no, just as nearly all of Sister Wendy's colleagues said that Piss Christ was an abomination. But what if we could be like this woman of the church? Could we see in the fire provocative questions about our forest management and our narrow-minded actions which seem to operate on the presumption that the forest is for our benefit alone?

Should we rethink the way we always put out all forest fires? Was putting out even lightning-caused fires like damming rivers or paving swamps, a misguided attempt to have nature the way we like it?

The questions seemed to run in endless circles. I finally put aside my art book and art magazine and went to bed.

The next morning the phone rang as I was eating breakfast.

"Hello?"

"Owen, Dick Siker. About that cat?"

"Yes?"

"Your dog didn't hurt her at all. She was shot through the neck. In fact, Spot saved her life."

FOURTEEN

"What?" I said, shocked and delighted. I looked over at Spot. He was lying on the floor in the corner, not sleeping but just staring at the wall like a monk enduring deprivations.

"All I know is that Pussy Cat was shot. The puncture I thought was from your dog's fang turned out to be from a bullet. I don't know the details. For that you'd want to talk to Dr. Selma Peralta down at the UC Davis Veterinary Hospital." Dick Siker gave me the number.

After I hung up the phone I turned to Spot and spoke in the cheery voice I used whenever I wanted to get him excited. "Hey, polka dot boy! Guess what?"

Spot didn't move, didn't even shift his eyes.

"Spot, c'mon over here!" I patted my thighs.

There was no reaction.

Anytime someone describes the emotions of their pets in human terms, other people call it anthropomorphizing. But those people either have never had pets or else they are incapable of forming close bonds with them.

My dog was depressed and filled with guilt over the belief that he'd done something terribly wrong to the lion.

And I was the one who'd made him feel that way.

I walked over and knelt down beside him. "Spot, I'm so sorry," I said as I touched his head and ran my hands over his neck. "I screwed up, big guy. You didn't hurt the mountain lion. You didn't cause the blood."

I knew Spot didn't understand my words, but I hoped he'd get my meaning. Yet, he didn't appear to know I was even there. I sat down on the floor, lifted his head onto my lap and rubbed his ears. Then I got up and fetched a bag of dog treats from my desk. I put them in front of his nose, but he ignored them and appeared lifeless. That, and the fact that he hadn't drunk any water to speak of in the last day, had me worried.

After a few minutes I got up, dialed the number Dick Siker had given me and spoke to a woman in the UC Davis Veterinary Hospital. She couldn't put me through to Selma Peralta as the doctor was in surgery. I explained briefly what I was calling about and she said I could meet Dr. Peralta in her office. She expected her back from lunch around 1:00 p.m. and she wasn't scheduled for anything until 1:15. That gave me enough time to make the two hour drive down from Tahoe.

"Okay, Spot, let's go check on a mountain lion." I tugged hard on his collar and he reluctantly stood and came with me to the Jeep, hanging his head the entire way.

Once in a rare while he had hung his head and let his eyelids droop because he was sulking, feeling sorry for himself over some slight. But today was nothing like that and it made me worry.

I made it to the university with just enough time to park, walk across the busy campus to the vet hospital and find Selma Peralta's office on the third floor.

I knocked on the closed door and, receiving no response, leaned against the wall to wait. A beautiful Hispanic woman came down the hall at a brisk pace. She was short like Ellie, with a frame so well proportioned that if you saw a photo of her you'd guess her to be of normal height. She wore a white coat that made her sienna skin look exceptionally rich and warm. By her demeanor I guessed her to be a woman with natural authority, the kind of person who knew exactly what she wanted in life.

"Dr. Peralta?" I said as she approached.

"Hello," she said, cranking her neck back to take in my height. "You must be Owen McKenna. My secretary told me to expect you." She reached up her miniature hand and gave mine a delicate squeeze. "Please come in," she said as she unlocked her office door.

We went into a small space crammed with books and looking more like an associate professor's office than what I expected of an animal doctor. She gestured toward a chair and I sat while she dug through some papers on the desk.

"I appreciate you seeing me on such short notice, Dr. Peralta."

"Please, call me Selma." She gave me a warm smile. "I'm sorry I don't have much time. I've got appointments stacked up as high as a giraffe. I understand you are the person who found the mountain lion?"

"Actually, it was my dog who found her."

"So I've heard. Must be an awfully big, strong dog."

"I don't know how far he dragged her up the mountain. But I thought he had caused the lion's injuries. Her fur was matted and caked with blood on her neck where he'd gripped her."

Selma smiled again. "You can forgive your dog. He caused none of the injuries that I found. Come, we have a few minutes. Let me show you."

We left the office, rode an elevator down to a basement level and walked down a corridor to a large door that was wide enough to roll a prostrate moose through. Selma tugged on the door and I reached out to help.

We entered a wide, brightly lit hallway lined with doors that had windows in them. Through each door I could see white rooms with white tables. In one room there was a group of students watching and listening intently as their teacher examined a large black animal. From my position I could not tell what kind of animal it was, but from the size I guessed it to be a calf.

At the far corner of the hall Selma unlocked one of the doors and led me into a room like the others. On a white table, lying on a vinyl covered pad, was Pussy Cat. Her head was down and her eyes were shut, looking very much asleep or unconscious. Even so, I stayed back.

Selma walked up and put her hand on the lion's neck. She checked a drainage tube and glanced at some electronic readouts on the wall. "Come on over," she said to me. "Don't worry, she's out. She couldn't hurt a bunny rabbit in the state she's in."

I walked over and stood close. The lion had been cleaned up. Large portions of her neck and been shaved and bandages wrapped nearly all the way around.

"Your dog presumably carried the lion by lightly clamping his teeth onto the back of the lion's neck. That is a typical way for a mother to carry her offspring. The M.O., so to speak, is one of gentleness. The skin is loose and the fur thick. There would be much to bite onto without substantially hurting the animal." The doctor pointed. "When we shaved her neck we found contusions here and here, consistent with being carried that way."

"So my dog caused none of the bleeding?"

"No." She lifted slightly on the lion's neck. "A single bullet entered under this bandage, here, and lodged against one of the cervical vertebrae. It rotated as it passed through the soft tissue and did considerable damage, primarily to the windpipe and esophagus, but we think we've made sufficient repairs. One of the smaller arteries was severed and that led to substantial loss of blood." Selma Peralta walked around the lion's head and lifted an eyelid. "However, if we can prevent infection and keep her stabilized, she will likely recover from the gunshot."

"Will you be able to release her back into the wild?"

"That's the major question. The psychological and physical trauma will have serious effects on her after she is released. Will she successfully hunt? Gain her strength back? For a predator to survive in the wild without succumbing to the elements or other competitors requires nearly picture-perfect health."

"You don't sound optimistic," I said.

"I'm not. Typically, such an animal will give up hunting and instead come into populated areas in hopes of finding food. If that happens she will be shot unless an appropriate zoo can be found to take her."

"Did you get the bullet out?"

"Yes. It is over here." She walked over to a counter, picked up a small jar and handed it to me.

I held the jar up to the light. The deformed slug was small, but hadn't disintegrated.

"Can you tell what kind of gun was used?" the doctor asked.

"I'm not positive, but it looks like a twenty-two caliber, far too small to effectively hunt big game with. I suspect that the shooter wasn't hunting. More likely it was someone who was shooting wildlife just for kicks. And, if the shooter is sufficiently sick, there might be more kicks in merely wounding an animal with small caliber fire and letting it die slowly than in killing it fast with a big round."

Dr. Selma Peralta looked ill.

"Sorry, I didn't mean to sound too macabre."

"No, you are describing the real world. People like me need to face such things."

"May I keep the bullet? I'll have some tests done, see if we can learn about the gun that fired it."

"Certainly."

"How much longer will the lion be in your care?" I asked.

"A week to ten days. Hopefully she'll be well enough to transfer to a holding facility for cats. Then, after two or three months she might be well enough to be released back into the mountains. We'll know in a matter of a few days. If she isn't up and angry by then we'll probably be out of luck.

"Angry?"

"Yes. The hope is that she'll be pacing and snarling at us, the feistier the better. A subdued cat can never make it back in the wilderness."

Selma looked up at the clock on the wall. "I better get going."

We left the room and took the stairs up a single flight to the ground floor.

"I have what may seem like an unusual request," I said to the vet as we left the building and walked down one of the campus sidewalks. "When the lion gets better, I'm wondering if we might let my dog see her."

Selma Peralta frowned at me, as if I were suddenly revealing some craziness that had previously escaped her. "I'm afraid I don't understand."

"Have you ever worked with search and rescue dogs?"

"No," she said. "I've read a bit about it, but never seen them at work."

"When they recover a dead body they get depressed, sometimes profoundly so. The dogs have a clear sense of mission and duty, and a dead find makes them feel like failures. I'm afraid that's what my dog is going through, and I exacerbated his depression by making him feel as if he were responsible for the lion's injuries."

"You're hoping that your dog will feel better if he can see the lion up and relatively healthy."

"Yes," I said. "If, during a search, a dog makes a dead find, we arrange a live find to cheer the dog up."

"You mean you fake it, have someone hide and let the dog find them?"

"Exactly."

"But it will take several days before we expect any noticeable improvement. Don't you think your dog will have forgotten all about it by then?"

"Possibly, but I think it will be worth a try."

We came to an intersection in the sidewalks and Selma Peralta indicated that she was heading toward the edge of campus where the parking lots were.

"You seem like a very dedicated dog owner," she said.

"No more than usual. I just have a very depressed dog. Perhaps you'd care to take a look. He's in my car over in this next lot." I pointed off to the right.

The vet nodded and we were at the Jeep in a minute.

"Hey, Spot," I said as I opened the rear passenger door. "I want you to meet Selma. She's a dog doctor."

Spot was lying on the seat. He did not lift his head.

I stepped aside so Selma Peralta could take a look. She leaned in the door and pet him. "Hi, Spot. I hear you're not feeling well." Selma gently ran her hands over Spot, feeling under his jawbone and under his armpits. "Now that I see his size I can understand how he dragged that lion up the mountain." She felt Spot's ribs. "Has he been drinking and eating?"

"Not to speak of. I think he's lost some weight."

The vet lifted Spot's jowls and looked at his gums, pressing her finger against them and watching the pink color slowly return. "He's pale and quite dehydrated," she said. He needs fluid." She looked at her watch. "I don't have enough time to..."

"I've taken enough of your time," I interrupted. "I'll bring him by my local vet."

Selma looked relieved. "Good," she said, turning back to Spot. "I don't want to alarm you, but you should do it first thing. The dehydration appears significant."

"I'll stop at Doctor Siker's the moment we get back to Tahoe."

Selma Peralta gave me a polite smile. "With fluid and time he'll get better. And, yes, I'll make sure he can visit the lion when she gets better. Do you have a card? I'll call when the time is right."

"Thank you, doctor."

On the way back up to Tahoe I caught a weather report that said the current high pressure zone over the Tahoe Basin would be hotter and last longer than previously expected. Further, we could expect even stronger afternoon winds than previously forecast. It was a troubling report, a prescription, especially after a long, dry summer, for deadly forest fires.

I went directly to Dick Siker's animal hospital when I got back to Tahoe. He took one look at Spot and agreed with Selma Peralta's assessment that my dog was in trouble. We left Spot in the Jeep and Dick brought out a large, clear bag of fluid with a tube and needle.

"You figure an IV will do the trick?" I asked.

"Not an IV. I'm not putting this into a vein, just under his skin. It will kind of slosh around in there until it is gradually absorbed into his system."

He inserted the needle under the loose skin at the base of Spot's neck, then gave the bag of fluid a gentle squeeze. In a few minutes the liquid was transferred and Dick pulled the needle out. "He's going to leak a little out of the needle puncture, but don't worry about it. Bring him home and make him rest. He'll be better tomorrow. Give me a call and let me know how he's doing."

I thanked Dick Siker and drove home.

The vet wasn't kidding about sloshing and leaking. Spot's neck skin ballooned when he stood up to get out of the car and it wobbled like an out-of-balance washing machine as he walked into the house. And instead of the gentle wet leak I expected to find in the neck fur, water dripped out at a rate that would prompt a quick call to the plumber if it were my faucet instead of my dog. I filled Spot's bowl with food, but he immediately lay down in the corner.

I unwrapped a new leather dog bone and while he didn't show any enthusiasm, he at least took it from me, a sign that we were approaching détente. After getting a beer, I sat down cross-legged on the floor next to him, lifted his head over my thigh and told him the story of Pussy Cat while he chewed on the leather bone and slobbered all over my pants.

It was late in the afternoon and I still hadn't had any lunch. I figured someone in the house should eat, so I went to the kitchen to grab a bite. I was pulling out sandwich fixings when my cell phone rang.

"Owen McKenna," I answered.

"Owen, this is Linda Saronna." Her voiced was rushed. "We've got a ground fire off High Mountain Road, just below Tallac Properties. It's small, about sixty feet by two hundred, but it's growing fast and heading up a meadow toward a large stand of dead Lodgepole pine. Not too far above the trees are several houses."

"I'm on my way," I said into my phone as I pulled Spot with me out to my Jeep.

FIFTEEN

I raced through town and headed out Lake Tahoe Blvd. toward a growing plume of smoke only to find that a squad car and two Eldorado County Sheriff vehicles with their lights flashing had blocked the entrance to High Mountain Road. I didn't see anyone I knew and the two cops standing there waved me off.

I jumped out of the Jeep. "My name's Owen McKenna. I'm assigned to this fire by Linda Saronna. I need to get through."

They looked at me blankly. "Sorry, buddy," one of them said. "I don't know any Linda whats-her-name. You're going to have to leave."

"She runs the Lake Tahoe Basin Management Unit of the Forest Service. She's in charge of this fire."

"Let me check," the cop said. He spoke into his walkie talkie. "Okay," he said in a minute. "Captain Mallory said he's parked by the last turn before Tallac Ridge Road. He wants you to find him when you get up there."

I got back in the Jeep, they stood aside and waved me through.

High Mountain Road climbs up a relatively small, forested bump that rises one thousand feet above the valley floor. Most people don't even notice it because it is so over-shadowed by the cliff face of Mount Tallac directly behind it. The housing development called Tallac Properties sits on the side of a ridge that extends out from High Mountain. The area looks down on Fallen Leaf Lake, a large, glacier-cut finger of water that stretches like a reflecting pond across the entire front of Mount Tallac. As Hollywood movie producers have discovered, Fallen Leaf Lake is perhaps the prettiest body of water in the entire Sierra Nevada.

As I drove fast up the shallow incline, the plume of smoke above me grew larger and darker. Where the road stopped climbing I saw a blackened meadow off to the side in the forest. The fire had already moved out of the meadow and into the trees that surrounded the neighborhood houses.

The first junction in the road was clogged with more squad cars and fire engines. I pushed the button to roll down the window as I eased through the congestion toward the fire. Firemen ran by me dragging a long hose. Loud radios squawked. People shouted. In the distance a child screamed. Behind the human commotion I heard the frightening sounds of the fire, the pop of green pine cones exploding, the cracking sounds of overheated branches, and the steady low roar of the fire wind.

I pulled the Jeep off the road and into the woods, out of the way of the firemen and far enough back that I didn't think the falling embers would land on it. As I walked toward the center of the activity it was clear that the fire had grown dramatically from what Linda Saronna described. She had mentioned a stand of Lodgepole pine above the meadow where the fire had apparently started. I saw that the trees were now fully involved and the flames roared a hundred feet into the air. Three groups of firemen directed their water cannons at the flames. I hurried forward and found Mallory next to his unmarked Explorer. He was yelling into a radio. He saw me and held up a finger. I trotted toward him.

"McKenna!" he called out as I approached.

We had to yell to be heard over the surrounding noise.

"Linda Saronna says you've been working with the Forest Service!"

"Tahoe Douglas F.P.D. hired me," I yelled back, "but it's obviously a group effort. How many houses are there on the other side of those flames?"

"Five or six I think," Mallory said.

Any evidence of arson?"

Mallory shook his head. "Nothing obvious yet," he yelled back. The whump, whump of an approaching chopper made talking even more difficult. "The way this sucker is growing our only concern right now is evacuating the neighborhood."

The chopper whirled into view. Swinging on a cable in a wide arc below it was a bucket. The chopper pilot made a tight turn and the bucket swung out over the flames. The water that showered into the flames looked like a tiny gray splash against the black smoke, although I realized it was probably thousands of gallons. The chopper continued its tight turn and dropped down to Fallen Leaf Lake for a refill.

"Have you seen Linda?" I yelled.

Mallory pointed through some trees. "She was next to a Forest Service rig over there a few minutes ago."

The light green Forest Service trucks were easy to distinguish from the red trucks of the South Lake Tahoe Fire Department. I ran over and found Linda conferring with Joey Roberts, one of the South Lake Tahoe F.D. Battalion Chiefs. Linda looked very distressed. The circles under her eyes were dark blue and her eyelids were puffy red. It looked like she had been crying, although I realized it was more likely the smoke. As I approached, a Tahoe Douglas Fire Department pickup roared up and jerked to a stop. Terry Drier jumped out and ran over to Joey Roberts.

He yelled as he approached. "Thought I'd bring some help from the Nevada side!"

Joey yelled back, "We've already got half the vehicles from this end of the lake on this torch job, but it doesn't look good. What did you bring?"

"I've got two Type One engines and five men," Terry shouted as a Nevada truck roared up.

"Your boys got Nomex suits?"

Terry nodded.

Joey got on his radio. "I need another strike team! Type Three engines! And get a tanker if you can!"

A fireman ran from the woods near the flames. He yelled over the roar of the fire and the fire engines. "I sent a team around the west side of the fire toward the houses! One structure is already involved! More are in danger. But the wind shifted toward my team!"

Joey spoke to Terry. "Can you suit up a couple of your men and send them around the east side? Have them check to see if there are people in those houses!"

While the firemen hurried about, I spoke to Linda. "Any indication yet if it's arson?"

"No," she said. "We haven't found anything."

"The tanker Joey Roberts called for," I said. "Is that a big truck? Will it be able to get into this forest?"

Just then a whistling noise filled the air as a huge burning tree crashed to the ground.

Linda Saronna yelled back, "A tanker is a plane! It can pick up water in Fallen Leaf Lake and carry a lot more than a chopper."

"Who first reported the fire?"

"A nine-one-one call came from a house in the neighborhood at the same time as our Angora Ridge spotter called it in."

At that moment Francisco ran up. "I found a match!"

The young man looked alarmed. "It was half burned," he said. "Right on the edge of the meadow where the fire started."

"Did you touch it or disturb the area?" I asked.

He shook his head. "No, no. I know better than that. I was following the edge of the burn," Francisco said to me, concern wrinkling his forehead. "From the burn pattern I thought I could discover where the fire had started. Sure enough, there was the wooden match, plain as day."

"You'll show the Fire Investigator as soon as possible?" Because we were in Eldorado County on the California side, the Fire Investigator was Bill Pickett, a man I'd met only a couple of times.

"I think Linda said that Mr. Pickett is in Hawaii on vacation," Francisco said.

Linda nodded. "That's right."

"Okay," I said. "I'll get Mallory. We can show him."

At that moment Linda got a call on her radio. She listened a moment, then said, "Frederick, Captain Mallory asked me if he could get some help with the press. He said there is a TV crew down the road and some reporters walking through the woods. Hurry. You know what to do." She clicked the radio off. "Francisco, can you go help Frederick? He's down at the High Mountain Road turnoff. Thanks."

He jogged off.

"I'm curious," I said to Linda. "What is it that Frederick will do regarding the press?"

"We just went over it yesterday, in fact," Linda said. "In dealing with the press it is important to tell them the truth but keep it narrow and without any speculation. Otherwise it inflames the reporter hoping to write an exciting story. When they ask if the fire was caused by arson Frederick will say, 'we don't know.' If they inquire about another note Frederick will tell them that he understands there was another note but that he hasn't seen it. The goal is to keep the arsonist from feeling like the press is another tool he can use to terrorize the local population."

"You speak of the arsonist as a 'he?'"

"Aren't they all?" Linda said, her exasperation clear.

Just then two firemen in bright yellow suits ran out of the smoke-filled trees just to the side of the wall of flames. One was carrying something large and dark flung over his shoulder. He picked his way carefully as he ran around a burning manzanita and stepped over a downed tree. The other fireman ran up to Battalion Chief Joey Roberts. His words came in bursts, punctuated by a fit of coughing. I heard him say something about a victim and smoke inhalation. He was cut off as Joey yelled into his radio.

An ambulance had been waiting down the street. It suddenly jerked forward, its siren turning on and off twice in quick succession to let the firemen in the street know it was moving.

The ambulance turned sideways in the street and stopped. The back doors flung open and two paramedics ran out carrying a stretcher. They sprinted into the smoky woods and met the other fireman halfway. The paramedics set the stretcher down in the blackened dirt and the fireman lowered his load down onto it. With a flash of movement they had the victim lashed down and the paramedics were off and running.

As they came near we saw the victim up close. She was middle-aged and wearing a light blue bathrobe. One foot had a maroon velour slipper on, the other foot was bare. Her skin was the color of old concrete. The paramedics slid the stretcher into the ambulance which immediately started forward. As it raced away, one paramedic strapped an oxygen mask over the woman's face as the other reached out and pulled the back doors shut.

I turned to Linda. She was pale and shivering and the shock in her eyes was startling. "I'm sorry, Linda," I said.

"Oh, my God!" she said over and over.

I put my hands on her shoulders and could feel tremors shaking her body. She grabbed the front of my jacket and bowed her head. Tears dripped onto her bunched knuckles. Watching them bring a fire victim through the flames was an upsetting experience to say the least. And I knew that Linda had been under a great deal of stress. Yet I wondered if there was something else that troubled this woman who clutched onto me.

SIXTEEN

The various agencies fighting the fire produced a massive assault that grew to two helicopters, one tanker, a dozen fire engines and what looked like a hundred men, half of them wielding chainsaws. Even so, it was well into the evening before they had cut fire breaks on both sides of the fire and containment started to seem like a believable proposition.

Several hundred acres had burned.

Along with two houses, just as the note said.

Linda Saronna eventually headed back to her office. Frederick and Francisco had long since disappeared, perhaps still keeping the press at bay.

Joey Roberts stayed in command of the fire, with the South Lake Tahoe departments and the Forest Service contingents on the scene. Terry Drier remained to help Joey, but sent one of his Tahoe Douglas teams and their truck back to their station on the east shore of Tahoe. I followed them as evening turned to dark night. When the fire truck turned into the fire station, I continued on past and headed up the mountain to my cabin.

It was late, but Street usually worked late. I dialed her number at the lab and she answered immediately.

"Thought it might be you," she said. "I just heard about the fire on the radio. Were you there?"

"Yes. It was bad. One woman was sent to the hospital with smoke inhalation."

"Do you think she'll be all right?"

"I don't know," I said truthfully. I didn't add that the only time I'd ever seen the gray color of the woman's skin was on dead people. "The good news," I said, eager to change the subject, "is that Spot didn't hurt the mountain lion." While Street almost shrieked with pleasure, I told her about my trip to the UC Davis Veterinary Hospital

When I finished, Street said, "So Spot was dragging Pussy Cat up the mountain to try and help her?"

"Only explanation that fits."

"Oh, my God, that's wonderful, Owen," Street said.

"Yes, it is," I said, looking over at my dog, prostrate in the corner. His water-balloon neck had dissipated, but he was morose as ever.

I said goodbye to Street, then coaxed Spot into eating a small amount of dog food while I resumed work on the sandwich I'd started so many hours before.

The next morning, Street came over. We sat together on the deck drinking coffee. Despite a breeze, a brown haze from the fire filled the Tahoe Basin.

"I heard on the radio that they couldn't revive the woman," Street said, her voice very sad.

"No." I'd already spoken to my doctor friend John Lee who pulls night duty at the Barton Hospital ER. "Her name was Joanie Dove. Doc Lee says she was home from work with a bad cold. The fire caught her napping in bed. By the time she awakened the house was in flames. She only made it into the living room before collapsing from smoke inhalation."

Street gave a little shiver in the chair next to me. "The second note said two houses would burn, didn't it?"

"Yes. But nothing about any people."

"Are they sure it is arson?"

"I called Terry Drier first thing and he said they called Diamond across the state line because Bill Pickett, the Fire Investigator from South Lake Tahoe, is on vacation. Diamond said the matches from the two fires look to be identical and the MO was the same. But this fire didn't reveal any gasoline."

"Did Ellie and her dog already check it?"

"No, we didn't need to call them. Turns out one of the South Lake Tahoe canine units is accelerant trained. A search revealed nothing."

Street put her feet up on the deck railing and gazed off over the water. "Maybe the gas at the first fire was the only way to assure that Jake Pooler would burn. But on the second fire no gas was needed because the woman was in her house."

"That could be," I said. "But this second death doesn't look like it was intentional. Joanie Dove was supposed to be at work, so how could the arsonist have known? And Jake Pooler's death might also have been an accident."

"True," Street said. "But in both cases it is possible that the fires were set to cause the deaths."

"Yes, it's possible. It just doesn't seem likely."

"I suppose," Street muttered, "that what will tell you will be if you can find any connection between Jake Pooler and Joanie Dove. If so, that would make the deaths more likely to be murder."

"Exactly," I said.

"Where did Joanie work?" Street asked.

"Heritage Title Company."

We were both silent a moment.

"There is one more wild card," I said. "But if I could find a link there it would be revealing."

"What is that?"

"Pussy Cat.

"How do you mean?"

"What if the arsonist was the person who shot the mountain lion? If I could find the gun that fired the bullet I might have my arsonist."

"That seems a stretch. Why would an arsonist shoot a mountain lion?"

"Good question. Maybe the guy was Jake's friend. They were out together and saw the lion. The guy pulls out his gun, which incidentally was too small a caliber to kill big game without an incredibly accurate shot. Jake doesn't want him to do it and they argue. The guy shoots the lion anyway and it runs away. Now Jake is very mad at the shooter. They fight, Jake gets gas spilled on him and dies when the shooter strikes a match."

I could see Street mulling it over. "It seems an improbable scenario, but pick up any newspaper and you see improbable scenarios happening every day." She stood up, walked over to the edge of the deck, turned toward me and leaned back against the railing. "What's that aphorism you talked about once? About the simplest explanation?"

"Occam's Razor. He was an English philosopher, Fourteenth Century, I think, who said that in any puzzle or mystery the simplest explanation is the likeliest to be the truth."

"So have you applied that to these fires and deaths?"

"I've tried," I said. "The problem is, I can't find *any* explanation that fits, let alone a simple one."

At that, Street walked over to where Spot was sprawled, bent down and rubbed his head. "Next time you rescue a pussy cat, you drag it to my house, okay? With me you're innocent until proven guilty."

With that, Street headed off to work while Spot and I drove into town to The Red Hut, breakfast restaurant extraordinaire.

"Hey, Mr. detective," a familiar voice said as I sat on the last open seat at the counter.

"Michelle, my belle," I said as she poured delicious smelling coffee into one of the thick Red Hut cups.

"How's the hound?" she asked as she craned her neck to look out the window. Michelle was a former champion skier who turned champion waitress when she reached the ripe old age of twenty-five and retired after competing in the last Olympics. Unlike a lot of Olympic skiers from Tahoe who go on to careers in the ski business, Michelle decided she wanted to focus on raising her two young kids, and working in a breakfast restaurant allowed her to get home just as they finished preschool. "I bet your dog is waiting with bated breath for a piece of your breakfast," she said.

"Bad breath," I corrected. "But yes, I'll have to save a few bites to take out to him."

"You want the usual?"

"Please."

"One Owen's Omelet coming right up."

Five minutes later she brought me an omelet with cheddar cheese, ham and green pepper inside and hash browns on the side. It looked and smelled so good I couldn't imagine saving any for Spot.

"I read about you in the paper," Michelle said. "About how you found the first body. That must have been gross, all burned."

"Yeah, it was pretty nasty," I said. "Speaking of which, is your uncle still working for the FBI?"

"Uncle George the shrink? Last I heard he was. But it's been a while since we've spoken. It's embarrassing how bad we are at keeping up. It's not like he lives on Mars or something. But since I had my boys, well, you know how it is. Hey, you want to talk to him about the fire and the arsonist?"

"Yes," I said.

"Here, I'll write down his number. My little brother and I used to go into San Francisco to visit him. Mom's way of getting us out from under her feet while she went shopping was to dump us on Uncle George. It's amazing how nice he always was about it." Michelle wrote his number on a napkin and gave it to me.

"Thanks," I said.

Later, she gave me a goodbye pat on the shoulder as I left with the last few bites of my breakfast in a doggie box.

Spot rallied a little when I approached smelling of omelet. "A small offering for your largeness," I said as I opened the box and offered it to him. He made one swipe with his gigantic tongue and the food morsels shot into his cavernous mouth like a slap shot from Gretsky's hockey stick. Then his tongue returned for a repeat trip into the box, smacking into the corners hard enough that I had to grip it with both hands. A drop of saliva hit my cheek.

"That does it," I said, wiping my cheek. "I'm sending you to finishing school for dogs. There's probably one in L.A." Spot put his head back down on the seat and went back to acting depressed.

Back at my cabin, I dialed the number Michelle had given me for George Morrell, the psychologist who did profiling for the FBI. George answered directly, no answering machine, no secretary. When I explained what I wanted he agreed to see me that afternoon.

As long as I was going to be in San Francisco, I remembered that Terry Drier had said that Arthur Jones Middleton could give me the "wacko environmentalist perspective" on forest management. Middleton wasn't available to talk on the phone, but a secretary took the call and said I should come to his house at 5:00 p.m.

I took Spot out for his walk, then left him in my cabin. It is a four hour drive across California to the Bay Area, and by early afternoon I was on the Bay Bridge heading to my old hometown, the place that San Francisco locals refer to as the City.

SEVENTEEN

I had just enough time to stop at the ballistics lab that was tucked into an old warehouse south of Market. I dropped off the slug that Dr. Selma Peralta took out of Pussy Cat's neck. The technician said he'd have a report for me in a couple of days.

Back across Market and the Financial District, I headed through China Town. After ten minutes of circling various blocks I found a parking space just below Russian Hill, wedging my Jeep into a spot on a street that pointed impossibly up like those near-vertical streets in a Wayne Thiebaud painting. It took a few minutes of walking and then backtracking to discover that the street number for George Morrell's office was not actually on a traditional street, but instead was where a street would have been if San Francisco had been built on the flat. The number led me up a steep cascade of trees, bushes and rocks that were bordered on both sides by stairways. The steps went up for hundreds of feet, boring twin tunnels through the steep arboreal darkness. The houses were a mixture of candy-colored Victorians and weathered cedar boxes with rooftop gardens. Between the houses were decorative gates opening on narrow passages that wound back through small, private jungles so lush it was hard to believe I was in an urban setting.

Morrell's house number was on a wrought iron gate in front of one of the Victorians, this one painted in two tones of peach with light blue trim. I paused to catch my breath after hiking up a couple hundred feet of stairway, wondering why my high-altitude fitness efforts didn't make a sea-level climb any less tiring. After a moment I pushed the button. I heard a door open behind thick foliage and a man came around a curved, brick path. He was broad through the shoulders, and narrow everywhere else. His clothing was California-chic, chinos, sandals, and a thin, off-white sweater with the sleeves pushed up onto his forearms exposing an expensive gold watch. He stopped and looked up at me.

"Good afternoon, Mr. McKenna," he said as he opened the gate and shook my hand. "I'm George Morrell.

"Please call me Owen."

He nodded. "George for me. Come in." He gestured toward the stairs that passed for the street. "Did you come from above or below?"

"Below."

"Oh, then you've had your exercise for the day." He grinned at me.

"Indeed," I said.

He led me along the brick path, through the large front door and into a formal entry hall about the size of my entire log cabin. "We'll talk in my study," he said, "that is if you don't mind climbing a few more stairs." He turned and smiled.

"Not at all," I said. I followed him up a curving stairway. "Do all FBI people live in such nice places?" I asked as we climbed in a half-circle to a wide second-floor balcony.

He chuckled. "All the ones who inherit as I did. But actually, I'm not an FBI employee."

"Oh? I thought your niece Michelle referred to you as such."

"I think Michelle finds it much more interesting to think of me as an FBI man than as a psychologist.

"You have a private practice?" I asked. We turned down a hall and went into a room at the end. Large windows looked out at the San Francisco Bay and the Bay Bridge.

"Used to," George said. "But after my mother died I had no more need for income and, well, private practice is interesting but not that interesting. Twenty years of it is enough." He gestured me toward a pair of large leather easy chairs. We both sat. George crossed his legs, laced his fingers together and propped them over his knee. Casual, relaxed, yet a touch intimate. I could see that people would feel comfortable telling him anything.

"Yet you do work for the FBI?"

"Only as a consultant. Frankly, they present me with such horrific but, dare I say, fascinating problems that I cannot resist."

"I imagine you've seen it all by now. Doesn't the macabre get wearying? The FBI must hand you some pretty ugly stuff."

"The worst of the worst. But that's the point." He leaned back in his chair. "We shrinks are all somewhat on the edge of the bell curve when it comes to matters of psychological balance. Why else would we choose such an occupation? The individual who follows a career of, say, growing roses or running a vineyard is fundamentally a different kind of person than one who studies tumors in rats. Neither, of course, is better. And the world needs both. But shrinks belong to the second group. The most bizarre manifestations of human behavior are what motivate me to get up in the morning. What sick mind will the FBI present me with next? And how can my analysis help them catch the individual?" He suddenly stood up. "Excuse me, but I forgot to offer you something to drink. Perrier? Lemonade?" He looked at his watch. "Not too early for scotch. I have what may be the largest private collection of single malts in Northern California."

"I'd love a beer if you have any," I said.

"Anchor Steam?"

"Perfect," I said.

George opened one of those miniature refrigerators and pulled out a bottle. He popped the top and set it and a tall glass directly down on a low, walnut burl cocktail table. Despite the fastidiousness made obvious by the perfectly neat and clean house, there were neither coasters nor doilies visible anywhere, something a guy who lived in a log cabin could appreciate. The cold Anchor Steam sweated immediately and the condensation ran down onto the nice table. Being a psychologist he probably lived by a Don't Sweat The Small Stuff mentality. And doing what he did for the FBI, he had plenty of Big Stuff to concentrate on. I sipped the beer.

Delicious. George poured himself a healthy belt of Laphroiag and returned to his chair.

"So what can I help you with, Owen?"

"You are what the FBI calls a profiler?"

"I review information on certain individuals that the FBI is particularly concerned about and from that information I construct likely personality traits and responses to various scenarios. Profiling isn't my favorite term, but yes, it refers to what I do."

"We used the term when I was with SFPD homicide," I said. "Periodically we worked a case in conjunction with the FBI. On two occasions where I was involved the FBI brought in a profiler to help them understand a killer's motivations."

"Interesting that you don't betray the usual animosity when you refer to the FBI," George said. "It's been my experience that cops universally don't like them."

"I've been an ex-cop long enough now that I'm largely over it. But it's true that some of my dealings with the FBI were rough. I remember one time where a Special Agent, fresh out of the academy, came into my case and pulled rank on me, flashing his law degree in my face. Then he proceeded to screw up my entire investigation with his inexperience. I certainly understand how cops develop a pejorative attitude about them."

"The suits."

"Yes, that's what we call them," I said. "But you have to get a little curl into your lip when you say it. Also, put an expletive modifier in place of the word 'the' and you'll have it just right."

George grinned. "So tell me how I can help you."

"I need to learn about firestarters."

"I assume this is about the arsonist up in Lake Tahoe."

"Correct," I said. "I've been hired to try and find the arsonist. The first fire was in Douglas County on the Nevada side. The Fire Investigator for Douglas County is Diamond Martinez, a good guy, but somewhat inexperienced. The second fire last night was on the California side. The South Lake Tahoe authorities are equally at a loss when it comes to tracking a crime without a traditional motive."

"You expect more fires?"

"Yes. Each fire was preceded by a note. The first fire involved no structures, so insurance claims are out and without insurance we don't have any kind of arson that we understand. The second fire burned two houses, but coming on the heels after the first fire, it doesn't seem as if insurance is any motive."

"So," George said, "you don't have a motive on these fires. But I read in the paper that they did find a body," George said.

"Yes," I said. "In the first fire I thought perhaps it was the dead man who lit the fire and maybe he accidentally burned himself as well."

"You considered self-immolation?"

"Suicide? I didn't give the idea much credence at first, but it became a possibility when we found out that the victim was in debt and that the gas can found at the scene might have belonged to him."

"Yet you now think it is murder."

"I'm not sure. There was a second note before yesterday's fire and that fire caused a second death," I said.

"Another death?" George's eyebrows rose.

"Yes. Like the first death, this one *could* be murder. Then again, the woman who died in the second fire was supposed to be at work and apparently called in sick. So we've got two deaths, and either one could be accidental."

"I see. Why don't you fill me in on the details," George said.

I went over the events from the beginning. George interrupted now and then to ask questions. In each case the questions were about small details such as whether the phrasing on the notes used active or passive verbs. And how many bystanders were seen at the fires.

"Let me tell you a bit about arsonists," George said when I was done bringing him up to date. "The firestarter who is easier to catch, the one who burns for money, is much less pathological than the other kind. Typically, the former is a person who gets into financial trouble and searches for a way out. If they are desperate enough and if they are not constrained by the kind of psychological mechanisms that help you and I to function morally and legally, they may see any number of ways out of their financial troubles, arson being just one of them. Once such a person chooses arson, they go about it the way you or I would, making various attempts to conceal their involvement, some clumsy, some clever. Often, to establish an alibi, they hire someone else to strike the match while they are away on a well-documented trip.

"Ironically, another example of the less pathological fire-starter," George continued, "would be a person who decides they need to murder another person. Perhaps the victim appears to be an obstacle to all that the murderer cares about. Or maybe the victim has incited uncontrollable anger in the murderer. Just as with the individual who has financial problems, the cold-blooded murderer searches for an appropriate way to commit the crime and they might settle on arson as the best method."

"So in both cases the arson is merely a means to an end," I said.

"Exactly." George sipped his scotch. "And because of that, understanding the crime and finding the perpetrator is much easier."

"But we may be dealing with a different kind of criminal?"

"I'm not certain, but that would be my guess," George said. "The person who lights fires for the thrill of it is an especially disturbing individual. We don't understand much of the pathology, but the fixation on fire is tied to an entire range of other problems." At this statement, George's eyes widened with enthusiasm.

"What kind of problems?" I asked.

"For example, let's look at serial killers. Typically, there are several manifestations of pathology that appear at an early age and continue into young adulthood. Bed wetting is one. Torturing animals is another. And fixation on fires and playing with fire is the third. We call this the homicidal trinity."

I thought of Pussy Cat when he mentioned animal torture. "Meaning that someone who grows up with all three characteristics is more likely to murder?"

"Yes," George said. "But not just murder in the sense of killing a certain individual."

"In other words, not murder as a means to an ends, but as an end in itself."

"Correct. The person who kills because they like to kill."

"So serial killers and arsonists who torch for thrills have something in common," I said.

"Yes. However, it is serial killers who exhibit the highest tendency to manifest the homicidal trinity. It is these people who are the hardest to catch. Their victims appear to have been chosen at random or as a matter of convenience."

"Do serial killers ever use arson as their standard MO?"

George nodded. "From what you've told me, the person you are after might not be an arsonist trying to solve their personal problems, but a thrill seeker. Further, if I had to guess, I would say that the deaths were intended."

"The killer wanted these people dead and figured out how to murder them with fire?"

"No," George said, shaking his head for emphasis. "I think it is worse. I think the killer didn't want those *particular* people dead, but he wanted to kill. The identities of the victims were random. As will be those of future victims."

I sipped beer and thought about what he said. "Is there a sexual component as well?" I asked.

"In most cases, probably. But, as Freud made so clear, there is a sexual component to all behavior."

"I guess I meant sexual deviancy in the sense of behavior that would make it easier to catch the killer."

"After you catch him, you may well see such a deviancy. But it might not be something that will aid you in finding him. First of all, you might not be able to discern its presence without considerable digging. And secondly, many people behave in ways that one would think of as deviant, yet they don't kill people nor do they light fires."

"I'm assuming that these deviant personalities don't always fit into neat little boxes," I said.

"In what way do you mean?"

"For example, maybe a killer exhibits the bed wetting, fire starting and animal torture as a child but doesn't become a thrill killer. Instead, he kills as a - what did you call it? - a problem solver."

"That's true. The pathology runs the gamut," George said. "Someone exhibiting the homicidal trinity could be on the edge, tempted but never acting on a homicidal impulse until they find themselves in a situation that would come close to driving the rest of us to kill. In that case, such an individual will go over the homicidal edge much sooner than you or I. But they are not killing for the thrill of it. Instead, they are killing for reasons similar to those that would make you or me kill."

"You make it seem as though the personality characteristics are so indistinct that we'll never find the killer."

"Oh, no," George said. "These personality characteristics are very distinct. And when you find your killer, if he has such characteristics they will be clear to you."

"You say, 'if' the killer has characteristics."

"Correct. It is important to remember that this is not a causal relationship. The horse who wins the Kentucky Derby usually has great conformation, long legs, powerful hindquarters. But if you see a horse with great conformation out in a pasture, it is unlikely you're looking at a derby winner."

I drank some more beer, wondering about the use of a metaphor that presented killers in such a light of greatness. "What other characteristics do serial killers present?" I asked.

"Oh, there are many of them, but because they are less common they are notable only when the main three are present."

"And they are?"

George paused. "I'm a bit reluctant to even mention them because making note of them is likely to bring innocent people under suspicion."

"But if," I said carefully, "I have reason to suspect an individual of murder and/or arson, and I find the homicidal trinity, then what else might I notice about the suspect?"

"Under those conditions," George said, "you might also make note of any speech impediment."

I immediately thought of Winton Berger, the kid who used to work for Jake before he was killed. "How about a minor lisp," I said. "Like, for instance, an SH sound in words where there is only the standard sibilant sound of the letter S?"

"Yes, that would qualify," George said.

I thought about it a moment. "Other traits?"

George hesitated.

I was reassured that there were some limits to George's apparent enthusiasm for the details of killer's personalities.

"You might find an abusive childhood. Especially physical and sexual abuse. You might also find someone who was orphaned as a child."

"You keep using the pronoun 'he'," I said. "Are all serial killers male?"

"That reminds me of the joke about privacy rights and bio-technology," George said, his enthusiasm back in force. "There is, in fact, a genetic marker that is present in well over ninety percent of serial killers. The question is to what extent should society act when a baby is born with this genetic marker?" George paused, grinning. "Of course, the genetic marker is the presence of the Y chromosome." George grinned again. "We don't yet know the reason for it, but serial killers and arsonists are overwhelmingly male."

"Why would the arsonist send us these notes?"

"Grandstanding. Boasting. Taunting. He is saying, 'look how smart and clever I am. I can alert you before I light the fire and you still can't catch me.'"

"But the notes might make it easier for us to eventually catch him."

"True," George said. "But that is part of the appeal of the dare. It makes it more exciting for the firestarter."

"The day I was hired, the paper made a small note of it. The next day someone left a toy stuffed dog on my doorstep. It was a Great Dane, the same as my dog. The toy was badly burned. Does that sound like a warning?"

George's face became serious. "Yes, it does. One can't know for certain, but I think you should take it as a serious threat."

"Any standard way of removing the danger of such a threat?

"Give up the case. Make it public that you are no longer looking for the arsonist. That will be quite a feather in his cap and he would likely leave you alone."

"And if I don't give up the case?"

George thought a moment. "The burned stuffed animal on your doorstep was a warning just like the notes. The killer has demonstrated that he acts after his warnings. I would expect that your dog is probably in danger."

"You mean like tossing poisoned hamburger into my yard? After all, my dog is large. Almost no one would dare to physically come after him."

"No, I wouldn't expect poisoning, although that is certainly possible. From what you've told me, I would look for a much more active threat."

"Like?"

"Like a fire," George said.

The thought made me suddenly nauseous.

"Are you okay?" George said.

"What you said is frightening. I left my dog home alone."

"I don't want to alarm you, but that is probably not a good idea until this is over," George said. "This killer might not limit himself to fire. If your home is in a place where it is not easy to sneak up and throw a Molotov cocktail, he can just as well sit a long distance away with a high-powered rifle."

I thought of Pussy Cat being shot and it made my throat constrict painfully. "Would it be okay if I used your phone? I left mine in my car. I'll put the call on my card."

"Of course, only don't worry about the card," George said. He gestured toward a small writing desk that had a phone on it. "I'll give you some privacy," he said and then left the room.

I called Street and briefly explained where I was. I told her what the psychologist had said and asked if she'd be willing to go up to my cabin and take Spot back down to her condo.

"Of course," she said.

"Thanks, Street.

"Don't worry, I won't let anything happen to his largeness."

"I appreciate it. I'll be home this evening."

I hung up the phone and George returned a minute later.

"I thought it would be smart to have my sweetheart look in on my dog."

"Good idea," George said.

"Your mention of the arsonist possibly using a gun brings up another situation we've had that might be unrelated, but also might fall into the animal torture component of the homicidal trinity."

"Oh?"

I told him the story of Pussy Cat.

George got very concerned, his face a network of worry lines. "I think you are dealing with a very disturbed individual," he said. "My guess is there will be more fires and more deaths. And I think that not only is your dog in significant danger, but you may be as well."

I thought about it as we sat in silence. "Do you have any ideas about how to catch this guy?"

"As far as serial killers go, there are no tricks. Standard police work is the best you have to go on. But as far as arson goes, there is one thing that often helps identify the man who torches for thrills as opposed to the other kind. And that is, the thrill-seeking firestarter stays around to watch."

I pondered that. "In the group of gawkers that always appears at any fire?"

"Yes," George said. "Very often the firestarter will be there, mingling with the crowd."

"I could review photos," I said. "Reporters and lots of other people take pictures of the fire. They might include the bystanders in their shots."

"Additionally," George said, "there are other people besides bystanders who watch a fire."

I looked at him hard. "You mean firemen," I said. I'd heard of the correlation, but it was still disturbing.

George nodded. "If you sort arsonists by occupation you find little or no deviation from an average sampling, except in one area. A slightly higher percentage of firemen are arsonists than one finds in the general population." He added, "Of course, this is a very small factor."

I finished my beer and George immediately stood up to get me another. "No thanks," I said. "I've still got another gentleman to talk to and the drive home after that. You've been very helpful," I said, shaking his hand. I added that he should send his bill to Douglas County, Nevada, then thanked him a second time and left.

EIGHTEEN

Because parking is such a problem in the City, I left the Jeep where it was, hiked down Russian Hill to Columbus, then walked to North Beach. I reached Telegraph Hill just as five o'clock drew near.

Arthur Jones Middleton the Sixth, the man Terry Drier called a wacko environmentalist, lived in an apartment building that would have been very modern back in the 50's and still looked contemporary today. According to the names engraved in shiny brass and mounted on the marble wall in the big entrance foyer, Middleton had the top floor.

There was an Art Deco brass security gate in front of a large front door made of hundreds of small beveled glass panels in a design that looked like a Picasso nude. Two video cameras watched me from above. I pushed the button opposite Middleton's name.

"Good afternoon, sir," a high voice said in what sounded like a Middle Eastern accent. "May I help you?"

"Owen McKenna here to see Mr. Middleton. I have an appointment."

"One minute, please."

I waited to be buzzed in. Instead I saw a bright sparkle of movement through the beveled glass door. It opened and a small, sturdy woman who matched the accent reached through and opened the brass security gate. "Mr. Middleton will see you now," she said.

She escorted me into a gold-plated elevator and we rode whisper-quiet to the top of the building. When the door opened and we walked into the entry it was like taking a time machine back a couple of centuries. The floor was polished, rose-colored marble. Golden wall sconces had a swirling motif that mimicked the gold stitching in the tapestries on the walls. Next to a tiny table with gold legs sat one of those chairs that Louis the Sixteenth used in his entrance room at his chateau. The chair had bowed legs and a back so straight that one wouldn't actually sit in it except when posing for a formal portrait. Above the chair hung a portrait, although not the kind where the subject sat in a chair. An oil about ten feet high, it was of a man wearing military regalia riding a white steed who was rearing up and pawing at the air. I didn't know the artist, but the detail and craftsmanship were impressive. The frame, an ornate gold molding eight inches wide, added to the drama.

"Sir," the woman said.

"Oh, sorry, just admiring the painting." I followed her through an arched opening into a living room which, in both art and decor, was the opposite of the elegant, traditional entry. The room was starkly modern with a lowered ceiling from which dozens of recessed, high-tech lights shined ovals on the floor. Floor-to-ceiling windows showed all of downtown. The Transamerica pyramid pierced the sky and dominated the skyline.

"Sir," the soft-spoken woman said. "Mr. Middleton will be with you in a moment. Please wait here." She left.

I stood still for a moment, wondering if my shoes were clean enough to proceed into the room which was carpeted with a thick, white nap softer than my bed. On the field of white sat a black Steinway. White leather couches were arranged at angles around a low, oblong, black marble table. The only color came from the art.

A large Keith Haring painting of red and blue stick figures hung on a white wall at one end of the room. Although made of simple lines, the figures were so energetic they almost leaped off the canvas. Near the piano was one of David Hockney's blue swimming pools, cool enough that it made me thirsty. Above the couches were a pair of ethereal flower photos by Robert Mapplethorpe. They were spectacular in their simple beauty and grace.

"You admire fine art?" The voice from behind me was deep and resonant.

I turned to see a man who was nearly my height, but rotund. He must have out-weighed me by fifty pounds. His gray wool pants were the same color as his close-cropped hair and beard. A white silk shirt draped his torso in such a way as to minimize a belly that suggested decades of the finest restaurants. His watch was expensive, though not ostentatious. On his feet were well-worn leather slippers. The overall impression was of a man who belonged to the aristocracy by birth.

"Yes, I do enjoy art," I said. I pointed to the flower photos in front of me. "Mapplethorpe's talent for finding beauty was so obvious, it makes you wonder why he ever did the brutal stuff."

"Well, Picasso did Guernica," he said, his voice booming like Paul Robeson's. "And Munch did The Scream. Or look at all those Francis Bacons. My word, I have nightmares just to think of them. You wonder about brutal stuff, think again. That is half of what art is all about."

"I suppose," I said, thinking of Sister Wendy and the Piss Christ and wondering if the arsonist thought of himself as a kind of performance artist.

Middleton went on, "And my dear friend Antonio Scarpetti, you know, sings for The Met? He sat once for Lucian Freud. The way the painting came out, Antonio looked like a torture victim from the Inquisition!" Middleton lifted his hand and sucked on a cigarette I hadn't noticed earlier. An ash fell to the white carpet. Middleton ignored it, making me wonder how the carpet stayed so white.

"I'm Owen McKenna. Pleased to meet you."

Middleton gave me a firm handshake. "You said something on the phone to my secretary about an investigation."

"I'm a private detective," I said. "I'm looking into the arson fires in Tahoe."

"How exciting." Middleton looked disappointed. "Tell me, Owen, before we get all serious, would you like to see more of my art?"

"Love to," I said.

"You're not squeamish, are you?"

"Well, Hockney's swimming pool made me a little seasick, but I'm over the worst of it."

Middleton took another draw from his cigarette and spoke, smoke issuing out with his words. "You are a fun one! Come, we'll go in the Japan room first." He led me through a wide sliding door made out of teak with rice paper panels. We entered a long narrow room lit by soft red silk lanterns. I now understood the difference in décor between the living room and the entry. Each room was done in a different style. "Today I was in a Japan mood," Middleton said, "so I had my breakfast in here." He gestured toward the walls with a big sweep of his cigarette. An arc of smoke hung improbably in the air like I'd seen once in a photo portrait of Salvador Dali. I looked down the room and saw dozens of etchings hung on what looked to be paper walls.

Middleton continued, "I have one of the most significant collections of Japanese queer art in all of America. What do you think?"

I wandered around and paused on several pictures. The prints were done in the standard style of erotic Asian art with fierce warriors and kings displaying impressive sexual acrobatics. But instead of young maidens, their partners were other men. Some of the prints showed group orgies engaged in activities far more inventive than any I had ever contemplated with women. Maybe straight guys just don't have that creative gene.

"Well?" Middleton asked.

"Very impressive," I said. "Do you collect any American landscapes?"

"Is that your favorite art? Then let me show you my Wild West room," he said, his big voice filling the room. He led me through another door.

My thoughts paused for a moment on the Wild West concept, but it turned out that the room was a straight-forward collection of cowboy paraphernalia. Riding tack hung on the walls next to a Thomas Moran. On a pedestal was a Remington bronze of a cowboy lassoing a bull. I turned and saw that Middleton had a Bierstadt. It was less majestic than most, showing a placid river running through a gentle valley, Napa maybe.

Middleton saw the painting I was looking at. "It's a small one, but nice, don't you think?" he said. He sat down on a big leather chair.

"I like it a lot," I said. "Tell me, what do you think Bierstadt was saying with these landscapes?"

"I think he wanted to paint the west as a holy place, someplace sacred that should be worshiped and otherwise left alone."

"Which is what the League To Save Lake Tahoe is all about, isn't it? Leave the lake alone?"

Middleton looked down. "You would have to bring up that subject, wouldn't you? Yes, now that you've mentioned it, that is sort of what we're about." He took a drag on his cigarette. "The Washoe Indians did that," he continued. "Worship the lake, fish and hunt, but do nothing else. They lived that way for centuries, and the lake was pure for centuries. Then Fremont came through and claimed to discover the lake. What a joke. Those macho white guys have been trying to pave it over ever since."

"You're not fond of development."

Art Middleton looked at me hard. "If I were in charge, I'd ban all motorboats on the lake and all cars in the basin. No motors at all. And the golf courses and private lawns! All that fertilizer goes right into the water! And they wonder why the water is turning green with algae. Fertilizer should be outlawed."

"That's a pretty severe position, isn't it?" I said.

Middleton made a harumph sound.

"Do you get up to Tahoe often?" I asked.

"Now and then. I have a place up there on the north shore, been in the family for generations."

"Drive a car?"

"Oh, of course. I have several. Don't be petty. But I don't fertilize. And my little truck and cars are gas efficient, not like those monster sport utility gas hogs everyone drives these days. I do have a conscience and I act on it."

"Tell me, Mr. Middleton..."

"Art."

"Art. Do you ever remember meeting a man named Jake Pooler?"

Arthur Middleton stood up, walked over to a window and stared out at the Bay. "He's the one who burned. I have the Tahoe paper mailed here. I'm not sorry, if that's what you're wondering. But unfortunately, I didn't have the pleasure of doing away with him myself."

"Why the animosity?"

Art paused. "Jake was a developer. I'm against development. We clashed at some meetings."

"Clashing at a meeting doesn't usually make you wish someone were dead."

Middleton turned from the window and gave me a steady gaze. "Owen, even though you are a straight man, you must have an idea about how many rednecks live in Tahoe. God, I swear if you acted queer up there your life expectancy wouldn't be long enough to chair an AIDS Awareness meeting. Anyway, the whole of the Tahoe Regional Planning Agency was deciding a development issue. I had just finished making a statement on behalf of the League To Save Lake Tahoe. Then Pooler had his turn at the lectern." Middleton stopped talking, his face turning red at the memory.

"What did he say, Art?"

It took a moment for him to get his composure. "Jake Pooler yelled out in that twangy voice of his, 'We don't need a bunch of rich, fat homosexuals coming up from the big city to tell us how to run our lives, do we?'" Middleton shut his eyes. When he opened them it was if there were flames way back in there behind the tears. "And then," Middleton continued, "can you guess what happened? People clapped and laughed. The upstanding citizens of Tahoe laughed at me and clapped at that man's homophobic remarks."

"Not all of them, surely," I said.

"Enough of them."

"Let me change the subject, Art. Do you know a woman named Joanie Dove?"

"No. Who's she?"

"We had a second fire yesterday. She died of smoke inhalation in her home."

"Oh, that's terrible! Did she suffer much? I hope not!" Middleton's reaction to the second death was the reverse of his response to Jake Pooler's death.

"Art, what do you know about the fire danger in Tahoe's forests?"

Arthur Middleton took several deep breaths. He closed his eyes for a moment, calming himself. "Just that the forests have been ruined by old, old management policies that are still largely in place."

"You mean the Forest Service?"

"I mean everybody. Forest Service, Tahoe Regional Planning Agency, local fire departments. They all do the same thing which is putting out fires. It's wrong, unnatural and it has destroyed the ecology of the forest."

"You would prefer that the forest burns up."

"That's the way it has been through all the ages until white man got here. And the lake was pure and the forest healthy until people interfered." Middleton was a bit more relaxed now that we were no longer talking about Jake Pooler. "Lightning struck and caused frequent fires in the basin. Those fires were like nature's cleaning service, clearing out the dead wood and excessive brush. They also kept control of the most fire-susceptible species like the firs.

"Now," he continued, "we have a fir-heavy forest, with the fire-resistant pines being forced out of their natural habitat. Because we put out all the fires, we have an unnatural number of trees, all competing for the scarce rains of summer.

"The firs especially end up stressed and vulnerable to the bark beetles. The bugs bore extensive galleries through the critical layers under the bark. That kills the tree which adds even more unburned fuel to the forest."

Art turned and looked out at the Bay. He continued speaking with his back to me. "Not only do regular forest fires clean out the fuel before it builds up to ridiculous levels, but fire kills the bark beetles. Putting out the fires allows an explosion of beetle populations which kill more trees and so on in a vicious cycle."

Art turned and looked at me with a new intensity. "The forest is now so heavy with fuel that a big fire will be catastrophic, burning right down through the soil and destroying the root growth that prevents erosion. Afterward, the first heavy rains will cause a massive runoff of ash into the lake. Lake Tahoe is now, for the first time in history, in a terribly precarious situation. And what is everybody doing? Still putting out fires."

"I don't know about that, Art. They are constantly doing controlled burns."

"Those pissy little burns are nothing in the big picture," he said, flipping his hand such that his cigarette flicked more ash onto the floor. "Think about where you've seen them. They burn in the areas that most threaten housing developments or the tourist areas."

"You don't think they should do that?"

"Of course they should. But they should expand the program a hundred times. A thousand times. And they should stop putting out lightning-caused fires."

"What else?" I asked.

"How many days can you stay?" He smiled at me. "Okay, Owen, I'll give you a few more thoughts. Because of the rules about soil compaction, local firewood cutters aren't allowed to drive into the woods in their pickups. So the worst areas are getting cleared much too slowly. Much of the lumbering is being done by helicopter, which is really slow and much more expensive. Meanwhile, the people who are getting firewood have to park on the road and walk in, a major inhibiting factor." Arthur Middleton stubbed out his cigarette butt, pulled out a gold lighter and lit another cigarette.

"Here is where I break from most of my environmentalist colleagues," Art continued. "Imagine this paradox. We don't want people to drive their pickups into the forest because the soil compaction is very bad for the flora, a point no one disputes. Further, the permit process for cutting deadwood is designed to control the use of public lands and prevent them from being abused. Yet both situations act as constraints on what we really need which is the fastest possible removal of excess deadwood. So these efforts to protect the forest actually contribute to the likelihood that Tahoe will have a catastrophic blowup which will destroy the very soil that the environmentalists are trying to protect."

"By blowup you mean a very big fire."

Arthur Middleton pointed his cigarette at me and sighted down it as if it were a rifle. "I mean a fire that could destroy a major portion of the Tahoe Basin in just a few hours. A fire that will be so big it will create its own flaming thunderheads that will consume any aircraft that try to drop retardant. A fire that will take out the fire trucks and the men fighting it. A fire that will jump the firebreaks, cross the highways, leave the forest and take down the towns." His eyes narrowed.

"Art," I said, "you make it sound exciting. Like you want this fire."

"Maybe part of me does," he said in a low voice. "The people of Lake Tahoe burned me. Still do. They scoff at what I've said about letting the lightning-caused fires burn." He turned around and looked at me. "They won't laugh anymore when I've been proved right."

"About what?"

"About the risk of a blowup. About the fire risk that has been created by the very policies designed to control fires, policies that have been in place for decades." Arthur Middleton paused, his intense gaze holding my eyes. "When Tahoe burns - and it will - some of those bastards will finally admit that I am right."

NINETEEN

I thanked Arthur Middleton the Sixth for talking candidly with me, then left. It was obvious why Terry Drier had thought that Middleton's perspective was extreme. By Middleton's own admission it was clear that he wanted Tahoe to burn, at least to some degree. And he was almost glad for Jake Pooler's death. But I couldn't believe he was the arsonist. Or Joanie Dove's killer. Maybe it was just hard to see a blue-blooded aristocrat pouring gas onto the ground and striking a match. Even so, the man had motive with Jake and, probably, opportunity with both victims.

It was late afternoon and I figured the rush-hour traffic would be stop-and-go over the Bay Bridge, so I went west on Lombard and then north over the Golden Gate. The traffic was slow, but I imagined going through Marin County to be the better route. As I cruised above Sausalito I thought that California had far more than its rightful share of beautiful scenery.

I went north around the Bay, past the entrance to Napa Valley, and caught up with Interstate 80 where it turns east into California's Central Valley.

In Sacramento the freeway splits in two with Interstate 80 heading toward Truckee and Tahoe's north shore while Highway 50 heads toward the south shore. I stayed on 50 and made the winding climb up 7,400 feet to Echo Summit. The sun had set long before and, when I came over the top of the pass, the lights of the Tahoe Basin spread out before me in a spectacular vista. Driving down the cliff edge into South Lake Tahoe was a bit like floating in on a small plane.

In a few minutes I was through town and turned up Kingsbury Grade to my office. Eager to get home to see Street, I hurried up to the second floor two steps at a time. Once inside, I picked the mail up off the floor and checked the answering machine. There was one message. I played it as I went through the mail. After a few words, I dropped the mail, hit the rewind button and started it over.

The voice was tinny and buzzed as if the person were speaking through a kazoo. The voice was in an upper register, although the buzzing made it impossible to tell if it was a woman or a man speaking in falsetto.

"You found the burned dog, but you must be either too stupid or too stubborn to understand the meaning or how serious we are. This is your last warning. Leave the fire investigation to the official agencies."

I played the message a couple more times, writing it out on a pad while I listened for some speech quality that might help me identify the caller. I could imagine the voice to be Arthur Middleton in falsetto. But was that only because I couldn't imagine Terry Drier or some other man in falsetto? I also thought the S sounds were somewhat furry. The speech impediment that George the psychologist suggested? Winton, the young man with the lisp who had worked for Jake Pooler? But after several listens, I realized the recording was too well disguised for any identification to be made from the vocal characteristics. Which still left syntax and grammar. It seemed the caller was articulate, although the first sentence was an awkward construction. Not much to go on. And what of the plural 'we?' Was I dealing with a group or was this an attempt to mislead?

The most peculiar aspect of the message was the part about leaving the investigation to official agencies. Did the caller worry that I was more likely to find him or her? It didn't seem likely. Another possibility – though even less likely - was that the caller might not be the firestarter at all, but rather someone in one of the so-called official agencies who wanted to have the glory of finding the arsonist himself.

I took the tape out of the answering machine, thinking I should turn it in to someone. I trusted Diamond completely. As well as Captain Mallory on the South Lake Tahoe PD. But would it be safe to give either of them the tape? There were many others in the Sheriff's Department or the Police Department or the Fire Departments who would then have access to it. Not sure, I slipped the tape in my pocket and left.

Driving away, I noticed headlights turn on from up the street and come up behind me. I couldn't see what kind of vehicle, but from their height and position I guessed it to be a sport utility vehicle. The headlights stayed with me as I drove up the east shore toward my cabin. The phone message had left me a little paranoid, but if the person behind me was the firestarter, I didn't want to lead him up to Street's condo where she and Spot waited. I made a turn off the highway, trying to get a glimpse in my rear-view mirror as the vehicle went under the streetlight. It was an old pickup, a mid-seventies Chevy from what I could see. The pickup followed me. I made two more turns and then sped back onto the highway, flooring the Jeep.

I've got the biggest engine package that Jeep sells which makes my vehicle faster than most anything on the road. Yet the pickup stayed with me. The pickup probably had the 350 V8 that Chevy was using in the seventies. Even so, my guess was that there was a lot of custom work under the hood of the pickup. Realizing that I wasn't going to speed away to an easy escape, I slowed and dialed Street.

"Hi, sweetheart. I just left the office to come home, but it looks like I've got someone on my tail and I don't want them following me to your place. So I might be a bit."

"Owen, what are you going to do? Do you think this is someone dangerous? Can you drive to the police station?"

"I would if I merely wanted to scare this guy off. But I'd rather learn who he is and what he wants." As I said it, the pickup came up on my rear, tailgating me close enough that his headlights made a mockery of my tinted glass. I stayed at an even forty-five, not wanting too much speed in case he did something crazy like ram me.

"Owen, this sounds very scary. Please be careful."

"I will. This guy might be the firestarter. I've got to find out."

Street didn't speak at first. "Could you at least get Diamond on your phone and arrange to meet him where the guy tailing you won't expect?"

"Good idea. I'll call you back as soon as I find out what's going on."

"Be careful," Street said. "I love you."

"You too," I said, uncomfortable with good-byes that sounded final.

I dialed Diamond and left a message on his pager. Not yet sure of the best tactic, I continued heading up the east shore. I next dialed Diamond's voice mail and told him I had a general plan to lead my pursuer into the Spooner Lake campground where I thought I could trap him. I hung up, hoping Diamond would call back before I got that far.

There were other cars on the dark four-lane highway. I stayed in the right lane and the pickup stayed right behind me while other cars zoomed around us on the left. We crawled away from Lake Tahoe, up the big incline toward Spooner Summit like two slow night bugs on a mission that the rest of the universe knew nothing about.

I got in the left lane and turned off toward Spooner Lake, a vague plan taking shape. If the territory was more familiar to me than to my pursuer, I would have an advantage. When I approached the Spooner Lake campground, I took the entrance turnoff at high speed and hit the gas.

The Jeep fishtailed and shot though the campground, the pickup following closely. I made some sudden tight turns and the pickup missed one of them, slamming into a bear-proof garbage dumpster. In my side mirror I saw the pickup back up, turn and come after me again. I had gained some precious yards and intended to stretch them out.

I turned onto one of the hiking trails that led out of the campground toward Spooner Lake. If my memory was correct, there was a fence with a gate that kept vehicles from leaving the campground. I went up a rise, then down, scanning to the sides to see the lay of the land. There was an open meadow to the right. Just before the gate I braked nearly to a stop, then turned off my lights. Without touching my brakes again, I turned off to the right and circled around through the darkness.

The pickup came over the rise and down the trail fast. He flashed by me and then hit his brakes at the last moment when he saw the gate. There wasn't enough distance and he hit the gate just as he came to a stop. I pulled out directly behind him, turned on my high beams and got out of the Jeep.

The pickup shifted into reverse, and the engine revved. The driver obviously intended to ram my Jeep. But his bumper had gotten hooked on the metal gate and his wheels spun fast, throwing a spray of gravel and dirt as they dug down into the ground.

The driver left his lights on and his engine running and got out into the wash of my headlights. I stood off in the dark.

He was a redneck cliché. A grubby, sleeveless undershirt was insufficient to cover his massive belly. Dirty jeans were held up by suspenders that arced over the fat and up toward tattooed shoulders. On his feet were scuffed, black combat boots. His eyes were bloodshot and seemed to glow pink in my headlights. He was a big man and there was a lot to look at. But my eyes settled on the tire iron in his right hand.

"Time to teach you a lesson, stretch," he drawled, staring off into the dark where he presumed I was standing.

TWENTY

The obese man with the tire iron chuckled as he advanced roughly toward me. My headlights lit him up like a stage actor, while I was invisible in the dark.

"What is this about?" I asked.

"This is about no more checking out the fires."

"Not while I've got this nine millimeter on you," I lied. Off on the highway behind me came the welcome sound of a vehicle slowing and then turning into the campground. Diamond must have gotten my message. "You don't move until I give you permission to move," I said.

The redneck ignored me and started to move away from his pickup, out of the Jeep's headlights. As his eyes searched the darkness for me, his grip on the tire iron seemed to tighten. He telegraphed a feral quality that frightened me. The most dangerous people are those who have nothing to lose. And the fat slob in front of me looked like a poster boy for those without any cares in the world.

He started to move again, watching and listening as Diamond's Explorer wheeled up behind me, headlights flooding me from behind.

Only, it wasn't Diamond. It was another old pickup.

The door opened and I heard the sickening sound of a pump-action shotgun.

"Now look here, Bobby," a nasally voice behind me said. "What if I hadn't gotten your call? I don't know if it'd be smart for you to go up against Mr. McKenna yourself. He coulda got the drop on you."

I slowly turned to look at the man behind me.

"Easy, boy" the man said, his voice almost falsetto.

The fat man started toward me, raising the tire iron. "He says he got a nine on him. I don't see no piece."

"Me neither," the man behind me said.

"Good. Now I can finish what I started," the fat man said.

"Not a good idea," I said.

"Why not?"

"Because, if I hurt you, your friend might want to shoot his cannon and in the dark he could hit you instead of me."

"Not likely," the nasal-voiced man behind me said.

"Which one of you is the firestarter?" I said, stalling for time while I tried to think of a strategy.

"Neither," the fat man said. He advanced on me, the tire iron held out at his side.

"Instead of trying to take my head off with the tire iron, why don't you drop it and we'll fight the old fashioned way."

"I don't think so," he said in a sing-song voice. He grinned, the headlights illuminating a sporadic assortment of brown teeth.

I considered sprinting off into the dark, but I didn't know how determined the man behind me was. A shotgun didn't need to be aimed accurately and it could still blow your head off. "Your friend can put down the cannon and join in. Two against one. Kicking my butt with your bare hands would be a lot more satisfying than cleaving my brain with the iron."

Judging by his giggle, the man thought that was a really good joke.

"Don't do it, Bobby," the nasal voice called out from the dark behind me. "Use the iron. Let's get this over."

Bobby came closer, the tire iron in the air.

"Last chance," I said.

He grinned once more, then his face got so serious and intense that it frightened me.

I had to get the tire iron out of his hand and I thought the best way would be to draw him out with a fake punch.

I stepped toward him and made like I was trying to get in a serious right jab. He swung hard with the iron. He would have easily broken my arm if I hadn't pulled away at the last moment.

The iron swished through the air next to my head.

I pretended to wind up a left hook, hoping to get him to step into me so I could grab him.

He was too quick with the iron and I misjudged my distance. The metal cut through the air like a scythe, grazed my side and made a ringing blow on the upper corner of my hip bone. The pain was excruciating. I grit my teeth and took the fast-moving wrist.

I grabbed onto the big, pudgy arm with both of my hands. He was already moving forward with the swing of the iron. I added a good pull to his momentum, bent down and caught his face with the upper crest of my forehead.

As his nose and few remaining teeth were lost to my head-butt, my focus had already shifted to the man with the shotgun behind me. Still holding the redneck's arm, I spun around behind him and brought the tire iron up tight against his throat. But he had already sunk into unconsciousness and sagged down, a massive weight for me to hold up. A biting, acrid body odor rose up and made me want to gag and drop him. But I continued to hold him up, as his body was my protection against the shotgun in front of me.

"Your turn," I said to the man with the shotgun, a man whose face I still hadn't seen. I tried to sound casual, tried not to show my heavy breathing.

"Don't move," he suddenly said. His voice was a squeak.

I heard him reach for the door of his pickup. Not wanting him to get away, I summoned strength I didn't know I had and virtually threw the limp man toward him. He hit the vehicle door and the other man simultaneously. The door slammed shut and the man with the shotgun fell back. I launched myself onto him, grabbing the gun.

As my fingers gripped the barrel, he fired the gun. The shock was as if the explosion went directly through my hands without the protection of the metal barrel. I was momentarily stunned. I regained my senses and wrested it from his hands. I threw the weapon into the darkness, picked the man up by his jacket and belt and slammed him up against his pickup. He didn't move as I patted him down.

When I was certain that he had no more weapons on him, I carried him into the headlights of his pickup for a good look at his face. He didn't fight back.

His complexion was gaunt, with dark bags under small eyes and a three-day growth of beard. I guessed him to be younger than me, in his mid-thirties, about the age of his obese companion. Although six feet tall, his frame was light enough that I could have thrown him through his windshield, such was my anger.

"What's your name?" I asked, my voice a ragged whisper.

"I ain't telling you nothing," he said.

"Yes, you are." Blood was running from where the fat redneck had lost his teeth on my head. It dripped into my left eye, angering me further. I lifted him by his belt and walked around the pickup, stepping on the prostrate body in the dirt so that I could ascertain that he was, indeed, unconscious.

I dragged the skinny man through the dark, stopping to pick up the tire iron and throw it into the darkness.

The fence around the campground was made of large cedar posts strung with wire. With my right hand, I grasped the hair of the man I was dragging. With my left, I grabbed the back of his neck. I indelicately placed his open mouth onto the top of a cedar fence post, his upper incisors against the rough wood. Leaning hard on the top of his head so that maybe two hundred pounds of me was pressing his upper teeth down into the end grain, I spoke slowly and softly.

"While you're playing beaver on the fence post, I'm going to ask you a question. If you answer to my satisfaction, I'll show my appreciation by not breaking off all your upper teeth at once. Do you understand? You can just grunt if you do."

He made a weak noise.

"Okay, here's the question. What is your name?" With a tight grip on his hair, I lifted his head three inches up off the fence post and held it there as if to smash it back down.

"Jeremy Dodger," he said, his voice tiny.

"And your companion?"

"Bobby Mackenzie."

"Why did he want to put the tire iron through my head?"

"We were paid to do it by Joe."

"Who is Joe?" I asked.

"The manager at the High River Saloon in Truckee."

"He do this often?" I asked. "Give you jobs like this?"

"Once or twice."

"How do I know you're telling the truth?"

"He paid us five hundred."

"Cash?"

"Yeah," he said. Drool was hanging from his open mouth.

"That proves nothing," I said. "Maybe he did, maybe he didn't."

Jeremy Dodger thought a moment. "He wrote down your address on a bar napkin. I gave it to Bobby so he could watch your office. I watched your cabin. When Bobby saw you first, he called me on Joe's cell phone so I could drive to wherever he followed you."

"Where is the napkin and the phone?"

"I don't know," he said. "Maybe in Bobby's pocket. Or his truck."

"Let's go have a look," I said. I half-walked, half-dragged Jeremy over to where Bobby still lay. I planted him face down in the dirt next to the fat man and kneeled on his back while I went through Bobby's pockets, ignoring Jeremy's cries of pain. Something cracked under my knee. One of his ribs maybe. I found nothing. We repeated the maneuver at Bobby's pickup only with me standing on his back while I looked in the truck. Jeremy groaned even louder.

The dome light was broken, so the only light was what came in from my headlights and Jeremy's headlights. But it was enough.

The phone was on the seat. I slid it into my pocket. A napkin was paper-clipped to the visor. I held it up so my headlights shined on it.

The logo said High River Saloon, and my office address was written in pencil. It would be easy enough to check the handwriting and see if it belonged to Joe. Easier still to check the number to which Joe's phone answered. I put the napkin in my pocket, bent down and lifted Jeremy up just as another set of headlights pulled up.

Diamond got out. He looked around at the vehicles, then settled his gaze on Jeremy and me. "It looks like I got here too late," he said. "Sorry."

"No problem," I said. "If you look on the other side of that truck you'll find a well-marbled side of beef named Bobby. Bobby is the brawn of this duo. Which suggests that Jeremy, here, is the brains and the beauty. Isn't that right, Jeremy?" When he didn't respond, I shook him.

"Uh, sure."

"Brains and beauty, huh?" Diamond said. "Can't wait to see the brawn." He walked around to the dark side of the pickup and poked at the prostrate body with the toe of his boot. He turned back toward me. "I guess I missed the whole play," he said.

"As drama goes, it was pretty weak."

"Maybe. But the denouement looks to have been exciting."

"Denouement," I said, repeating his 'day-new-mah' pronunciation which, knowing Diamond, was probably accurate. "I thought you were still focusing on English for your second language."

"Can't hurt to learn some others. It's French for outcome. Besides, I got that word on a cop training tape at work. Surviving Street Fights. The announcer referred to taking away the suspect's weapon as the key to a positive denouement."

I gave Jeremy a little shake. "What do you think, Jeremy? Have we achieved a positive denouement?"

"I dunno," he said.

"Let's put him in the back," Diamond said.

I held Jeremy's wrists behind his back while Diamond cuffed him. Diamond walked over and opened the back door of the Douglas County Explorer. I pushed Jeremy in headfirst and shut the door.

Diamond got in Jeremy's pickup and jockeyed it so that the headlights shown on Bobby. Then the two of us rolled him over.

"Look at that," Diamond said. "This beef is missing some teeth."

Together, Diamond and I cuffed Bobby. I let Diamond do the honors of double checking his body for weapons. Then we lifted him up and slid him into the back of the Explorer, his head in Jeremy's lap.

"Aw, man, he's getting my pants all bloody! God, his teeth are coming out!"

"Your five hundred bucks will buy him a new one," I said.

After we shut the door, I told Diamond what had happened.

"You're thinking of paying a visit to Mr. Joe at the High River Saloon?" he asked.

"Out of your jurisdiction, so I guess I'll have to."

Diamond shrugged. "Let me know what you find out," he said as he walked over to each of the two pickups, reached in, turned them off and pocketed the keys.

I followed him out of the campground, thinking about Joe in Truckee.

Jeremy said Joe had given them five hundred dollars to dissuade me from my investigation. Seemed like a lot of money to waste. Be good to find out more, but it would have to wait. Street was still with Spot. As I thought of her, I pictured the faceless Joe having hired someone else to watch my cabin. Anybody could have seen Street go pick up Spot, then followed her back down to her condo.

I floored the accelerator and shot up the highway. I pulled up to Street's condo a few minutes later, jumped out and ran to the door, key in hand.

Street was sitting and reading in front of the fireplace, the fire sparking and crackling. Spot was next to her, his head draped over her knee. His eyes were half shut indicating heat intoxication.

Street looked up and her eyes immediately went to my bloody forehead. She jumped up. "Owen! What happened? Are you all right?"

I wiped at the dried blood with my forearm and gave her a weak smile. "Just a scratch received in the course of achieving a positive denouement," I said.

TWENTY-ONE

The next morning, I sat in my big chair and drank my coffee while I looked at the Bierstadt painting. It was so overdone, the mountains, the waterfalls and the God-like light in the clouds around the peaks. Yet I was drawn to it as one is drawn to all excess of beauty. It was as if Bierstadt said of his painting, 'If a little beauty is good, more must be better.' He made the subject of the painting less a mountain landscape and more an essay on beauty. It seemed that beauty was sacred to Bierstadt, and the excess of it in his painting was like the excesses of gothic cathedrals. No depiction of sacredness can be too grand for the worshipful parishioners. I looked up from the book and swept my eyes across the lake. The beauty before me was not as loud as the beauty in the painting, but it was just as sweet. To burn it up was like burning my church. And when people were in the church as the flames engulfed it, the crime was beyond outrage.

I realized I'd been breathing fast, and the tension through my body was palpable. Maybe it was time to take it out on someone.

An hour later, I parked directly in front of the High River Saloon in Truckee. The place was crammed between a Laundromat and a beauty salon in a low-slung, dark, clapboard building. Outside were parked two pickups and two Harleys.

Spot and I walked up to the front door of the bar like we did it every morning. I pushed in through actual swinging half-doors like those on an old-west saloon in the movies.

The inside was dark and stunk of wet wood and malted hops gone bad. I walked across an uneven wooden floor, past a pool table with a trio of fat biker types playing eightball.

A broad man a good two or three inches over six feet was behind the bar, rinsing glasses. He had on a white, short-sleeved shirt. The sleeves were rolled up high, exposing large biceps. Over the shirt was a gray banker's vest, open at the front. The effect was a little Victorian elegance over casual Film Noir. The pockmarks on his face were obvious from a distance. He telegraphed tension, and it bunched the powerful muscles of his neck and shoulders.

"Hi, Joe," I said as I walked by.

He instantly looked up, no doubt wondering who I was and how I knew his name.

"Lose your phone?" I said. I slid the phone onto the bar and walked past him down the long stretch of mahogany.

"Hey, man," the bartender said, his eyes stealing a furtive look at Spot. He picked up the phone. "Where'd you get this? Somebody stole it right off of this bar."

I ignored the man and took Spot to the opening at the end of the bar where the hinged section lifts up so that bartenders can come and go. I lifted the hinged piece up and over, then touched Spot on the shoulder and pointed to the opening.

"Sit-stay," I said. Spot sat. He wasn't the smartest dog in the world, but he made up for it by being practically the biggest. And he'd learned well a few of the tricks I'd taught him. I pointed to the bartender. "Watch him."

Without budging from his haunches, Spot turned and focused on Joe.

It is an impressive sight when a 170 pound dog with pointy ears and very large teeth turns his attention on a single person without letting anything, man or beast, distract him. His normally lugubrious eyes become laser weapons and his panting tongue flicks little drops of saliva toward the would-be prey just as if he were entering a pre-prandial Pavlovian response.

The result is that the person being watched usually melts. I've seen big guys with loaded guns go limp under Spot's intense gaze.

I was glad for the exercise because it was a good way to change Spot's mood.

I left Spot and walked back up the bar to where Joe stood. Behind me, the pool players stopped poking at the balls and watched my dog, their pool cues in suspended animation.

"What the fuck do you think you're doing?" Joe said.

I was surprised. If my dog flustered him, he didn't show it.

I pulled out the napkin that had my office address on it. "Did you write this?" I asked.

"Fuck you," the bartender said.

I turned toward Spot, almost winking, as we were about to show off his most impressive trick. "He's trying to sound tough, Spot. Maybe you should show him we mean business."

At this, Spot stood, lifted his lips in a snarl and gave forth one of the deepest, most impressive growls in the history of the earth. Spot kept up his chest-shaking volume as he walked up the aisle behind the bar toward Joe.

Spot bends his legs a little when he does this, so it appears he is stalking his prey. But the intensity is so out of proportion to merely collecting dinner, that it seems instead as if he is about to exact a terrible revenge.

Joe betrayed the tiniest of quivers. He glanced at the bar, possibly wondering if he could vault it.

I was ready to leap over the bar myself just in case Joe pulled out a weapon.

Spot was now only ten feet away from Joe. The amplitude of his growl ratcheted up another notch, and his lips pulled back further revealing teeth that would give pause to a grizzly.

"Okay!" Joe said. A distinct tremble ran through his body. "What do you want?!"

"Enough, Spot," I said.

My dog immediately stopped growling, looked at me and, for the first time since the Pussy Cat incident, vigorously wagged his tail.

"Damn it, Spot," I said. "When you wag, it spoils the whole effect."

Spot wagged some more. His tail knocked a large, plastic tonic bottle off a shelf. It hit the floor, bounced and rolled away.

"Sit," I said.

He sat once again. At least now, the wagging tail swept the floor and was somewhat subdued. I couldn't blame him, really. He knew his growl was majestic acting, the dog world's version of Laurence Olivier playing Iago.

Joe leaned on the counter below the bar. Tiny drops of sweat on his face glowed in the recessed light like little glass beads.

Again, I gestured at the napkin. "Did you write this?"

"Shit!" Joe said. "I knew they wouldn't..." he glanced at Spot and then stopped.

"Tell me about it," I said.

"Yes, I hired them," Joe said, his voice cracking. He leaned heavily on the counter. His breathing was labored. "I gave Jeremy Dodger five hundred and your address and said he was to convince you to drop the fire investigation."

"You thought he'd intimidate me alone?"

Joe hesitated. "I assumed he'd bring Bobby along for the ride."

"Why did you hire them?"

"I was paid to," he said.

It was the answer I expected. "By whom?"

"I don't know."

"You'll have to do better than that," I said, anger welling. I wanted to turn Spot loose on him.

"My instructions came over the phone. I don't know who paid me."

"Guess." I was getting very irritated.

"I still don't know."

I lifted up my knee and braced it against the underside of the bar. In a quick, fluid movement, I reached over the mahogany slab, grabbed the fabric of his shirt and vest and yanked him off his feet and over the bar. It is a dumb move, because if the person being yanked has any sense, he can box your ears, punch your throat or poke out your eyes. But I was angry and I sensed that jerking a 200 pound man off his feet would have an intimidating effect.

I was right.

Pulled into a sprawling position over the mahogany, Joe stammered, "I'm telling the truth! I got a message about it on my machine! A woman's voice. The money came through the slot in the door. A thousand bucks. Ten C-notes. Wrapped in a piece of newspaper. I gave five to Jeremy. Honest. I'll give you the rest if you want!"

It felt good to see him frantic with fear. But the information about the high voice was unnerving. "Tell me about the person who called."

"I don't know how to describe her. Her voice was distorted. Kind of tinny and buzzing."

"Like the sound of a kazoo?"

"Yeah! A kazoo! I knew it sounded like something I'd heard before."

I let go of his shirt and vest and pushed him back over the bar. "What did she say?"

"Just that she was going to put an envelope through my door slot with a thousand bucks in it. I was to hire someone to persuade you to stop looking into the fires. Then she told me your office address. It was her idea that I keep five hundred for my trouble." Joe was panting. He paused and took a couple of deep breaths. "If I didn't do it, she was going to shoot my balls off. So I figured, no skin off my back if I do it, so why not? It didn't occur to me that you would... you know, figure out who had sent Jeremy. What happened? Your dog get them?"

I ignored the question. "Could the voice have been a man speaking falsetto?"

He thought a moment. "I don't think so. It was pretty high."

"Why did this person pick you?"

"I don't know. I guess it's common knowledge that some pretty rough types hang out here."

I glanced at the pool players still taking cover behind the pool table. When I turned back I saw the beer taps. "I'll take a Sierra Nevada Pale Ale."

"Yeah, sure." He wiped his hands off on his pants, got a glass and filled it. His hand shook as he set the beer on the bar. "It's on me."

"No, I insist," I said and got out three ones and set them on the counter. I sucked down half of the dark amber brew, then licked the head off my upper lip. "I'll take the five hundred, too."

Joe swallowed. He glanced at my dog. "Uh, sure," he said, slowly. He bent over and reached for a drawer beneath the counter.

"Real slow," I said. He looked at me and saw my hand under my windbreaker as if I had a weapon.

He pulled out the money and set it on the bar.

I drank more of my ale. "You know a woman named Joanie Dove?"

He shook his head. "Who's that?"

"She died in the Tallac Properties fire."

"Never heard of her."

"What about Jake Pooler?"

"Sure. Everybody knew Jake." Joe leaned back against the counter behind him. His eyes flicked toward Spot. "Jake used to come in here after work for a bump or two. A shame about him getting fried in that fire."

"Did you like him?"

"He was a customer, what can I say?"

"You wouldn't want to light him on fire? Just for kicks? Or send Jeremy and Bobby to do it?"

"Look, man," Joe said. "I made a mistake sending them after you. I'm the first to admit it. But I wouldn't burn nobody. I'm a moral guy."

"What does that mean?" I asked. "You go to church?"

Joe hesitated. "Yeah, sure. I go to church."

"Can you think of anyone else who might have wanted to burn Jake Pooler?"

Joe threw his head back in laughter. Spot looked at me, concern on his face, then looked back at Joe.

"Look, man, there's probably a couple hundred people who wouldn't lose any sleep over that man's death. He was the biggest S.O.B. in this town."

"Give me some names," I said. "People who'd like to see him gone."

"Well," Joe said slowly. "A lot of men in this town have wives who spent some time with Jake."

"Why?" I asked. "Was he a real charmer with the ladies?"

"Must have been," Joe said. "Either that, or he was hung like a moose. And some of those husbands for sure would have wanted him turned into toast."

"Who can you think of?"

Joe started fidgeting, clearly uncomfortable. He glanced again at Spot who sat there watching us, blocking Joe's escape.

"Names," I said again.

"Well..." he said, "Jimmy MacIntyre has a real cute little wife, a young brunette, five-four, hundred five pounds." Joe moved his hands through the air, outlining a curvy woman. "I know for a fact that for several months last summer she was spending afternoons in the sack with Jake."

"How did an older guy like Jake get her into an affair?"

"You know, the usual. Young woman meets an older man who seems so worldly compared to her husband. The older guy uses all the right words. Next thing, the young woman is all limp in the knees, dreaming about romantic love. She never realizes that all the bastard wants is to get into her pants."

"You're saying Jake was a sexual predator?"

"Absolutely. Except, instead of using a knife for persuasion, he used sweet talk. It wasn't until Jimmy's wife discovered that Jake had two other ladies going at the same time that she went back to her husband. Yep, ol' Jimmy MacIntyre, he especially had a bad thing going about Jake."

"Does he live in the Truckee area?"

"Yeah. Out by Sugar Bowl ski area. He's a maintenance guy on the chairlifts. You'll find him in the book."

"Who else would have been happy to have Jake gone?"

"Like I said, just about half the men in Truckee. Hell, in all of Tahoe, for that matter. Let's see. There was Dan Turner and Wally Grossman and Big Moe Walsh over at the lumber yard. And, of course, there was that kid who worked in Jake's office, what's-his-name."

"Winton Berger?" I said.

"Yeah. Jake brought him in here a time or two. God, you should have seen the way that kid looked at Jake. From what I saw, lighting Jake on fire wouldn't satisfy that kid. More like cutting off the old man's balls would be Winton's style."

"Did Jake have a fling with Winton's girlfriend?"

"Of course," Joe said as if I weren't paying attention. "It was sad, when you stop and look at how hard she fell for Jake. She was built like a garden rake, skinny and plain as the workday is long. And her hair was this stringy stuff, it looked like old spaghetti. I'll never forget, it was only about three weeks after Winton first brought her around. One afternoon she meets Jake in here by herself. They have a few bumps and for the next month or so she is in here early, waiting for the old jerk, this sappy look of bliss on her face like big daddy is some kind of drug or something. When Winton found out, he threw a brick through my front window. I had to talk lawsuit before he paid for it."

"Did he threaten Jake or anything?"

"I don't know. He's pretty poor, so he probably couldn't do anything that risked his job."

I ruminated on that while I finished my beer. I was getting up to go when I asked the bartender, "Anyone else notable? Someone Jake really wronged? Someone who threatened Jake?"

"Well," he said with a smirk, "there was that fireman."

"Who?"

"I forget. It was a few years ago. This guy was on the department here in Truckee and got into an argument with Jake. Right over there by the pool table." Joe pointed. "The fireman was a brave sonofabitch, I'll give him that. He duked it out with Jake even though Jake was near twice his size. Now, Jake wasn't what I'd call a real skillful fighter, but he was big and he could throw a mean punch. 'Course, Jake was old enough to be the fireman's father, but even so, Jake cleaned his clock. A couple of the fireman's friends had to carry him out. His eyes swelled shut from Jake's blows, and he was yelling that he was going to come back and burn Jake's ass."

"Were those his words, 'burn his ass'?"

"Yeah. It stuck in my mind because of the word 'burn' coming from a fireman."

"Do you remember his name?"

"No. Like I said, it was a while back. There was a group of them that would come in after their shift. One of them was Larry Riverton, and he's still on the department up here. I could call him."

"Let's do that," I said.

Joe got on the phone and dialed a number off a three-by-five card he had push-pinned to the wall. "Hey, it's Joe over at the saloon. Lemme talk to Larry." In a moment he said, "Hey, Larry. Joe. Got a question. Remember that fight here a couple years ago where Jake Pooler decked that fireman? Yeah, you helped carry the poor sucker out. Right. Do you remember his name? What? No, just curious. We're having us one of those reminiscing conversations. Hey, thanks. Your next beer is on me."

Joe hung up the phone and turned to me. "I guess the guy left the Truckee Fire Department shortly after that fight. Went to work for one of the South Shore departments."

"What was his name?"

"Terry Drier."

TWENTY-TWO

Spot and I left the bar and walked up the street. I had more suspects for Jake's murder than I knew what to do with and none for Joanie Dove's.

Jimmy MacIntyre, Winton, Terry Drier and half the male population of Tahoe apparently had it in for Jake Pooler.

I had a lot of questions to ask Terry Drier. He previously said he'd met Jake Pooler, but nothing more. But I was already in Truckee, so it made sense to first question Winton as well as Jimmy MacIntyre, the man whose cute wife apparently got lost in Jake's allure.

When I got to the building that housed Jake Pooler Construction, I told Spot to sit at the base of the stairs. I hiked them two at a time and found the lights on and the door unlocked. When I pushed in through the weathered door the dead man's secretary Betty Williamson quickly closed a file folder and slipped it into the top drawer of her desk.

"Mr. McKenna!" she said, a little too much enthusiasm in her voice. "Why, what a surprise!"

"Good morning," I said. "You are working hard even though Jake is gone."

"Oh, well, you know, I'm struggling to collect on some of these receivables. Lenora Pooler is going to need all the money she can get, what with funeral expenses and all."

"Is Mrs. Pooler going to keep the business?" I asked.

"I don't imagine so in the long term," Betty said. "But there's people owe us money and we deserve to get what's coming to us."

"Will you still be getting paid while Mrs. Pooler decides how to dispose of Jake's assets?"

"Well, now that you mention it, I haven't thought about that. I've always handled the payroll, including writing out my own check. I figure out the FICA, state and federal withholding, unemployment and so forth. And I sign the checks. So I suppose I'll keep doing that for the time being." She looked at me hard. "You knew he was dead the last time you came by, didn't you?"

"Yes, but I had to inform the widow first. What about Winton? Is there still work for him to do?"

"My land, yes, if he would only show up! Just yesterday I took delivery on the roofing material for the Rewald's. The trusses and sheathing are up of course, so the shipment was just the cedar shingles. But when I saw bill of lading, I almost fainted! They came C.O.D. Custom cut, fire-proofed cedar shingles for a roof with something like fifteen dormers. It was Winton who placed the order. He must have forgotten to send the letter of credit! So I had to interrupt Mr. Rewald down at his venture capital firm in Santa Clara. What with all the faxes and bank guarantees, I'm up against the wall trying to keep track of it all. And that boy Winton taking off at a time like this! Good heavens, what am I going to do?" Betty looked up at me, her eyes searching mine.

"You say Winton hasn't shown up for work?"

"No! Two days, now. And he just lets the answering machine get it when I call. If I didn't know him so well, I'd be worried. I know he's angry about Jake and is staying away out of spite. But little does he know that the fallout is all landing on me." Betty folded her arms on her desk and bent her head down, forehead on forearms. Her gray hair hung forward off her head, just touching the cluttered desk top. Then she lifted up, her tight face red. "I'm sorry, Mr. McKenna. I guess this is all getting to me."

"Betty," I said, moving in closer, using a soft voice. "I thought I should talk to Jake's friends. Maybe I could get a clue as to

what happened. Could you give me the names of the people who
were closest to him?"

Betty burst into laughter, then caught herself. For a
moment I thought the skin over her cheeks would break. "Mr.
McKenna, you don't understand. Jake didn't have any friends. He
was, how shall I put it? He was an unpleasant man at best. It wasn't
like he and Lenora ever received dinner invitations or anything like
that."

"He must have been friendly with somebody."

Betty shook her head. "Not the way I use the word. I suppose you could go over to the High River Saloon and ask around.
Jake used to stop there after work."

"I thought I'd stop by Winton's house. Can you tell me his
address?"

"Sure. He's down by Carnelian Bay somewhere. I've never
been there myself. Let's see, I've got the number in the payroll file."
While she flipped through a file drawer, I picked up a phone book
off her desk and looked up MacIntyre. There was a James MacIntyre listed in Soda Springs.

Betty handed me a Post-it note. "This is Winton's address."

I wrote Jimmy MacIntyre's number next to Winton's.

"Thanks, Betty. Oh, one more thing. Did you ever hear of
Joanie Dove?"

"No. Who's that?"

It was the exact same response that Joe the bartender at the
High River Saloon had given me. I thanked her again, said goodbye
and left.

I didn't know the street that Jimmy MacIntyre lived on,
but the bartender said it was out by Sugar Bowl Ski Resort. It made
sense to go there first and catch Winton on my way back home.

Jimmy MacIntyre lived in a run-down eight-unit condo. I
stepped past a broken plywood contraption that used to hold a
grouping of six garbage cans. Now the ugly, bent cans sprawled at
odd angles, the garbage pulled out and ripped apart by bears.

I stepped past the mess, found the MacIntyre unit and rang
the bell.

The woman who answered was cute and petite, with perky hair cut shoulder length so that it would bounce like a cheerleader's. No doubt she was the wife who'd been Jake's sexual target. "Hello," I said. "I'm looking for Jimmy MacIntyre."

"Oh, no. Is he in trouble again?" She wiped her hands with a pink and blue plaid dish towel.

"May I speak with him, ma'am?"

She stuck a corner of the towel in the back pocket of her tight jeans, then stuck her hands on her hips. "You're with the probation department, right? I don't understand why they're always switching officers. Just when Jimmy was starting to get comfortable with Mr. Webster, they changed him over to Mrs. Tasminski, or whatever her name is. Now you. What gives?"

I realized that the mistaken association would get me answers better than any other. "Is he home?"

"No, he's at work. Where he's supposed to be. I just talked to him on the phone, so I know he's not out running around." Her tone had an edge to it, as if she were an innocent wife, victimized by her husband's transgressions.

"Where is work?"

"Oh, come on! As if you people don't know everything about Jimmy!" She pointed toward the mountains. "Over at Sugar Bowl, remember? Chairlift maintenance in the summer? Snowcat driver in the winter? Ring a bell, now?"

"Thanks, ma'am."

Fifteen minutes later I found Jimmy MacIntyre climbing down from a chairlift bull wheel. He held several tools in his left hand and hopped his right hand from one ladder rung to the next until he reached the ground.

"Jimmy MacIntyre? My name is Owen McKenna. I'd like ask you a couple of questions if you have a moment."

Jimmy bent over and dropped his tools into a large tool box that was attached to the back of an all terrain vehicle, the kind with four over-sized, knobby tires and a seat and handlebar arrangement like on a motorcycle. "Ask all you want. It don't mean I'll

answer." He sounded gruff and angry. It was a big, bad world and
Jimmy wasn't finding an easy way through it.

"I'm investigating the east shore fire. I wonder if you knew
the victim, Jake Pooler."

Jimmy was bent over the tool box, fishing for something.
"If I did, I would have kicked his fuckin' ass, that's for sure."

"Did you ever meet him?"

"No."

"You didn't light him on fire in revenge for him sleeping
with your wife?"

Jimmy jerked his head up to look at me. He held a large
wrench in his hand. His knuckles were pale and hard under the
grease. He shook with anger. "I wish I had! But somebody else beat
me to it."

"You sound serious, Jimmy."

He moved a step toward me. The wrench seemed to levi-
tate a few inches as if his hand were struggling to hold it down. "I am
serious," he hissed. "I would've burned him if I'd had the chance. I
don't care what would've happened. I coulda spent the rest of my
life in prison, but it would've been worth it." Jimmy turned and
looked up at the mountain. He breathed deeply. His voice was
lower when he spoke again. "I guess it was lucky for me that somebody else got him first."

It was a short conversation, yet I saw no point in continuing. I regretted having faced Jimmy with his demons, but having
done so convinced me of his innocence. His anger was so all-con-
suming that I didn't think he could lie while under its influence. I
thanked him for his time and left.

I drove back to Lake Tahoe on 89, past Squaw Valley and
Alpine Meadows ski areas. When I got to Tahoe City, I headed
around the north side of the lake to Carnelian Bay, one of a long
string of resort communities that consist of a jumbled mix of expensive vacation homes and old cabins. A fancy restaurant, a ski rental
shop and a condominium complex filled the remaining spaces.
Across the lake, 25 miles to the south, I could see the ski runs of
Heavenly. Despite the Indian summer they were still white from

the last snowfall, protected from the warm winds by their north-east orientation and their high elevation.

Winton Berger's address turned out to be one of six tiny cabins that comprised the Big Sleep motel. A sign advertised weekly and monthly rentals and I surmised that the cabins were too small to compete with other accommodations for the typical tourist. Winton's cabin was number 4.

I found him out back, sitting on a tree stump sipping a beer. A short distance away was a dirty barbecue pot with a small pile of charcoal under the grill. The corners of a couple briquettes were white, but it looked like they had gone out.

"Hi, Winton. I'm Owen McKenna. We met at your office the other day."

"Yeah, I remember." He glanced up at me, then back at the charcoal. "Only, it ain't my office. Never was, never will be. I quit." There was a slight lisp on the S in 'was' and the C in 'office.'

"Why? From what I gather, it would be a much nicer place to work now that Jake's gone."

"True," Winton said. "But I'm sick of everything connected to that jerk. And ol' lady Betty, she ain't much better. She's either in love with Jake or ready to cut his throat. All I hear about is Jake this and Jake that. It's even worse now that he's burnt toast. I can't stand it." Winton looked over at the charcoal in the pot. "Fuckin' shit's gone out." Without getting up, he lit a kitchen match and tossed it onto the little pile of briquettes where it flickered weakly. Then he picked up the lighter fluid and squirted a long stream that arced through the air to the charcoal. The fluid burst into flame. Winton kept the stream going while the flames grew into an inferno.

I stepped back before my hair was singed.

Winton stopped squirting. "Damn charcoal never lights the first time." He held the lighter fluid can up and looked at the label. "I should just use gasoline." Winton set the can on the ground and looked up at me. "Of course, gas has this little problem." He gave a nervous giggle. "If you squirt it like that while the fire is burning, the fire races up the stream and the can explodes. I saw that happen to a friend once when we were little. Lost three fingers on his right hand." He giggled again. "But that charcoal sure did light the first time!"

"You like to play with gas?"

"What does it matter? You gonna try and stick me with Jake's murder? Good luck, 'cause I was in Reno the whole time. My friend can vouch for me."

I stepped to the side and sat down on another stump not far from Winton. Uncle Owen sitting down for a chat. Friendly. Caring. You could tell me anything. "Who said it was murder?" I asked.

Winton paused. "It only makes sense. Fucker deserved to be murdered. And there are a lot of guys out there who'd do the honors. Besides, Jake wouldn't have killed himself, accident or not. He wasn't the type." Winton poked at the charcoal with a long stick. "If I killed Jake I woulda done it the same way. Set a fire to make it look like an accident. With all them environmentalists fighting that Smoky Bear shit about not letting the woods burn, it wouldn't look like murder. More like a war about fire policy."

It is unnerving when you realize that you've underestimated someone. I suddenly had the sense that Winton was choosing his words not to express his feelings so much as to manipulate mine.

"Winton," I said, "Did you ever know a woman named Joanie Dove?"

He hesitated just a moment. "No. Who's that?"

I looked at Winton, disbelieving.

He smiled at me.

"Joanie Dove died in the second fire," I said. I watched him carefully.

"What fire?"

"In Tallac Properties."

"Where's that?"

"On the south shore," I said.

"Oh," he said.

"Winton, do you know where Jake kept his gasoline cans?"

He took his time answering. "I don't know. On his truck, I guess."

"Any idea where his truck would be?"

"No. Maybe at his house?"

I wondered how close Winton was to Jake's life. "Do you go there much?"

"Never been there."

"But you know where he lived, right?"

Winton shook his head. "I met Mrs. Pooler once when she came into the office, but that's all I know of his family life."

"It was rare, her coming to Jake's place of work?"

"Like I said, she only came once when I was there."

"What was her reason that time?" I asked.

"Same as why she always called on the phone. Screaming about what she was going to do to the bastard."

"Did she ever threaten to kill him?"

"Worse," Winton said, looking off into the woods, remembering. "Once I answered the phone the same time as he did. Before I got it hung up I heard her yell that she was going to cut his pecker off."

I pondered that. "Now that you've quit your job, what are you going to do?"

"Don't know. I got a friend who drives truck for a cement company. Maybe he can get me some work."

"Do you plan to stay in the area?"

"Why? You gonna charge me with a crime?"

"No. But we may have more questions."

"We?"

"Me. The Truckee Police. The Douglas County Sheriff's Department." I stood up.

Winton craned his neck to look up at me. "You're about as tall as Jack's beanstalk." Then he seemed to grow more sullen. "You want to ask more questions, come and find me. Maybe I'll be here. Maybe I won't."

As I left I thought that Winton Berger could certainly be the firestarter, but it didn't have the strong resonance I'd come to expect over my years of interviewing suspects who turned out to be guilty. Revenge as a motive for killing his boss was possible but not convincing. And there were some things that didn't fit. Why, for example, would Winton spend a thousand dollars to have me roughed up? First of all, he didn't look to have financial resources. Second, wouldn't he just torch my cabin instead?

On the way home I called Lenora Pooler.

"Mrs. Pooler, this is Owen McKenna calling. I just have a quick question. Did you know Joanie Dove?"

"Who's that?" she asked.

It was becoming boring, this answer to my question about Joanie Dove. Everybody had a reason to kill Jake Pooler, but no one would even admit to having heard of the second fire victim. It didn't suggest much promise of finding a connection between the two.

TWENTY-THREE

I had used up most of the day and learned next to nothing. My one big breakthrough was when I decided that Jimmy MacIntyre, the spurned husband of one of Jake's conquests, didn't do the old bastard in. Which possibly narrowed my list of suspects down into the three figure range. I decided I should investigate the second victim while I was on a roll. But it was late, and as I drove south around the lake I was already mentally cataloging my wine selection and trying to match one up with the filet mignon in the fridge.

"What do you think, your largeness?" I said to Spot who was lying in the back seat. "Shall I open the Caymus cab?"

He swung his eyes toward me for a moment, the lower lids drooping and revealing pink crescents of flesh. Then he looked away.

"Okay," I said. "I know you prefer beer, but trust me on this one, will you?"

Spot tucked his nose under the crook of his paw and pretended to sleep.

Being a detective, I knew that the excitement at the High River Saloon was not enough to sustain him through the day and he was back to being depressed over Pussy Cat. I believed that Dr. Selma Peralta would call as soon as the mountain lion was well enough to see Spot. His guilt would have to wait. The thought reminded me about the bullet they'd taken from Pussy Cat's neck. It wasn't yet five o'clock. The ballistics lab might still be open.

I got through on my phone.

"This is Owen McKenna calling to check on a bullet I dropped off. Any chance you've run the tests?"

"Yes," a gruff voice answered. "We finished this morning. Hold on, let me grab the sheet." I heard what sounded like clipboards being juggled. "Here we are. It was a twenty-two caliber, that much is clear. But unfortunately it was damaged by the impact and by the surgeon's tongs. And if the victim is deceased, then I should point out that there is no coroner's mark, a fact which you should point out to the county authorities. Very unprofessional."

"The victim wasn't human, so no coroner was involved."

"Oh. I thought..."

"It was a mountain lion. Veterinarians don't usually think to be careful of how they handle bullets."

"Oh," he said again. "I didn't know."

"Don't worry. Anything else?"

"Yes. The bullet was substantially deformed by impact with bone. Yet we find traces of right hand grooves. But it was not possible to determine a land and groove ratio. So it could have been fired from any number of rifles."

I thanked him and hung up just as I approached my turnoff. Dinner was but a thousand feet up.

Street called as I was putting the steak on the grill. "I wondered if you'd like to have a picnic with me in the morning after I get off work. I'll have some maggot data by then."

"Of course," I said.

I was lounging in the sun on the deck when Street pulled up the next morning.

"I found the perfect place the other day," she said as I got into her VW after cajoling Spot to scrunch himself into the back. "I've been wanting to take you there ever since." She turned and gave me a mischievous grin. "You're going to love it."

"I was certain of that," I said. "So I brought a libation to help us celebrate." I opened my day pack and gave her a peek at a bottle of Beringer Meritage. Street waved her eyebrows in appreciation.

"So what did your creepy crawlers tell you?" I asked as she drove off.

"I took the standard approach of dividing the maggots I collected from the body into two groups. I killed one group to fix their development. The other group I allowed to mature. That process is not complete, so I'm not certain of the species and hence I'm only making educated guesses.

"I ran the numbers on several scenarios, adjusting for the temperature data the hygrothermograph recorded down in the Highland Creek ravine. It's not an exact science. Closer to art in some ways. But each way I add it up I still come up with the same time of death."

"Which is?"

"I believe Mr. Jake Pooler died between eight and ten p.m. on the night of the first forest fire," Street said.

"The same time as the beginning of the fire?"

"Right. I can't say the fire killed him. But being that the times coincide, it is likely. Has Diamond gotten an autopsy report yet?"

"Not that I know of," I said. "But I'll bet it shows smoke inhalation. Which would make it murder."

We were driving through South Lake Tahoe. Street turned up Ski Run Blvd. toward Heavenly Ski Resort. At the parking lot, she went around and on up Keller and then parked on a side street between two angular houses with beautiful views of the town and the lake beyond.

I let Spot out. Street reached into the back of the car and pulled out a telescoping aluminum rod with a large curved plastic hook on one end.

"Looks like a boat hook," I said.

"Right. It belongs to my neighbor. He's out of town. He always says I can borrow any of his stuff."

I looked around at the mountain. "Not too many boats up here."

"Well," Street said, demonstrating. "In this collapsed position it makes a good staff for hiking. But if you get out of line, I can telescope it all the way out and use it to reel you in." She popped the catch, extended the pole and gently hooked the hook around my neck. Then she pulled me toward her, hand over hand, until our lips met in a moist kiss.

"Effective," I mumbled against her mouth.

Street released me, collapsed the boat hook to its short dimension and pulled her backpack out of the car. "Come. Our picnic awaits." She hiked up to where the neighborhood road dead-ended against the steep mountainside. There was a narrow trail that went into the woods. Spot ran ahead, eagerly sniffing out the recent movements of forest critters.

I followed Street up the trail.

She had the cuffs on her khaki shorts rolled up to mid-thigh, and above her hiking boots were red wool socks that came to mid-calf. She'd rolled up the sleeves of her red flannel shirt so that her thin forearms were revealed. Her skin glowed.

I showed proper restraint and kept my hands to myself.

"This picnic that waits for us," I said. "Is it in your backpack? All I brought is the wine."

"The food is in my backpack," she said. "The picnic is up on the mountain."

"The difference being?"

"Oh, I don't know. The right setting, weather, companionship, you know what I mean. This particular picnic features an amazing view. Speaking of which, you shouldn't be walking behind me on this narrow trail. I'm blocking everything and I've been here before. This is my treat. You should go first."

"No, I'm fine," I said. "Besides, the view from here is very nice."

Spot came running toward us down the trail, more pleasure in his demeanor than I had seen since his persecution over Pussy Cat. He did a quick stop in front of Street. She reached out and gave him a pet. He about-faced and trotted back up the mountain.

The trail went around a giant boulder and the forest suddenly gave way to the steep open ski run that fronts the lower part of Heavenly.

Called The Face, it is, in winter, 1,700 vertical feet of Black Diamond skiing, one of the meanest mogul runs in the country. I remembered that its monster bumps were like a thousand buried VW Beetles.

Coming upon it now, without snow, emphasized how steep the terrain is. "Tell me we're not hiking up The Face," I said, my legs protesting at the thought.

Street turned and grinned. "What'sa matter? I thought you liked vigorous exercise."

"Some kinds," I said, holding her eyes a moment.

"Anyway," she said, "we're going across, not up."

Street cut across the slope with Spot ranging out in front of her. He looked back now and then to check that he was going in the same general direction. I followed, enjoying the view across Lake Tahoe, but mostly watching Street hiking at an angle upslope a few yards in front of me.

She was a diminutive woman, not so much in terms of her five foot five inch height, but in her slenderness. Yet despite her small stature, there was no frailty about her. Many times people had been surprised when they asked her to join them on a ski or bike outing only to find that Street had more stamina and guts than anyone else in the group. She was like a sapling, thin and graceful, yet strong and tough.

But feminine. Although Street thought she was too thin, I knew well her luxurious curves.

We came to a line of trees, stepped through them and out onto another ski run. This one was called Gunbarrel and was as steep as The Face. Here, Street turned and headed straight up the mountain.

"Hey, sweetie," I called. "You made a wrong turn. Aren't we supposed to go this way?" I pointed vaguely downhill.

"Just a little farther, hon," she said. She seemed to be angling toward one of the chairlift towers on the high-speed quad that races skiers up the mountain in winter.

I followed, my lungs working hard. Spot looked back and saw Street's change in direction. He loped toward her.

Street stopped at the chairlift tower and waited for me to join her.

"This the picnic sight?" I said.

"No," she said. "When I was looking up the mountain the other day, I noticed that one of the chairs on the downward cable was stopped next to one of the lift towers." She pointed up above our heads. "Voila."

"I don't get it."

"Our picnic," she said. She reached onto one of the welded steel rungs on the tower and, holding her boat hook staff in one hand, began climbing.

"Street, wait. Let's be reasonable. Shouldn't we discuss this first?"

"What's to discuss?" She was already ten feet up and moving fast.

"This lift tower must be fifty or sixty feet high. That's a dangerous height."

"You ride the chair all the time when you're skiing," she called out. "You never said anything about it being dangerous."

"But then I'm just sitting," I said. "And there's snow below when you're skiing. Now you're climbing and there is nothing below but boulders and dirt."

"I can't hear you," Street said. She was thirty feet above the ground. Spot looked up at her and whined.

"I said that if you fall you won't hit snow, you'll hit rocks," I yelled.

"I won't fall," she yelled back. "Come on up. I don't want to eat alone."

I looked at Spot. "Too late for me to be a show-off," I said to him. "So if you don't mind waiting down here, I'll throw you a scrap of lunch. If I live to eat it, that is." I rubbed his head, reached up onto the steel rungs and began climbing after Street.

Chairlifts seem much higher when one isn't skiing. As I rose high above the ground I felt ill at ease. Many times I've stood on the edge of a cliff and gazed down hundreds or even thousands of feet and felt secure. But dangling from steel is not like standing on granite. My nervous system was on alert. Spot, as if sensing my concern, whimpered from down below. But Street was above me and I needed to at least make an attempt to maintain the tough guy facade I'd been working on for so long.

"I almost fell asleep in the hot sun," Street said when I finally got just below her at her perch near the top of the lift tower.

I looked down the mountain. The steep slope of the Gunbarrel ski run made it seem as if we were a thousand feet above the lake. Then again, maybe we were. I pretended it was no different than standing at the railing on my deck.

"Spot was worried about you," I said. "I took a moment to reassure him."

"Right," Street said.

"We're going to eat while hanging onto these lift tower rungs?" I asked.

"No, silly. We're going to have a relaxing picnic on the living room couch." She pointed to the chair that hung out in midair, next to the tower. It was on the downward cable and pointed down the mountain toward the lake.

"But Street," I said, keeping my voice calm. "The nearest edge of that chair is four feet out. You don't want to leap that far when you're sixty feet above the ground."

"Which is why I brought this." She reached out the boat hook and snagged the side rail of the chair. By pulling on the hook, she swung the heavy four-person chair a couple of feet toward us. It hung crooked under the pull of the boat hook. Street then reached into her backpack and removed a short coil of rope. She tossed one end of the line around the rail on the chair, made a large loop through one of the steel rungs on the chairlift tower, and tied it off.

Next, she took the boat hook and laid it horizontally from the rung on the lift tower across to the back edge of the big chair. Grabbing it and wiggling it vigorously to make sure it wouldn't shift, she put some weight on the boat hook, reached a leg out into space and, as I watched speechless, made a little leap onto the chair. The air in my lungs suddenly seemed to lack oxygen.

"Come on, Owen. You've got long legs. This will be a small step for you."

I shook my head in disapproval. "Heavenly is going to send up the chairlift police. We'll be incarcerated for riding the chair without a lift ticket."

Street held up her backpack, trying to tempt me. "All the food is out here on this chair."

"But I've got the wine," was my weak reply. We looked at each other. Her eyes were demonic. I climbed up another two rungs, leaned on the boat hook and stepped through space out to the chair.

I moved awkwardly as I lowered myself into a sitting position.

"Now," Street said. "If you rotate the loop of rope holding the chair, you can untie the knot and the chair will swing back so it hangs straight."

"Sure, I knew that," I said, still getting accustomed to the height and position. I did as she said and let the chair swing out to its natural position.

We were now facing down the mountain toward South Lake Tahoe and the lake. Put skis and boots on my feet and snow on the ground and I would have felt normal. But without, it took some getting used to. Street pulled down the safety bar and I immediately felt much more secure.

I reached into my pack, pulled out two of my best wine glasses, propped them between my legs and busied myself with the corkscrew.

Street unwrapped deli sandwiches and opened a bag of potato chips. Being that the chair was designed for four skiers, we had plenty of room. Street turned sideways with one of her legs folded under her. I poured the wine and we toasted.

"Here's to rescuing the damsel in distress on the chairlift," I said.

"Oh, Owen, I'm so glad you did!" She sipped her wine, then leaned over and gave me a hug.

At that moment Spot whined.

We both leaned over the edge of the chair and looked. He was sitting on his haunches at the base of the tower, staring up at us.

"Okay, Spot. Catch." I broke off part of my sandwich and tossed it down. It separated into pieces of roll and turkey and tomato as it fell. Spot snapped at more than one and missed them all. It took him all of a second to inhale them off of the ground.

"You didn't think I'd forget him, did you?" Street pulled some Hostess Twinkies out of her pack.

"Street, I'm not sure that food is approved by the American Kennel Club."

"Let's let Spot be the judge of that." She pulled off the plastic wrapper. "Hey, Spot!" She tossed one of them down to him. He caught it in the air. The sound was something like a plug of whipped grease getting sucked into a Hoover vacuum cleaner.

"I don't believe you did that," I said, doing my own fast work on my sandwich and potato chips.

"Any more news on the firestarter?" Street asked.

"Not much in specific except that I have a lot of suspects with both motive and opportunity."

"What about studying the general characteristics of arsonists and applying those to your suspects?"

"I've tried and it doesn't narrow them down much." I gave Street a brief recap of my visit with Arthur Jones Middleton the Sixth, my interrogation of the bar manager in Truckee and the other people I'd spoken to. Then I told her what I'd learned from the psychologist in San Francisco.

"The homicidal trinity sounds bizarre!" she said. "Imagine that such a strange group of behaviors are so commonly present in serial killers. The animal torture and playing with fire make sense.

But bed-wetting! It makes you wonder how the brain is set up that those patterns connect to thrill killing."

"Yes," I agreed. "To a psychologist, the brain must be a dark labyrinth." I munched more of my sandwich and washed it down with wine. The chair swung slightly, reminding me that we were dangling above the world. "What about insects?" I said. "Do they ever exhibit aberrant behaviors?"

Street sipped some wine. "Not much. For all their complexity, bugs are relatively simple. They don't manifest psychological pathology in the way that we think of it. They are more tightly controlled, their behavior hardwired into their brains. They eat, rest, reproduce and care for their young. All other behavior is an offshoot of one of those basic Darwinian drives."

"Same for people, don't you think?"

"I suppose," she said.

"Are there any bad bugs? Criminal bugs?"

"Well, bugs can get pretty nasty. For example, there is a type of scarab beetle that invades an ant colony and then absorbs the scents of the ants and their surroundings. The beetle is so good at it that the ants don't recognize it as a predator. The beetle then roams through the colony freely eating the offspring of the ants. But I guess it wouldn't be criminal behavior any more than that of a hunter who dons camouflage clothing and goes into the woods to shoot deer."

"What about within a species?" I asked.

"Bugs will steal from or even kill their own kind, but not in the sense that we think of as criminal. Within a species, they are merely fighting over food or a potential female mate."

"There aren't any true deviants? No serial killers?"

"I don't know if any research has been done in that direction. I suppose that now and then a bug goes astray. Possibly due to a mutation or an injury to its nervous system."

"What would the other members of its species do when confronted with such a bug?"

"In most cases, nothing," Street said. "Most insects are relatively solitary. They come together only to mate. But among the social insects, the ants, bees, wasps and termites, there could be a group response to a deviant member of their community."

"What would the response be?"

"It would depend on the circumstances. But in the case of a severe transgressor, they would possibly attack and kill it."

"Ah, there is justice in this world," I said.

"Here and there," Street said. "Speaking of which, how shall we do justice to the remainder of this wine?"

"I think I can manage it," I said.

"It's not too much wine for an early lunch?"

"A big guy has big fuel requirements." I upended the last of the bottle into my glass. I glanced over at the gulf between the chair and the lift tower. "Besides, this will help give me the faith to make that leap."

"Kierkegaard's Leap of Faith," Street said.

"To Kierkegaard," I said, holding my glass up.

Street held hers up and we clicked.

TWENTY-FOUR

The next morning Spot and I headed out early.

I knew nothing about Joanie Dove except where she had lived and worked. I thought I'd start with her neighbors.

The Tallac Properties neighborhood where the fire had raged through was a wreck, two houses burned to the ground, the forest devastated. The houses that weren't burned were covered with ash and soot, their once-neat yards dark with debris. I left Spot snoozing in the Jeep and went to the house nearest the charred hulk of Joanie's and rang the doorbell. The place looked deserted. Like so many houses in Tahoe, it was probably a vacation home, empty most of the year. I rang two more times and eventually moved on to the next house.

No one answered at the second house so I walked down to the third.

This time a young woman answered the door. She was tall and slim and held a remarkably pudgy, wide-eyed baby in her arms. The woman turned her body back and forth, rocking the baby vigorously enough that I wondered if the child was wide-eyed because it was nauseous.

"Yes?" she said.

"Hi, my name's Owen McKenna. I'm looking into the fire on behalf of the fire department." I handed her one of my McKenna Investigations cards. "May I ask you a few questions?"

"Sure."

"I'm sorry about your neighbor Joanie Dove. Did you know her?"

"Not well. But she was very kind. What a horrible thing it must be to die in a fire." The woman shook her head which made for an unusual movement on her already-twisting body. The baby glanced up at mom's face then stared even more intently back at me. It looked about to spit up. I moved a half step back.

"Did she ever talk to you?"

"Just a little, here and there," the woman said. "We'd say hello coming and going, that sort of thing. And when we moved in, Joanie came over with a fresh-baked apple pie. God, it was so good! I asked her for baking tips and Joanie said her personal secret is to always use half again as much brown sugar as any recipe calls for. Did you know that about brown sugar?"

"Uh, no, actually," I said. "I didn't."

"Anyway, she seemed to be an awfully sweet person. Gentle and soft-spoken."

"What about family? Any that you know of?"

"Just a sister. Quite a bit older than Joanie. She lives out in Kirkwood."

"Do you recall her name?"

The woman shook her head again. That, with her twisting body, was making me dizzy. I could only imagine what the baby was going through. "Wait," she suddenly said. "Mrs. Mortensen, that was it."

"First name?"

"I don't remember."

"Did Joanie have any friends who knew her well? People you often saw going to her house?"

She shook her head again. "Not that I ever noticed."

I looked beyond her head and stared at the house to steady myself for a moment, like a seasick sailor staring at the horizon in pitching seas. I pointed through the trees at the second house that had burned, a place that looked as if it had been large but was now just a huge mound of ashes with a few charred timbers poking out. "How about your neighbors in the other house that burned? Do you know them?"

She glanced over at the burned house. "I've never known exactly what their name is, but it sounds like Spacocinni." The woman grinned mischievously, looked down at her baby and waggled her nose in the kid's face. "We call them the Spaghettios, don't we, pumpkin?" She turned back to me. "They haven't even been up to take a look. The only person I've seen was an insurance adjuster. You know how it is with rich people. It's just one of several vacation homes they have. They're probably back in Sicily or someplace."

"Thank you," I said. "My number is on my card. If you think of anything else, please call, okay?"

This time she nodded vigorously, and the up and down with the body twisting was too much. The kid vomited across the front of the woman's shirt. I left fast.

Information had a Mrs. Lydia Mortensen in Kirkwood, and when I called and introduced myself, she invited me down, giving me directions from the Kirkwood turnoff.

I drove out Christmas Valley and headed up the highway at the end of the canyon. The road climbs up to Luther Pass and then makes a gentle descent down into Hope Valley, a spectacular mix of aspen stands and open glens at 7,000 feet of elevation. The aspen trees had turned a brilliant golden yellow and the leaves shimmered like discs of gold in the breeze. Surrounding the valley are snow-capped peaks. Snow melt from the recent storm had swollen the rapids of the Carson River and I paralleled the rushing water up the valley. Further west I followed the road up the side of Red Lake Peak. Nearing the top of Carson Pass I drove into a winter landscape. The storm that had dropped a few inches at my cabin on the east shore of Tahoe had made a major impact in the high country to the south of Tahoe.

The plows had pushed the snow into berms eight feet high and it was still September. It was easy to see why the higher passes to the south are closed in the winter. Too much snow. Coming around a curve I could see the jagged ridge line of the California

Alps to the south, and beyond them, the 13,000 foot mountains of Yosemite.

Just above Carson Pass loomed Round Top and The Sisters and all of them reflected, like a picture postcard, in Caples Lake which hadn't yet frozen. I continued over the dam and turned in to Kirkwood.

I followed Lydia Mortensen's instructions all the way in past the ski lifts and then out toward the golf course. She lived in a new house, light gray with brown trim.

Lydia, a sturdy woman in her mid-fifties, was outside shoveling snow when I pulled up. I parked in the street. Spot was still sleeping in back and didn't move when I got out.

"I swear, you just can't find kids who want to work anymore," Lydia said as I approached her. "I pay well, but shoveling is too much work for kids raised on video games." She looked up at me and I could see the dark bags around her eyes. She'd obviously been through hell in the last couple of days.

"Did it snow again last night?" I asked. "We've had nothing in Tahoe since the storm last week."

"Mr. McKenna," she said in an admonishing tone. "You are Mr. McKenna, right?"

I nodded and reached out my hand. We shook. Her grip was firm.

"Mr. McKenna, this is Kirkwood," she continued. "Snowiest ski resort in North America. Last year we had fifty-four feet of snow. Do you know how often it has to snow to add up to fifty-four feet? I figured it out. Thirty inches a week for five months straight. Of course, sometimes it snows sixty or seventy inches in one storm, which leaves room for a few sunny days. Other periods, it snows all the time. So, in answer to your question, yes, it snowed last night. And it'll probably snow tonight. And these neighbor kids are worthless. I just bought this place last year. Joanie wanted me to move up to Tahoe from Sacramento, but I didn't want to be too close to Joanie, didn't want to crowd her. So I came to Kirkwood. It was so cute, I couldn't resist. But I'm already thinking of moving down below Heavenly on the Nevada side. Maybe just south of

Carson City in Gardnerville. My God, last year the snow here was as high as the house." She pointed dramatically up toward the top of the roof. "We were like a walled city. The streets and driveways were just tunnels in the snow.

"I could get a little ranch," she continued non-stop. "I looked into it, you know. They have these beautiful places down below the mountain. But this place," she pointed at my feet, "the driveway right where you are standing is at eight thousand feet. I've got one of those special maps that I looked it up on. You know what that means? That means that while I'm shoveling snow, those people in Gardnerville are listening to songbirds. I watch the giant rotary snow plows go roaring by while the Gardnerville people are watching wild mustangs running across the desert under Job's Peak.

"I'm sorry, I'm talking your ear off. Why don't you come inside, Mr. McKenna. I'll make you some tea."

I followed her into an immaculate house with spectacular mountain views out the windows, and sat on a gray divan while Lydia Mortensen made us a pot of tea.

"I've got some oatmeal biscuits, Mr. McKenna," Lydia called out from the kitchen. "Would you like one?"

"No thank you," I said. Oatmeal had always seemed like a food one ate for no purpose other than to build character. I didn't see any reason to start on that now.

Lydia came out with two mugs on a tray. Between them sat two lumps of gray stuff on brown napkins. "I brought you a biscuit, anyway, Mr. McKenna. You are a big man, and you need lots of food." She sat down on a love seat opposite me. "Now my sister Joanie, she was an amazing cook. Could that girl bake. No biscuits for her, let me tell you. My God, her Danish pastries were to die for!" She picked up a biscuit and took a large bite. Her jaw muscles bulged like Arnold Schwartzenegger's as she chewed. She looked at me expectantly.

I picked up my tea and sipped it. "Delicious," I said.

"Aren't you going to try your biscuit?" she said through a full mouth.

"I'd love to, Mrs. Mortensen, but I just ate a huge lunch. Tell me," I said, changing the subject, "do you have a photo of your sister that I might look at? I never met her."

"I... on the piano," she muttered.

I stood and fetched a silver framed photo. When I came back to the divan, I realized she was crying.

"I'm sorry, Mrs. Mortensen. I know this is hard for you." I sat next to her on the loveseat, put the framed photo down on the low table and took her hand in mine.

"She... she was my only family." Her words were interrupted by choking sobs. "It should have been me. She was the good one, I was the selfish one." She cried harder.

I massaged her hand. "I don't see why you would think that," I said.

"It's true!" Lydia blurted. "I've always been selfish. Me, me, me! And all I do is talk! As a result, nobody ever liked me. Everybody liked Joanie! Just ask the people at her work. They always ask her out to the shows and over to their houses for dinner. Just last week Joanie was telling me about going to a birthday party for one of her boss's kids. A girl named Lucy. My God, what I would do to have someone want me at their kid's birthday!" She broke into another fit of sobbing.

"Do you live alone, Mrs. Mortensen?"

"Yes. Ever since Herb passed on seven years ago. He was an older man. We were married sixteen precious years. He was a dear and left me well-provided for." Lydia sniffled. She reached for a Kleenex and blew her nose.

"Was Joanie married?"

"No. Never was. She was kind and sweet and certainly attractive enough. Here, look at her picture." She picked the framed photo up and handed it to me.

The fortyish woman in the photo had shiny brown hair in a Betty Crocker cut and a gentle smile. "Did Joanie have any kids?"

Lydia pulled her hand from mine and stared at me. "I just told you she never married." Her tone was indignant.

"Oh, of course you did," I said.

"I was barren and she was single," Lydia said, her crying beginning again. "But there again, I was selfish, and she was giving. All I did was sulk about my inability to have children, while Joanie took in all those foster kids. I can't even count how many over the years."

I sipped the last of my tea. "Did Joanie have any enemies?"

Lydia acted shocked. "What are you saying?"

"Someone who would want to hurt her? Someone who was angry with her?"

"You mean, someone who would burn her house down? What are you, nuts?!" Lydia stood up and stared at me. "It was a forest fire! It was an accident! I can't imagine what you are suggesting. Joanie was a beloved person. No one would want to hurt her!"

"I'm sorry, Mrs. Mortensen. I'm only trying to be thorough. The fire was started on purpose. Just like the other one."

"It was?" Lydia sat back down, a stunned look on her face.

"Mrs. Mortensen, almost certainly you are right. Even though the fire was caused by arson, Joanie's death was probably not intentional. But bear with me for a moment. Pretend that someone did want to harm her. Or maybe just scare her. Can you think of anyone who had a disagreement with Joanie? Or maybe someone who was envious of her? Someone at work who didn't get the promotion that Joanie got, that sort of thing. Does anyone come to mind?"

Lydia Mortensen slowly shook her head. "No. I can't imagine that there is anyone in all of Tahoe who'd want anything but the best for Joanie."

"How long has she lived in Tahoe?"

"Let's see. It will be three years this Christmas. I mean, it would have been." The tears started to flow again. "God, all I've done since her death is cry like a baby. But she was all I had left in the whole world." She sobbed harder.

"Did you say that Joanie lived down in Sacramento before moving to Tahoe?"

Lydia nodded, tears dripping off her cheek faster than she could mop them up with tissue.

"What about her life there? Was there anyone who might have been angry with her?"

"No. It was the same then as now. Everybody loved Joanie."

I was getting frustrated. To hear Lydia and Joanie's neighbor tell it, Joanie was more loved than a saint. "Mrs. Mortensen, I don't mean to be rude, but you're not being realistic. No one can get through life without irritating others. A very good person like Joanie may not irritate many, and it may not even have been Joanie's fault when someone felt angry with her. But life doesn't run perfectly smoothly. You know that from your own experience. So please think harder."

Lydia just sat there shaking her head, tears pooling in the corners of her eyes.

"Let's think of this a different way," I said. "Did you ever spend much time with her?"

"Of course," Lydia said, displeasure in her voice. "When we both lived in Sacramento we played cards once a week and often went to movies. When Joanie moved to Tahoe I came up and stayed with her for weeks at a time."

"In all those times, did anyone ever raise their voice at Joanie, or argue with her?"

"Not to speak of."

"I don't just mean to speak of," I said, trying to stay calm. "I mean at all. Ever."

Lydia Mortensen looked exasperated with me. "Well, I remember a time the newspaper kept going missing off her front step. When Joanie spoke to the boy about it he got mad at her as if she were accusing him of being dishonest. But that wouldn't be cause for lighting a forest fire now, would it?"

"Not for you or me, Mrs. Mortensen. Was this newspaper boy in Sacramento or in Tahoe?"

"Tahoe. Not long after she bought her house."

"Speaking of which, how was it that Joanie afforded such a nice house?"

"Oh, Joanie was very frugal and she always had a good job. She saved every penny. Plus, there were all those foster children over the years.

"The foster children were when she lived in Sac?"

"Yes. The money from it was terrible, but she saved it all."

"Did she leave a sizable estate?" I asked.

"She had a decent savings account, a few stocks and the house. Of course, the house is gone, but the insurance agent says there won't be any trouble collecting the insurance."

"How is her estate to be handled?"

"I get one third, the Tahoe Women's Center gets one third, and The League To Save Lake Tahoe gets one third."

I pondered that for a moment, seeking motive, not finding much. "The foster children you mentioned. How many of them were there?"

"Oh, gosh. She must have had kids in her house for twelve or fifteen years. Two at once most of the time. Most would get moved every few years, so I suppose it added up to a dozen or more."

"How did she work it with her job?"

"Same as other single mothers. It was difficult at first, convincing the agency she could do it. But they could tell she was dedicated. And after the first year, they kept calling to see if she'd take more kids. Anyway, she'd get the kids off to school, then Nattie, the neighbor lady, would be there to baby-sit when the kids came home until Joanie got home from the title company. After a few years, Joanie got good enough at her job, she could do much of the escrow work at home, so she'd leave work early most days and meet the kids when they were through with school."

"Did she ever have any difficult foster kids? Any who fought with her or were particularly rebellious?"

Lydia gave me a skeptical look. "Do you have kids, Mr. McKenna?"

"No." I could still see the vomiting baby from a couple hours earlier. "I've never had the pleasure."

"I can tell. If you did you'd know that all kids at one time or another are difficult and rebellious. All kids fight with their parents at some point. Now, if you're thinking one of those kids would grow up, track Joanie down in Tahoe and then light her house on fire, you're wasting your time. Mr. McKenna, we're talking about children to whom Joanie was a loving, devoted mother."

"I'm sure you're right," I said. "One more question?"

"Certainly."

"Have you ever heard of a man named Jake Pooler?"

Lydia shook her head. "No, I'm sure I haven't."

"If Joanie had ever had any dealings with any man, do you think she would have told you about it?"

"Absolutely. Joanie didn't have much time for men. If there had ever been one around, I'd have known. You can count on that."

I thanked Lydia for all of her time, complemented her again on her hospitality.

"You still didn't eat your biscuit, Mr. McKenna. I'll put it in a bag for you." She ran and got a baggie, carefully folded the biscuit inside and pressed the package into my hand.

I thanked her again and left.

When I turned out on the highway, I remembered the biscuit in the baggie. I pulled it out and held it up. "Hey, a treat for your largeness."

Spot sat up, sniffed the biscuit, then lay back down.

"As you wish," I said, then tossed it out the window.

When I got back to South Lake Tahoe, I stopped at Heritage Title, the company where Joanie had worked. There were several women inside a single large room. One was a secretary at a desk in the front, the others were at desks arranged in a square formation in back. One of the desks was empty. All the women were on their phones while they flipped through folders, sorted papers, amended contracts, dug in file drawers, punched calculators and took notes.

I waited at the secretary's desk. With a phone wedged between her head and shoulder, she was speaking to a client while she wrote in an appointment book with her right hand and worked a computer mouse with her left. She smiled at me and held a finger up to let me know she'd be with me in a minute.

For a guy who has to concentrate just to brush his teeth, this office was a lesson in the real difference between the sexes. It wasn't strength or social skills or cooking techniques.

It was multi-tasking.

"Yes, sir?" the secretary said.

I gave her my quick intro and explained that I wanted to speak to whomever had known Joanie Dove the best.

"Oh, Joanie was the nicest person. We're all still in mourning. Let's see. I guess Sonoma knew her best."

"Sonoma?" I said, wondering if I'd heard correctly.

"Yes." She turned and pointed to a thin woman with a tight helmet of blond curls who was maybe twenty-three at the outside. "She's our youngest escrow officer, but is she good or what. She's closing as many per week as Annie and we've only had to refile one set of documents since she started and even that was because of a mistake that Fidelity Mortgage made. Sonoma didn't know Joanie as long as the rest of us, but she and Joanie really hit it off. They had lunch together all the time." The secretary waited until Sonoma got off the phone. "Sonoma? Do you have a second?"

I was directed back and introduced to Sonoma who stood and shook my hand. She sat in her high desk chair and I sat in a low-slung vinyl contraption that brought me almost level with her. I explained that I was looking into Joanie Dove's death and wanted to ask some questions about her.

Sonoma was kind and forthcoming throughout my interview, and when I was done I'd learned precisely nothing. Saint Joan was a wonderful person, sweet and kind to a fault, and no amount of digging could change that.

I thanked Sonoma and left, walking out into a day that was as hot and dry as any in August, an amazing contrast to Kirkwood in the high mountains to the south.

As I drove away, I realized that I'd failed to find any connection between Joanie Dove and Jake Pooler. If their deaths were not accidental, it was going to be hard to establish motives that made any sense. A motive for Jake alone was easy enough. But Joanie was the opposite of Jake. It appeared there were as many people who loved Joanie as there were people who hated Jake.

I was just approaching Stateline when my phone rang.

"Owen?" a taut voice said when I answered. "This is Linda Saronna at the Forest Service." She sounded so tense it was as if someone had a gun to her head.

TWENTY-FIVE

"Hello, Linda," I said. "What is wrong?"

"I wondered if you could meet me," she said, ignoring my question.

"Certainly. At your office?"

"Uh, no. Could you come to my house this evening at eight?"

"Of course," I said. It was clear from her tone that she wasn't asking me for a date. "Linda, what's this about?"

"I'm not sure," she said. "But I might have some information about the arsonist."

"Do you suspect who this person is? If so, tell me now. This is too important to wait."

"I don't want to harm someone who may be innocent. We need to talk first. It's only a hunch, based on something I just heard."

"Where are you now?"

"I'm in Truckee." As she said it I heard road noises in the background, a car honking, the roar of a truck. "I was in the..." She suddenly stopped talking. When she resumed, her voice sounded perfunctory and business-like. "Can you, today? Good, because the burner keeps kicking out. Maybe it's the pilot or something. If I lose heat for just one night this time of year my pipes could freeze and burst. Let me give you directions. You know Windsor Shores on the way out toward Emerald Bay? Turn right at the sign and drive down toward the lake. There's a bunch of vacation homes scattered through the forest. A quarter mile in, you'll see mine on the right. It is a little green cabin with a green metal roof. Drive slow because it is tucked in under a thick stand of white firs and it's easy to cruise right on by without noticing. Okay? Thanks so much for your help." She hung up.

Someone must have suddenly appeared, someone Linda didn't want overhearing what she was saying to me. She said she was just "in" someplace. If I were to make up a scenario that would fit, I'd guess that she'd been in some building where she'd overheard something revealing. So she went outside and called me on her cell phone. As she spoke to me, the person came out and Linda switched gears so that the person in question wouldn't be aware.

As I drove home, I wondered what she could have overheard. I thought about the fire that killed Joanie Dove. Linda Saronna had been so distraught that day, even before we knew that a woman would die from the fire. Did Linda know Joanie? Or was it something else? Something she was afraid to talk about? Now she was calling me with a desire to talk. Maybe she'd been doing her own investigating in the mean time.

A disturbing thought intruded. Could Linda be the fire-starter? In many ways, she didn't fit. The psychologist had said that nearly all arsonists were men. But if she were, and if she didn't intend to kill Joanie Dove, that would explain her distress when the firemen carried Joanie Dove out from the fire.

One thing was for certain. Linda's stress was significant, palpable even over the phone. But I wouldn't find out more until eight this evening.

I pulled into Terry Drier's Fire Department, intending to ask him about his altercation with Jake. Before I could even come to a complete stop, he was out the door, jogging toward me. "Damn it, Owen, where have you been? Either I get no answer or your phone is busy."

"Sorry," I said. "What's wrong?"

"We got another note. This one came by fax, while I was out for lunch. Come in and take a look."

I left Spot in the Jeep and followed Terry inside.

The printing was the same as before, although slightly degraded by the fax transmission. There was nothing printed at the top where the sender's name and number normally appeared.

The message was short.

The next fire will be a test of
precision. Can I light a fire that
takes just three houses out of a bunch?

Terry was very agitated. "The phone company can trace this, right? You can get a court order or something and find out the telephone number it was sent from?"

"Yes," I said, studying the paper. "It can't hurt to know, but it won't tell us who the firestarter is. This guy is smart. He'd use a pay phone and hook up a laptop computer or something to send the fax."

"So what are you going to do?" Terry sounded exasperated with me, as if the fires were my fault. "We're paying you good money, and for what? Everything's gotten worse, and I can't even find you when I need you."

"I'm making good progress," I said. "There was one thing that came up, however, that you could help me with. Did you know Jake Pooler?"

"Like I told you before, I met him. But that was all." He glanced down for a moment.

"That's not what I heard at the High River Saloon in Truc-kee, Terry. Joe told me about you and Jake getting into a fisticuffs. In fact, Joe seems to clearly remember you threatening Jake, saying you were going to burn his ass." I sat down on the edge of Terry's desk. "Do you still not remember?"

Terry's jaw muscles flexed, relaxed, flexed again. He looked away. His voice was low and angry when he spoke. "We exchanged some words. Then the asshole sucker-punched me. I was up against the wall, trying to get some air. Next thing, all the guys on the Truc-kee FD are egging me on, saying Jake deserved to be laid out. So I went in swinging while I was still gasping for air." Terry looked out the window at the mountain above. "It was the most humiliating moment of my life. An old guy beating the crap out of me. I didn't mention it because I've been trying to forget about it ever since."

"What about Joanie Dove, Terry? Is there a humiliating moment with her that you've been trying to forget?"

Terry turned from the window and looked directly at me. "I'm sorry I wasn't forthcoming before, Owen. I am now. No, I've never met Joanie Dove. Never heard of her until her death in the Tallac Properties fire."

I believed it to be true even as I realized that he still could have lit the fire that killed her.

Terry and I spoke for another hour, going over every aspect of my investigation. I told him everything that I knew for a fact, but nothing that I had surmised, not the least of which was that he was one of my prime suspects. I also left out the phone call from Linda. Whatever it was that she was going to tell me was nothing I needed to speculate about with Terry. He'd know soon enough.

TWENTY-SIX

When it was time to go see Linda, I didn't want to take Spot as he'd already spent enough of the day in the car. I was afraid to leave him at my cabin, so that left Street as the obvious alternative.

Spot sat to my side as I knocked on her door.

I heard a noise and saw a darkening of the peephole. The door opened.

Spot wagged eagerly at the sight of Street. Yet he remained sitting, his tail sweeping her doorstep clean.

"Pardon me, ma'am. I'm wondering if you'd be willing to take in a homeless dog. Just temporarily, of course."

Street pretended to look around before seeing Spot. "Oh, you mean this little cutie?" Street grabbed his jowls with both hands, pulled them out like wings and steered his head back and forth. "Look, he's a fighter bomber!"

Spot wagged harder.

Street let go of his lips, took his ears and bent them over like a broken nun's cap.

"Now he looks just like the Flying Nun!" She leaned forward and hugged Spot, their heads side by side like dancers. "Okay, your largeness, give me a pooch smooch. Now let's you and me go inside and watch a Father Knows Best rerun or something."

She turned, pulling on Spot's collar and led him in.

I followed them in and explained that I was going to see Linda Saronna from the Forest Service and would be back soon. We kissed and said goodbye.

It was dark by the time I got around the south end of the lake and headed back north toward Emerald Bay.

Just past Camp Richardson my phone rang.

"Owen!" Terry Drier said without identifying himself. "We've got a fire report! In the forest near Cascade Lake. Just south of Emerald Bay!"

"Can you be more specific? I'm right nearby."

"The call came from a house in Windsor Shores. A man said he could see big flames through the trees."

"I'll be there in a minute," I said.

I hung up just as the wail of a siren reached my ears from somewhere down the road behind me. The engine roared as I floored it. My Jeep has auxiliary headlights. I flipped them on and punched up the high beams. When the Baldwin Beach entrance flashed by, I hit the brakes, slowing for the steep upcoming curves. The tires screamed as I cranked into the turns going twice the limit. In a few moments the Windsor Shores sign appeared suddenly in the dark and I half slid into the entrance, wheels spinning. My headlights lit up a wide swath of black forest and I shot down the narrow road, bouncing and slamming over ruts and potholes. As I came around the first turn my gut clenched. Up ahead, beyond my headlight beams, the forest was making its own light.

A distant orange glow made silhouettes of the trees. The glow turned brighter and more yellow as I got closer. Then the yellow turned into a distinct wall of flames. I heard the roar of fire wind over my engine.

Suddenly, I was at the fire. I stomped on the brakes and jerked off to the side of the road.

Not far in front of me was an inferno. It engulfed a hundred foot swath of forest. Directly in front of the advancing flames was a small green house with a green metal roof.

TWENTY-SEVEN

I jumped out of the Jeep and ran toward the house.

The heat was searing. I lifted the front of my windbreaker up and held it in front of my face.

"Linda!" I yelled as I plunged closer to the house and the wall of fire just behind it. "Linda!"

My voice was impotent against the roar of the flames. The forest cracked and spit under the assault. Flaming debris rained down around me. Bits of smoldering wood left arcing smoke trails as they curved to the ground like fireworks.

The back of the tiny house was in flames as I reached the front. Shaded somewhat from the flames, the heat was less intense. I dropped the jacket fabric from my face and tried the door. It was locked.

Although I knew that an oxygen-starved fire could explode when a source of air reaches it, I didn't hesitate to raise my leg and kick in the door.

Black smoke gushed out as the door flew in against an inside wall.

"Linda!" I yelled again, as I dropped to my hands and knees. The smoke was still thick and I dropped onto my belly and put my nose and lips to the floor. There, the in-rushing air from the open door kept the smoke away and I was able to take a breath. "Linda!" I kept yelling as I belly-crawled through the smoke-thick living room. I couldn't see where I was going, nor could I get a sense of the house layout. But I knew that there were back rooms already on fire. If Linda was in one of them...

I hit a wall, and, nose and lips still to the floor, I turned left thinking there had to be a doorway nearby. Some firelight was coming in through a window, but the smoke was so heavy it was nearly black inside.

I ran my fingers along the wall as I crawled. They soon hit some moulding that ran vertically. A door frame. In it, a closed door.

I sucked a breath off the floor, stood and groped for the doorknob. Without thinking, I grabbed onto it. The pain from the hot metal was like electricity. I jerked away. Then, still holding my breath in the sea of smoke, I kicked the door in.

It broke far more easily than the front door. The door slammed open, hit something and bounced back.

I was yelling Linda's name when the room exploded.

TWENTY-EIGHT

I didn't know where I was.

It was dark, but orange light flickered somewhere. After a minute I figured out that I was lying on my back. Sirens screamed. Truck engines roared. From several directions came the sound of men yelling. I tried to turn and look but my face seemed plastered against a tree trunk.

What was I doing here?

My body felt on fire. I looked down without moving my head. I wasn't burning, but some coals glowed red on my jacket. I tried to brush them off, but couldn't manage the coordination. I rolled my eyes the other way. The nearby trees were on fire. I forced my eyes to turn further. There was a little house in the woods. It, too, was on fire. One side of the house had broken off and sagged down like a fiery lean-to. I tried to turn away, but I couldn't make anything move. I turned my eyes a different direction.

Lying in the woods next to me was a door. It burned with a yellow flame that was bright against the dark soil.

Someone grabbed my arm and started dragging me. Parts of me hurt as I bounced over rocks and roots. Other parts of me were numb. Two men ran up and set a stretcher down on the ground. One took my head and shoulders, another my feet. A third stood over me, straddling my middle. He reached down and looped his hand through my belt. Somebody shouted.

"Ready? One! Two! Three!"

In one smooth motion, they lifted me onto the stretcher. In moments I was in an ambulance, and it bounced and lurched away.

I tried to speak to the attendant next to me, but my mouth wouldn't make the words. I worked at it, concentrated on making my lips move. He sat there, a concerned look on his face, as I tried to talk.

But no words came out. If the attendant smelled the burning flesh, he just assumed it was flesh already burned, not burning still. He didn't know that a coal had burned through my clothing and was now burning into the flesh of my stomach.

The pain concentrated my mind. I remembered the time I accidentally flicked a piece of glowing charcoal into the top of my shoe. This pain was much worse. I could think of nothing else. I couldn't even try to remember why I might have been in the middle of a forest fire. My only focus was my belly flesh, burning away under the insistent glowing coal which was lost under my layers of clothing. I concentrated on that coal until I passed out.

TWENTY-NINE

I awoke in a hospital bed.

For a long time I lay still, reconstructing what I remembered, trying to imagine what I did not. I had a lot of room to imagine because what I remembered wasn't much more than my name.

People moved about in the hallway. I saw a policeman standing guard. It was light out my window. Then it was dark. Sleep came and went. I couldn't place the intervals. I couldn't place the day. Now and then a nurse would come and do things to the tubes. One time, she noticed that my eyes were open. She left and I heard her talking to someone else. A doctor came in and poked at me here and there. He shined a light in my eyes and ignored me when I tried to express my displeasure. But with no words coming out of my mouth I couldn't expect him to pay attention.

At one point I awoke to see Diamond staring down at me.

"Yo, gringo," he said. "You talking yet?"

"Meh...be," I said. The word was almost unintelligible, but he smiled.

"You've been out two days.'Bout time you start talking. We've got questions."

"Pro...bly," I mumbled. I then attempted to rattle off a veritable torrent of words, not one of which Diamond understood.

"Hey, look, buddy," Diamond said, leaning in close. "Doc says you ain't got a stroke or nothing else serious. Just a real bad concussion. I guess the explosion basically knocked your brain senseless, but they expect a good recovery."

I could see that Diamond thought he might be talking to a vegetable, but he was giving me the benefit of the doubt.

"Besides your head being knocked silly," he continued, "you're going to have a macho scar on your stomach. Seems a coal got on your belly and tried to burn its way to China. Doc said they had to cut out some flesh and pull you back together with twenty pound test. Anyway, take care of your head and it won't be long before you're back to your normal perspicacity."

I tried to repeat his big word, but it came out like perspiration.

"You get your rehab butt in gear, Yankee. I'll be back manana."

When Diamond left I could tell he'd decided my brain was fried. He had no clue that I could actually think a little bit. What I couldn't do was talk. My verbal center was down for the count. I couldn't put my thoughts into clear words. And even if I could have, I couldn't get my mouth around them.

What scared me, though, wasn't the way Diamond reacted to what was wrong with me, but something else in his face. I worked on it for awhile, coming up with some vaguely disturbing scenarios, but it was then I realized that not only couldn't I talk, but I couldn't track my thoughts, either. All of my 'what if' scenarios turned into something more like cartoons than real life. Eventually, I went to sleep, aided, probably, by one of the drugs they were slipping into my IV.

By the following morning I'd improved dramatically. My thinking was only somewhat muddled, and my speech was mostly clear. Nevertheless, I couldn't simply talk, but instead had to think about each word as I said it.

Diamond came back just as I finished nibbling at my first solid food since the explosion. He sat down on the edge of the bed. Intense concern made worry lines where his brown skin used to be smooth.

"Morning," I said with only a slight thickness to my speech. I'd been secretly practicing.

"Your brain back?"

"Yes. It sort of was yesterday." I spoke very slowly, forming each word with care. They still came out slurred as if the dentist had shot me full of Novocaine. "I just have trouble talking."

"Good. Keep you from yakking my ear off."

"Right," I said. "I can tell something bad happened besides the fire. Did Linda die?"

Diamond bit his lip. "We found her remains in the bedroom you tried to bust into. She was on the bed. Funny place to be when your house burns up in the middle of the evening. Especially when the house was overloaded with smoke detectors, including one in the bedroom. More than one person said they have personally heard Linda say that she puts fresh batteries in them every six months and never waits until they start beeping. Seven smoke detectors in a five room house. And there was general agreement that Linda was not a nap taker."

"So why did she die in her bedroom?" I asked, working through the sentence with care.

"Don't know. Forensics might have something in another day. Meanwhile, tell me if we've figured this out. You were going to see Linda, right?"

I nodded. "She said she had something to tell me. Something she heard about the arsonist."

"That's what we thought," Diamond said. "Explains why you were in the vicinity when the fire broke out. Next question. You saw the fire and kicked in the front door. The house was already on fire, but you went in. Not finding Linda, you kicked in the bedroom door. It opened fast, hit the wall or something and bounced back at you just before the explosion. Am I right?"

"I'm a little vague, but that fits from what I remember. How did you figure it?"

"The bedroom was superheated from the fire," Diamond said, "ready to burst into flames. But because the walls were still intact, the room was oxygen starved and hence no fire. When you kicked in the door, the rush of oxygen made the room explode." Diamond shook his head as he looked down at me on the bed.

He continued, "Having the bedroom door bounce back saved your life. It took the brunt of the explosion which drove the door and you out through the front picture window and beyond the burning house. It was an old house and it had solid doors. If the bedroom door had been a hollow core, you'd be history. Even so, the door had a dented imprint of your arm and shoulder and head."

"Did the fire burn three houses like the note said?" I asked, forming the words carefully.

Diamond nodded. "Six or seven in the vicinity, but only three burned. Guy knows what he's doing." Diamond's tone was depressed, his face somber.

"Linda's death is worrying you," I said.

"No, it has to do with Street."

"Which was going to be my next question. Have I been unconscious every time she's visited or what?"

"As far as I know, she hasn't visited." Diamond leaned forward and put his hand on my forearm. "I haven't seen her anywhere. Was she going on a trip or something?"

"No. She's at her condo taking care of Spot," I said. But as I said it, I felt confused, trying to remember how I'd left things before the fire and not being able to come up with a clear memory.

"She's not at her condo," Diamond said.

"What do you mean? You've checked?"

"Yes. After your accident I went to get her. Spot was locked inside, but Street was gone."

"You went inside," I said, a numbness creeping into my psyche.

"Yes. I had to force the lock. Lucky for me, Spot knows who I am. I left him there the first night. Then I took him home to your cabin."

"You've checked Street's lab?"

"Yes. She hasn't shown up the last three days. I also talked to all of her neighbors. No one has seen her.

"Did you call Glennie at the paper?"

He nodded.

A powerful wave of nausea swept over me. "Where do you think she is?"

Diamond looked at me intensely. His black eyes were moist at the corners. "It's only supposition at this point, Owen. But I'm afraid she might have been kidnapped by the arsonist."

THIRTY

I was stunned.

A tidal wave rose unannounced from the depths, breached the breakwater, slammed up against the castle and ripped out the foundation. I struggled to breathe, the flood choking me, my entire life lost in the torrent. My mouth opened and closed silently, then again as if the movement would bring me sweet air. Or sustenance. Or some revelation that it was all wrong, that Street was coming down the hospital hallway, about to turn the corner and come into my room, her smile glowing, her sparkling eyes crinkled against her own high wattage.

But Street didn't appear and I couldn't get air and the tidal wave was sweeping me out to sea.

I realized that Diamond was talking. "I checked your office and cabin," he said, "and it was the same. No sign of Street. And no note. No message on the machine at your office. You still don't have an answering machine at home, correct? I looked around, but I didn't see one."

I was reeling. I shut my eyes against the pain.

"Is there any chance that Street might have suddenly left?" Diamond asked. "Maybe to visit a friend? Something comes up and she decides to split and call you later?"

I struggled to come to the surface. I worked my mouth to answer Diamond's question. "No," I said. "She was staying with Spot. The farthest she'd go would be to step outside to the barbecue or something. She knew Spot was in potential danger. She wouldn't have left him."

As I said it, I realized the incredible oversight I'd made. If the killer wanted to get to me through Spot, it would be a thousand times more effective to target Street instead. And if I wanted to protect Street, my first impulse would be to leave Spot with her and tell her to keep him at her side at all times whether she was inside her condo, answering the door or out on her deck. Instead, I had focused on protecting Spot. Street had probably gone outside to investigate a sound and carefully locked Spot in behind her!

My brain pounded with pain. I'd been so stupid!

Rage coursed through me. I turned toward the wall, away from Diamond, away from the world.

A killer had sneaked into my most private, special place, a personal world I shared with Street and no one else. A universe of love and comfort and understanding where no thoughts were too secret to confide, no fears too large to discuss and no triumphs were too small to celebrate. The killer had taken her, taken the only person in the world I lived for.

I turned back toward Diamond. His eyes showed worry as I laboriously sat up and swung my feet out of bed. He put out his hands as I inched forward on the edge of the bed, gathered weight on my feet and slowly stood up, rising well above him. My clothes were hanging in a little half-closet. I untied my gown and let it drop to the floor as I reached for my clothes.

Diamond was already out the door, grabbing a nurse as she walked by. She turned, saw me in my nakedness and gave a little scream. The policeman who had been guarding me came in and tried to reason with me.

I ignored him.

Moving at my fastest was moving very slowly. Even so, I was most of the way dressed when Diamond came back with three people in white coats, one probably a doctor and the other two nurses.

They made lots of protest and scurried about. Diamond spoke on his mobile phone. A nurse stuck her head out of the hospital room and yelled at someone down the hall. The policeman stayed back, his arms held out like a gorilla. But he let the others make the commotion. Even though we were in his town and Diamond was a mere sheriff's deputy from another state, he deferred to Diamond.

At one point the one who acted like a doctor even held her hand out in front of me, then realized the folly of it. The other nurse stepped forward, but then he, too, stopped. There are advantages to being a half foot taller than anyone else in the room.

When I finished dressing, I realized what was missing. I turned to the doctor. "My gun," I said.

The doctor turned and looked at the nurses. They all acted like they didn't know what I was talking about. I took a step toward the doctor. "Get it now, please."

The policeman stepped forward and spoke to Diamond. "Shall I stop him, sir?"

Diamond made a guffawing noise in the back of his throat. "You wish." Diamond turned to me and put his hand on my arm. "Owen, you don't have a gun, remember?"

I shut my eyes, the rage and confusion overwhelming. How many years had it been?

Diamond directed me out of the room and led me to the parking lot.

THIRTY-ONE

As I walked out to the hospital parking lot I realized I'd left my Jeep near Linda Saronna's house. Yet there it was, at the end of the second row. Diamond must have arranged for it to be brought over.

My first stop was Street's condo.

I pushed past the crime scene tape and let myself in.

I did a poor job of searching for evidence, shocked as I was with the enormity of what had likely happened. Nevertheless, I satisfied myself that Diamond's idea of the events was close to the mark. Street had no doubt answered the door and left Spot inside to protect him. There was no sign of a struggle, so she must have felt comfortable enough to step out on the porch and close the door behind her.

Maybe she even knew the kidnapper.

Again, I chastised myself for such stupidity. It was my fault.

I left and drove up the mountain to my cabin.

Spot was glad to see me, but still morose. He sniffed me everywhere, no doubt trying to determine what the hospital smells were all about. I didn't pay him much attention. Then he lost interest and lay down on the rug in front of the wood stove.

My first call was to Glennie.

"Owen!" she nearly yelled. "My God, I was so worried! I came by the hospital to see you, but they had an armed police guard who wouldn't let me in! Are you okay? We heard that poor woman's house exploded when you were inside!"

Something about her enthusiasm raised a little red flag in the back of my mind.

Could Glennie be lighting the fires in order to get exciting scoops for the paper?

For that matter, could she have kidnapped Street because of jealousy over my affections?

"I'm okay," I said carefully. "Glennie, I need a favor."

"Of course. Anything you want."

"Can you see what photos you can find of the fires? I'd like to see both those taken by reporters as well as any taken by bystanders. I thought you could run a little notice in the paper asking for fire photos."

"Consider it done. I'll put it in tomorrow's edition. Is there anything else I can do?"

I realized that she had no idea Street had been kidnapped, assuming, that is, that Glennie was innocent. There didn't seem to be any point in bringing it up now. "No thanks, Glennie," I said.

I looked up the number for Jake Pooler Construction and got tight-faced Betty on the first ring.

"Betty," I said slowly, forming my speech with as much precision as possible. "This is Owen McKenna."

"Oh, hi, Mr. McKenna!" Her voice was as cheery as a game show host. "Is something wrong? You sound kind of, I don't know, bedraggled."

"I am," I said. "Tell me, Betty. Have they found Jake's truck yet?"

"No. Not that I ever heard."

"Has Winton come in?"

"No. And let me tell you, that boy is going to get an earful when..."

"Thanks, Betty," I said, and hung up.

Spot and I were at Winton Berger's cabin on the north shore sixty minutes later.

I left Spot in the Jeep as I had a bad feeling about what was to come and I didn't want him in harm's way.

Winton's front door was shut and there was no sign of any lights in the windows. Nevertheless, a TV or radio was broadcasting a game, so I knocked loudly. No one in a building that small could have missed it, yet there was no response.

I knocked again, louder still.

"Get outta here!" a drunken voice yelled.

"Winton!" I yelled back. "It's Owen McKenna. We need to talk."

"Fuck you! I'm busy!"

"Winton!" I called through the closed door, "you can talk to me or talk to the police. What'll it be?"

There was no response. The game boomed through the cabin walls and into the forest. I pounded on the door again, hard enough to make the wood crack.

I was about to turn to walk around the back side of the cabin when the door jerked inward an inch, slamming against the chain. A rifle barrel jabbed out of the dark opening, eighteen inches of blued steel that angled up and nearly touched my chin. I paused, leaned back a few inches and saw a dark hole smaller than a pencil.

.22 caliber.

"Listen up, Mr. Beanstalk! A man's cabin is his castle! Now get your ass outta here before I shoot it off!"

The rifle wavered to my right. I leaned to the left, grabbed the barrel and jerked the rifle out of the door opening.

"Ouch! Goddamn you!" he screamed, then slammed the door. The lock clicked shut.

I slid the rifle's bolt action, ejected the round and put it in my pocket. From inside the cabin came the sound of soft, fast footsteps. I set the rifle down on the front step and ran around the cabin. A movement caught my eye in the forest beyond.

Winton was running through the trees.

I tried to sprint after him, but my body still felt broken. Why had I left Spot in the Jeep!

The skinny kid could run like a mountain cat. He easily out-distanced me and disappeared in the trees.

I was about to give up when I heard the roar of an engine. I ran toward the sound, ducking low branches and rushing around trees and was rewarded with the sight of Winton driving away, tires kicking up dirt and rocks as he fishtailed away up an old logging road.

His vehicle was huge and white and shiny, with dual rear wheels.

Jake's pickup.

He flashed up the mountain and disappeared.

THIRTY-TWO

I ran back past Winton's cabin, picking up the rifle from where I'd left it by the door. I threw it in the back of the Jeep so I could have the ballistics lab check it for similarities to the slug that was taken out of Pussy Cat.

The driveway to Winton's cabin was a dirt patch among widely-spaced trees, and I spun my wheels as I shot into the woods. It took a minute to find the place where Winton had parked Jake's truck. The tracks he'd left were clear abrasions in the dirt and I was able to follow them, bouncing and shaking, over the rough terrain that led up the slope above the cabins and the highway.

After a mile the dirt trail came to another, bigger road, probably a logging road from years past. It had a rocky surface that did not show his tracks. I assumed that Winton would want to avoid going farther up the mountain because he might come to a dead end and he would be trapped. So I turned to follow the logging road down the mountain and was back at the north shore highway in a few minutes. There was no sign of Winton and I knew I'd lost him.

I was about to drive back to Winton's cabin and search it when my phone rang. It was Terry Drier saying they'd just gotten another fax. I decided that Winton's cabin could wait.

Terry handed the fax to me the moment I walked in the door of his station.

Now that Detective Owen is conscious,

he should know that I have Street Casey.
Wow, what a little fighter that girl is!
It took some work, but I convinced her to
give me some information that would
make you believe this kidnapping is for real.
She said that not long ago she talked about
bugs named Achorutes Nivcolas. How's
that for specific information?
The next fire will be the blowup you've all
been waiting for. It will take out over eighty houses.
P.S. This isn't about ransom. This is about
punishment. Street will be in one of the houses.

My head felt about to explode.

This was the first time anyone had harmed Street since I'd
known her.

Because of me!

Street's kidnapping was worse than the kid at the Wells
Fargo Bank. It blew out my rational fuses, burned through my logic
circuits.

Justice was no longer some concept handed down from the
Magna Carta. Justice had morphed into a singular vision – Owen's
Jurisprudence – a vision that put my hands on the kidnapper.

I'd break the long heavy bones first just to hear the sounds,
deep and loud. Next, I'd work over the soft tissues, organ damage
being particularly painful. Finally, I would seize the neck. There
were seven cervical vertebrae. How many could I grind into pow-
der before he expired?

I turned toward Terry, wondering if these notes didn't just
come to him, but from him as well. He must have seen something
in my eyes or in the clenching of my fists, for he stepped back.

"Owen? You okay? You need a soda or something?" As he
spoke, he maneuvered slightly closer toward his office door.

I thought also of Winton. He might not have been drunk
like I thought. It would have been easy for him to get the note faxed
after he drove away in Jake's truck. The note could even have been

pre-written. Winton might have been waiting until he knew I was conscious and out of the hospital.

"Owen?" Terry said again, a worried look on his face.

"Yeah," I said. "I'm okay."

"I know it's upsetting," Terry said. "Anything we can do to help you on this, just let me know."

"Thanks."

I left and called Diamond, filling him in on my encounter with Winton as well as the latest fax.

Later, my evening blurred into a tormented night, crazed sleeplessness mixing with demented dreams.

The next morning Diamond stopped by my cabin. "First thing I did as soon as I saw the fax was call the FBI. They're hard to interest when we have nothing but a missing persons report. But when we get hard evidence of a federal crime, they start acting like grown-ups. Special Agent Ramos says he'll be wanting a full interview with you."

"Fellow Mex?"

"More gringo than Mex from what I can tell. Talks like he was born in America, and I heard he got his law degree at an Ivy League school. He looks at me like I still got cabbage stains on my shoes." Diamond looked down and cocked his shoe. "Then again, maybe I do. Anyway, he's probably a good guy to have helping to look for Street."

I stared out at the lake and the mountains beyond. The hot weather had melted nearly all of the snow from the storm, even at the higher elevations. The only white patches I could see were a few places on northeast-facing peaks, snowfields that often existed year-round.

The distances across the lake were too great to see any houses. But the south end was where the most significant groupings of houses were and hence the likeliest places where the arsonist would set the next fire. Street could be in anyone of them. Even if we had a carte blanche search warrant, it would be impossible to search even one percent of them in the next day or two. And all the other fires had come soon after the notes were delivered or faxed. The time to save Street was nearly gone.

"We also got the forensics back on Linda Saronna," Diamond said.

"Any direct evidence of murder? Or is this like Jake Pooler and Joanie Dove, another supposed accident?"

"This one is definitely murder," Diamond said. "The coroner determined cause of death to be smoke inhalation."

"Like Joanie Dove."

"Right. But Ms. Saronna had contusions on both wrists and one ankle. They were deep enough to have survived the charring of the fire. The ulna bone on her right arm also showed marks."

"Meaning?"

"Ligatures. She was tied to the bed. She fought the ropes so hard that she produced bruising down to the bone. It could eventually help us to convict the killer. Sometimes victims do that. The ones that struggle the hardest leave behind the most evidence."

"What was she tied with?"

"They're not sure. I don't know the technicalities, but apparently synthetic polymers like nylon leave certain traces when they burn, and no such traces were found. So that rules out standard climbing ropes and water-ski ropes both of which are common up here in Tahoe. The best guess is that it was probably a cotton rope. The charred remains would then be hard to distinguish from her clothes which, according to her colleagues, were all cotton."

After Diamond left I thought it best to start learning what I could about Linda Saronna. If it was just another accidental death or a thrill-killing as George the psychologist thought, then learning about her would do little good. But there was still the chance it was murder with a purpose, in which case having a third victim multiplied my chances of finding some connection between the killings. Furthermore, any information could bring me closer to Street's kidnapper.

I thought it would be easiest to start at Linda's work. I took Spot with me and drove to the Forest Service.

Inside, the secretary was red-eyed and wiped her nose as I approached.

"I'd like to speak to Frederick, please. My name is..."

"Owen McKenna," she interrupted. "We all know you now that the news talks about you every day." She sniffled. "I'm so sorry about Street Casey. I hope you find her soon." She picked up the phone and punched some numbers. "Frederick? Owen McKenna is here to see you."

Frederick came out in a few seconds. He, too, was red-eyed. He no longer looked like the clean-cut young man with lots of energy and enthusiasm. Instead, he looked beaten down and enormously sad. "Come on back, Owen. We can talk at my desk."

His office was a cubicle made out of carpeted panels five feet high. When we both sat down, our knees nearly touched.

"Sorry for the melancholy atmosphere. The last few days have been pretty rough for all of us here. Linda was like a mother to me and to most of the crew as well. And today when Patty Sherman told us how Linda died – Patty's brother knew because he is a policeman – that did us in all over again." He pulled a Kleenex from a box and blew. "I heard you were hurt pretty bad trying to help Linda."

"I'm better now."

"I'm real sorry about your girlfriend. Any news?"

I shook my head. "What I came here for is information about Linda. General stuff that you might know as well as anyone."

"You mean her job? Or her personality?"

"Anything you can think of. What she did, talked about, her loves, her family, friends, where she went on vacation."

Frederick nodded. "I don't know where to start."

"Start when you first met her. Your impressions then and now. Anything that comes to mind."

He thought a moment. "Linda was one of those good, honest people who would tell you exactly what she thought. Sometimes it could be a little harsh when she critiqued you, but she always did it gently and without any meanness whatsoever. She was just frank. And sometimes her frankness could be really funny."

"How do you mean?"

"Like after a meeting with the Tahoe Regional Planning Agency she'd say, 'old so and so is so stiff I bet he hasn't been laid in six months.' Or she'd say that watching environmentalists trying to save the forests is like watching Nineteenth Century barbers pulling teeth. The cure is worse than the disease."

Frederick talked about Linda Saronna for twenty minutes. He sketched in detail a dedicated career woman with few friends, a woman whose passion was the forest in general, first, and Lake Tahoe forests, second. A woman whose idea of a vacation was fly fishing in remote forests of Northern California like those near Mt. Shasta. She gave herself to everyone at work but not, apparently, to her two ex-husbands.

I interrupted at that point. "She was married twice?"

"From what I've heard, yes," Frederick said.

"Do you know how long ago?"

"Not really. When she was in her twenties, I think. My sense is that neither marriage lasted more than a couple years. But I don't think there was any animosity there. She remained friendly with at least one of her ex-husbands. They sounded like good friends."

"Any kids?"

"No. But she loved kids. I guess she took in a foster kid some years back."

That got my attention. *My first connection between two of the three fire victims.* "Do you know anything about the child?"

"No. That was long before I got here."

"Did Linda ever talk about the kid?"

"No. I only remember one comment. She had a dog a few years ago, when I first started. Some terrier/schnauzer mix that she'd rescued from the pound. She was trying to give it away right after she hired me. I asked her about the dog thinking maybe I'd take it. She said no way she'd give it to me, that it was a bad dog. I said how bad, and she replied, 'you want to know how bad this dog is? I'll tell you. This dog is so bad he makes even my foster kid seem nice.'" Frederick paused. "Are you thinking her foster kid might be the arsonist?"

"I don't know, Frederick. I'm just trying to learn as much as I can."

"I suppose you could ask Sheila. She's been here the longest, even longer than Linda was. She may remember more."

"Is she here?"

"I think so. Let me check." He got her on his phone. "Sheila? Are you free for a few minutes? I want to introduce someone to you. Be there in a sec."

Frederick brought me to a corner office similar to the one Linda had occupied. He introduced me to Sheila, a large, beautiful black woman with clear rich skin the color of Hawaiian Koa wood. As with the Mexicans, it was a lift to my spirits at seeing Sheila adding some color to a community as white-bread as Tahoe.

Sheila gestured me into one of the chairs at the side of her desk. She turned, leaned her elbows on skirted knees and spoke to me, her black eyes moist and warm. "I've heard of you, Mr. McKenna. I'm so sorry about your lady friend being kidnapped. And I want you to know that we're all grateful about the way you tried to save Linda. What can I help you with?"

"I'm investigating the fires and Frederick just told me that Linda Saronna took in a foster child some years back. I'm wondering if you can tell me anything about the kid."

"I'm afraid I can't be very helpful. I only met him once or twice. His name was Tommy. I forget his last name. Or maybe I never knew. He lived with Linda for two, two and a half years. Tommy was around twelve. And this was maybe twelve years ago. He was a problem child, always in trouble at school. He got suspended a couple of times during the period he lived with Linda. But Linda loved him very much, tried everything. And even though the State of California is supposed to pay all expenses, she brought in two or three therapists at her own expense. I asked her about it once. I was worried she was spending her entire salary on counseling for the boy. But she wouldn't hear of it. She said that if you knew the child's history you would justify any expense."

"Can you tell me what Tommy looked like?"

"Skinny. Long, brown hair, always in his face. He had terrible posture, stood so bent it was like he was about to break in half. I remember thinking at the time that he looked like a troublemaker."

"Sheila, do you know if Linda kept any photos of Tommy here at work? I realize it was a long time ago, but maybe there would be something tucked away in her desk?"

Sheila smiled and shook her head. "I went through her desk just yesterday, looking for a Planning Commission report that she wanted me to work on. I looked everywhere before I found it in the secretary's file. I'm sure I would have noticed any photos of Tommy."

I stood to leave and Sheila stood as well.

"May I ask what you do here at the Forest Service?"

Sheila smiled. "Oh, I'm sort of the stage manager behind the scenes, making sure all the props for the magic tricks are in place."

"You've been here a long time?"

"Twenty years. Longest of anyone. They offered me Linda's job before she came, but I declined. I don't like spotlights and center stage comes with all the responsibility. I prefer to work the curtain ropes and such. I'm very happy being number two. I just hope that when they find a new number one that he or she is even half as good to us as Linda was."

"Thanks so much, Sheila," I said as I left.

I felt torn in two by the stress, half of me ready to give in to terminal sadness, the other half ready to go to war. One thing was for certain: if the second half of me was still primed when I found out who had Street, no amount of legal maneuvering would save his sorry ass to enjoy a legal execution.

THIRTY-THREE

Spot ignored me on the ride home. I tried to be nice to him, but I think he sensed that Street had disappeared from his life. Having that happen on top of me disappearing for days and his earlier mistreatment over Pussy Cat made him permanently melancholy. He lay in the corner of the cabin and wouldn't budge even when a moth landed on his head.

Meanwhile, I tried to see the murderer as a problem foster kid named Tommy who grew up and killed his foster mother in revenge for perceived misdeeds. Or, killed both foster moms if, as I suspected, Tommy had lived with Joanie Dove in Sacramento before being assigned to Linda Saronna.

The logical next inquiry would be to go through the foster agencies and see if Tommy had ever lived with Joanie Dove. But it would probably take days to get through the privacy rules that the agencies adhere to. I thought I would first try Joanie's sister, Lydia Mortensen. She might remember if Joanie had a foster child named Tommy. She might even have pictures of Joanie's foster kids, pictures that I could show to Sheila and see if she recognized any of them as Tommy.

I'd written her number down the last time I called her.

"Mrs. Mortensen," I said after I'd identified myself over the phone. "You met most of Joanie's foster kids, didn't you?"

"Yes, certainly. I think I knew them all."

"Were any of them boys?"

"Half or more, as I recall."

"Do you remember any of their names?" I asked, not wanting to say the name Tommy in case her memory was suggestible.

"Well, now, let me see. There was William, of course. I'll never forget him because he got so mad once when I called him Billy. 'My name is William!' he yelled at me. Imagine that, a little boy of four or five yelling at me like that!

"And then there were the twins, Tim and Tom. There was also..."

"Mrs. Mortensen," I interrupted. "The boy named Tom. Did people call him Tommy?"

"Oh, no, that would have been too confusing. We all were careful to call him Tom."

"I don't understand why it would be confusing," I said.

"Because of the other Tommy."

"There was a second Tom?"

"Yes. He was older than the twins."

"How old?"

"Well, let me think," Lydia Mortensen said. "He wasn't in middle school yet. I remember because where Joanie lived the middle school was just down the block. But Tommy was still taking the bus to grade school. So I suppose he was nine or ten."

"Do you remember how long ago this was?"

"Oh, dear. Besides the twins, he was her last foster child. A very difficult boy. Headstrong and surly, always blaming the world for what happened. I know Joanie loved him, but she couldn't handle him."

She hadn't answered my question, so I tried again. "How long ago was this?"

"Well, it wasn't long after the agency relocated Tommy that the twins Tim and Tom went back to their natural mother who had gotten out of some kind of drug rehab. Joanie was without kids for the first time in years. I guess it was about fourteen or fifteen years ago that she had Tommy."

"Did Joanie ever take pictures of the kids?"

"Yes! She always had a camera going. Whenever I visited her house during those years chances were there'd be a flashbulb going off in my face at some point."

"Where might I find some of those pictures?"

"Mr. McKenna, I'm so sorry. They burned up in the fire. Joanie kept all her photos in a toy box in the bedroom closet. She pulled it out often. It was red with a gold latch. She called it her treasure box."

"Did she give any of the photos to you or anyone else?" I asked.

"No. Joanie never did that for some reason. But it fits with her personality. She was very interested in everyone else, but she didn't think anyone would be interested in her life. In fact, the only photo I have of any of her kids was one of Joanie and Suzanne. Suzanne was my favorite of all her foster kids. Like a niece to me. God, I cried when she went off to college in Florida."

"Mrs. Mortensen, you say that Tommy blamed the world for what happened. What was it that happened?"

"Actually, I never knew the details but Joanie said he was orphaned in the Freel Fire. I always remembered the sound of the words. Oh, my! Now that I've said it, I'm realizing for the first time what it means. I haven't thought of it in years. Do you suppose that maybe he grew up and..." She stopped talking for a moment. "But it doesn't seem like something he would do. He was a willful boy, as I remember. But I can't see him lighting fires. Even so, it is a disturbing thought, isn't it, Mr. McKenna?"

"Yes, it is." I was thinking of the words, Freel Fire. "Do you think Joanie meant the Freel Peak Fire?"

"I'm not sure," Lydia Mortensen said. "But when Joanie referred to the Freel Fire it certainly sounded like a family name."

"Can you describe the boy?" I asked.

"Well, it was an awfully long time ago. He was, you know, a typical boy. Ran around a lot. Always throwing or kicking something. He made lots of noise."

"You mean he was verbally loud?"

"No, more like he took up a lot of space for a skinny kid. Physical space. Psychic space. He was a demanding child, somewhat sullen, definitely not happy. And he wet the bed. It always sounds like a small thing. But let me assure you, Joanie found it very difficult."

"What did he look like?"

"Like I said, he was skinny. He had brown hair like a mop almost. It went in every direction. And there was something in his eyes I didn't trust."

"Thanks, Mrs. Mortensen."

My next call was to Jake Pooler's secretary, Betty Williamson.

"Betty, do you know anything about Winton's childhood?"

"Why, no. I don't know anything about Winton's personal life. Why do you ask?"

"Did he ever mention parents or siblings?"

"No, I don't think so."

"What about holidays? Did he say where he was going for Christmas or Thanksgiving?"

"As far as I remember, if Winton wanted to celebrate any holiday, he would get together with his friends and drink beer."

"Can you think of any of their names? Someone who knew Winton?"

"Just that girl that he saw for awhile."

"His girlfriend?"

"Used to be," Betty said. "Before Jake got to her."

"What is her name?"

"Rosie. I don't think I ever knew her last name. You could check at the Truckee Gift Company, the little shop where she works."

Not wanting to call and possibly scare Rosie away, Spot and I drove up to Truckee and found the Truckee Gift Company on a side street lined with tiny boutique shops. I decided to take Spot with me to the store as he can be a real ice-breaker with women.

When I got to the store, a plain young woman with half a dozen earrings in one ear and little stud in one nostril was standing behind a small counter. She was pricing candles that were shaped like fir trees. She had straight stringy hair tucked behind her ears and wore an olive dress that looked like it was made of old paper.

"Excuse me, are you Rosie?" I said as I stepped into the doorway.

She looked up and her eyes immediately went to Spot who was standing at my side. When I want to be certain he doesn't scare anybody I keep my fingers in his collar, no leash necessary because of his height.

"Yes?" Rosie said, glancing at me, then looking back to my dog.

I decided my official investigator status would intimidate Rosie so I said, "I'm from Jake Pooler Construction. Betty Williamson and I have been worried about Winton Berger because he hasn't shown up at work or called. Betty thought you might know where to find him."

Rosie was still staring at Spot. "Is he friendly? Can I pet him?"

"Sure. He won't hurt you."

Rosie came out from behind the counter and tentatively reached out her hand for Spot to sniff. Her eyes were wide.

"Any idea?" I prompted.

"What?" She stroked the point of Spot's head with two fingertips as gently as if he were a new-born kitty.

"Any idea where I might find Winton?"

"No."

I thought it wouldn't hurt to expand my white lie. "Rosie, an older woman was in yesterday, said she was Winton's mother. She wondered where he was. I didn't know what to tell her. Have you ever met his mother?"

Rosie reached out both hands and, very delicately, scratched behind Spot's ears. "I haven't seen Winton in weeks." Her voice sounded distant. She was in doggy rapture.

I repeated the question. "Did you ever meet his mother?"

She shook her head. "I didn't think he had a mother. I thought Winton was a foster kid all his life." She took her index finger and very carefully stroked Spot's nose. "God, I didn't know that Mr. Mondo was based on a real dog."

"Mr. Mondo?" I said.

She tilted her head toward the wall behind her as she leaned forward and ran her hands down Spot's neck. Spot looked up at me, his eyes no longer sad.

I looked at the wall behind her, wondering what she meant about Mr. Mondo.

Rosie reached her arms around Spot's neck and hugged him. I was looking at the wall inside the shop.

On the bottom shelf were two stuffed animals. Long legs, thick chests, big heads. White with black spots.

Harlequin Great Danes just like Spot and identical to the one that was burned and left on my doorstep.

"Rosie, when was the last time you sold a Mr. Mondo?"

"We haven't. Too expensive. We got them in almost six months ago, so lots of people have looked. But eighty-nine ninety-five? Gimme a break. I told Mrs. Kato she should only get one, but did she listen? No way." Rosie was now kneeling in front of Spot, her arms up around his chest. His head hung over her shoulder.

Rosie continued, "She insisted on getting three of them. And this was after the Sierra Nevada Board Game. She didn't listen to me on that, either. When is she going to learn?"

"You say you had three Mr. Mondos?"

"Yeah." Rosie's head was turned sideways against Spot's chest as if she were listening to his heartbeat.

"There are only two on the shelf," I said. "Where's the third if you haven't sold it?"

"Stolen. Mrs. Kato thinks it was on my shift. Says I spend too much time in the bathroom. But I think it was on her shift.

Besides, it was on her shift that the deposit was stolen just before she closed, what was it, a week ago? It only makes sense that if someone is lifting the deposit off the desk when she goes in the storeroom to check the back door, wouldn't they grab the Mondo dog at the same time?" Rosie was now standing at Spot's side, bent slightly, her arms as far around his chest as they would go, which meant her fingertips were just touching each other.

"At least, I should be glad she doesn't think I stole him," Rosie said. "Why would I want a Mr. Mondo? Especially now that I know the real thing is available." She stepped back to get a better look. "What is his name?"

"Spot," I said. "Rosie, do you have any idea where Winton would go?"

She shook her head vacantly. "No. I don't know."

I tugged on Spot's collar, getting ready to leave. Spot resisted. He didn't want to go. "Thanks, Rosie," I said.

"Spot," she said wistfully as we drew away. "That's great. Good to meet you, Spot." She called after us, "How much do Mondo dogs cost, anyway? Are they expensive?"

I called back, "Yes, but it's not the cost to buy them, it's the cost to feed them."

We left Rosie standing in the sidewalk, staring after us.

THIRTY-FOUR

The next morning was warmer and drier. I turned on the radio and the forecast called for increasing winds out of the southwest. The phone rang just as the announcer particularly cautioned about the fire danger. It was FBI Special Agent Ramos asking to come by my cabin.

When he showed up I had already assembled an appropriate group: Diamond was there to represent Douglas County. Captain Mallory of the SLTPD and Captain O'Reilly of the Truckee PD were also present. I wanted each law enforcement agency to share all information that could help find Street, and I knew the FBI would never agree to it in advance. So I had to spring it on him.

Ramos was irritated as hell and threatened to walk out. I said, fine. I'd tell everything I had to Diamond, Mallory and O'Reilly and Agent Ramos could find out from them later.

Fuming, he stayed.

The meeting was stiff and formal with Agent Ramos acting more like he was participating in a deposition than in a discussion with other law officers about a sick perp.

I gave them everything I had on the fires.

I started with the foster child named Tommy orphaned in the Freel Peak Fire. The fact that Tommy appeared to have lived with both Joanie Dove and Linda Saronna and that the child was a discipline problem who also wet the bed. The fact that the child's description matched that of Winton. The fact that I'd seen Winton play with the lighter fluid and the fire. The fact that he appeared to present himself to be dim-witted when I believed him to be bright.

I continued with Winton's .22 rifle and the mountain lion named Pussy Cat, shot with a .22 at about the same time the first fire was started, the fire that killed Jake Pooler who was Winton's boss.

I told them about Jake Pooler's affair with Winton's girl-friend and hence, Winton's motive for killing Jake. Further, Winton had Jake's truck from which the gas can used in the first fire had likely been taken. Lastly, I explained that the burned, stuffed dog left on my doorstep was almost certainly stolen from a store where Winton's ex-girlfriend worked.

After a couple hours of questions and suppositions and theories, we all agreed that the evidence against Winton was only circumstantial, that there was nothing to directly tie him to the arson fires or the murders. But we also agreed that both the quantity and quality of the evidence was overwhelming.

Agent Ramos said he could obtain a search warrant for Winton's cabin.

O'Reilly said that he would get a warrant for Winton's arrest for the theft of Jake's pickup. There was a problem in that the truck had not been reported stolen and Winton had used it in the past for Jake's business, but O'Reilly thought he could take care of it.

Once Winton was brought in we were certain he would cave under questioning.

I gave Agent Ramos Winton's rifle and told him that the deformed slug found in the mountain lion was at the ballistics lab in San Francisco. Ramos said he'd have the tests on the rifle completed in a couple of days.

As they left, we knew that within a couple of hours every law officer in California and Nevada would be looking for Winton Berger.

The phone rang a few minutes later.

"Owen McKenna," I said.

"Owen, it's Glennie. You didn't tell me about Street. I'm so sorry! You must be dying inside!"

"It's hard. I'm mostly numb," I said.

"Is there anything I can do?"

"Just the photos of the fires if you can find any."

"That's why I'm calling. I've tracked down several. Should I bring them by your cabin? They're not very good, but perhaps you'll spot something in them."

"Yes, please."

"Okay. I'll be there in thirty minutes."

When Glennie showed up she gave me a hug. "Owen, I'm so sorry. Do you think Street will be okay?"

"I don't know, Glennie. I don't know."

"Here, let me show you the photos." She pulled out a yellow Kodak envelope and spread out a bunch of prints on my kitchen counter, grouping them into three sets.

"These are from the first fire when Jake Pooler died. They were taken mostly from the highway below your cabin. As you can see, our staff photographer was focusing on the fire, not the bystanders. Plus, it was at night. So it's very hard to see any faces.

"The next pile is the Tallac Properties fire where Joanie Dove died." Glennie was obviously in reporter mode, telling me a chronology that I knew better than anyone. "This fire," she continued, "was during the day. The bystanders are better lit but still hard to make out.

"This third pile is the fire that killed Linda Saronna, again at night. Not many bystanders and very hard to see. Some of these were taken by one of Linda's neighbors. All the others were taken by the paper's photographer."

Glennie dug in her purse. "I brought you a magnifier to help you see." She handed me a little box with a lens on one side and a light bulb inside. "Just set it on the photo and push the button on the side."

I tried it on one of the photos. It made a dramatic difference, but it would still take a lot of studying to get anything out of the photos.

"Obviously, I'm going to need to go over these slowly," I said. "Can you leave them here?"

"They're yours," Glennie said. "You let me know if there is anything else I can do, okay?" She forced a little smile and left.

It had been a long day and I was so fatigued I thought I'd be worthless at studying the photos. But Street was out there someplace.

I got a pen and note pad, sat down at the counter and went to work using Glennie's lighted magnifier.

In terms of identifying faces, the photos ranged from barely promising to completely hopeless. But I went through each one, slowly and carefully, making two lists.

When I was finished, the first list contained all possible identities of the people in the photos. Some stretched my imagination, but if I had a vague idea of a person's identity, I wrote down their name.

The second list was positive IDs and it contained only a few names, most of whom appeared in just one photo each. Glennie, Diamond, Captain Mallory, Frederick Mallicoff and South Lake Tahoe Battalion Chief Joey Roberts were all on this list. One person appeared in three photos taken at the first two fires and that was Linda Saronna.

I studied her pictures again. Although hard to see, I could tell that the fires were very traumatic for her, so obvious was the distress on her face. Did she already suspect Tommy/Winton during that first fire? Was Tommy/Winton in any of these photos? He could be, for I saw Winton in every obscure and blurry human form before me.

There was one more person on my list. He was in many photos and they represented all three fires. More disturbing than the number of photos, however, was the look on his face in several of the images. It was a look I could only describe as excitement.

Terry Drier.

Of course, being a fireman, Terry Drier had a reason to be at all of the fires. And fires are exciting, even if in a negative, horrifying way. But two of the three fires were on the California side of the lake, out of Terry's normal territory. Then again, Frederick had explained to me that the Mutual Aid Plan had all fire-fighting agencies helping each other.

I tried to imagine Terry lighting the fires and found that it didn't seem impossible. I tried to imagine him kidnapping Street, and while it was an outlandish thought, it would be easy for him because Street would open the door for him. And Spot knew Terry as well, so he wouldn't have been alarmed.

Then there were the warning notes. Why did they come to Terry's fire department? Why not the Forest Service? Then the notes switched to faxes. Was Terry feeling too much risk with the notes being "delivered?" Did he arrange the faxes to put some distance between him and the other warning notes? It would have been more complicated sending a fax from someplace else, from another machine without anyone knowing.

Then I realized a potential misdirection.

They might not have been faxes at all.

Terry could have written the notes as before, then run them through the fax in the "copy" mode. The version that comes out of the fax is exactly like an actual fax transmission. And if his machine has a log feature that lists incoming faxes, it could have been disabled.

I picked up Glennie's magnifier and looked again at Terry's face in the photos.

George the psychologist had suggested looking at photos to find the arsonist. George had also reminded me that firemen are slightly more likely to be arsonists than the general population.

Was I wrong about Winton?

Was the whole thing with the foster child Tommy just a coincidence?

George had also said that the arsonist was sending the notes as a kind of braggadocio, saying, 'look how bold I am and you still cannot catch me.'

Terry was the person who hired me. Wouldn't that be the ultimate in boldness if he turned out to be the arsonist/murderer/kidnapper?

Numb with fatigue and more confused than ever, I finally went to bed. I listened with dread to a howling wind, warm and dry, and cried for Street.

THIRTY-FIVE

The phone rang at 7:00 a.m.

"McKenna?"

"Yeah," I said. I sat up sweating from a nightmare about Street being tied to a bed.

"This is Agent Ramos. We got into Winton Berger's cabin. We haven't found him yet, but he's our perp."

"What do you have?"

"Maps. Fire locations. Enuresis. "

"What is that?"

"He wets the bed," Ramos said. "Under his regular sheets are towels and special rubber sheets below that. They stink of urine."

"So if he shot Pussy Cat, then we've got the homicidal trinity," I said.

"Right," Ramos said. "Playing with fire, torturing animals and wetting the bed. And we found evidence that directly links him to the fires. He has maps of Tahoe up on the wall. All three fire locations were marked with notes about how the fires would burn. Very accurate descriptions."

"You think the murders are thrill-killings?" I asked.

"Probably not, what with the evidence you've got that he had possible motive with all of the victims. But they could be. Regardless of which they turn out to be, we've got the evidence for it. Speaking of which, we left all the evidence in place and didn't put up any crime scene tape in hopes he'll return. Once we bring him in, we'll hit him hard. From your description of his personality, no way will he resist us. He'll be on death row as fast as we can hold the trial."

"Let's hope we find him fast," I said. My confidence was at an ebb. I didn't believe that Winton would be caught before he lit the next fire.

As I hung up I was thinking about what could make a person evil. Nature or nurture? Possibly there was nothing more stressful while growing up than being orphaned in a fire. How old was Tommy when the Freel Peak Fire happened?

I tried to recall Linda Saronna's words. Something like fifteen years ago. A woman died. No mention of a child.

I got Frederick Mallicoff on the phone.

"Frederick, I need some help, some research that you could probably do faster than anyone else. And I need it fast."

"Anything you want, Owen."

"Linda mentioned a forest fire to me. She called it the Freel Peak Fire. Said it was the worst the Tahoe Basin had ever had. About fifteen years ago. Sheila might know where to start your research. Find out everything you can about it and call me."

"You got it."

My next call was to Ellie.

"Owen, I heard about Street," she said when I told her who I was. "What can I do?"

"I want to borrow Natasha and keep her with me for awhile. I think Street is being held in a house somewhere in South Lake Tahoe. If I can narrow down the location, maybe Natasha can search her out."

"She's here just waiting for you," Ellie said.

Spot and I jumped in the Jeep and were out of Tahoe and down at Ellie's ranch in Gold Country an hour later.

Ellie gave me a squeeze and a kiss and directed Natasha to the back door of the Jeep. The little German Shepherd jumped in promptly, then turned and cried as she realized her master wasn't coming.

Ellie's eyes were moist as we drove off, but she gave a brave smile. I think she sensed that we all, Natasha included, were in a very dangerous situation.

I was coming up through Kyburz when Frederick called.

"I've got the basics on the Freel Peak Fire. There might not be much more info available and I thought you wouldn't want to wait while I kept searching."

"Right," I said. "I'll be going through town in a while. I'll stop by."

Frederick was at a copy machine near the reception desk when I walked into the Forest Service.

"Hi, Owen," he said. "Let's go where we can spread out some maps."

I followed Frederick into the conference room. One wall was covered with a giant map of the Lake Tahoe Basin. Frederick ignored the big wall map and pulled some rolled maps from a bin in the corner.

He unrolled two of them on the table, his arm muscles flexing dramatically. "These maps are older than the wall map. They show fire tracks from the previous couple decades." He set paperweights on the edges of the curled maps to hold them down. The two maps made a single image of the south shore. He pointed toward Freel Peak which, at nearly 11,000 feet, is the highest mountain in the Tahoe Basin.

"The Freel Peak Fire was a blowup. It took place fifteen years ago next week. Both in terms of acreage burned and buildings burned, it was the worst fire Tahoe has seen since the arrival of white men. But that little statistic belies the real significance of the fire."

"Which is?"

"Which is that what actually burned, bad as it was, was nothing compared to what should have burned given the conditions at the time. But by some miracle, the wind shifted suddenly and dramatically. The roiling air masses brought a solid rain from skies where no rain had been predicted."

"We've all seen that happen in the Sierra."

"Yes," Frederick said. "But this happened just as the fire got going. It was perfect timing. Luck at its extreme."

"Yet you called it a blowup."

"It was." Frederick opened his folder and flipped through some of his papers. "One eyewitness account said it was a small ground fire one minute and then twenty minutes later the forest exploded. The trees went off like bombs and no man-made intervention could stop it as it raced up the mountain.

"Where did it start?"

He pointed to the map. "It started near the Freel Creek Elementary school and grew slowly into the Freel Creek Subdivision neighborhood. Fortunately, officials got all the nearby houses evacuated before the fire exploded. Once the firemen realized they had a blowup on their hands, they backed off. There was nothing further to do."

Frederick pointed to arrows on the map. "The fire raced up the mountain at speeds estimated to be as high as fifty miles per hour. The updraft was so intense it created its own thunderhead fifty thousand feet high which produced lightning that started several other nearby fires."

"Rain and hail?" I was still trying to understand how such monstrous fires worked.

"Yeah. One report said there was hail the size of golf balls. And this from a storm that was created by a fire." Frederick leaned over the map. "The fire tracked through here, just to the east of Trimmer Peak and then went all the way up to the treeline below the saddle between Job's Sister and Freel Peak. During all this the air masses were shifting and strong rain came in from the southwest, rain that wasn't so intense as thunderstorm showers but was long-lasting and thoroughly soaked the entire Tahoe Basin."

"Total damage?"

"Fifteen houses, ten thousand acres and one fatality."

"Linda mentioned a woman," I said.

"Right. Apparently she was hiking with her son when the fire started and she took refuge in a mining cabin on a ridge over Star Lake."

"I know that lake. Under the peak of Job's Sister." I said.

"Yes. She soaked herself and her kid down in the lake before hiking up to the cabin." Frederick glanced among the papers and scanned down one of them. "His name was Tommy Reynolds. The Hotshots parachuted in and got the kid out."

I noticed confirmation of the name Tommy. "But mom didn't survive," I said.

"No. They should have stayed in the lake."

"It sounds like a good idea," I said. "But Star Lake is over nine thousand feet of elevation. The water probably never gets any warmer than forty degrees. You'd die of hypothermia in a few minutes."

"Yeah, I suppose you're right," Frederick said.

"What was her name?"

Frederick again looked down the paper in his hand. "Melissa Reynolds."

"When Linda mentioned the fire to me, she said a woman died. But she didn't mention Tommy Reynolds. Sheila said that Linda's foster child was named Tommy. I think they were one and the same."

Frederick was surprised. "Wow, what kind of a coincidence is that? Or do you suppose Linda somehow arranged to take in that particular kid because his mother died in a forest fire?"

"I think the latter," I said. "I also think that the reason she didn't mention him was that she suspected him of being the arsonist and she didn't want to bring attention to him until she was more certain."

Frederick frowned. "If he is the arsonist, then that means he burned his foster mother to death. What a sick bastard! If she suspected him, why didn't she say something?" Frederick straightened the papers he'd collected. "Then again, to be fair, Linda might not have known about the boy surviving. Her foster child might not have been the same Tommy." He tapped on the pile of papers. "I went through all the newspaper articles, several eyewitness accounts, and both fire department and Forest Service reports. While they all mention the fatality of the woman and the damage to buildings, only the newspaper articles mention the boy. I guess the official agency reports aren't interested in the human interest angle. And Linda moved to Tahoe maybe a year after the fire. I'm not sure when. If she didn't read the old newspapers she might never have known about the kid."

"Other people would have talked about it."

"Not necessarily," Frederick said. "Think of when skiers or boaters die here in Tahoe. It happens every year, but locals don't talk of such accidents much at all. Ever since I moved up here, I've learned that it's kind of an unspoken rule that certain subjects are taboo in an economy dependent on tourism."

"True," I said. "I can see that people would not have wanted to speak to Linda about local tragedies right when she had just moved here and was excited about her new job. But I'm going to assume that a strong possibility exists for the boy who survived the fire being the same boy that Linda took care of. I also assume he might be the arsonist. Such assumptions can be wrong, but, if logi-cal, can help us find the firestarter more quickly."

"Truth is stranger than fiction," Frederick agreed.

"Frederick, in your opinion, what would have happened if the wind hadn't shifted and the heavy rain hadn't come in?"

He puffed out his cheeks and blew air in a big sigh. "The worst you could imagine. A hundred houses and thousands of addi-tional acres might have burned. As it was, the fire wind caused dam-age to some houses that never felt heat. Without the rain, the fire wind would have been much worse as well."

"What do you mean, fire wind?"

"When a forest fire creates a large updraft, air has to rush in from the side to replace the hot air shooting into the skies. The fire wind is not hot, but it can be so strong that it blows down trees and buildings, fueling and exacerbating the fire. From what I read in these reports, if the Freel Peak blowup had progressed without the sudden change in the weather, the resulting firestorm would have been like what happened in World War Two when we fire-bombed German cities. South Tahoe would have looked like Dresden, decimated by a firestorm."

As Frederick talked, I visualized Winton squirting lighter fluid into the charcoal flames, talking dumb in an effort to mislead me.

"Is there any substantial difference," I asked, "between then and now in terms of the fire danger and our ability to fight it?"

"Well, our strike teams are better equipped and better trained. And we have more patrols and brush rigs than we used to."

"I don't know what those are."

"Oh, sorry. Patrols are basically glorified pickups with water tanks on them. And brush rigs are what we call Type Three trucks, the ones with four-wheel-drive. In the business of fighting forest fires, mobility and speed are everything. Our access to choppers is better. And our fire science is better. We simply know a lot more about how forest fires burn.

"On the other hand, fuel levels are higher in the forest. The drought of a few years ago left tens of thousands of dead trees that still haven't been cleared out. And there are many more houses out there, all made of wood, I might add. Further, there are many more people at risk."

"If someone lit a similar blaze today, what do you think would happen?"

"I can't even imagine. The main portion of South Lake Tahoe has only two escape routes, Highway Fifty east or Highway Fifty west. There is no effective way to move a sizable population. A lot of people could burn."

"Frederick, I want you to call me if you get any other thoughts on where this guy may strike the next match. You probably heard about the last note?"

"Yeah. What was it? Eighty houses or something? I'm sure the threat is very real. But I can't see such a specific figure. Having enough control over a fire to burn one or two houses made sense. But anything close to eighty doesn't seem possible to predict. Most of the neighborhoods that big have a lot more houses. And once a fire is going to burn more than ten houses in such a neighborhood it seems it would be too unpredictable to plan how far it would go. But if I were to guess, I'd say the arsonist would be looking at Kingsbury Grade. Especially if the wind shifts a touch to the north. That area is very vulnerable to fire in a northwest wind.

At that moment Sheila stuck her head in the door. "Oh, hi, Mr. McKenna. I don't mean to interrupt. But I thought you should know that the Mutual Aid Coordinator took the advice you gave me, Frederick. The chopper will stand at Red Alert on the Tahoe Keys meadow until further notice."

"Sounds good," Frederick said.

Sheila turned to go.

"Sheila," I said. "I've got a quick question. I was unsuccessful at locating any pictures of Linda's foster child, Tommy. I'm wondering if you thought you'd recognize him today?"

"Well, I suppose he must be all grown up and look a lot different." She grinned at me. "But I bet I'd recognize that little troublemaker's mug anywhere, anytime. He made an impression on people, let me tell you." She stopped and looked at me, eyes wide. "Do you mean to tell me you think the arsonist could be..." Sheila broke off and looked horrified.

"It's looking like that, yes."

"Have you found him?"

"Not yet. But when we do, we'll want an ID. It'll be the final piece of evidence."

It took Sheila a moment to respond. "Sure. Just let me know." She was turning to leave the conference room when Francisco burst in shouting, "Another fire was just reported! Over by the airport!"

THIRTY-SIX

Frederick dropped his papers, pushed past Sheila and was out the door. Francisco and I followed at a run.

The Forest Service was in total pandemonium. People were shouting and running in all directions. I figured I could try to get information while I drove, so I sprinted to my Jeep.

Spot and Natasha were thrown about as I careened out of the parking lot at high speed and headed down Highway 50. My phone rang and I grabbed at it.

"Hello?"

"This is Mallory. We've got a fire."

"I heard. Over by the airport?"

"Yeah. It started in the tall grass near the airport turnoff."

"How bad is it?"

"Sounds like they've got it almost out already. Sergeant Polk spotted the blaze right after it started. A vehicle raced away as he pulled up. He would have given chase, but he figured that his first duty was to try to stop the fire. Another squad was nearby and an Eldorado County Deputy came a minute later. All three officers went into the meadow with the extinguishers they keep in their vehicles. Kind of like trying to put out a big fire by pissing on it, but it made a critical difference. Two fire trucks got there soon after and hit the flames hard before the wind could whip it into something bigger. Just a sec..."

Mallory put me on hold, then came back shortly. "Just got the report that it's out, Owen. Burned less than an acre. Those boys did good. They'll stay on the scene for awhile, though. This wind is blowing like a son of a bitch. Never know when that sucker sparks back to life."

"Any idea how it started?" I asked.

"No. Probably like the others, though. Walked out there and struck a damn match."

"I don't suppose Sergeant Polk got the plate?"

"Hell, yes. It's a California number. We're running it as we speak. What?" Mallory said to someone else then came back to me. "Here it is, Owen. Vehicle's registered to a California corporation, name of The Jones Company."

"That's informative," I said.

"Right."

"How long to get a list of corporate officers?"

"Shit, McKenna, I'd ask a private dick that question."

"Good point. Maybe I can pull it off the Internet. What about the vehicle make?"

"Polk said he was so focused on the plate as it sped away that he didn't get the make. All he knows is that it was a white pickup."

"A dooley?"

"What the hell is that?" Mallory asked.

"One of those big ones with dual rear wheels."

"Oh. I'll ask Polk. Shit, I got a red light flashing. Gotta go."

I drove to the fire site and saw that while there were no flames, smoke issued from a wide swath of burned meadow. It was easy to see that it could have expanded into a major fire. Although, I had to agree with Frederick that if a bigger fire was what the fire-starter wanted, then he would have waited until the wind shifted to the northwest.

Then again, maybe that was how he intended to only burn eighty houses. Light a smaller fire.

There was nothing else to do in South Lake Tahoe, so I drove home. Natasha and Spot had been in the Jeep a long time and needed to run.

Treasure came running as we pulled up, her toy-poodle legs moving in a blur. I let Spot and Natasha out and the three dogs ran in figure eights.

Mrs. Duchamp came out of her house wearing some kind of tight white outfit that showed just how well-fed she was. She looked like the Michelin tire man in high heels.

"Yoo hoo, Treasure," she called out in a sing song. "Yoo hoo."

I waved.

The dogs went in and out in a complicated pattern as if they were trailing invisible streamers and were weaving them into a complex braid. Then Treasure broke rank and shot up the street toward Mrs. Duchamp.

When I got inside, I picked up the phone and dialed Jake Pooler Construction. I wanted to find out if Betty knew the registration and license number of Jake's pickup. The phone rang several times and then was picked up by an answering machine. I left a message for Betty, asking her to call me at home ASAP.

Next, I tried Captain O'Reilly of the Truckee PD. He was the one who was going to get a warrant for Winton's arrest based on the theft of Jake's pickup. That was before the FBI had found maps of the fires in Winton's cabin. Nevertheless, he would have looked up the truck's registration.

A cheerful secretary informed me that Captain O'Reilly was out on a call. She could put me through to dispatch if it was an emergency. I asked if anybody else would know something of Jake Pooler's truck. She had no idea. She took my number and said she'd have O'Reilly call as soon as he checked in.

I got a beer and sat down, exhausted.

My heart ached for my sweetheart and I felt powerless to help her. Almost for certain, Winton had her in some house in the path of his next fire, maybe out near the airport.

Was she tied up the way Linda had been? I struggled to breathe as I visualized Street lashed to bedposts. The thought was so suffocating it felt like it would crush my chest. Yet Street was counting on me to find her. I could feel it. If she was still alive, she would believe that I'd never give up. And so I couldn't.

I felt that I was at a second major turning point in my life, a kind of defining moment where my choices and actions were critical and could drastically alter the outcome of my future and Street's.

The first major turning point was when the kid came running out of the Wells Fargo Bank. In the space of a few seconds, I made a choice that turned my world bleak. By no official mandate, yet as if by decree, my life as a cop was suddenly over just as I had reached my prime. My very existence became tenuous.

But, following some instinct, I left the city for a different environment, one as opposite from my background as I could find. Instead of pavement, there'd be forest. Instead of crowds, there'd be space with few people. Instead of street gangs, I'd find children playing innocent games. Instead of pickup basketball, there'd be skiing and mountain biking, boating and hiking. Instead of sea level fog, I'd find high altitude sun.

Of course, there was another side. Tahoe has no symphony or opera, no art museums or professional theater, no cultural diversity or racial diversity, no ocean, no significant architecture, few restaurants.

But that was part of moving to a place where everything was different.

I started a second career and rebuilt my life. Day by day. I wasn't happy, but that kid and the image of his blood and brains spilling out onto the sidewalk faded. Gradually, my life took on shape and form.

Then I met Street and color came back into my world. I had a reason to live, better than all the ones that had come before. My center came back. I felt a balance, fresh energy, a new sense of purpose.

It had been going for several years, this new, wonderful life. The best years I'd ever had. The tragedy of that kid had given birth to something wonderful for me, and though I'd do anything to give him his life back, to restore him to his family and friends, I was eternally grateful that he'd set in motion a chain of events that led me to Street.

And now...

I drank my beer angrily, pounding it down in hard swallows that hurt my throat, then letting the bottle drop to the rug. I stared at the dark glass of the woodstove. Without a fire behind it, the glass was like a smoked mirror reflecting the cold, empty, lifeless room.

If only I knew she was all right. If only she could get a message to me. If only...

I sat up straight.

I jumped up and got a copy of the last fax the killer had sent. Partway down were the words about Street. Words that the killer knew would prove he had her in his possession.

'She said that not long ago she talked
about bugs named Achorutes Nivcolas.'

Was that it? A message of some kind?

I remembered that she mentioned that bug or something similar the night Ellie stayed over. We had been looking at the Bierstadt painting. Street had said that these bugs lived in the landscape of the painting. Something like that.

So when the kidnapper demanded she give him some information that only she would know, information that would prove he really had her, she gave him a bug's name.

Why? She could have chosen any of a thousand bits of private information, things only the two of us shared. Bugs were just one thing we talked about. It identified her, certainly. But did it do more? Did it have another meaning?

I went over to my bookshelves. Street spent enough time at my cabin that she had her own shelf of books including one on entomology. I got it down and looked up Achorutes nivicola. In the index were listed several page numbers for this critter which, I noticed, was not spelled correctly in the fax. Was that a clue? Had she purposely misspelled it for him? Or was it his mistake?

One of the page numbers was in bold. I flipped to the page and found the bug mentioned halfway down.

Achorutes nivicola was the genus and species name for a particular Springtail which was only one of 150 species in the state of California. Although they are not really fleas, they are commonly referred to as snow fleas because they sometimes swarm in enormous numbers on snow. I checked all pages listed in the index.

The book went on to explain the various habitats where snow fleas live including soil, leaf litter, decaying wood, fungi and other damp places. In great detail were descriptions of the actual bugs, the size of their body parts, the segments of their antennae, and the spring-like mechanism that makes the bug, despite not actually being a flea, jump like one.

What could it mean? When Street mentioned these bugs the night Ellie was over, we were looking at the Bierstadt. Was that part of a clue?

I got out the big art book and flipped to the reproduction, Bierstadt's The Sierra Nevada In California. I virtually had the painting memorized – could have painted it from memory if I were an artist – but I studied it anew.

I went over the clouds, the shafts of sunlight, the jagged mountaintops. Below the rock, snowfields gave way to streams, waterfalls and lush forests. According to what I'd read, snow fleas could live almost anywhere in the picture.

I studied every aspect of the image, trying to think about it in terms of snow fleas. But nothing came to mind that would give me the identity of the killer or the location where Street was being held. I went back to the entomology text and read everything there was about snow fleas. No ideas came to mind.

Possibly, there was nothing there. Street was not a calculating person. Nor was she a game player. She didn't do crossword puzzles or play word games. In fact, cleverness and clever people were not attractive to Street. So it was entirely possible that the snow fleas were merely an identifier, nothing more, something to prove that the kidnapper did, in fact, have her.

But I didn't believe it.

For Street was very bright, and she was a fighter. The combination would have her thinking of how to help me find her and/or find the killer.

I finally gave up, shutting the book with a thud. Any clue Street had sent with the snow fleas message was beyond me tonight.

I called the dogs in and went to bed. When I finally nodded off, I slept like Street on a bad night, wrestling the sheets and blankets, twisting them into ropes so tight a princess could have dangled them from the tower window and made her escape.

THIRTY-SEVEN

My last dream was filled with fire and I awoke hard, frightened and alert before dawn. I turned on the coffee and dialed up Morning Edition on public radio. I was impatient, waiting to get a detailed weather report. I had fire on the brain. Winton was loose and would try again. The worse the wind, the more difficult it would be for fire fighters to keep houses from burning. One of which was likely serving as Street's prison. If Winton had his way, Street would burn, the fourth victim on his death row.

I thought about Frederick's comment on the wind.

Yesterday, he had pointed out that if the firestarter wanted a wind like we had now, he would have already lit his fire as the wind had been blowing continuously for several days. Then, it turned out Winton did light a fire, but it was put out in minutes. Now I wondered if the tables had turned. If the wind changed, would that be a good sign? Or did it not matter?

Winton lit his fire and was foiled. He'd probably light another and another until he succeeded in burning whatever neighborhood he wanted. Which led to a very unwelcome thought.

Maybe the fire by the airport was a diversion.

He knew that the Forest Service and several fire departments would now be throwing much of their resources into watching the neighborhoods by the airport, thinking that he would try again.

All while he may be preparing to start his major fire somewhere else.

I reached for the phone, ready to call Mallory and Terry, Frederick and Sheila, when I realized it was 5:30 a.m. Maybe I should think about it for a few minutes and wait until six o'clock before waking everyone with a frightening thought that might be way off base.

Finally, the Morning Edition half-hour break came and KUNR in Reno gave a full update on the weather. It was as bad as I could have imagined.

The day was supposed to set high-temperature records for all of the Tahoe Basin. The winds, already strong, were going to pick up further and, toward afternoon, switch around to the northwest. This would make the northwest-facing slopes of the south shore, slopes like Kingsbury Grade especially vulnerable to a fire.

The announcer took care to add that the fire danger in Tahoe's forest was as bad as it had ever been and that everyone should be particularly careful regarding all potential sources of ignition.

The fire marshals of every community had issued fire warnings. There could be no matches or cigarettes used out of doors. No barbecuing was allowed. No fires of any kind were allowed indoors, whether in fireplaces or woodstoves because of the danger from sparks coming out of chimneys. No vehicles were allowed off paved roads or parking lots except in residential driveways because the hot catalytic converters could ignite grass. Anyone engaged in any activity that could potentially start a fire, no matter how benign it seemed, would be cited.

I turned off the radio and went out on my deck.

But for a gibbous moon hanging in the sky, it was still dark out. The air, at least for now, was cool. Spot and Natasha had followed me outside and the three of us stood at the deck railing, me looking down at the black water a thousand feet below, and the dogs vigorously sniffing the predawn air. Natasha had her nose through the railing while Spot had his over the railing. I was thinking that when the first forest fire began, Spot had been looking over the railing and growling from the very same place.

He suddenly did it again.

Natasha looked at him, realizing that one of the sounds or smells on the wind was out of place. She gave a little yip and spun around, wondering, looking at Spot for a clue. Spot stuck his nose high in the air, turned, ran back to the rear of the deck where it faces the street and let out a huge bark.

"What is it, Spot?" I said.

Sometimes he does a weak point, not lifting a paw, but reaching forward with his nose and straightening his tail. His growl intensified. I followed Spot's line out into the darkness of the street and saw a reflected glint of light, a sparkle of chrome, where there should be none.

An engine suddenly started and revved. Headlights came on and the vehicle came toward my cabin at high speed. I opened the deck gate and ran into my drive as it roared by and rocketed down the road. It was night and the vehicle went fast, but I was able to see it clearly in the moonlight.

A large, white pickup with flared fenders and dual rear wheels.

The pickup Winton had stolen after Jake Pooler was killed.

A dozen questions crowded my thinking as I ran for the Jeep. How long had he been watching my cabin? Was he planning to burn it with me and the dogs inside? A Molotov cocktail through the window could have turned it into an inferno before I would have known what happened. Were we alive only because I was unable to sleep?

I opened the back door of the Jeep and the dogs leaped in. In another second I had it running. I burned rubber backing out of the drive and again as I shifted forward.

The pickup was out of sight down below the first curves. I thought I could catch him before he got to the highway, a two-mile drive that I knew better than anyone. If not, Diamond or one of his colleagues could pick him up. I reached for my phone.

It wasn't there. Damn!

I'd brought it inside last night and left it by the bed. Too late to go back. But if I could drive fast enough...

The dogs struggled to keep their footing as we careened right and left. I pushed it as hard as I dared, almost skidding out of control on one hairpin curve. But Winton must have been the better driver because when I got to the highway he was gone. There were no taillights in either direction.

I remembered my own trick.

He could have shut off his lights and been driving by the weak light of the moon. If so, he would have to hit his brakes eventually because the highway comes to sharp curves regardless of which direction you turn out of my road. The only way to avoid braking would be to drive slowly and downshift hard before the curves. But I didn't think Winton would drive slowly knowing I might be right behind him with my own lights off, too.

I considered making a guess, picking a direction and seeing if he'd gone that way. But I thought that the fifty percent odds weren't worth it. Better to wait.

I couldn't watch both left and right at once, so I turned onto the highway and stopped. Now I could gaze in one direction while my rear view mirror covered the other. Any flash of red taillights should be obvious regardless of where they came from. And there were no other cars on the highway to confuse me.

It came from behind, a red light that flashed in the mirror as brief and distant as a firefly. I threw the Jeep into gear, skidded around 180 degrees and shot down the highway.

I drove dangerously fast, but after a few miles I realized that I'd lost him. He could have turned off on any number of roads. Or he might have parked in a dark spot and waited until I passed by.

Without my phone I discovered that phone booths are hard to find. Eventually, I came upon one in Roundhill and, after waking Diamond up, reported the events to him.

I drove random patterns through side streets, checking neighborhoods from Cave Rock to Stateline. Soon, I saw a Sheriff's vehicle and then another, joining me in the search. Both drivers waved at me even though I couldn't see who they were in the dawn light.

I finally gave up and went home. I stopped at Street's condo on the way to pick up one of her scarves which I could use to scent the dogs when the time came to have them search houses. I put it in a plastic bag and stuffed it under the front seat of the Jeep. When I got to my cabin, my phone was ringing.

"Owen McKenna," I said.

"Owen, Mallory here. Getting back to you on the pickup driving away from the airport fire."

"The one where the plate was registered to a corporation?"

"Yeah," Mallory said. "The Jones Company. Only it wasn't one of those doolies or whatever you called it. It was a white Toyota pickup. Medium size. Anyway, the sole stockholder of The Jones Company is Arthur Jones Middleton the Sixth."

My confusion was so great I could barely think. Was it Art who'd set the fires and kidnapped Street? Was it Art in Jake's pickup? No, Mallory had just said that Art's truck didn't have dual rear wheels.

"You there?" Mallory said.

"Yes." I took a deep breath. "I'm going to be real eager to talk to this guy."

"Be my guest. We picked him up at Embassy Suites Hotel ten minutes ago."

THIRTY-EIGHT

Captain Mallory led me to his jail cell.

The man inside started talking when we were still some distance away. "Are you Mr. McKenna? Art told me about you. Said you were real tall. Thank God you're here! Can you get me out of here?" Although his voice was tiny and airy as a whisper, the man talking was tall and robust, almost as big as Arthur Jones Middleton. Shave off his trim little moustache and he'd look like him as well.

Mallory looked at him, then at me. "I don't get it. This isn't Middleton?"

"No. I don't know who this is."

"I tried to tell you!" the prisoner almost screamed. "But you and your boys wouldn't listen! 'Up against the side of the car! Hands behind your head! Spread 'em wide!'" The man looked about to cry. "Then it was 'shutup!' And 'you'll talk when we ask you!'"

Mallory shook his head. "He's driving Middleton's wheels, he's got Middleton's wallet on him. The ID matches for chrissakes. What the hell are we supposed to think?" Mallory turned to the prisoner. "Try again. What's your name?"

"Lawrence Raphael. And it's *my* wallet."

"What are you doing impersonating Middleton?" Mallory said. "How did his ID end up in your wallet?"

"We're friends. He has two IDs. He likes me to be able to charge to his account. An ID makes it easier."

"Where's your ID?"

"I lost it about six months back. When I realized I hadn't really used it in years, I didn't get around to replacing it. Art said that if I was going to be his..." Lawrence looked down. "Art takes care of me. I don't need my own ID."

Mallory unlocked the jail cell and opened the door. I followed him inside and Mallory shut the gate behind us.

"Let's go through this again," Mallory said. "You can repeat your story for McKenna's sake." Mallory walked up to the bigger man, crowding him.

Lawrence Raphael stepped back and hit the wall of the cell. It was obvious that even though Mallory was a smaller man, he intimidated Raphael.

"Why did you light the fire?" Mallory said.

"I told you! It was an accident!" He was frantic, his eyes darting toward me then back to Mallory.

Mallory gave me a knowing look.

"I swear!" Lawrence Raphael yelled.

"Easy, Lawrence," I said. "Calm down. Mallory isn't going to hurt you."

"Are you sure?" Raphael was shaking.

I didn't see any point in saying that the danger would come from me if I thought he had Street somewhere. But at the moment it didn't make sense.

Mallory spoke. "Why don't you tell McKenna what happened. From the beginning."

Raphael's face was covered in beads of sweat. "Like I said, it was an accident."

"You admit to starting the fire yesterday?" I said.

"Yes, absolutely. It was the most frightening thing!" Raphael swallowed and wiped his brow. "I was driving along highway fifty and this terrible gust of wind nearly blew my truck off the road. I was fighting the wheel, trying to get back in my lane when my cigarette blew out the window. Christ, I could use one now." He rubbed his eyes with his fingertips. He shook with nervous twitches.

"Anyway, I saw the direction my cigarette blew and I was terrified because there was all this tall grass and all those warnings on the radio. So I pulled over and went to try and find it. But before I located my cigarette, the grass had already started burning. I tried to stomp it out, but the wind was so strong it just kept growing. I felt so lucky when that police car came down the road. But then I realized he would think I was the arsonist! I knew I would be arrested!"

Lawrence Raphael closed his eyes and shook his head. "I ran. I'm embarrassed to admit it, but I got frightened, ran back to my truck and drove away.

"Later, I drove back by and was so glad to see that firemen had arrived and put out the fire! My God, what if it had grown into a forest fire! People could have died!"

I watched him as he stepped sideways past Mallory and moved around the cell, nervously touching the bars, rolling his shoulders, reaching up and rubbing the back of his neck. His voice was low and calm when he spoke again. "I didn't know what to do. I wanted to turn myself in, but I knew my story sounded so... ridiculous. And I thought they would hurt me."

"Because of homophobia," I said.

"Right."

"Did they?"

"Hurt me?" He glanced at Mallory. "No. But they've been very gruff. They were rough searching me. Then they handcuffed me. My wrists still burn. It was the most humiliating moment of my life. Being treated like a common criminal."

I thought he was going to cry. "Lawrence, you should know that accidentally starting a fire is a crime. Not the same as arson, but it is a serious crime nonetheless."

"As is running away from a police officer," Mallory added.

"I thought you'd believe me, Mr. McKenna," he said, his words thick.

"Maybe I do, Lawrence. But you have a lot more explaining to do. Captain Mallory said you had wooden matches on you. Why? Doesn't Art's truck have a cigarette lighter in it?"

"It does, but I've always used wooden matches." He wiped his eyes with his hands. "Lately, I've been getting them from Club Tropic. Art and I go there Friday nights to listen to jazz. Their match boxes have a Bird of Paradise design on them. They add the right touch to my cigarettes."

Lawrence found a tissue in his pocket, blew his nose and seemed to relax a bit.

"And when you drive and smoke," I said, "do you always keep the window open? Even in forest fire country?"

"I can see now how stupid I was. But yes, I generally do."

"Where were you going?" Mallory asked.

"I was going up to Art's house. He's coming up today."

"Lawrence," I said. "Art's place is on the north shore. Wouldn't you drive up Interstate Eighty to get there? Why come up Highway Fifty to the south shore? It's a longer drive."

"I just do it for variety sometimes. Don't you ever do that? Take different routes to keep from getting bored?"

"If you were going to the north shore, why were you at Embassy Suites on the south shore?"

"You won't believe me, I know it. But I checked in last night because I thought I might get up the guts to turn myself in this morning. I wanted them to know that I was not the arsonist and that they should keep looking for someone other than me. I called Art last night from the hotel and told him what happened. I know he's worried sick about me. Now, he doesn't even know where I am."

The door opened at the end of the hall. A cop walked in followed by Arthur Jones Middleton.

"Lawrence!" he boomed in his big voice as he trotted down the hallway. "My God, are you okay?" he said as he got to the jail cell. Arthur looked at Mallory. "Officer, my name is Arthur Middleton. Lawrence is my friend. You can release him to me."

"He ain't going nowhere until the FBI gets here. Then he's going with them."

"But he's done nothing. The fire was an accident."

"Art," I said. "Lawrence is going to be dealing with the cops for a time. They're just following rules."

"Yeah," Mallory said. "Rules about starting fires, carrying a fraudulent ID, resisting arrest, evading a police officer. Gosh, we're strict. We got rules about everything."

"But I'll post his bail."

"Bail won't be set for some time," Mallory said.

"Well, can I at least talk to him?" Art said. "Mr. McKenna, can you reason with this man?"

I looked at Captain Mallory.

"Sure." Mallory finally said. He turned toward the cop who had escorted Art in. "Sergeant, stay with Mr. Middleton. Give him five minutes with the prisoner." Mallory unlocked the cell door. As we were stepping out, Art tried to walk in. Mallory put out his hand. "Sorry, Mr. Middleton." Mallory locked the cell door behind us. "He stays inside and you stay outside."

Art stepped to the jail bars and reached through them to Lawrence Raphael. They embraced silently as we walked away.

"What do you think?" Mallory said when we were back in his office.

"He's not our man," I said.

"You got some logic behind that thought or is this a gut thing?"

"Gut. His story about staying at Embassy Suites because he was working up to turning himself in, it's too goofy. If he were lying, he'd be sure to sound more reasonable."

Mallory chewed on the inside of his cheek as he looked at me.

"I wouldn't let anyone in the department think you've got the arsonist. Keep them all alert."

"You got any more advice?" Mallory said, his eyes narrow. I could tell he didn't like my input. Especially when he thought I might be right about Lawrence Raphael.

"Yeah. Although the fire could come anywhere, I would keep a focus on the Kingsbury area and work on your evacuation plan. My guess is that Winton Berger is still the real arsonist.

THIRTY-NINE

I was driving out of the police station when the weather report came on. In a grave voice, the announcer repeated much of what I'd heard early in the morning including admonitions about the extreme fire danger. He then said that the low pressure system that had been lingering to the north of Tahoe and generating the strong southwest wind was finally moving. The wind was expected to shift to out of the northwest. However, due to an unusually hot high pressure system moving into Northern California, the wind would not bring any cooling trend at all. If anything, the wind was expected to increase in velocity and temperature.

I thought of Frederick's wind analysis.

Would the Kingsbury area be at even more of a risk? Should I start driving the neighborhoods, looking for something that could alert me to Street?

Thinking I would ask him, I turned and drove to the Forest Service.

The receptionist said that Frederick was out.

"Will he be back soon?"

"I don't know. He left about an hour ago. He had one of our inspection clipboards and was in a big hurry."

"What is an inspection clipboard?"

"Just like a regular clipboard. We use them out in the field for doing dead tree counts and such."

"How about Francisco?"

"Sure, he's in. I'll buzz him."

Francisco came out in a few seconds.

"Hello, Mr. McKenna, what can I do for you?"

"Actually, I wanted to speak to Frederick, but I'm told he is out. Do you know when he'll be back?"

"I haven't any idea."

"Do you know where I might find him?"

"No. Maybe he took a break and went to the Tahoe Keys club. He works out a lot. I'll call him at home and see if he might be there." Francisco stepped into the conference room, picked up the phone and dialed. After a minute he hung up. "I guess he's gone. Let me try his cell phone." He dialed again, then left a quick message asking Frederick to call him. "He must have it turned off."

"Where else would he go?"

"Besides home or the club? I don't know."

"If you hear from him, have him call me, okay?"

"Sure."

As I walked out of the Forest Service I thought about Frederick and Francisco. Were either of them possible arsonists? Frederick certainly knew as much or more about forest fires as anyone else. If anyone could burn a set number of houses, it would be him. And for all I knew, Francisco might know fire science as well as Frederick.

Of course, we had a mountain of evidence pointing toward Winton Berger. There was the homicidal trinity to begin with. He played with fire, wet the bed and, possibly, tortured animals, shooting Pussy Cat with his .22. In addition, he had motive with Jake, stole the man's pickup, and as a foster child had possibly been placed with both of the other victims, Joanie Dove and Linda Saronna.

Even so, I wanted to check on Frederick and Francisco. Like Terry Drier, they were too close to the action to ignore. But unlike Terry, both Frederick and Francisco were reasonably close to the age of Tommy, the boy orphaned in the Freel Peak fire, the boy who, I was convinced, had changed his identity before becoming the arsonist and kidnapper.

I went back into the Forest Service building and asked to speak to Sheila. I was shown to her office in a moment.

"Yes, Owen," Sheila said. "Please have a seat." She pointed to the chairs in front of her desk.

"May I shut your office door?"

Sheila raised her eyebrows. "Of course," she said.

I shut the door and sat down. "I'm wondering how well you know Frederick and Francisco."

"Just in the way we all know each other here. I talk to them at work and at occasional Forest Service functions. You know how it is. But I don't go to parties much, so there may be others who know them better. What is it you're wondering?"

"I'm wondering if either of them could be the arsonist."

Sheila's eyes grew wide. "You must be kidding."

"Please understand that I'm just trying to be thorough. I have to rule out all possibilities."

"Well, I'm certain you can rule out both of them. They are good, decent hard-working boys. I can't imagine either of them burning down the forest. They respect the forest far too much. Besides, didn't you say you thought that Tommy, the foster child Linda raised, was your main suspect?"

"Yes. You met Tommy as a boy. You don't think either Frederick or Francisco could be a grown up version of Tommy?"

"Heavens, no. Francisco is Latino. His skin is way too dark. And Frederick doesn't look anything like Tommy. Tommy was a scrawny, slovenly kid, the opposite of Frederick."

"What about their childhoods? Could either of them have been foster kids?"

"You don't give up easily, do you?" Sheila said.

"Like I said, I have to be certain."

"Neither of them were foster kids. Their parents are alive and well."

"You know them?"

"Not to speak of, but I've met Francisco's parents when they visited him a year or so ago. Very nice people from the Bay Area. Francisco brought them to work one day to show them around."

"And Frederick?"

"He is from Bakersfield. His parents retired to Costa Rica. I haven't met them in person. But I know of them. Frederick gets phone calls from them here at work now and then. I spoke to his father once on the phone. And once, when Frederick had just moved, they didn't have his new address. So they mailed a postcard to him here at work. I remember that it was a beautiful picture of tropical birds with the beach and ocean in the background. Frederick seems to have a good relationship with them. He's visited them in Costa Rica two or three times since he's worked here."

I spoke to Sheila some more, then thanked her and left. She'd said enough that I was back to concentrating on Winton Berger.

Back in the Jeep, I pet the dogs and pondered my next move.

Although it appeared that the shifting wind would place the greatest fire danger on the south shore and hence that would suggest that Street was captive on the south shore, I had no idea where to look. I kept thinking that something Winton had said or done would hint at the location of his next fire. But as I went over everything I knew, I couldn't see any clue. The FBI had already searched his cabin and his workplace. Until we found Jake's pickup, there was little else to go on.

But how thorough was the FBI? It occurred to me that after they found the rubber sheets and the fire maps, evidence solid enough for an easy conviction, they may have given up searching for anything else. At best, they'd be less meticulous. Was there anything else to learn from his cabin?

Despite the fire danger on the south shore, I decided it was worth heading to the north shore to do my own search.

I drove up the west side of the lake, past the fire-scorched forest where Linda had died, around Emerald Bay and on up to Tahoe City. At the Tahoe City stoplight, I took a right to follow the shoreline and continued on another fifteen minutes to Winton's cabin.

The sightlines from the cabin to the highway are wide and open, so I parked some distance away behind a group of trees. It would seem stupid for Winton to go back to his cabin now that the FBI had searched it, but even brilliant psychopaths sometimes do stupid things. If he was inside, I didn't want him to see me coming.

Of course, Agent Ramos would have put a sentry out in the woods to watch for Winton's return. The same man would see me and report back to Ramos, but I didn't care. The FBI would follow the law which meant they had to wait to see if Winton would lead them to Street. Whereas I was going to make him tell me.

As every K9 handler knows, a dog is more intimidating than any cop with a gun. I opened the back door and let Spot out, leaving Natasha inside with a worried look on her face. Even though she could do wonders in a search and rescue, I knew that she wasn't trained as a police dog. Of course, Spot wasn't the greatest police dog either, but he'd been trained in the basics and, as always, what he lacked in skills he made up for with his size and enthusiasm.

Spot and I walked into the forest and approached Winton's cabin from the side that had no windows.

As I got closer, I saw a curl of steam from the gas vent pipe. It didn't seem cool enough that the heater would be on. Did that suggest that he was inside, using hot water so that the water heater would have turned on?

I stopped behind a large tree and held Spot's collar so that he was somewhat concealed. No sound or movement came from the cabin. But the steam continued to issue from the vent.

Maybe he was in the shower.

I wanted to give him as little warning as possible, so I decided to go in fast.

FORTY

I went in low so I'd be under his gunfire. As my foot hit the door near the deadbolt, I was nearly horizontal and moving fast. The door exploded inward with a loud, cracking boom. Wood splinters filled the air as I slid across an oily carpet.

"Spot," I yelled. "Find the suspect!"

Spot bounded in after me, his ears quivering with excitement, his eyes intense.

I spun around. The main room was empty.

To one side a bedroom door stood open. Spot ignored it, which meant it was empty. He ran to another open door. The bathroom. He sniffed then turned back. There was no more intensity in his manner. Which meant only one thing.

We were alone in Winton's cabin.

It took a minute for my adrenaline surge to quiet down and my heavy breathing to subside as I checked the bathroom, the bedroom and the bedroom closet. Back in the main room, I slowed down and took a closer look at the contents.

In one corner were a stovetop, refrigerator, and sink with a warped chipboard counter attached to its side. On the counter were three boxes of ammunition. Two were .22 caliber. One was 30.06.

In another corner there was a small desk and an old file cabinet next to it. On top of the file was a coil of white cotton rope.

The rope that tied Linda Saronna?

To the other side, a tall, narrow bookcase was filled with clothes, some folded, most just stuffed in. On the bottom shelf there were just two books. One was a large hardbound volume titled

'Fire Science.' Next to it was 'The Arsonist's Mind: An Examination of the Psycho-Sexual Deviance of Firestarters.' I flipped through the volumes. They were impressively complex. Winton was surprising me. Written sideways on the inside covers were Winton Berger's initials, the W.B. formed awkwardly the way a child might make them and retraced so that they were virtually engraved into the paper.

I wondered why the FBI's sentry hadn't already appeared. Had he called in reinforcements? Was a carload of suits about to arrest me? Either that, or the man on watch had broken the rules and taken a lunch break. I went back to my search.

Next to the bookcase was a narrow desk. From the top of the desk sprouted a lamp on long metal arms supported by springs. The lamp was turned to shine on the main feature of the room.

Maps.

Six topographic maps had been matched edge to edge to form a huge picture of the Tahoe Basin. I turned on the desk lamp. The wash of light was bright on the maps and I scanned them for any marks that would refer to the fires.

The first thing that caught my eye was an X written in pencil. Next to it were penciled notations and arrows. It was on the east shore, near the highway below my cabin, almost exactly on the spot where Jake Pooler had burned to death.

Looking elsewhere, I saw another X in the area near the south shore neighborhood of Tallac Properties where Joanie Dove had perished from smoke inhalation.

A third X marked Windsor Shores on the west shore where Linda Saronna had died tied to the bed posts. From each X were penciled arrows. To the best of my memory, it appeared they showed the direction the fires had burned.

Near each fire were carefully penciled notes explaining the wind direction, the burn patterns, the type of trees predominant, the percentage of dead and downed trees and the tree density.

I went over the maps slowly, from left to right, top to bottom. There was no fourth X.

Turning from the map wall, I went through the rest of the room. In one corner was a rolled-up sleeping bag, foam pad, cookstove and a water filter pump. Next to it on the floor was a boom box. A pile of cassette tapes spilled behind it. Not far away was a plastic crate that held cross-country ski boots with Goretex gators stuffed inside them.

After I'd gone through all the furnishings, I looked for other places where Winton might hide anything that could provide a clue to the location where he held Street captive. I looked in the file cabinet, refrigerator and in the cupboards. There was nothing.

I searched the bedroom and bathroom and the result was the same.

Sitting on Winton's desk chair, I tried to think like him. If he had a notebook or a pad of paper where he detailed his future plans, where would he keep it? In Jake's pickup? But the fires started before he stole it.

I leaned back and noticed a trapdoor in the ceiling.

Bringing Winton's chair over, I climbed up, slid the panel aside and stuck my head up in the attic. It was dark and musty.

I got down and found an extension cord that went to a window fan. I unplugged the fan, plugged in the desk lamp and held it up into the attic opening. Shining it around, it was easy to see a thick layer of dust all around the trapdoor opening. The dust hadn't been disturbed in years.

Again, I sat in Winton's chair and thought it through. If I wanted to hide something, the obvious thing would be to put it where no one would think to look. Yet, as I looked about the cabin, it seemed I'd thought of everything and looked in every place.

Then I realized his strategy.

He wouldn't hide something where no one would think to look. He'd hide it where no one *wanted* to look.

I went back into the bedroom and pulled the covers off the bed. The stink of old urine filled the room, burning my nose like ammonia.

The sheets were as Agent Ramos described them. There were towels under the sheets. And under the towels was a rubber liner. As I lifted them off, I could see where the FBI, turned back by the disgusting stench, had just lifted the corners.

Under the rubber liner was the mattress, an old, lumpy pad printed with blue pinstripes. It appeared soiled but dry. I felt around the fabric and found a slit cut along one of the printed lines. Reaching inside and under the padding, I found a notebook.

It was an antique book of maps. Old topographic maps.

I set it on Winton's desk and paged through it. There was a master map that showed the Tahoe Basin and surrounding parts of north-eastern California and western Nevada. It was divided into a grid with each section numbered. The numbers corresponded to the maps within the book.

I quickly paged through several of the maps.

Just as on the wall map, near each of the three fire locations were red X's with arrows showing how each fire had burned. Again, I didn't see any fourth X that would tell me where the next fire would be.

Flipping back to the master key map, I noted that there were twelve maps covering all of the Lake Tahoe Basin. I bent forward and studied each map up close. I let my eyes wander over the mountains that circle Lake Tahoe, remembering from countless hikes the lay of the land, interpreting the elevation lines to determine how steep the slopes were and how far the various cliffs plunged.

At first, nothing unusual caught my eye. The maps were similar to modern topographic maps with curving lines that showed contours of equal elevation. Various areas were in green, depicting forest. Other places were in white which designated areas above the treeline or rocky enough that no forest would grow.

I was looking at the mountains around Emerald Bay and their three thousand foot faces when I saw a small insignia that looked like a drawing of an old oil derrick. According to the elevation lines it was at 8,600 feet. Checking the map key I saw that it marked a mine.

On an impulse, I looked up at the newer map on the wall. A glance across the same region showed that no mine was marked.

I went back to the old maps in the book and searched for another mine. In a moment I found one in what is now the Desolation Wilderness. Going back to the new maps revealed that, once again, the mine did not show.

Apparently, the mines had been closed or forgotten before the new maps were drawn, or else they were locations that the newer map makers didn't feel were important enough to put on the new maps.

As I continued to study the old maps, I found other mines and a few cabins that were not marked on the new maps. But I saw no more X's.

So was this the reason for the old maps? Did Winton use them because they showed the locations of old mines?

There was obviously something significant about the maps that I still hadn't seen. I continued studying them, scanning left and right, up and down. I spotted it on the second to the last map, a region that included Freel Peak and its companion mountain, Job's Sister.

Another red X.

The X's designated the fire locations. We'd had three major fires, not counting the small one at the airport. This X was the fourth.

It was in South Lake Tahoe, just off Westwood Trail near the Freel Creek Elementary School. Next to the red X was a single word written in pencil and underlined.

Blowup.

Around the word flowed penciled arrows and an irregular outline lightly shaded with diagonal lines. Nearby was writing, again in pencil, 'Original Freel Peak Fire, constrained by unexpected rain.'

Another irregular outline was drawn in red pencil. This one had the same general shape as the former, but was three times as large. Next to it, in red pencil was written, 'Repeat of Freel Peak Fire with same north wind but no rain.'

The weather report had said the wind was going to shift to out of the northwest sometime in the afternoon.

I glanced at my watch. 1:00 p.m. I pulled Winton's dirty drapes aside and looked out the windows. The nearby pines were waving in the wind. As near as I could tell, it was a northwest wind.

I picked up Winton's phone and dialed 911.

"Nine one one emergency," a woman said.

"This is Owen McKenna calling with a fire emergency. I work for the fire department," I said, seeing no reason to differentiate between different departments in different states. "Please patch me through to Captain Mallory on the South Lake Tahoe Police Department."

"Sir, is this fire near your address in Carnelian Bay?"

I tried to sound calm, but it came out closer to a yell. "Ma'am, I know of no fire on the north shore. This is another fire on the south shore and I will tell Mallory about it just as soon as you connect me."

"Sir, we are required to get a description and address."

What I said next was rude and abusive, but it worked.

"Yes, sir. Please hold."

I stared at the arrows Winton had drawn from the red X. They went across several inches of the old maps, around the side of Trimmer Peak and on up toward the saddle between Freel Peak and Job's Sister. But it wasn't a fire in the mountains that made the prospect of a blowup so frightening. It was what the fire would go through before it even got to the steep slopes.

It took a minute to compare old maps and new maps.

According to Winton's arrows, the fire he was planning would burn through most of what was now the Freel Creek Subdivision neighborhood.

From their origin at the red X, the arrows broadened out unlike any of the arrows he'd drawn to represent the other fire locations. I had no idea how many houses this potential blowup would encompass, but I'd been through the Freel Creek Subdivision neighborhood on a few occasions. If my memory was correct, there were certainly several dozen houses at risk. Maybe a hundred or more. Winton had demonstrated by his previous fires that he knew exactly what he was doing. If he intended this one to be a blowup, it almost certainly would turn out to be one.

How many people would perish if he lit this fire?

And where was Street? Was she in one of those houses? In the fire's path?

I heard several clicks on the line. Then, "I'm still trying, sir." Then, "I'll have you connected in a moment."

I had no doubt that, thinking me a crank caller, she was directing officers to intercept me at the same time she was trying to get Mallory.

"Here is Captain Mallory, sir," she finally said, and then Mallory was on the line.

"McKenna!" he barked. "What the hell is going on?"

"I'm in the firestarter's cabin on the north shore."

"Is that where Winton Berger lives?"

"Yes. I'm calling because the Kingsbury location isn't accurate. If he hasn't already lit his next fire, he is about to. According to a map I found in his mattress, the ignition will be someplace near the Freel Creek Elementary School."

"What?!" Mallory sounded truly shocked.

"Hello?" another voice got on the line. "This is Diamond Martinez. Owen, are you there?"

"Yes, Diamond." I repeated what I'd told Mallory. Then I continued. "Winton's maps show that this fire will be a repeat of the Freel Peak blowup from fifteen years ago, the fire that killed his mother. That was made possible by an unusual wind, strong and warm and out of the northwest. Now we've got the same thing happening, winds picking up and coming out of the northwest," I said. "I'd consider the entire Freel Creek Subdivision neighborhood at risk."

"Goddamn it!" Mallory yelled over the phone. "Are you saying we should move out of the Kingsbury area and evacuate the Freel Creek end of town?"

"Yes. I'd get every unit you have and go door to door. Start at the lower elevations and work your way up."

"How many hundred kids are in that school? Goddamn it!" he said again.

At that moment there was another click and a fourth voice got on the line. "Captain Mallory? This is Fire Marshal Joey Roberts. I'm told you've got something for me."

"I've got Owen McKenna and Diamond Martinez from Douglas County Sheriff's Department on the line," Mallory said. "Tell him what you told us, Owen."

I repeated myself again.

"Excuse me," Roberts said. "We've had no reports of fire. And we've put on two more lookouts since the fire that killed Linda Saronna. One up at Heavenly and one on Tahoe Mountain. Along with the Angora Ridge lookout, that makes three on the south shore. I just spoke to all of them and they see no smoke anywhere in the basin. Now you want me to send men and rigs to the Freel Creek Elementary School based on a guess about the fire-starter?"

"This ain't a guess, Joey," Mallory said.

"I send even one strike team to one part of the basin, it would jeopardize our readiness everywhere else. Maybe this fire-starter is setting us up. Maybe that's what he wants."

"Owen," Mallory said. "You still stand by your assessment?"

"Yes," I said.

"Joey," Mallory said. "You better do it. Owen's been wrong before, but I'm not betting on it this time. You've got a reasonable warning about a potential blowup. Hate to think what the town will say afterward if you didn't act on that warning."

There was a pause. "Okay, consider it done," Roberts said and hung up.

"You better be right, Owen," Mallory said before he hung up.

"Diamond, you still there?" I said.

"Yes. You're in the gringo's lair, huh?"

"Yeah."

"What's your next move?" Diamond asked.

"I'm looking for a clue to Street's location. She's got to be in the fire's path."

"If it could be a big fire, then she could be anywhere in a big area. If you get any sense at all of where we should start looking, call me right away?"

"Thanks, Diamond."

I continued to sit in Winton's chair, staring at his maps, trying to think as he would.

He's trying to orchestrate the biggest fire in the history of Tahoe.

Why?

His note said the fires were punishment for crimes against the environment. I now knew what those crimes were.

The government and its Smoky Bear policies put out all fires which deprived the forest of its natural cleaning process. No fires meant a drastic buildup of fuel levels. Which meant that any fires that did occur tended to be much worse than they otherwise would have been.

The epitome of that was the Freel Peak Fire fifteen years earlier. The blowup raged out of control and killed a woman. Her son Tommy became an understandably recalcitrant foster child, a psychically wounded survivor who grew up angry, nourishing his anger into an obsession. He changed his name to Winton Berger, took a job working for Jake Pooler all while he focused on his obsession with the Forest Service, the very agency that kept in force policies that destroyed his earlier life.

His hatred grew while he made his plans to exact his revenge.

His first victim was Jake Pooler, an abusive boss who stole his girlfriend.

The next two victims, Joanie Dove and Linda Saronna, were probably killed because they had been his foster moms and they tried, unsuccessfully, to be substitutes for his real mother. Further, they represented the authorities he blamed for his real mother's death. Linda had even worked for the Forest Service.

So he hatched a plan to exact his revenge.

Linda Saronna must have heard about him and, realizing that he was living in Tahoe under a new name and working for the first man killed in the fires, suspected that Winton was the arsonist.

Then came the fire that killed Joanie Dove, and Linda's suspicions grew. But either her suspicions came too late, or else it was her suspicions that caused her death. Either way, she burned.

Now there was to be one more victim to punish me for trying to find the killer.

Street.

But where was she?

I looked again at the maps. As the topographic lines morphed into a mountain landscape in my mind, I thought of the Bierstadt painting. In essence, it depicted a mountain paradise not unlike what Tahoe must have been before white man came. As I saw it in my mind, I thought of the words on the last fax, words that Street had given him.

Achorutes nivicola.

Snow fleas. Minute insects, unrelated to real fleas. They lived in moist soils, decaying organic material, near fungus, under fallen leaves. And they swarmed on snow.

We'd been looking at the Bierstadt picture when Street mentioned the snow fleas, so I kept thinking that it contained a clue. But there were countless places in the Bierstadt landscape where snow fleas could live. And even if I could pinpoint a location, there were few places in the Bierstadt picture where I could find a corresponding place in Tahoe. It made no sense. Besides, much of the Bierstadt landscape was covered in snow, and in Tahoe in the fall there was almost no snow left from the previous winter.

But there was *some* snow.

Did Street's mention of snow fleas mean she was near snow?

I stared at the map. Looking over the area he had marked to burn in his next fire, there was only one place where there was snow this time of year.

The snowfield I could see from the deck of my cabin.

I looked out Winton's window. Across the highway was a condominium complex, obscuring any view of the lake. But up above, in the distance, were the mountains of the south shore.

The snowfield was little more than a white speck from such a distance. But I knew that it probably was hundreds of feet across. It sat in the shadow of Freel Peak and Job's Sister, probably around 10,000 feet, and was not too far from Star Lake.

There was no marking on the map for snowfields. But I knew roughly where it was. And at that spot the map showed a mark for a mine and another structure I took to be a mining cabin.

I thought back to what Frederick had told me about the Freel Peak Fire.

He'd said that the woman who died soaked herself and her son in the water of Star Lake and then took cover in an old mining cabin.

If Winton was going to recreate the fire, then maybe he planned to recreate his mother's death in the mining cabin.

Street.

I tried to stay calm, tried to think despite my hammering heart and breath that came in staccato bursts.

If Winton had her captive in the mining cabin near Star Lake there had to be a way to drive up to it, as hiking up to a lake at over 9,000 feet was not something he could reasonably do while dragging Street against her will.

Four-wheel-drive trails were often depicted as dotted lines on topo maps. The Forest Service had reclaimed many of them over the years by blocking them with logs and other erosion-prevention measures. Those routes were often marked on maps as 'old Jeep trails.'

I looked over the newer map on the wall. Not only did it not show any Jeep trail leading up to the snowfield, it didn't even show the mining cabin, suggesting it might not even exist anymore. Had it burned in the Freel Peak fire of fifteen years ago? From the way I remembered Frederick describing it, Winton's mother had died from smoke not fire and the cabin may very well still exist.

Then how did Winton get up to it with Street?

Was I wrong in thinking that he was recreating the Freel Peak Fire, wrong in thinking that he would want to burn Street in the same cabin in which his mother had died?

Again, I went over the old maps in the book that smelled of urine.

The coloration showed areas of forest separate from areas that were mostly rock. When I followed the topo lines away from Star Lake and the nearby snowfield, I found a long cliff face with a narrow, but nearly level stretch of barren ground just below the cliff. Farther to the side was an open area void of trees. According to the map key, this was a large meadow at roughly 9,500 feet. On the other side of the meadow there was a Jeep trail.

I traced the dotted line down a ridge where it turned and descended a steep face in a series of switchbacks, zig-zagging down to a forest at about 8,000 feet. At the bottom, the trail meandered through forest and glen until it intersected Highway 89 near the top of Luther Pass.

Was the old Jeep trail still there?

I looked up at the newer wall map for the same area. Scanning the highway, forest and ridgeline made it clear that it was no longer marked. Which suggested it had long since been overgrown.

But how did Winton get up there? Was the trail still in use? Or did Winton have his own secret route? I'd find out shortly.

In Winton's pen jar on his desk was an Xacto knife. I used it to cut the appropriate portion of the new map off the wall, grabbed the old map book and left.

At the broken front door was a coat rack with a collection of baseball caps on it. I grabbed one for its scent and was just stepping through the door when a cop car pulled up at the end of the driveway. Another stopped down the road behind my Jeep, blocking it. Two officers jumped out, guns raised, feet spread in the stance.

"Drop what you're holding! Hands above your head!" the leader said.

I kept walking toward them. Spot was tense at my side. I gave him a touch to calm him.

"Stop or I'll shoot!"

"No, you won't," I yelled back. "Call Captain Mallory on the SLTPD. I'm Owen McKenna investigating the fires for the Tahoe Douglas F.P.D. You can call them or the Forest Service. Or call Captain O'Reilly on the Truckee PD."

The cops kept their guns on me. "Spread 'em and we'll check your story out." His eyes went to Spot.

"What I'm going to do is slowly reach into my pocket and show you my license. Then..."

"Shit!" the second cop said. "He could be carrying!"

I could see their trigger fingers tightening on their guns.

"Then," I continued, "I'm going to get in my Jeep and drive to the fire. If you don't move your cruiser I'll ram it until I can squeeze by."

"Nine, one, one got a suspicious call from this address."

"That was me," I said, softer now as I drew close to them. "I also kicked in the front door," I said as I pulled out my license and held it up. "This is the residence of Winton Berger the arsonist. He is no doubt lighting another fire as we speak. This one will be over by the Freel Creek Elementary School on the south shore."

As I spoke, the radio on the first cop's belt squawked. He punched a button. I couldn't understand the words, but they were angry. The cop said a few words and then let his gun down.

"Seems you're okay," he said. He turned to his partner. "The south shore is marshalling everything they've got in the Freel Creek area, all based on what this guy told them. He must be legit."

The second cop protested. "But this guy committed a B and E. He admitted it. We can't leave the scene."

"You're free to go," the first cop said, as he glanced at Spot. "What the hell kind of dog is that, anyway?"

"A Mondo dog," I said as Spot and I got in the Jeep where Natasha waited.

FORTY-ONE

I got Diamond on the phone as I raced around the lake. I told him my suspicion that Street was being held in a mining cabin up near Star Lake and under the peaks of Freel and Job's Sister.

He wanted to know the exact location and I explained that I wasn't sure and was operating off of an old map that might not be accurate. Nevertheless, he said he would try to pull strings with the fire agencies and see if he could send the chopper waiting on Red Alert up to scout it out. I told him thanks and concentrated on speed as I went down the west shore.

Then I called Glennie at the paper.

"Hello, Glenda Gorman speaking."

"Glennie, I need a favor."

"Hi, Owen. Anything you want."

"I need you to look in the archives for any articles on the Freel Peak Fire. It was fifteen years ago this week. A woman died in a mining cabin up near Star Lake. A little boy was rescued. What I need is any indication of the location of the trail up to the cabin. I need to drive up there and I don't know how to go. Can you help me? This is an emergency." I gave her the number of my cell phone.

"Absolutely," She said. "I'll get right on it and call you back in a few minutes."

I was going around Emerald Bay when Diamond called back.

"Owen, we've got a report of a fire. It was started in the tall grass near where Freel Creek runs under Westwood Trail. The wind has already whipped it into the nearby meadow where it flashed into a large wall of flame. It's now out of control and raging toward the Freel Creek Elementary School."

"Which means the chopper has to work on the fire and not look for Street," I said, feeling desperate even as I understood their priorities.

"Right. Sorry, Owen."

He had to get off.

The phone rang again immediately.

"Owen, it's Glennie. I'm very sorry, but I couldn't find anything about any trail. There were a couple of articles on the fire. They mentioned the woman who died. But there was no mention of any mining cabin or a little boy, so maybe I missed an article. But our microfiche records are pretty good, so I don't know what to think. I'll keep looking. If I find anything, I'll call back."

We said goodbye and hung up.

I listened to the radio and pieced together what was happening as I drove into South Lake Tahoe and raced out toward Echo Summit.

As orchestrated and practiced twice during the previous week, three hundred and twenty-seven children, ages six through eleven, filed in orderly lines out of their classrooms and into buses that were streaming up Westwood Trail past the wall of fire and whipping into the parking lot. The children boarded the buses en masse and were all taken down Westwood Trail toward the state line where they were brought to the Crescent V shopping center parking lot, an area deemed safe from nearly any forest fire.

Meanwhile, South Lake Tahoe Police and Eldorado County Sheriff's Deputies descended on the nearby Freel Creek Subdivision and were evacuating the entire area.

As I went past the airport where Arthur Middleton's friend had accidentally started his fire, the trees opened up and I had a view across the big open valley that comprises South Lake Tahoe. A couple miles to my left rose an ugly plume of smoke. It was moving into the sky so fast that I saw dramatic movement in the tiny moment of my glance.

Four miles out of town I came to Meyers. I turned off Highway 50 just before it starts to climb up Echo Summit. I made a hard left onto Highway 89 and shot out Christmas Valley. The dogs had been riding with their heads out the rear windows, but I was soon going fast enough that both dogs pulled their heads in, shaking as if to get the wind out of their ears. I pushed the buttons to roll the windows up.

A thousand feet above me to my right, a line of cars crawled down the cliff road from the Echo Summit pass. Tourists unaware that their picture perfect vacation land was on fire.

I looked at the maps as I drove. According to the old Topo map, the trail I was looking for turned off the highway a few miles after the road began its long climb up to Luther Pass. Both the new and old maps had several elevation lines stacked one on top of the other showing a tall, steep slope coming down to the highway. The trail apparently snaked around the base of that rise.

When I came to an abrupt rise, almost a cliff, I figured it must be the spot even though there was no sign of trail from the highway.

I slowed to a crawl, pulled across the highway and onto the opposite shoulder. Roadside grass and brush obscured any path.

Where was the trail that Winton used?

I could spend thirty days looking and still not find it. And if the fire progressed as I thought, I probably had less than thirty minutes to get to Street.

Which meant that an old, overgrown trail was infinitely better than nothing.

I looked at the brush and focused on the lay of the land underneath, looking for what could have been a trail before everything grew up. Directly next to the steep slope was a reasonably flat spot, the only place that looked like a possibility. The drawback was that there was a patch of manzanita in the way and a good-sized boulder sat just behind it, no doubt fallen from the slope above or put there by the Forest Service to close the trail. I got out of the Jeep, climbed over the manzanita and stood on top of the rock to see farther into the woods.

Everything was overgrown, but the old outlines of the trail were clear. Further, the large trees on either side of the trail were denser farther from the road. Less light from above meant thinner brush. It looked passable if only I could get through the manzanita and past the boulder.

Heavy manzanita is a maze of tangled, wooden branches so tough and dense that it is impenetrable to nearly everything except chain saws and bulldozers. Fortunately, this was a small patch and I thought I might be able to blast over it. But first the boulder had to go.

I got down on the ground with my back to the rock and pushed. It rocked, but that was all. I tried a different angle with the same result.

Archimedes said he could move the earth if he had a long enough lever. Searching the nearby woods produced a length of thin log which I dragged over and wedged between the boulder and a nearby tree. I grabbed onto the far end of the log and leaned into it. The lever action rocked the boulder, but I couldn't quite roll it out of the way. If I had more power I was certain I could do it.

I saw the dogs watching me.

That was it.

Inside the back of the Jeep I had some nylon line I used for tying odd items to the roof rack. I let the dogs out and they ran around while I worked some knots and loops into place. When I was done I looped the makeshift harness over the boulder and stretched out the line.

"Spot! C'mere, boy." Spot came running with Natasha at his side.

Spot and I sometimes play tug-of-war. When he gets tugging, I growl at him and he goes into overdrive, showing me time and again that my 210 pounds is no match for his 170 pounds equipped as he is with four feet and claws like studded snow tires.

I got him into position and gave him the line. We tugged and I growled and Natasha ran and grabbed onto the line in front of Spot. I growled some more and Spot growled back, startling Natasha who jumped in fear. But when she saw he was growling at me and that it was only a game, she sunk her teeth back into the rope and tugged. I couldn't begin to hold against their pull and the rope jerked tight to the boulder. Growling louder, I ran around and leaned against the log lever.

The boulder rolled away like a giant bowling ball. I called the dogs off as the boulder dropped into a depression to the side of the trail. With the line wrapped around it, it looked like a mysterious medieval weapon flung down from above.

"Into the Jeep!" I said and the dogs, excited at these sudden games bounded through the open door, Natasha running so fast she couldn't stop on the back seat and slid under Spot's chest.

I backed up to gain some distance and gunned the Jeep toward the hidden trail.

We hit the manzanita fast. The bouncing and scraping was severe and there was a screech of ripping metal as the plants tore something from the Jeep's underside. But I wasn't slowing down to check. We got past the manzanita and dove into the dark forest.

I picked up the old Topo map again and glanced at it as we raced up the old overgrown trail. All I could see was that the mine entrance was on a steep slope and there was a square on the map indicating a cabin or building built over the mine shaft. The elevation of the mine was approximately 9,500 feet, so I had over 2,000 feet to climb.

Branches slapped at the Jeep and scraped its underside. I set down the map and concentrated on driving.

We bounced and jerked through forest that was getting thicker with firs crowding out the Lodgepole and Jeffrey pine. In places, the trail was populated with young trees. At those times I floored the accelerator and we crashed over them, bending the flexible trees to the ground and snapping off the stiffer ones. Soon, we shot up a steep rise and burst out onto a meadow. The dried grass and wildflowers of late fall were four feet tall and I had to guess at the location of the trail.

The meadow was like a sea. The grass and wildflowers flowed around the hood of the Jeep like the bow wave before a boat. I risked driving even faster and aimed for a spot across the meadow that looked like a logical place for the trail.

As the waves of grass parted before me, looking ever more like water, I concentrated on where the trail would be under the flowing grass, trying to force myself to see through the illusion.

In some ways it was like art. The illusion was stronger than the truth. Perception is reality. When I looked at the Bierstadt painting I saw only a mountain landscape when, in fact, I was looking at a photo reproduction of a canvas covered in paint.

I realized I was heading up an old, abandoned mountain trail all because I'd forced myself to see through other illusions. Winton's cabin looked empty. Yet it contained a map book under urine-soaked sheets. Winton's last fax had used Street's words about the snow fleas to verify her imprisonment. Yet, I now believed that underneath them was a message saying she was held near a snow-field. Much of the case had been illusory, like a painting of a mythical place. As I drove through the large sea of grass, I had another thought, unbidden and unwelcome, and it suggested a larger, darker, venomous illusion.

I swerved as the realization hit me, an impact as sudden and shocking as if an unseen boulder had stopped us dead.

It was always there and I'd missed it.

It changed everything. I'd made some wrong assumptions and therefore my conclusions were wrong. I thought I was seeing clearly an entire landscape of human behavior. But now that I was finally looking *through* the image, the killer's brush marks became visible and the illusion was revealed.

And another person was dead because of it.

I tried to concentrate on my driving, slowing as we came to the end of the meadow and bounced back into the forest, accurate in my guess for the old trail location.

The trail went up another rise which abruptly crested. We plunged down a winding path that descended into a deep broad valley. Freel Peak loomed on the other side. The dogs were thrown about as we lurched around curves. Eventually, we were going back up again, higher than before.

We climbed up a rocky slope with magnificent firs so big that they had probably escaped the clear-cutting of the Tahoe Basin back during the Civil War. I guessed that we were approaching 9,000 feet. Soon, we would crest the ridge above us and be able to see down toward South Lake Tahoe. I heard clinking on the roof of the Jeep and then saw black hail falling around us. It took me a moment to realize that they were cinders, lofting in the updraft from the fire down the other side of the mountain and dropping from the sky in advance of the flames.

How large had the fire grown in the few minutes since I'd seen the smoke plume?

Mixed in with the tiny black chunks were larger pieces. Most of these pieces were smoking, leaving little smoke trails as they plunged to earth where they would, in classic forest fire behavior, start new small fires to be the advance guard for the big one coming behind.

The old trail led straight to a slope so steep there was no way to climb directly up it. I stepped hard on the brakes and the dogs hit the back of the front seats. Looking right and left I saw the switchback I had passed several yards back. The wheels dug in as I jammed it into reverse. The Jeep's engine roared under my right foot and we shot back. Shifting again, the wheels spun and we moved forward with a short lag between inputs at the controls and movement of the vehicle.

Switchbacks force you to come to a near stop to turn 180 degrees as you crawl up a mountain. Any attempt to speed between the turns comes with substantial risk because slopes steep enough to require switchbacks are also steep enough to roll your vehicle all the way to the bottom if you should slip a wheel off the trail. I took it as fast as I dared.

The rain of black cinders grew heavier as we approached the top of the slope. The land was mostly open now with large distances between the trees. And the trees were Whitebark pines, somewhat stunted, which told me I was over 9,000 feet with not much farther to go. Several small fires dotted the slope above me. I was on the lee side of the mountain, so there was no wind. The baby fires grew upslope toward the big unseen mother fire on the other side of the mountain. Behind each crest of flame was a blackened path. One of the fires was in the middle of the trail.

I gunned it between switchbacks and blasted through the flames, thankful that the rear windows were still up.

Three more switchbacks brought me to the saddle. I jerked to a stop at a view that would have made Dante pause.

Before me stretched the Lake Tahoe Basin. But instead of the crystalline blue of the lake, there was an angry black thundercloud that rose from the valley below into the sky miles above me. It was the worst sign. The fire was already so big that it was creating its own weather. The fire's updraft had blasted into the cooler air of the upper atmosphere, creating a thunderhead that was now self-sustaining. Down the mountain orange licks of fire flashed. They looked small enough until I gauged their size by the trees they were devouring. At the present elevation of the fire, the fuel was Jeffrey Pine, mature trees 150 to 180 feet tall.

The smoke cloud shifted and revealed that the licks of flame were all part of a united front higher than the trees.

The wall of fire was 200 feet high and moving toward me fast.

I forced myself to look away. The trail stretched across the saddle to the mountain above me. It climbed up the slope and crawled along the base of a tall cliff that loomed above. In the distance was Star Lake. Below the cliff, in the near constant shade, was a large permanent snowfield.

Street's snow fleas.

A half mile away the trail dead-ended at a small mining cabin.

Street.

I was so relieved to see her probable location.

But she was directly in the path of the fire raging up the slope from below.

I gunned the engine and raced up to where the trail ran along the base of the cliff. I'd just gotten near the cliff when a loud pop came from below the Jeep. The Jeep lurched and pulled to the side.

I knew it was a blowout. But I thought I might be able to continue on the rim in four-wheel-drive. Then another tire blew. I wondered if I'd driven over something extremely sharp. The question was immediately answered.

The windshield exploded.

FORTY-TWO

We were pinned down below the cliff, easy targets from anywhere up on the rocks.

I leaned next to the side window and looked up. The nose of Jake Pooler's pickup peeked over the top of the cliff. It was parked on the very edge. As I scanned the palisades above us it was obvious that the rocks held a thousand places to hide. Even if I'd had a rifle I would have been unable to defend us.

The left rear passenger window exploded.

Natasha cried out. I spun around to check her. She appeared okay, just afraid. How could he shoot out the windows on the left side of the Jeep when he was up above us to the right? Then I understood.

He was shooting through the roof.

He had a serious weapon, definitely not a .22, to be able to do that kind of damage.

I had to get the dogs out of the Jeep, away from the line of fire. But if I opened the door, they would hang around the Jeep, a carnival shoot for the killer. There was only one way to get them to run away fast without coming back and that was to give them a mission. I opened the glove box and got out Winton's baseball cap that I had taken from his cabin.

Another shot exploded the window next to me and the bullet pinged through the dashboard. I held up the cap for the dogs to sniff. "Smell it, Natasha! Take a good whiff. You, too, Spot!" I made sure they each stuck their nose into the cap. "OKAY, FIND THE SUSPECT!" I grabbed their noses for emphasis. "TAKE

HIM DOWN!" I didn't know if a search and rescue dog like Natasha would know that command. But Spot did.

At that I opened the door as another shot plowed through the roof and took out the far rear window on the other side of the Jeep.

The dogs took off, Natasha a blur and Spot not far behind. The scent must have been strong because they didn't even have their nose to the ground. Perhaps Winton, sweaty and nervous, had gone the same way. The dogs ran up the trail along the base of the cliff, moving so fast that I knew they were safe for the moment. It would be nearly impossible for a sharpshooter to hit such fast-moving targets.

But when they followed Winton's scent around the side of the cliff and up onto the top where he had probably walked, they would be easier targets. It would be easy to draw a bead on them as they approached straight on and hit them from a comfortable distance. I hoped that the killer was on the other side of Jake's truck and that it would shield the dogs from his view.

I could help by distracting him.

I jumped out of the Jeep and ran toward the base of the cliff.

A human is a much easier target than a fast moving dog. So even though the cliff was close, I ran in a jerky fashion, tracing S shapes as I crossed open ground.

I thought the base of the cliff held cover for me, but before I got next to it I'd be an easy shot. I ran unpredictably, jerking right, then left, then more left to throw him off, my legs pumping fast. Although I heard several bullets hit the dirt nearby, I made it unscathed.

I took a moment in cover against the vertical rocks, sucking air and wondering exactly where above me he might be, when a large falling cinder landed at my feet, smoking like a fresh-puffed cigar. I looked down the mountain.

Under the angry, roiling, blackened cloud, the huge wall of fire was coming up the mountain at maybe 40 miles an hour. Lightning flashed and thunder rumbled in the fire-created storm, punctuated by heavy cracks like artillery shells or Fourth-Of-July fireworks. I realized the loud cracks were the moist trunks of trees superheated by the blowup and exploding like popcorn. My eyes followed the upward movement of the flames and traced the fire's direction.

Heading straight for Street.

I only had a few minutes.

But if I ran toward the cabin, I wouldn't get far before my chest was perforated by lead, mushrooming from the point of impact and shredding my insides. The only way Street would survive would be if the dogs could get to the killer, or at least divert his attention from me long enough for me to run away. But if he was waiting for the dogs, watching, with his finger on the trigger, I was out of luck. Maybe I could get him talking.

"FREDERICK!"

"You can't get to her, Owen! Give it up!" Frederick yelled from the rocks above me.

"You almost pulled it off, Frederick," I yelled back. "You want to know what was most impressive? It was the bed sheets. You put your own stinking sheets on Winton's bed, didn't you? You put your fire books on his shelf. It was your initials in those books, written sideways inside the cover. So you turned them around, added a little ink to the upside down F and the F.M. becomes W.B. Then you put your map book in his mattress where no one would dare look. Very smart. But Winton Berger didn't deserve to die, Frederick."

"He's a casualty of my war against the Forest Service! So are you."

I could visualize Frederick gripping the rifle in his muscular arms. Francisco had said that Frederick worked out a lot. What better disguise was there for a skinny kid with bad posture and a mop of hair than to build himself up, stand straight and wear his hair short and combed up in a little flip. Bad teeth can be capped. Not even Sheila recognized him.

I didn't suspect until Glennie said she couldn't find any mention of the newspaper article that Frederick told me about. It was an article that didn't exist. Everything Frederick told me about the young orphan came from his own memory. Telling me was part of the thrill, the daring boastfulness that the FBI psychologist had said was a trademark of some killers.

I yelled up to the cliff above me, "So, you plan to shoot me with Winton's other gun, the thirty-ought-six? And after the fire rages through and they find his burned body, they'll think he shot me and was then killed by his own fire."

"You've got it."

I had to keep him talking another few minutes. If the dogs could take him down, then I could get to Street.

"Why'd you shoot the mountain lion? Just for kicks? Does it feel good to inflict pain?"

"It's part of nature, Owen! If the Forest Service let the fires burn naturally, animals would die naturally. Putting out fires lets animal populations build to unnatural levels. Better to shoot them."

"Why Street, Frederick? She never hurt you. Let her go."

"*You* hurt me, Owen! I asked you to leave the fires alone. When you didn't, I made it clear that you were getting in over your head.

"When I discovered that Winton Berger worked for Jake, I went to the store where Winton's girlfriend worked. She told me that Winton had been a foster child. Just like me. It was perfect. So I stole the deposit and the stuffed dog. If you had obeyed my warning and dropped the case, I would have triumphed. If you didn't, Winton gets blamed postmortem and I win anyway." As he spoke I realized how easy it was for him to create fictitious parents in Costa Rica. Arranging postcards or phone calls was simple and effective.

Frederick continued, his shouted words seeming to hurl down on me like cinders from the fire. "You could have honored my request, Owen! But you didn't, so Street's death is going to be your punishment. You'll have the pleasure of watching the cabin burn with Street inside."

"It won't happen, Frederick. They're sending in tankers and choppers. They'll have the fire out before then." I felt the futility of saying it as the wall of fire continued to race up the mountain and the sky began to rain flaming debris.

Frederick didn't say anything. I worried that he was watching for the dogs. Dogs run fast, but it was a long way around and up onto the cliff. It would be another minute or two before the dogs could get to him. I needed to keep him focused on me. "Everyone knows you lit the fire, Frederick," I shouted. "They'll connect you to the theft at the gift store."

A loud laugh echoed through the mountains. "No, Owen. In a jar in Winton's kitchen, they'll find the store's deposit ticket and three hundred dollars from the same batch of money I paid the bartender with to send the roughnecks after you."

"What about Jake's truck?" I said, stalling for time. "Your fingerprints are on it."

"If any prints survive the fire, they'll be Winton's. I wore gloves."

I was hoping that Natasha's nose wasn't *too* good. Winton's body would be somewhere up near Frederick in order for it to look like it was Winton who shot me dead. I was hoping that Natasha would follow Winton's scent trail to Jake's truck and assume that Frederick was the target. If she realized at the last moment that Frederick didn't match the scent of Winton's baseball cap and backed off, I doubted that Spot would be that smart. Give him a scent trail that leads to a single man in an open landscape, and I was fairly certain he'd make the mistake and assume it was the same person. Furthermore, Frederick had no doubt handled Winton's body and had his scent on him anyway. It might be enough.

I kept shouting. "It was you sitting in the truck outside of my cabin this morning, wasn't it? Was Winton already dead by then?"

"Well, what do *you* think, Mr. Detective? You're supposed to be smart. I saw all those art books inside your cabin. What do you think?"

The idea that Frederick had been inside my cabin was nothing like the outrage of kidnapping Street, but it was one more violation. "I think Jake Pooler may have been a lousy father, but that doesn't mean he or anyone else deserved to burn to death."

"YES HE DID!" Frederick yelled at the top of his voice. "HE ABANDONED ME AND MY MOTHER! NEVER GAVE HER A CENT! AND WHEN SHE WENT TO HIS HOUSE, HE STRUCK HER ACROSS THE FACE! I WAS THERE! HE DESERVED TO DIE IN THE MOST PAINFUL WAY! AND LET ME TELL YOU, HE FELT MORE PAIN THAN YOU CAN IMAGINE!"

"So is that why you killed your foster mothers? Did they strike your real mother?"

"They may as well have. They presumed to take her place! My mother was as close to perfect as a person can be. No one could replace my mother! She died because of the fire policies of the Forest Service. Her last moments on earth were terrifying! She held me below her, kept me away from the smoke, gave her life for me!" Frederick's voice cracked.

He continued, "Those other women could never know what it's like to give your life for a child. They didn't know sacrifice. They used me. I was just a job! They didn't love me! They took me in for the money even though they had never known poverty." He paused.

I looked down at the fire. It was coming too fast. I couldn't wait any longer for the dogs to get to him.

Frederick started talking again, his voice high and keening, his words plaintive. "What kind of person would do that to a child? Take him in like chattel? The government pays the rent and the foster parent gives the government space to put the unwanted kid. Living with them was like being put in a storage garage. That's all I was. Chattel in a storage garage! For that they had to be punished..."

His last words were fading in my head as I silently sprinted away along the base of the cliff, heading toward the cabin. I hoped he would keep talking and not look down at least long enough to let me get some distance between us. The dogs were no longer in sight, having gone around a curve at the base of the cliff. They were probably clawing their way up the side of the rocks and across the top of the cliff toward Frederick. In the meantime, where would he go? Was he still trying to explode my brains with a bullet? Or would he head back down toward the cabin to use Street as a hostage? If so, I had to get there first. I was already running up the slope at top speed, but I tried to push myself faster.

I came to the snowfield and headed across it, grateful that the snow was firm enough to keep me from sinking in. I crossed tracks where the dogs had preceded me. Instead of following their steep ascent toward the shooter, I ran on toward the cabin, aware of an increased rain of cinders from the fire below. As the coals fell they trailed streamers of smoke so that it looked like the mountain gods were throwing a birthday party for the coming fire.

A new sound permeated the alpine landscape and it took me a moment to figure out what it was. A low hum seemed to float through the trees. As I ran it grew in volume until it became a dull roar. Finally, I understood that it was the fire itself, roaring as it attacked.

The cabin seemed to get no closer, hovering at a distance no matter how fast I ran toward it. Then, over the fire roar and my own panting, I heard an unnatural voice, carried on the freak air currents.

"MCKENNA, YOU'RE GOING TO BURN WITH EVERYONE ELSE!"

I stopped, turned and looked up the slope that rose to the cliff.

He stood there, a lone, distant figure silhouetted against the dark sky, his rifle aimed at me. The black eye of his scope obscured his face behind it. Down the slope below him but moving up in a blur was Natasha. Not far behind was Spot.

Frederick must have sensed the approaching dogs. He turned toward them and raised his rifle. I watched, horrified, expecting to see the animals hit the dirt. Several puffs of dust popped out of the ground near the dogs. But the dogs didn't go down nor did they slow down. That's one of the amazing differences between dogs and men. Shoot at men, they dive for cover. Shoot at dogs, they keep coming at you.

Frederick put down his rifle and held out his arm. I thought I saw a flicker of light against the black cloud. It was then I noticed a red object on the ground next to him.

Gasoline.

He lowered his arm to the grass and the ground seemed to burst into flame.

The flames raced down the mountain in a line, a line, I now knew, he'd drawn by pouring gas out of the can as he walked. Behind the thin line of gas-fired flame, dried grass and shrubs quickly caught and burned.

I stopped, frozen by the sight as the dogs continued toward the man, a growing line of fire separating them.

The dogs never paused.

Natasha powered through the fire as if it didn't exist. She gave a little leap and flew through the flames. Frederick must have expected the fire to intimidate the dogs, and was not prepared. His rifle was still down and he didn't have time to aim and shoot. He swung the rifle butt up as Natasha launched her attack.

From my distance I could not see in detail, but Natasha changed direction in the air as his rifle hit her and she went down near the edge of the cliff. She bounced once, tried to scramble on the steep, loose scree, then slid down the rock and off of the cliff.

Spot leaped through what was now a larger line of flames. He reappeared on the other side, moving fast. Frederick lifted his rifle again, preparing to hit Spot as he had the much smaller German shepherd. Spot launched and the man swung his weapon. I couldn't see where the rifle butt hit my dog, but I could see that it made no difference. Spot hit the man high, teeth to the shoulder, and took him down like a play toy. The rifle arced through the air as man and dog slid down the rock and disappeared from my sight.

As I turned away and ran on through the raining cinders to the cabin, a thought hit me like a punch to the solar plexus.

The line of gas that Frederick had lit afire went straight to the cabin.

FORTY-THREE

I saw the padlock on the outside of the door as I ran up to the cabin. Big and shiny silver, it looked like something on an $8,000 mountain bike, impenetrable to ordinary tools. It held shut an industrial-strength clasp that was bolted through the split-log door and would withstand the kicks of a bucking horse.

"Street!" I yelled. "Are you in there?" I rattled the door, smelling gasoline on the wood.

I heard a muffled reply, but couldn't make out the words over the roar of the forest fire coming up from below. It was enough, however, to satisfy me that she was inside.

Turning, scanning the cabin for a vulnerable opening, I saw the fire line that Frederick had lit. The flames had come down from the cliffs and were coming fast for the cabin. I ran around the cabin, smelling gas on the outer walls. The only window was boarded up with heavy plywood. There was no time to get Street out. She'd be in flames in seconds.

I ran away from the cabin toward the approaching line of fire. Of course, he'd poured the gasoline far from the snowfield so that the snow was of no use. When I was close enough to guess where the invisible gasoline trail was leading the fire, I found an area of relatively loose, open ground, and I dropped to my hands and knees.

I started where I thought I smelled gas and dug like an animal, digging my hooked fingers through the dirt and throwing it out between my legs. My fingers immediately hit hard rocks and woody debris, but I ripped the stuff out of the ground.

The firebreak I made was six feet long and went perpendicular to the approaching fire, but the little trench was only a foot wide and six or eight inches deep. I had no idea if it would work. When I knew I was down to a few seconds, I moved away to an area where I thought there was no gas and dug some more dirt, scooping it up in my arms. I ran to meet the flames racing down the gasoline trail and, just as the fire got to my firebreak, I dropped the armload of fresh dirt on the fire, hoping that it would help to overwhelm any residual gas fumes oozing out from deeper soil.

I stood a moment, panting, adrenaline burning my arteries, as the fire stopped and didn't jump my little firebreak. I held my jacket up, ready to beat the ground, but it seemed I'd killed the fire for the moment. Frederick was still nowhere in sight. Nor were the dogs. Perhaps all of them had fallen off the cliff.

The forest fire was closer and bigger and would be on the cabin shortly. The falling cinders had increased their tempo. I realized that if one of them landed on the gasoline trail or on the gas-soaked cabin, Street could burn immediately.

I threw myself at the cabin. In a moment I knew I wouldn't get through the door without a crowbar. I had a tire iron back at the Jeep, but it was a half mile away. This whole part of the mountain was going to be gone in just a few minutes.

Moving to the boarded window, I jumped up and got my fingers around the top edge of the plywood. I scrambled my feet up the log wall and jerked with all I had against the plywood. I could feel the wood bend, but the nails held firm. Maybe the plywood could be kicked out from the inside, but not pulled away from the outside.

Again, I made a complete circuit of the cabin, trying the log walls, feeling for movement that could indicate loose wood somewhere. But there was nothing. If I'd had the Jeep nearby, I would have risked major injury to Street by trying to bash it through the cabin. But trying to tear through a log cabin with bare hands was impossible. I backed up from the cabin and looked around the forest, hoping to find a miracle boulder up the slope, waiting for a small push to send it rolling down through the cabin wall. Or a tree that had broken and was leaning against another tree, waiting for a tiny shove to send it crashing down through the roof. But there was nothing.

I went back around the cabin, looked at all four walls, then up at the roof.

The roof.

I ran to the back of the cabin, toward the corner where the ground was highest. My timing was off as I leaped from a small rock. But I got one forearm and elbow up over the eave. I did a crooked pull-up with my other hand on the roof's edge and, raking my feet against the log walls, I boosted myself up on the roof.

The corrugated tin roof was nearly rusted through in places. I ran around the roof and found a place where I could get my fingers under an edge of the metal. Finding a loose piece, I jerked and tugged, ripping out some nails until I folded back a two foot section of metal. The old cedar planks underneath were set with one inch gaps between the boards. I tried to see between the gaps, but the cabin below was dark.

I yelled to Street, "I'll have you out in just a minute, sweetheart!"

I heard her making noise, but it was unintelligible. She may have been gagged. Then again, the roar of the approaching fire was so loud that I would not be able to hear words anyway.

As I raised my foot to kick down at the boards, it occurred to me that Street could be below them and be hit by any falling wood. So I kicked softly at first, then harder until the first board gave with a crack. I bent down and jerked it up and out and threw it off the roof. The second board was tougher, but it too came off without falling in on Street.

The light coming through the opening was insufficient to see much inside the dark cabin. I stuck my head down and looked around. Street was sitting on the floor, leaning against a wall. She was no doubt tied up, but it was too dark to see. She shook her head as if trying to get the gag off and the dim light caught the whites of her eyes. I will never forget the terror in her look.

"One second, sweetie." I reached my foot in and set it on a cross beam that bridged across the rafters. Street made a guttural sound that betrayed panic, reasonable considering the circumstances. But I'd get to her in a moment.

I lowered myself down through the small opening I'd made in the roof, standing on the beam. Then I transferred my hands to the beam and swung down, hanging from the beam so I could drop to the floor.

Although she was gagged, Street gave out the most horrifying scream I had ever heard. I suddenly understood that it was not panic at her situation, but a warning to me.

There was a rule we had when I was on the force in San Francisco years ago. It applied anytime we were confronted with a situation unlike what we'd been trained for.

New Predicament? Don't React.

Think First, Then Act.

I hung there from the beam, looking around in the dark cabin for someone else. But of course there was no one, the cabin was locked from the outside. Some other danger. Street continued making noise and jerking her head toward the floor below me. I looked below my dangling feet as my eyes adjusted to the dark interior.

The mine.

The dark, gaping hole took up the entire corner of the cabin. There was a ladder that disappeared into the ground, but I would have missed it and fallen into the yawning earth, how far I couldn't tell.

"Thanks, Street," I grunted as I went hand over hand on the beam until I'd cleared the hole. I dropped to the dirt floor of the cabin.

The gag was an old T-shirt. It came off easily and Street coughed and gasped. I quickly kissed her and held her cheeks in my hands, then bent to the white cotton cords securing her. One went around her wrists, holding her hands in front of her and the other cord went from her ankle to a ring in the wall.

The knots were tight and I could tell by the moisture in them that Street had been working on them with her teeth. I had to cut them with my pocketknife. I helped her stand up and was about to say that I could boost her up through the roof when she collapsed. If my arm hadn't been around her back she would have hit the dirt. As it was, I lowered her back to the dirt floor and leaned her back against the rough log wall. The bastard probably hadn't given her any food from the beginning. She was no doubt dehydrated as well. I'd have to carry her out. Which meant I needed to widen the hole in the roof. Or kick out the plywood over the window.

"I'm going to make some noise, sweetheart." At that I ran and jumped up to kick the plywood over the window. The jarring up my leg was a painful jolt and nothing happened. I switched to using my shoulder, but with the same result. I backed up farther and carried more speed, aiming closer to the corner to concentrate my blow in a smaller area. When I hit I felt nothing move except my shoulder bones. I did, however, hear the squeak of nails moving in the wood.

Encouraged by the sound of progress, I struck the plywood over and over, switching shoulders when I got too sore and then going back to my foot. Eventually, I popped the plywood off and the dingy cabin was suddenly filled with heat and swirling smoke and orange light from the forest fire. I climbed out the window to have a look.

I was on the upward side of the cabin, in the lee of the wind and fire. The smoke made the entire sky dark. Cinders rained like a hailstorm. When I looked around the corner the wall of fire had come to within two hundred yards of the cabin. I ducked back behind the cabin as the implications sunk in.

We were trapped.

There was no way we could outrun a fire that was coming like a freight train and was as wide as the mountain.

Trying not to think about the dogs, I climbed back through the window. "Street," I said in as calm a voice as I could manage. "There is a forest fire coming. I'm going to help you get down into the mine."

She gave me a single, silent nod. Her eyes showed a great sadness. Her body was slack against the cabin wall.

I didn't think she was strong enough to clamp her arms around my neck and hold her own weight, so I scooped her up over my shoulders in a fireman's carry. Her arm was around one of my shoulders, a leg around the other shoulder. I put one of my arms over her leg and arm and pinned them to my chest. Then I walked over to the hole in the earth.

Despite the extra light coming in the window, I could see nothing as I looked down. It looked like the ladder descended into nothingness

I used my free hand to grab the top rung of the ladder, tentatively reached a foot out and tested our combined weight on the ladder. It held and I went slowly down into what seemed like the black heart of the earth.

We bounced a little each time I let go with my free hand and quickly grabbed the next rung. It was slow going, but I knew we'd hit something soon because the ladder, although heavy-duty, couldn't be infinitely long.

About twenty feet down my feet hit dirt. I scraped my feet along the ground, feeling my way. There would have to be a tunnel or another hole so that one could descend in stages.

I put my hand along a rocky wall and moved sideways. When I'd gone six or eight feet and not come upon another hole I knew there was enough space for us to sit down and rest while the fire blew over.

Street slumped as I laid her down in the dense darkness. I lifted her up into a sitting position. "We'll be safe here while the fire blows over," I said, making it up, not having a clue as to what would happen in this hole when the firestorm torched the cabin above. I touched Street's cheek and it was wet with tears. "Don't worry, sweetheart, we'll be okay."

"But not Spot," she said. "He's out there someplace, isn't he? You wouldn't come after me without him." Her cries were loud in the relatively quiet hole.

"I'm going up to check," I said, my throat thick. "Don't move." I left before either of us could say anything more.

I found the ladder and nearly ran up it toward the dim circle of light above. I vaulted out the window and ran into a blast of heat and smoke.

"SPOT!" I yelled. "SPOT! NATASHA!"

The smoke cloud swirled down to the ground obscuring the nearby forest. I ran out from the cabin and hit the full blast of wind. Hot sparks hit my neck. I turned and saw a wall of fire rear up as if it were alive and furious at my impertinence. The heat on my skin was searing and the roar stung my ears. Then the wind reversed direction as the firestorm sucked the nearby air into a monstrous column of rising flames. The fire lifted higher and then, as if gathering strength for a strike, surged down to the ground. The flame raced toward me like a crashing wave. I jumped behind the cabin, took a breath and threw myself face to the dirt.

The wave of flame surrounded the cabin, then receded as the front of the gas-soaked cabin burst into flames. The grass nearby was burnt black. The forest above the cabin hadn't yet caught fire, but with the next wave of flame it would all be an inferno.

"SPOT! NATASHA!" I yelled again. But it was hopeless. If I didn't hurry, the cabin wall with the window opening would soon be in flames and I'd burn, too. The wind shifted again and smoke filled the air.

"SPOT! ARE YOU THERE? NATASHA!" Unable to see or breathe, I gave up and boosted myself up on the window sill to climb inside. Then I heard a sound.

I turned my head to hear better.

A whimpering cry.

I jumped back to the ground and ran out into the smoke, then fell to the ground and put my lips to the dirt to try to find clean air to breathe. I got some air in my lungs and lifted up to yell. "SPOT! SPOT, I'M OVER HERE. FOLLOW MY VOICE, SPOT! NATASHA, COME!"

I bent down and again breathed air next to the ground as the choking smoke raged and roiled through the air. The roar of the fire was closer. I couldn't see the flames so dense was the smoke. But an ominous orange glow diffused through the air.

I yelled again for my dog, over and over, trying to keep talking so he could sense direction by my voice. I didn't think a dog's nose was of any help navigating in a forest fire. And the fire was too close now for any more chance of the air clearing enough to see.

I moved a bit farther from the cabin, reminding myself not to lose my orientation. I needed to be able to reverse direction and find the cabin in the blackout.

"SPOT! ARE YOU THERE, BOY?!" The orange glow in the air was brighter. Three or four more seconds was all I could wait. At any moment, the fire could cough another wave of flame toward me and it would be all over.

"SPOT!" I tried again.

Another whimper.

"SPOT!" I ran farther into the woods.

The whimper came louder.

To my right.

I turned and ran, screaming Spot's name.

Movement in the forest.

Spot came slow, his breath audible before I could make him out. He sounded like he was gargling or choking, trying to suck air through a wet sponge.

Then I could see him through the smoke.

He was dragging Natasha by the nape of her neck.

Her rear legs were pushing, trying to help.

I ran to them. Spot let go and Natasha sagged to the ground, alive but severely wounded. I wasn't sure, but it looked like her front legs were broken. Her jaw was no doubt broken as well judging from the blood and the way it hung at a peculiar angle. She also had a wet, bloody wound on the skin around her neck, although I realized that was from Spot picking her up and dragging her all the way from the base of the cliff.

Trying to be gentle, I scooped her up. "C'mon, Spot, we gotta run or we won't make it."

I plunged into the black smoke, trying not to breathe, running without reference. Dead reckoning. Either we hit the cabin or we hit the fire. Or maybe the fire got to us first.

An orange glow grew bright. I ran to where I thought the cabin was. It appeared out of the smoke. It was fully engulfed. Orange flames surged out of the black sky as I jumped behind the back of the cabin. I put my jacket over the flames on the window sill and, holding Natasha tight to my chest, did a roll through it.

"Spot, are you there? Spot?" I called out into the black smoke cloud. Spot stuck his head in the window. He coughed and wheezed. "Spot, jump through. C'mon, boy, hurry!"

He pushed off the ground and put his front paws on the window sill, then pulled them away from the heat.

"Spot, you have to jump."

He didn't know my words, but he understood what he had to do. Whining, he took a turn back into the smoke and then came at the window with some speed, leaped and easily cleared the sill.

"Spot, come here. Lie down. I'm going down this ladder. Stay here and keep your nose on the ground to breathe." Again, he got the gist of it and did as I said, his jowls puffing with his coughing, choking breaths.

I stepped onto the ladder and lowered myself into the black hole in the earth. "We're okay, sweetie," I called down.

"Street, I've got Natasha," I said when I got to the bottom. "She's hurt on her jaw and front legs, so I'm going to set her on the ground next to you. You can pet her, but don't bump her legs."

I scrambled back up the ladder. Spot had shifted so his nose was hanging over the edge and down into the fresh air of the hole. "Okay, your largeness," I said, rubbing his snout and head roughly. "You're too big to carry, so I hope you remember that time you climbed the stepladder next to the fridge and took that steak I had defrosting on top of the fridge. Remember?" I had him up and standing next to the hole. "Same principle," I said, "but this time in reverse. Ready?"

The forest fire was on the cabin now, the roar like a train on an overpass above. Flaming chunks of wood fell from the roof, with hot sparks exploding in the air. We'd gone from a black smoke cloud to being surrounded by bright yellow light, searing like a million heat lamps.

I put one arm around Spot's narrow abdomen and pulled him tight to my own stomach. "Okay, bud, rear feet over here on the ladder rungs. That's right. Now the front feet. Good boy. I'll hold you from behind and below. Down we go. Hurry or we're going to be grilled like well-done steaks."

Spot resisted and I had the thought that for maybe the first time in his life he was scared.

"We've got about five seconds left, Spot. We have to move. NOW!"

He didn't like it, but I think he knew that if he didn't come willingly I was going to let go of the ladder and pull him down in a free-fall. We were down maybe eight rungs, just below the grade of the cabin floor, when the roof collapsed.

It seemed as if the cabin exploded, with the heat burning us from above and pieces of fire crashing down the hole beside us.

I kept a tight grip on Spot and we continued down the ladder, half stepping, half falling.

A large piece of burning wood rocketed down right after Spot and I made landfall. I picked it up by an unburned end and used it like a torch. Its light was sufficient to see the long tunnel that went from the bottom of the hole back into the mountain. We moved back into the tunnel away from the falling debris. When my torch burned out, we sat in the dark.

I didn't know how long Street could go without food and water, but Natasha gave her a focus and she held the German shepherd, pet her nose and whispered into her ear while I held Street with my arm around her shoulder.

The inferno roared above destroying everything in its path. After a while I heard a lot of whimpering cries coming from Natasha. As I tried to reassure the dog, I realized that some of the cries were from Street.

I tried to soothe her, but without success. When she spoke, she was largely incoherent and I knew she was in bad shape.

Twice I climbed partway up the now broken and burned ladder and was turned back by the heat.

By the glow on my watch I could see that we four had sat in the tunnel at the bottom of the hole for six hours.

Eventually, I heard the muffled thwop-thwop of a chopper.

"You guys sit tight," I told them, speaking of them in plural in an effort to keep Street thinking about Spot and Natasha and not about the fact that we could die down inside this mountain. "I'm going to go hitch a ride." Street mumbled something unintelligible and I crawled back down the mining tunnel and climbed up the broken, charred ladder.

The cabin was gone, replaced by a dark sky, brilliant with stars. A half mile away was a hovering chopper with a bright searchlight. The light shined on the burned-out hulk of my Jeep. Perhaps the boys in the chopper assumed that the Jeep pointed the way, for the chopper slowly came my way.

They missed me on the first pass, going by my frantically waving arms without a pause. When they came back on the second pass, they flew directly over me and I stood in the beam like a night bug blinded by a giant flashlight.

The chopper settled down on a flat spot about sixty yards away. Before it had come to a complete rest, several men rushed out, flashlight beams weaving through the air.

The first one to reach me was Diamond.

"Gringo? You okay?"

"Yes," I said.

"Street?"

"She's alive, in bad shape, but alive." I pointed to the opening of the mine shaft. "She's down at the bottom. She needs to be carried out on a stretcher."

Diamond shouted commands to the other men and they ran back to the chopper to get a stretcher. "What about Spot?" he asked.

"He's okay. I'll need to help him up. But one of your men can carry the other dog, a German Shepherd. Tell whoever does it to be careful. The shepherd's got a couple of broken legs and a broken jaw. What happened to the town?" I asked, fearing the worst.

"It is pretty bad. A lot of houses burned. But the evacuation went well. As far as we know, no one has died."

"Except Winton Berger. He was killed by the arsonist."

"I thought you said..."

"Frederick Mallicoff was the arsonist. He brought Winton up here and killed him."

Diamond squinted against a cloud of smoke that wafted from the smoldering logs that once made up the cabin. "Winton was set up."

"Yes."

"And the arsonist?"

"Spot took him down just before the forest fire got to us. Spot made it back to cover. The arsonist didn't."

The men came running back with a stretcher. I led them down to Street.

EPILOGUE

The parking lots at U.C. Davis were nearly full and we had to drive to the farthest corner to find a space.

"Are you up to walking a distance in the rain?" I asked Street. "Otherwise, I can drop you off and you can wait for us."

"I'm a little stiff, but I'll be fine," she said. "The walk will do me good. Besides, I love rain. Snow, too. Judging from this weather it must be snowing furiously up in Tahoe."

I ran around to her door, opened the umbrella and held her hand as she got out.

"Look how much better he is after seeing Natasha," Street said as I let Spot out of the back. "He's looking around, sniffing the air, almost acting like his old self."

"Indeed, he is. It's like doing a live find after a dead one. Turns their spirits around."

"Do you think she'll be okay?"

"Natasha? Yes. The surgeon told Ellie that her jaw and legs should heal completely in a couple months, her shoulder a month or two after that."

"I'm glad," Street said.

We didn't speak anymore as we walked across the rain-wet asphalt and then onto the gently twisting paths that wound through the beautiful campus. Street moved slowly but without much apparent pain. If her wrist bandages hadn't been poking out from below her sleeves, she would have looked normal.

Dr. Selma Peralta showed us down to a basement room in the vet hospital. "The mountain lion is nearly healed," she said. "Tomorrow, she'll be transferred to a holding facility up in the mountains of Alpine County. If she does well and shows a proper aversion to humans, she'll be released into the wild in a couple of weeks."

"What do you think her chances are?" Street asked.

"Quite good," Dr. Peralta said. "The best thing is that she is angry. That is a good sign. Remember that she can reach through the bars. So please stand back. She may be relatively small, but she is a powerful predator."

We turned a corner and walked toward a room that was similar to something in a zoo before they replaced cages with more natural habitats.

Pussy Cat paced back and forth, frustration and anger emanating from her like smoke. I held tight to Spot's collar.

Spot pulled forward when he saw her.

"Spot, that's Pussy Cat!" Street said. Then to us she said, "Do you think he recognizes her?"

Dr. Peralta answered. "Everything about this meeting is different, but yes, he'll still recognize her scent even without her fur being filled with smoke and ash."

Pussy Cat paused for a moment and looked up at Spot who stood a foot taller. A low, moaning growl rose up from her throat. She went back to pacing, more intense than before.

Spot lifted up his tail, a sign of pleasure. He pulled forward against my hold, stuck his nose toward the cage and gave a small woof.

Pussy Cat whirled and threw herself up against the bars of the cage. She stood on her hind legs and snarled, her mouth open and fangs bared. A powerful front paw flashed between the bars and cut through the air an inch in front of Spot's nose.

We all jerked back.

Spot growled and barked and wagged. He glanced at me, then looked back at Pussy Cat. His tail was on high speed.

Dr. Peralta spoke first, her voice a bit shaky. "Is that what he needed? To see that she's okay?"

"Yes. That was perfect. Thank you." I pulled Spot away. "Come, your largeness. The good doctor has work to do."

Street took the other side of his collar and helped me pull him down the hall. As we left, he strained to look back. His tail was held high and he pranced.

About The Author

Todd Borg lives with his wife in Lake Tahoe where they write and paint, ski and hike. Learn more about him by visiting toddborg.com.